ALLEN

AUTHOR OF *LUNAR DESCENT*

LABYRINTH OF NIGHT

ACE · 0-441-46741-5 · ($5.99 CANADA) · $4.99 U.S.

**THE GREATEST
QUESTION IN THE
SOLAR SYSTEM IS
ABOUT TO BE
ANSWERED...**

"ONE OF THE HOTTEST
NEW WRITERS OF HARD SF
ON THE SCENE TODAY!"
—Gardner Dozois, editor,
*Isaac Asimov's Science
Fiction Magazine*

Ace Books by Allen Steele

ORBITAL DECAY
CLARKE COUNTY, SPACE
LUNAR DESCENT
LABYRINTH OF NIGHT

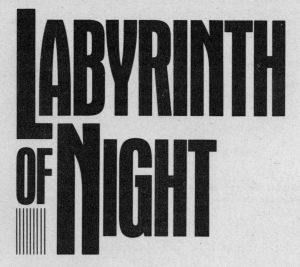

LABYRINTH OF NIGHT

ALLEN STEELE

ACE BOOKS, NEW YORK

Grateful acknowledgment is made for permission to reprint material from the following:

Return to the Red Planet by Eric Burgess, copyright © 1990 by the Columbia University Press, New York. Used by permission.

Powershift by Alvin Toffler, copyright © 1990 by Alvin Toffler and Heidi Toffler ; used by permission of Bantam Books, a division of Bantam Doubleday Dell Publishing Group, Inc.

Mars by Percival Lowell, copyright 1895 by Percival Lowell; Houghton Mifflin and Company, Boston.

"The Waste Land" by T.S. Eliot, from *Collected Poems, 1909–1962*, copyright 1936 by Harcourt Brace Jovanovich Inc., copyright © 1963, 1964 by T. S. Eliot; reprinted by permission of the publisher.

"I Know You Rider" is reprinted from the *Folksinger's Wordbook*, compiled and edited by Fred and Irwin Sibler, copyright © 1973 by Oak Publications, New York.

The War of the Worlds by H.G. Wells, copyright 1897 by H.G. Wells.

This book is an Ace original edition, and has never
been previously published.

An earlier and substantially different version of the first part of this novel
appeared in *Isaac Asimov's Science Fiction Magazine* in September, 1989.

LABYRINTH OF NIGHT

An Ace Book / published by arrangement with
the author

PRINTING HISTORY
Ace edition / October 1992

ISBN: 0-441-46741-5

Ace Books are published by The Berkley Publishing Group,
200 Madison Avenue, New York, New York 10016.
The name "ACE" and the "A" logo are trademarks
belonging to Charter Communications, Inc.

PRINTED IN THE UNITED STATES OF AMERICA

10   9   8   7   6   5   4   3   2   1

This one's for Frank Jacobs . . .
who wouldn't take no for an answer.

ACKNOWLEDGMENTS

The author extends his appreciation to the following persons for their assistance in the research and development of this novel: Koji Mukai, Tom Scheelings, Randy Kennedy, Phil Unger, Bob Liddil, Gardner Dozois, Sheila Williams, James Patrick Kelly, Kent Orlando, Doug Ferguson, Malcolm Hopker, Mike Nugent, Gary Freeman, and Bob Eggleton. I'm also grateful for the continued support of Deborah Beale, Charon Wood, Ginjer Buchanan, Carol Lowe, Susan Allison, Martha Millard, and Shelly Powers. Special thanks, as always, are also due to my wife, Linda.

Most of the scientific background and technological extrapolation has been drawn from the published papers of the first three "Case For Mars" conferences, held at the University of Colorado in Boulder between 1981 and 1987; much of the rest was gleaned from such diverse sources as space-science and astronomy texts, newspaper clippings, and interesting plastic model kits. However, the most controversial source for this novel is its very springboard for inspiration: the so-called "Face" and the nearby "City" in the Cydonia region of Mars.

Most of the details of these alleged "alien artifacts" were derived from two books which have been published about the subject: *The Monuments of Mars*, by Richard C. Hoagland and *The Face on Mars*, by Randolfo Rafael Pozos. While some of the theories and conjectures about the Cydonia anomalies have been included in this novel, others have been left out, and more than a few are completely the product of this author's imagination.

In real life, the oddities which were photographed by the NASA Viking orbiters in 1976 have been either hailed as certain proof of extraterrestrial intelligence or dismissed as wild-eyed pseudo-science. The truth probably lies somewhere between the opposite poles of fact and fantasy; the verdict isn't in yet, and perhaps won't be conclusively delivered until the first manned expedition is made to the Cydonia region. We can only hope this happens within our lifetimes.

For the purposes of this work, the Face and the City are treated as if they do indeed exist, but this should not be misconstrued as wholehearted endorsement of the "Face on Mars" theories; the author neither claims to be a believer nor a disbeliever. This is intended as a work of science *fiction*, nothing more nor less.

Your acceptance of the underlying premise, or your skepticism of the same, are both welcome.

> —*Rindge, New Hampshire;*
> *Sanibel, Florida;*
> *St. Louis, Missouri;*
> *September, 1987–December, 1991*

Prologue

"No one would have believed in the last years of the nineteenth century that this world was being watched keenly and closely by intelligences greater than man's and yet as mortal as his own; that as men busied themselves about their various concerns they were scrutinized and studied, perhaps as narrowly as a man with a microscope might scrutinize the transient creatures that swarm and multiply in a drop of water.... Yet across the gulf of space, minds that are to our minds as ours are to those beasts that perish, intellects vast and cool and unsympathetic, regarded this earth with envious eyes and surely drew their plans against us...."

—H. G. WELLS
The War of the Worlds
(1897)

Hal Moberly gingerly stepped on a round stone divot in front of a red door deep underneath the Martian surface, closed his eyes, and waited to die. Instead, the door slid grindingly aside, towed along coasters by pulleys at least as old as recorded history. Hearing the door move, the NASA geologist opened his eyes and took a deep breath. Through the now-open door, beyond the oval of light cast by his armor's lamp, lay the darkness of Room C4-20.

"Thank God," he murmured. "I'm still here."

Shin-ichi Kawakami watched from Cydonia Base's monitor center, located outside the City on the rock-strewn, wind-stripped red plain. Around him, other members of the team were hunched over their stations, concentrating on their instruments. "We copy that, Hal," the Japanese exobiologist replied. "Stay in the doorway for a few moments and let the pod sweep the room."

Next to Kawakami, Paul Verduin watched as the radar in Moberly's suit sensor pod—a sausage-shaped package mounted on the armor's right shoulder—mapped the interior of Room C4-20. The radar's feedback was input directly into Verduin's computer, which in turn assembled a three-dimensional image of C4-20 on his screen. The new room was 40 feet long, 21 feet wide, and 8 feet high. There were apparently no furnishings in this chamber, but the Dutch astronomer noticed that the computer had painted the room's walls as being irregular, rippled and unsmooth.

From her station behind them, Tamara Isralilova kept vigil on the armor's internal monitors. Moberly's Hoplite II armor was less like a garment than it was a vehicle. A spinoff from the military armor used by American and Russian heavy infantry units, the Hoplite suit weighed a half-ton and resembled an egg which had sprouted semirobotic arms and legs. Within its cocoonlike interior, Moberly's body was covered with biosensors.

"Respiration, EKG, blood pressure, brain alpha patterns all rising," the Russian doctor reported. "He's extremely nervous, Dr. Kawakami."

"Don't inject him with anything, Tamara," Kawakami replied. "I would rather have him nervous than somnambulant at this juncture." He glanced over Verduin's shoulder. "What's in there, Paul?"

Verduin shook his head. "It resembles a normal chamber, except that the walls seem irregular. Lumpy. And look at this." He pointed to the spectrographic readout. "Metal, not stone. Light aluminum-steel alloy of some variety. We have not seen anything like this yet."

Don't keep me in suspense, guys. Moberly's voice came through their headsets. *Are there any booby traps here?*

Kawakami and Verduin traded glances. An unnecessary question. Each chamber of the underground labyrinth had been booby-trapped, and already one person had been killed. Moberly was really asking if there was anything which would annihilate him the moment he entered the new chamber. Verduin shrugged, then shook his head. "Go ahead, Hal," Kawakami said. "Take two steps into the room and stop. Also increase your white-light intensity a little bit so we can get a good picture."

As Moberly stepped through the door into Room C4-20, the TV image transmitted from his armor's chest-mounted camera brightened. Kawakami and Verduin watched the monitor screen between their stations. The walls, toned like burnished copper, were intricately patterned, interlaced with whorls and swirls as if cut by a jigsaw. Very strange. Other chambers in the Labyrinth contained wall designs, but none as complex or extensive as these. The camera swiveled to the far wall and stopped. *Hey!* Moberly yelled. *Do you see that?*

"Yes, we see it," Verduin replied excitedly. Isralilova turned to look at the monitor. After staring at the screen for a moment, she cast a rare smile at Kawakami.

What they saw of significance in the last wall of the new chamber was nothing at all. There was no door in the far wall.

"That's it," Kawakami whispered. "The end."

Then Verduin glanced down at his console and stopped grinning. Cupping his left hand over his headset mike, he pointed at his screen. Kawakami looked and felt his elation vanish.

"Electromagnetic surge," Verduin whispered. A computer-generated red line in a window on his screen had suddenly spiked in its center. Before Kawakami could ask, Verduin answered his next question by pointing at a more regular blue line underneath the red spike. "That is his suit voltage. The red line indicates an exterior source. The surge happened the moment he stepped in the room. I cannot isolate the source, but it is definitely from inside C4-20."

They heard a familiar grinding sound in their headphones, picked up by the armor's exterior mike. Everyone looked up. *The door's closing,* Moberly said. *There it goes.* The TV image on the monitor screen shifted sharply as Moberly turned around, now showing the door to the corridor quickly shutting itself. Moberly lurched forward a step, but the door was sealed before he could reach it.

Everyone in the module took a deep breath. Although it had been anticipated that the new room would reseal itself once Moberly was inside, there was still a palpable sense of foreboding. Hal was obviously keeping his own fear under tight rein—the professional cool of a scientist-explorer, typical of a man who had hung a framed picture of Sir Richard Burton above his bunk—but the people at the other end of his comlink were at the edge of their nerves.

They remembered what had happened to Valery Bronstein . . . and they were all too aware of the solitary grave that lay on the small hill behind the base.

Still, Kawakami thought, it's not going to do Hal any good if we begin to panic. "All right," he said. "It knows he's in there." His fingers found the keypad in his lap and punched in two digits. Arthur Johnson and Miho Sasaki, the American and Japanese co-leaders of the expedition, were on standby in the corridor outside C4-20. "Team Lima-Two, do you copy?"

We're here, Shin-ichi. Arthur Johnson's voice was stressed. *The door just shut. What's going on in there?*

Kawakami was about to answer when another sound overrode the comlink: not static, not the usual crackle of electromagnetic interference from the pyramid. Something formed and rhythmic, as natural and yet unexpected as a coyote howl in the midnight desert. "Listen," Isralilova said. "Do you hear that!"

"Shh!" Kawakami hissed. Music. Formless and random, even grating, but undeniably music, lifting from the alien caverns like the sullen riffs of a subway jazz player, as if an avantgarde musician were lurking somewhere inside the chamber. Weird, yet somehow appropriate . . . and nonetheless threatening.

Are you getting this? Hal Moberly quietly asked.

Kawakami glanced at the CD-ROM deck above his console. "We're recording it, yes, Hal," he replied. "Stand by. Wait for our next signal."

The team's senior scientist had no doubt what the sounds signified. In some way, this was the Labyrinth's final test. Yet this was something entirely new. Before now, everything beneath Pyramid C-4 had related to equations and common sense. How can anyone ask a piece of music, alien or otherwise, to explain itself as an obvious statement?

Kawakami looked at Verduin. The other scientist met his gaze, glanced back at his console, then silently shook his head. Instinctively, they both knew the hard truth, although neither one of them had the courage to openly speak it.

Hal Moberly was not going to emerge from C4-20 alive. And there wasn't a damned thing they could do about it. . . .

Waterville, New Hampshire:
August 31, 1730 EST, 2029

The Blackhawk was an older helicopter, on the verge of retirement but still in use by the government for low-profile odd jobs. Its military markings had been removed, so it was appropriate for flying Dick Jessup from central Massachusetts to Waterville Valley. When Jessup had asked why he simply could not drive to the concert site, the copter pilot had grinned. "I don't think you want to do that, sir," Lieutenant Orr had replied.

Now, after a one-hour jaunt from Worcester Municipal Airport to the resort town, Jessup could see why. Traffic was backed up for miles on the highways leading into Waterville Valley, tucked in the foothills of the White Mountains. An estimated crowd of 70,000 music-lovers surrounded the huge outdoor stage of the New England Bluegrass and Jazz Festival. Orr circled the vast sprawl of people, tents, and cars before setting the Blackhawk down on a packed-earth landing pad inside the fenced backstage area. A couple of roadies dashed out to meet Jessup as he climbed out, then backed off, confused that the helicopter's lone passenger was not a performer. One of them made a call on his wristphone and a few minutes later the stage manager stalked over, convinced that Jessup was a high-rolling gate-crasher. It took a few minutes for Jessup to settle the dispute; it was not until the stage manager made a phone call to the promoter and verified that Jessup was there as an invited guest that he calmed down. Jessup was relieved; he did not want to produce his government I.D., which would have ended the dispute more quickly but also would have raised some uncomfortable questions.

On the other hand, the stage manager seemed irritated that he couldn't have Jessup arrested by the security guards. "Just get that bird of yours out of here," he snapped, pointing at the Blackhawk. "We've still got people flying into this place."

"Okay," Jessup replied. "Can you tell me where Ben Cassidy is?"

"He's onstage. You can talk to him when his set is over. Now get your chopper out of here."

Jessup waved to Orr and gave him the thumbs-up, and the pilot pointed at his watch and lifted two fingers. Two hours. That was sufficient time. Jessup nodded, and the Blackhawk lifted back up into the clear August sky. Jessup turned back to the stage manager, but he was already walking off to harangue someone else. Jessup wondered if he ever listened to the concerts he ramrodded, or if he was merely in this business because it gave him an excuse to be a jerk.

Jessup found his way to the stage and walked up the stairs to a small area between a stack of equipment boxes and a table covered with folded rally towels and bottles of mineral water. Roadies and various hangers-on moved back and forth around him; he felt out of place, wearing his beige business suit and tie, among the jeans and T-shirts which were the uniform for this Labor Day weekend gathering. Too much like a government official on official government business. People shied away from him as if he were an IRS agent there to audit the gate receipts. Jessup was sure that, if he were to identify himself as a NASA administrator, it would not make any difference. Not with anti-space sentiments growing as they were now . . .

He turned his attention to the lone figure on the stage, a burly figure sitting on a wooden stool with his back turned to Jessup. Ben Cassidy was performing solo, as usual, with no backup band. He was a middle-aged man—balding, beard turning white, the creased and heavy-browed face of a longshoreman turned itinerant musician—plainly dressed in baggy dungarees with shirt sleeves rolled up above his elbows, hunched over the keys and digital fretboard of a Yamaha electronic guitar.

It seemed impossible to Jessup that one person could entertain the vast ocean of faces that lapped at the shoreline of the stage, that his music would not be drowned in the tide of humanity. Yet, as Cassidy played, Jessup found himself empathetically melding with the current: the crowd, the mid-afternoon heat, and above all else the music which flowed from Cassidy's guitar. He was coming out of a blues number—Jessup, who had briefly been a blues fan in his college days, vaguely recognized it as Muddy Waters's "My Dog Can't Bark, My Cat Can't Scratch"—and was gliding into free-form improvisation.

As Jessup listened, he became increasingly fascinated. At first it seemed as if Cassidy was simply dog-paddling, thrashing without direction on the same couple of chords. Then he added a keyboard solo to the bass refrain and began holding a dialogue between the two sets of chords, shifting back and forth like an actor single-handedly conducting a conversation between two characters. When it seemed impossible that Cassidy could carry this on much longer, the musician added a third refrain, a lilting lead guitar riff which joined into the mesh of notes, joining a consensus of musical opinion. The crowd near the stage, mesmerized by this performance, shouted and applauded their approval, but Cassidy—huddled over his instrument, face almost pressed against his instrument—did not look up, or even seem to notice that he had an audience.

Jessup, listening and watching, suddenly realized why he had been sent to recruit Cassidy. He had heard the tapes of Hal Moberly's encounter with Room C4-20. Jessup had wondered if Arthur Johnson was losing his mind when he had suggested Cassidy's name; it had seemed improbable that the scientist would want anyone for Cydonia Base other than another scientist. Now, hearing Cassidy's guitar, Jessup understood. His improvisational style was disturbingly similar to the music of Room C4-20.

Jessup's right hand moved involuntarily toward the inside pocket of his suitcoat before he stopped himself. The folded message inside would wait until he met Cassidy backstage after his gig. Abruptly, Jessup hated himself. He had studied Cassidy's record, knew that the musician had been a draftee during Gulf War II. No one should be conscripted twice.

No choice, though. The final puzzle of the Labyrinth had to be solved, at any or all costs.

Cassidy ended his instrumental piece and, as the crowd went wild, he stood up for a moment to take a quick, solemn bow and reflexively scoot his stool back a couple of inches. As he did so, he glanced behind him and saw Jessup standing in the wings. Their eyes met and locked for an instant. Jessup caught the cool, appraising glare, the downturned mouth within the beard. Then Cassidy turned his attention back to his guitar and his audience.

He pensively warmed up with a couple of notes, then edged into his next number. Jessup recognized the song immediately as "Uncle Sam Blues."

Kennedy Space Center, Cape Canaveral, Florida; October 4, 0800 EST, 2029

The unmanned cargo shuttle *Constellation* was an old bird, the last of its breed. Built in the early 2000's to ferry the final components of the first-generation Freedom Station into orbit, it was the last of the Rockwell "Delta Clippers" to be rolled out to the launch pad. Its sister vessels were now on display in the National Air and Space Museum in Washington, the KSC visitors center on the other side of the Cape, and the Marshall Space Flight Center in Huntsville.

The *Constellation* was still flying, though, partly because no one at the Cape had the heart to put the last of the Delta Clippers out to pasture. The second-generation McDonnell Douglas "Big Dummies" were more efficient workhorses, but they were mostly owned and operated by Skycorp and other space companies. Although NASA flew third-generation SSTO spaceplanes for most orbital missions, there was still a need for the *Constellation*'s more capacious cargo hold. But everyone at the Cape knew that the *Constellation* was near the end of her days; at twenty-nine, she was a grand old dame who was tired of hauling freight. In another year or so, she would be taken off the flightline, her innards cannibalized for any reusable parts and her empty hull shellacked and mounted on a concrete parapet at another NASA facility, posing for tourist snapshots and collecting bird droppings on her fuselage. Nobody lives forever.

Tomorrow morning, though, she would be flying again. Ten days earlier, the *Constellation* had been rolled out to Pad 2-A near the northern end of the Cape for the loading of its cargo and the pre-launch checkout. Her cargo was not explicitly listed in any of the manifests, nor was its orbital destination being disclosed. Flight 29A-NM was a classified military mission for the United States Navy, so even its exact launch-time was traditionally kept secret from the public under longstanding Department of Defense guidelines. Security was tight at Pad 2-A for this launch.

An elevator glided up the core of the Rotating Service Structure and stopped at the fourth level; the hard-hatted pad technician in the cage with August Nash pulled back the metal-grate door and stood aside.

"Right through there, Colonel Meredith," he said deferentially. "Do you want me to wait until you're through with your inspection?"

"No," Nash said. "Thank you again ... ah ..." He pushed back his horn-rim glasses and allowed his gaze to drop to the ID badge pinned to the pad rat's white jumpsuit: ROBILLARD, J.E. "John," he finished. "I'll take the stairs down when I'm finished here. Just leave a jeep behind for me, if you would."

"Very good, sir," Robillard said. Nash nodded and was about to step out when the technician stopped him. "Sorry, sir. Your hood ... ?"

Right. The white nylon hood that hung from the back of Nash's head-to-toe whiteroom jumpsuit. Nash silently cursed himself; a small mistake like this could blow his cover. The jumpsuit was to keep dust from contaminating the pristine environment of the RSS whiteroom. A real Air Force colonel would know better than to enter this area without drawing the hood over his head.

"Of course," he murmured. "Sorry." He pulled the hood over the Air Force cap that covered his gray-dyed hair. His fake eyeglasses, with their utterly useless lenses, slipped down the bridge of his nose and almost fell off; he caught them with the gloved tip of his forefinger and pushed them back, then closed the neck flap along its Velcro seal. Stepping off the elevator, he turned and waved to J. E. Robillard. "Be seeing you."

"Sure thing, Colonel." The pad rat waved back agreeably as he pulled the grate shut with his left hand. As the elevator began to drone back down through the swingaway service tower, Nash turned and gently pushed through the translucent flap of the heavy plastic membrane which insolated the whiteroom.

Cold air, pumped outward to maintain positive-pressure on this side of the membrane, brushed against his face. After the high-eighties scorch of the launch pad outside the RSS, it was a welcome chill. Just ahead was an open man-sized steel hatch: SIDE 4 DOOR, read the sign on the door. NO SMOKING. As if anyone in his right mind would dare strike a match this close to over one million pounds of liquid oxygen and hydrogen contained in the shuttle booster. Nash stepped though the hatch, and in front of him lay the objective of his assignment.

The long, vertical maw of the *Constellation*'s cargo bay loomed before him, nestled up to the airtight confines of the RSS whiteroom. The Level 4 access platform had been extended from the tower until it stopped just inside the open bay doors; here, all was white and reflective silver, dust-free and so immaculately clean that a germ would die of starvation. And there, securely fastened to a pallet within the cargo bay, were two large pill-shaped objects, each wrapped in gold Mylar film.

A cargo technician, similarly robed in a white jumpsuit, knelt at the edge of the service platform, studying a datapad in his hands. He looked over his shoulder at Nash as he came through the hatch; the obvious question was unspoken, but plain on his face. "Colonel Joel Meredith," Nash said briskly. "USAF Space Command." As if he had every right to be here . . . which, in the sense of the lie, he did. He nodded toward the twin gold saucers. "How're you doing today?"

"Fine, sir." An uncertain pause. "Just fine."

"Those are the birds?"

The cargo tech, a middle-aged black man with a trim beard, didn't take his eyes from Nash's face. "Uh-huh," he said noncommittally. He gently folded the datapad. "They're the ones."

The cargo tech seemed to be paying a little too much attention to his guest. Nash ignored him, although he felt the man's eyes running across his face, looking closely at his ID badge. Nash took a couple of steps closer, looking up and down at the payload compartment.

Despite the bulk of the insulation, he could tell that the two objects nestled within the *Constellation*'s cargo bay were aeroshells. Yet they weren't the same size aeroshell normally used by OTVs which aerobraked in Earth's atmosphere before rendezvousing with Freedom Station or one of the other low-orbit space stations; these were smaller, very similar to the fuselages of Martian landers. And while there were a score of off-white stencils on the Mylar wrap, locating fuel and electrical ports, there was nothing which explicitly identified them as military spacecraft. But if his intelligence briefing had been correct . . .

"When did you shave off the mustache, Colonel?" the technician asked.

"Hmmm?" Nash glanced at the other man's ID badge—HUMES, T.S.—and immediately returned his attention to the *Constellation* as if to ignore the tech's question. Yet the nervous twinge he'd felt from the moment he had first seen the technician was still there.

"When I last saw you, you had a mustache," Humes said. He hesitated, and added, "Four months ago."

"Oh, that was a while ago," Nash drawled. "Got tired of the soup-strainer, that's all."

The company's file photo of Air Force Colonel Joel K. Meredith had shown him not to have a mustache. If it had, Nash would have cultivated one to match, since he had been given the assignment to penetrate Pad 2-A three weeks ago. But Meredith's photo was a relatively old one, taken at least six months earlier. Although Meredith seldom visited the Cape, his last pre-launch inspection had been exactly four months ago. It was possible that Humes remembered him because of a mustache he might have grown since the file photo had been taken.

Sure, people can grow and shave mustaches in a period of four months. Even without a mustache, Nash looked enough like Meredith to pass inspection; temporary exodermic alterations by the mug-doctors at Security Associates had matched his face to that of the colonel's. The real Colonel Joel K. Meredith was conveniently taking a vacation in the Smoky Mountains with his family; surveillance reports had placed him only yesterday at his summer home just outside Gatlinburg, Tennessee. Although Nash's phony face and bogus credentials had been sufficient to get him into KSC and out to Pad 2-A for a last-minute inspection, he was aware that it would take only a few well-placed phone calls to completely blow his disguise.

So far, nothing had occurred to raise anyone's doubts. But if someone became suspicious, even for a second . . .

"Uh-huh." Humes stood up and, in an all-too-casual manner, ran his gloved hands down his thighs to straighten out the wrinkles in his jumpsuit. "Well, if you'll excuse me a minute, Colonel . . ."

"Coffee break?" Nash asked. Humes quickly nodded, his sudden grin obviously faked. "Sure. Go right ahead."

Nash continued to peer closely at the aeroshells, allowing Humes to ease past him. There was a phone on the wall behind them; Nash let the technician get halfway to it before he whirled and, curling in his knuckles, slammed the heel of his right hand into Humes's neck just below his left ear.

Humes toppled to the platform, knocked cold by the karate chop. Nash knelt over him, tested his pulse to make certain that he was still among the living, then grabbed his shoulders and hauled him away from the edge of the platform, just in case Humes awoke in a daze and wandered in the wrong direction.

Nash hated to have had to punch out the pad rat's lights; at least half-a-dozen somnambulant KSC security guards had waved Nash through the checkpoints solely on the basis of his phony ID before this one lowly pad rat had tumbled to the ruse, acting on nothing more than the fact that a person he had last seen several months earlier was then wearing a mustache. "Someone should give you a raise," he whispered as he dropped Humes next to the fire extinguisher.

Now the clock was ticking. Unless he cared to kill Humes—which was the last thing Nash had in mind—it was only a matter of time before the technician regained consciousness and blew the whistle. Nash had to be through the checkpoint at KSC's west gate before then. But Robillard had left a vehicle for him just outside the pad's perimeter fence, and Nash was wearing his street clothes beneath the jumpsuit. In fifteen minutes, with luck, he could be out of the space center and on the highway to Titusville, where the Security Associates private jet was waiting for him at the municipal airport. He would be cutting it close, but . . .

Never mind that now. The assignment came first. His fake eyeglasses held a tiny nanocamera in its frame, capable of storing three images in microchip memory. Since he was now alone on the inspection platform, though, Nash could afford to use the miniature 35mm camera he had hidden in his inside jacket pocket; its resolution was much sharper than the blurred images produced by the nanocamera. Unzipping the jumpsuit, he pulled out the hand calculator which disguised the camera and spent the next fifteen seconds hastily photographing images of the twin aeroshells in the *Constellation*'s cargo bay. With the last available frame, he snapped a quick picture of Humes—for his own amusement, as well as the remote possibility that Control might want proof that he had not thrown the poor man to his death from the service tower—then he tucked the camera back in his jacket and zipped up the jumpsuit.

Nash took a last glimpse over his shoulder at the *Constellation* as he stepped over the technician's legs. It wasn't part of his job to be second-guessing either his employer's wishes or the client's reasons for wanting information. Nash was the legman, pure and simple. Get inside, obtain the info desired, and get out again without being caught. That's all there was to it.

And yet, and still . . .

The part of Nash's mind that used to work for the CIA wanted to know what was so important about another payload which, if his briefing had been correct, was ultimately destined for Mars. Sure, the mysterious objects were destined for Freedom Station, for final attachment to the next outward-bound cycleship which docked at the U.S. space station. But why did they have their own aeroshells? What was the secret cargo that the Air Force was sending to Mars?

He hurried through the hatch and plastic membrane and began jogging down the adjacent stairs to the bottom of the launch tower. You'll never know, Nash told himself, and it's none of your business anyway. . . .

For the second time during this job, he was wrong. His involvement was only beginning.

PART ONE

"The Cydonia region is also of great interest because of some unusual surface features, areas where great blocks of rocks stand out starkly from the surrounding plains. One of these blocks bears an uncanny resemblance to a simian face. This has been explained as a fortuitous chance of lighting. However, there have also been suggestions, based on another image at a slightly different angle, that the shape is quite real and is related in several ways to nearby features on a geometrical basis. There have been suggestions that the 'face' on Mars is evidence of extraterrestrial intelligence at some earlier epoch laying down a purposeful pattern on the planet's surface. Whether or not this shape is fortuitous or designed or is another example of anthropomorphic Mars remains to be seen when the area is again surveyed, and in more detail, by one of the upcoming missions to Mars. . . ."

—ERIC BURGESS
Return to the Red Planet
(1990)

RED PLANET BLUES

Excerpt from "The Labyrinth of Cydonia"; *The New Solar System (Version 6.0). McGraw Hill Hypertexts, 2032:*

SCROLL: The first clues that extra-terrestrial intelligence had entered the solar system in the ancient past were largely ignored by the scientific community. When NASA's Viking I space probe rendezvoused with Mars on July 20, 1976, the spacecraft's orbiter circled the planet, conducting the most extensive photographic mapping of Mars *(see Chapter 2)*. During Orbit 35, the Viking's camera caught the first image of the Face, in the Cydonia region in Mars' northern hemisphere, on the edge of Acidalia Planitia. PRESS ENTER, PLEASE.

(Animation of Viking I approaching and orbiting Mars fades to the first vague photograph of the Face; footage of NASA's Viking team gathering around monitors at the Jet Propulsion Laboratory in Pasadena, California.)

SCROLL: Although the Face was immediately noticed by the Viking Imaging Team, it was dismissed as being a natural formation caused by wind erosion. However, a few scientists and earthbound space explorers followed up on the enigmatic Frame 35A72. Calling themselves the Independent Mars

Investigation Team, the dozen members asked an unpopular question: Was the Face evidence that a spacefaring interstellar civilization had once inhabited Mars? PRESS ENTER, PLEASE.

(An orbital panorama of the Cydonia region; graphic lines are overlaid on the photograph to show the relationships between key objects; frame zooms in to focus on separate details in the montage.)

SCROLL: The informal group examined Viking photos of Cydonia over the next decade, now enhanced by a computer-generated processing system called SPIT, or Starburst Pixel Interleaving Technique *(see Appendix 2)*. They made a number of intriguing discoveries. Lying 11.2 kilometers west of the Face there was apparently a City composed of four major pyramids arranged equilaterally in a cluster measuring 4 by 8 kilometers around a central City Square. A few kilometers south of the Face, another large structure was located, labeled by the group as the "D&M" Pyramid (after Vincent DiPietro and Gregory Molenaar, the pyramid's discoverers). Like the City, it appeared to be aligned toward the Face. Since the D&M Pyramid seemed to have an unevenly defined fifth side on its northeast flank, apparently a large crevasse had been opened in one side of the pyramid, possibly caused by meteorite impact. Alignments between the City, the D&M Pyramid, and the Face appeared to comprise two adjacent sides of a right angle—a triangle, further evidence that the formations were artificial in origin. In addition, the group calculated that sunrise on Mars occurred during the solstices from directly to the east of the Face, so that the sun could be seen rising above the Face from the City Square. PRESS ENTER, PLEASE.

(A series of photos and film clips: a meeting during the first "Case For Mars" conference in Boulder, Colorado; the cover of a report titled "Unusual Martian Surface Features"; a hilltop radiotelescope dish; the headline of a supermarket tabloid, Weekly World News: *THE FACE ON MARS—A NEW SHOCKER!)*

SCROLL: The Independent Mars Investigation Team made their findings public during the 1980's, only to be met by skepticism, and even hostility, by the majority of the space science community. Although the question of whether extraterrestrial intelligences existed was being debated and explored, most SETI research concentrated on detecting radio signals from distant stars, such as Project META in Harvard, Massachusetts *(see Chapter 15)*. The idea that evidence of E.T.'s existed within our own solar system was considered ludicrous by most experts. To its dismay, the group saw media exposure of the Face relegated largely to sensational tabloid headlines, lumped in with Bigfoot sightings and reports that Elvis Presley had returned in a UFO. PRESS ENTER, PLEASE.

(Film clip of a C.I.S. Proton rocket lifting off from a pad; animation of unmanned Russian and American probes coasting into orbit around Mars; footage of the first-generation Mars ship of first American-Russian manned expedition being assembled in low orbit around Earth near Freedom Station; footage of the landers being released from the H. G. Wells above Mars; film clips of Arsia Station in the Tharsis region being assembled.)

SCROLL: While advocates of the Face theory pushed for a return to Mars to investigate the mystery in Cydonia, renewed Mars exploration was eventually begun in the last years of the

20th century by the United States
and the Commonwealth of Independent
States. Unmanned probes, including
NASA's Sample Return Mission, led
to the International Mars Project
which landed man on the red planet on
August 12, 2020 *(see Chapter 2)*. Arsia
Station, the first permanently manned
base, was established by the first expedition just south of the equator, approximately 4,700 miles from Cydonia.
But the reasons for the first missions
had more to do with international politics than scientific inquiry, and
the Cydonia enigma remained a low-
priority assignment. Even with men on
Mars, it was another eight years before
the controversy was finally laid to
rest by the first human visit to Cydonia. PRESS ENTER, PLEASE....

1. The <u>Shinseiki</u>

One-and-a-half A.U.'s from the Sun, Mars glides through space, a rust-colored desert world caught between the placid blue-green beauty of Earth and the immense, multicolored maelstrom of Jupiter. On Earth, it's early summer in the northern hemisphere, but for Mars summer has ended in the northern latitudes; frozen carbon-dioxide and water have caused the small white icecap at the plant's north pole to expand again while, south of the equator, it is high spring and the ice pack at the south pole has all but vanished.

As the sun rises over the central meridian, water vapor causes thin, filmy clouds to spawn in the vast canyons of the Valles Marineris, which are quickly evaporated by the new day. For a brief time the winds rise, kicking red sands into the sparse atmosphere before the wind reluctantly retires again, if only for a while. Mars is a slumbering world, gradually stirring from its rest; as autumn settles on the northern hemisphere and the days get colder, there will be fewer naps for the red planet. Soon the sandstorms will begin and vast curtains of scarlet, wind-borne sand will cloak much of the world, shrouding even the high caldera of Olympus Mons, the great shield volcano northeast at the Valles Marineris.

The Martian day lasts slightly longer than Earth's: twenty-four hours, thirty-nine minutes, thirty-five seconds. This is one of the few real similarities between the two worlds. Its atmosphere is composed principally of carbon-dioxide and has a density of seven millibars in the Amazonis Planitia, as compared to Earth's atmospheric density of one thousand millibars at sea level. Mars has no "sea level"; its seas and oceans evaporated millions of years ago, and the lack of atmospheric pressure means that free-standing water simply could not exist.

21

High summer at the Martian equator is when the ground temperature has risen to a sweltering 62 degrees Fahrenheit at the equator; during winter, the temperature can plunge to 172° below zero at the north pole.

A long time ago, an all-but-forgotten American vice-president named Daniel Quayle made the following observation about Mars during a TV interview: "Mars is in essentially the same orbit. Mars is somewhat the same distance from the Sun, which is very important. We have seen pictures where there are canals, we believe, and water. If there is water, that means there is oxygen. If there is oxygen, that means we can breathe."

Dan Quayle was stupid. Mars is not Earth's twin brother with a bad skin problem. This is a cold world. This is a harsh world.

But by no means is it a lifeless world.

Forty million miles from Earth, the NASDA/Uchu-Hiko cycleship S.S. *Shinseiki* coasted on the last leg of its outbound flight to Mars, gracefully spinning on its central axis like a three-vaned weathercock.

Nine months earlier, three interplanetary vessels had fired their nuclear-thermal engines and launched themselves from Earth orbit, following identical trajectories toward the red planet. Once having escaped Earth's gravity well, beyond the orbit of the moon, the vessels rendezvoused in deep space. The three ships linked together at the multiple-target docking adapter at each forward bow so that each vessel lay 120 degrees apart from the other, forming a pinwheel two hundred forty feet in diameter. Long heat radiators accordioned outward from the ends of each of the three arms, and reaction-control jets fired to spin the pinwheel clockwise to produce one-third Earth gravity within the two cylindrical habitation modules that lay behind the solar-thermal dishes on each arm.

In this way, once again, the *Shinseiki* was created, just as it had been twice already. Elsewhere in the vast distance separating Earth and Mars, its two sister cycleships were on other stages of the Mars Run; the U.S.S. *Percival Lowell*, the American ship operated by Skycorp, was on the long, lonely return flight from the red planet, and the S.S. *Sergei Korolev*, the C.I.S. ship jointly operated by Glavkosmos and Arianespace, was being refitted for launch from the Mir space station in Earth orbit. Every five-to-ten months, depending on orbital conjunctions between the two planets, a different cycleship returns to Mars, with the three of them forming a long, cycling bridge between the worlds. This time, it was the *Shinseiki*'s turn to visit the planet of the war god.

On this visit, though, the *Shinseiki* carried more than relief crews, consumables, replacement parts, and mail. In hibernation deck B of Module Two, five men were being administered drugs to wake them from their long sleep. Above them, on the other side of Arm Two's long truss and sheathed in layers of protective gold film, were the two aeroshells which August Nash had photographed in the payload bay of the *Constellation* many months earlier.

And on the opposite end of Arm Two, in a storage compartment in Module One, was a guitar.

Ten months after he first had spoken with Richard Jessup, Ben Cassidy found himself watching a cup of coffee spill in a way that he had never seen coffee spill before in his life. He had just settled into a chair in the cycleship's wardroom—a chair which pulled out along a slender, jointed rail from underneath the hexagonal table and unfolded like a box top—and the Japanese commander, Minoru Omori, had placed the paper cup of coffee on the table near his elbow. Dick Jessup, who had taken a seat across the table from him, had held out a briefing folder to him; when Cassidy had reached to take the folder, his elbow knocked over the cup.

The coffee spilled in slow motion, as if caught by time-lapse photography. It tipped over at a weird angle and the coffee sloshed out at a slightly curving trajectory; like a blob of brown mercury, the liquid seemed to follow a path of its own making, slopping to the left. Cassidy found himself staring at it as Jessup made a grab for a paper towel from the galley counter behind him. Jessup sopped up the mess before it reached Cassidy's lap, then looked up and noticed the dazed look on the musician's face.

"Coriolis effect," he said. "It's caused by the ship's rotation. Don't worry, you won't be here long enough to have to get used to it."

"Oh," Cassidy murmured. "That's great."

"How are you doing? Got your bearings yet?"

"Yeah. Sure. Doing fine." Of course he was doing fine. He had just come to the realization that he was in a Japanese spaceship in orbit around Mars, about 40 million miles from everything he had ever known or loved, where even a cup of coffee doesn't spill right. And how are you doing today, Dick?

Cassidy watched Jessup as he got up and walked to the galley to throw the towel into the recycling chute. The first impression Cassidy had of Jessup, when they had first met in Waterville almost a year ago, was that the man was a suit and little more: tall, dark-haired, whipcord-thin, conservative in every sense, having little or no sense of humor, patronizing to an offensive degree. Another bureaucrat, indistinguishable from the average IRS accountant or post office clerk. Yet, while there was was obviously more to Richard Jessup than met the eye, he was still an enigma to Cassidy. Of course, Cassidy had been asleep during most of their relationship, so maybe it was a little early to pass judgment . . . but he didn't like Jessup during their first encounter, and he still had no reason to trust the man.

Behind him, he could hear the amused snickers of the Marines, two tough guys from the 1st Space Infantry who had been revived from the zombie tanks in the hibernation bay shortly before he had. Biostasis had been part of their training; anyone who had never before been in drug-induced suspended animation for nine months was obviously a woosie. So it was okay for them to laugh, these professional badasses leaning against the bulkhead in the subdued half-light of the wardroom.

"Got them zombie shakes," he heard one of them whisper.

"Too much rock 'n' roll, man," his buddy replied.

Screw you both, Cassidy thought. To hide his embarrassment, he glanced up at the wraparound bank of screens suspended above the table. One of the screens showed a computer-enhanced image of Mars as captured by a camera at the *Shinseiki*'s hub. As he watched, one of the cycleship's three spindly arms glided past the bloodshot eye of Mars, surrounded by blackness and tiny blue readouts.

He blinked at it. Yeah, it was Mars all right. Now, what in the name of God was he doing here?

Captain Omori, the *Shinseiki*'s commanding officer, carefully placed another cup of coffee on the table in front of Cassidy and unfolded his own chair at the table. Jessup sat down at the table again, cleared his throat, and flipped a page on his clipboard. "Thank you all for being here," he said. "Like you, I'm still recovering from the tanks. . . ."

One of the Marines snickered again. "Tanks for nuthin'," he said.

The squad commander, Colonel Carter Aldiss, had taken the fourth seat at the table. He was a middle-aged man with a graying crewcut and a perpetual don't-fuck-with-me look in his eyes; like the two other Marines, he wore a blue jumpsuit with the embroidered eagle-and-starscape patch on the 1st Space Infantry on his chest. He glanced up from his papers and coffee and muttered, "Shaddup, Spike."

"Yessir, Colonel."

Jessup nervously cleared his throat again. "So I'll turn over the floor to Captain Omori, who'll update you on our mission profile. Captain?"

"Thank you, Dr. Jessup." Minoru Omori was a heavyset, round-faced man who looked as if he smiled once a year, just for kicks. "Welcome to the *Shinseiki*, gentlemen. My two crewmen, First Officer Massey and Executive Officer Cimino, extend their best wishes and also their apologies that they are not here to greet you personally, since they are otherwise involved on the bridge. Ms. Cimino wishes for me to tell you, though, that she enjoyed looking after you while you were in biostasis, and that's she's looking forward to doing so again during the return leg of our voyage."

Unexpectedly, Omori grinned and laughed. Jessup responded with a polite, uncertain smile. "Maybe she enjoyed asking us to cough," one of the Marines whispered.

"Cut it out, Goober," Aldiss said.

"Yessir, Colonel."

"To continue . . ." Omori, formal again, pulled a datapad from his jumpsuit pocket and tapped in a couple of commands. The overhead screens blinked and replaced the TV images from the outer hull with a computer-generated diagram of the *Shinseiki*'s approach to Mars. "The outermost curve represents our present trajectory. When we reach the periapsis at seventeen-hundred hours, Landers One and Two will be launched. The landing party for Lander One needs to be at airlock One-Two-Delta at fifteen-thirty hours for suitup and boarding."

"That's us, Ben," Jessup murmured. Cassidy nodded. He was still thinking about the spilled coffee.

"The relief crew for Arsia Station, the main base near the Noctis Labyrinthus region, will be boarded on Lander Two at fifteen-forty-five hours from airlock Two-Two-Charlie," Captain Omori went on. "These people are unaware of your presence, since they're secluded in another part of the ship. Before then, at fifteen-hundred hours, the outbound landers will be launched from Arsia Station. They will intercept the *Shinseiki* at eighteen-hundred and will dock for the return voyage. By then, of course, both of our landers will have been launched and will have completed aerobraking and landing maneuvers. During a normal timetable, we would execute periapsis burn for Earth encounter thirty minutes later, at eighteen-thirty, but for this mission we will have a minor glitch in the targeting computer, causing a disagreement in the primary AI interface."

A smile touched the edges of Omori's lips. "Nothing critical it will be, naturally. The targeting computer will have simply told the firing system that the course is in error and the major system will go down, aborting the burn. An unforeseen accident. It will cause us to fire the OMS for an emergency low-orbit insertion. This will give us enough time to question the main AI neural-net and sort out the problem without losing our REO window. Both Arsia and Cydonia commands will be apprised of the unfortunate circumstances for the delay." Omori's smile grew broader. "Of course."

Cassidy, confused by the explanation, heard the Marines chuckle and saw Aldiss stretch back in his chair in satisfaction; Jessup tried to hide a smug grin. Cassidy ignored the soldiers and stared straight across the table at Omori. "Excuse me, Captain," he said softly, "but what the hell are you talking about?"

Omori stared back at him and became taciturn once more. "An unforeseen occurrence, Mr. Cassidy. Nothing which should concern you."

"Nothing which should concern me. Right." Finally, his mind had started to clear. He had been warned that an aftereffect of biostasis was mental numbness. The frontal lobes were the last part of the brain to recover from the pharmaceuticals—clinically derived from the herbs that Haitian *houngan* had once traditionally used to sedate and enslave people as *zombis*—now used for deep-space hibernation. But it was not unlike the cerebral fuzzout of a cocaine high. In fact, you could almost enjoy the buzz. . . .

Cassidy shook his head: *Stop that.* Questions which over the last few hours had lingered unspoken in the back of his mind now galloped to his attention. He looked at Jessup. "Who are these guys?" he asked, cocking a thumb at the Marines lurking behind him. "You told me that there was going to be a science team on this ship. Where are they?"

Jessup shrugged innocently. "Module One, the other side of the ship," he said with unruffled complacency. "They're the ones on their way down to Arsia Station. Why?"

"*Why?* I was told they were coming with us to Cydonia Base. You said that yourself back at the space station."

Jessup blinked. "I told you that nine months ago, Ben. Things have changed since then. That's a completely different team . . ."

"Okay, so where's *my* team?" he insisted. "The guys I met before they stuck a needle in my arm and told me to count back from one hundred."

The Marines chuckled again; Cassidy found himself getting mad. "What're the Marines doing here? And what's this shit about unforeseen accidents and delayed burning, uh . . . return retroangular whatever the hell you call it . . ."

"Yeah," said the Marine whom Aldiss had called Spike, a skinny guy leaning against the hatch. "It's rectal return burn, man."

Cassidy turned around in his seat and stared at the kid, who was still laughing at him. "You're in the Marines, right?" Spike, grinning hugely now, nodded his head. "Guess you know a lot about having a burning rectum, don't you?"

As the other Marine broke up, Spike's face melted into an angry glare. The musician ignored him and switched his attention back to Jessup. "What's going on here?" he demanded.

"Well . . ." Jessup sighed and looked down at his hands. "As I was saying, there was a change in the mission which you were not informed about before we left Earth. Security considerations . . ."

"Screw that. You got me out here on the pretense that I was to be part of a scientific expedition. Now I suddenly find I'm the one-man Marine Corps Band for a bunch of grunts." Cassidy angrily shook his head. "I don't know much about how these things are arranged, but I can figure that this was planned well in advance. You've been yanking me along, haven't you?"

"Ben, I . . ." Jessup shut his eyes and blew out his cheeks. "Okay, I'll admit it. You were kept in the dark about certain aspects of this mission, and now it's time to let you in on it. Most of it, at least."

Cassidy started to object, but Jessup raised his hand. "Wait.

Let's get through this first. Colonel Aldiss, this is as good a time as any to brief your team and Mr. Cassidy here."

Aldiss nodded his head. "Spike, Goober, you can open your orders now."

While the Marines peeled open the seals on the folders they'd been issued upon entering the wardroom, Aldiss continued. "Last January, while this mission was still being prepared, the Russian cycleship *Sergei Korolov* entered Mars orbit and dropped supplies to Cydonia Base. It was a scheduled run, but what was unexpected was that one of their cargo landers contained two AT-80 Bushmaster autotanks and one combat armor suit. Big surprises, needless to say."

Captain Angelo "Spike" D'Agostino whistled softly. "Bushmasters are nasty business, Colonel. And what kind of CAS?"

"New type, so there's not much info on it. Adapted for Mars environment—the Bushies were modified the same way—but the suit looks like a variation on the Hoplite I armor which the First Space used during the Descartes Station raid a few years back. Probably a little less swift on its feet, considering the higher gravity."

"Higher gravity than the Moon?"

"Right. Check your material. The CIA specs are all in there. In any case, those are the first weapons to be mobilized on Mars, and they came complete with a Russian military advisor, Major Maksim Oeljanov—you'll want to read the dossier they've got on him, too. Of course, Minsk has claimed that the armor is there in case there are any surprises from the Cooties. In any event, we're not taking any chances on the Russians wanting to force a takeover of Cydonia Base . . ."

"Whoa, wait a minute," Cassidy interrupted. "Isn't it against some U.N. treaty about placing weapons in space?"

"The U.N.'s a long way from here, man," D'Agostino murmured without looking up from his file.

Aldiss cast a stern look at the captain, but nodded his head. "There's no proof that the Russkies have any such intentions. . . ."

"Yeah, but two Bushies and a CAS make a pretty strong argument," D'Agostino commented. "The Russians have been getting pretty cocky lately."

"Yeah, well, maybe that's because the yahoo we just put in the White House has been getting pretty cocky himself," Cassidy said.

"Let's not get political about this, shall we?" Jessup said quietly. "In any case, Colonel Aldiss' RDF squad—"

"Falcon Team," Spike said pointedly. "Call us by name."

"Or don't call us at all," Goober added.

"Right. Falcon Team is here as an ace in the hole. Look, Ben, there was a science team assembled for Cydonia that was supposed to be on this flight, but it was bumped back to make way for Steeple Chase . . . um, as this operation has been codenamed."

"That's right, buddy." Lieutenant William "Goober" Hoffman—a tall, lean Alabama boy with a shaved head—slapped his hand with condescending comfort on Cassidy's shoulder. "Just think of us as your guardian angels."

" 'Death From Above,' " D'Agostino murmured from behind his folder. "Just kicking ass and writing down names."

"Terrific." Cassidy's eyes rolled up. "Jessup, are these characters going down there with us? If they are, you don't mind if I just wait up here until they're finished shooting up the place, do you?"

Aldiss shook his head. "We won't be on the lander with you, Mr. Cassidy. The team will remain here for the time being."

"For the—?"

"Yes, sir," Aldiss said in a tone which suggested that he would answer no further questions. "All we expect you to do is keep your mouth shut about our presence here once you arrive at Cydonia Base."

Cassidy squinted at the colonel. It didn't make sense. If the Marines were here as a counterforce to the Russian armor on Mars, then what purpose was served by the Rapid Deployment Force remaining on the *Shinseiki*? He opened his mouth to venture another question, but Jessup seemed to read his thoughts. Slowly standing up from his chair—apparently he, too, was still getting used to the Coriolis effect—he cleared his throat and picked up his clipboard.

"Colonel, I'm sure that you want to complete this briefing alone with your men and Captain Omori." Aldiss nodded and Jessup looked over at Cassidy. "Ben, if you'll come along, I'll reintroduce you to an old friend."

"Great." Cassidy stood up and watched his chair fold itself back underneath the table. "Then maybe after that you'll gimme back my guitar."

He followed Jessup down a ladder into the storage compartment below the wardroom. Jessup reached up to close the hatch cover above them. "They're probably the best the First Space has to offer," he said quietly. "You could have been a little more civil to them."

"I volunteered to be part of a scientific experiment, not a USO show . . . though 'drafted' is probably the better term."

"Maybe it's better if you think of yourself as a volunteer, regardless of the circumstances." The bulkheads of the narrow compartment were lined with recessed lockers. Jessup pushed past Cassidy and traced his finger along the numbered cabinets until he located one in particular. "But I'll offer you some advice."

Cassidy walked over and watched as Jessup unlatched the cabinet. "What's that?"

Jessup pulled out a long bundle wrapped in opaque silver Mylar and gently handed it to Cassidy. "When we get down there, do exactly what I tell you, but don't head for the habitat. I'll arrange for you to be taken to a safer place. . . ."

"Why?"

Jessup gazed expressionlessly at him. "There's some shit that's about to hit the fan." He raised a forefinger before Cassidy could speak. "I can't tell you what it is right now. Just do as I say and you won't get hurt. Okay?"

Cassidy stared at Jessup for a moment, then unzipped the seal on the bundle and looked inside at his Yamaha guitar. "What do I do after that?"

"Do your job, that's all," Jessup replied with a shrug. "It's what we brought you here for. But till then, just go where we tell you to go. Understand?"

"Uh-huh." Cassidy deflected his nervousness by running his fingers over the neck of his instrument. He didn't want to admit it, but the craving was back. Just like it always had been, those times when he was unsure of himself, of his talent. "So, to paraphrase the immortal Frank Zappa, I just shut up and play my guitar."

"That's not a bad idea," Jessup said.

Exerpt from *Manifest Destiny and Mars: A History*, by David L. Zurkin. Duggan & Sons, Publishers, Boston, 2034:

Even as the news media were spreading photos of the City and the Face across every screen and page, at Arsia Station preparations were already underway for an extended expedition to the alien necropolis. The *Edgar Rice Burroughs* expedition of 2028 had made little more than a flyover and a brief touchdown at the Face, and although the airship was the fastest means of long-range transportation available on Mars—unlike ground vehicles, it didn't have to contend with the planet's rugged terrain—it did not have the cargo capacity or crew complement necessary for long-term exploration of the site. Meanwhile, scientists on Earth (along with the general public) were clamoring for more information about the City. It was because of the haste in which the expedition was mounted that a dispute arose: Who had the primary right to explore the ruins?

Although the prior establishment of Arsia Station was an international effort, different nations had contributed the components of the settlement and had aided in the discovery of the site. The *Burroughs* was registered to the United States, but her two-man crew, W. J. Boggs and Katsuhiko Shimoda, were respectively American and Japanese. Was the United States the prime discoverer of the Face, since Boggs had been flying the airship, or was Japan, since Shimoda had been the first one to spot the pyramids? The Mars tractors which brought the second expedition to Cydonia were Russian-made, but the leaders of the Arsia Station science team, Shin-ichi Kawakami and Paul Verduin, were Japanese and Dutch, while the co-supervisors of the newly established Cydonia Base—Arthur Johnson, Sasha Kulejan, and Miho

Sasaki—were American, Russian, and Japanese. Although the scientific equipment which was cannibalized from Arsia Station's labs and transported to Cydonia Base was largely American-made, the habitat modules had been built by the European Space Agency while the ingenious portable waste-recycling plant was a product of the C.I.S., and so on.

In ideal circumstances, this would have been a testament to international space cooperation. Indeed, the members of the Mars settlement had long since learned to disregard the matter of who contributed what. Boggs and Shimoda, in fact, refused to take official credit for "their" discovery, pointing out that it was the Viking Imaging Team which had first located the Face in 1976 (a self-effacing statement which would later have dire repercussions). But on Earth, the sponsoring governments did not view matters in the same light. When Mars had been a way-station for further planetary exploration and its resources were considered nearly limitless, the U.S. and the C.I.S., Japan and the Europeans were completely willing to share the wealth. But the City, the unexplored culture and technological artifacts of the aliens (nicknamed the "Cooties" by Boggs, an appellation which was made to stick by the news media) was not seen to be part of the bargain.

Unfortunately, international space law had yet to evolve to cover exploration or salvage or extraterrestrial artifacts. The closest applicable document, the Protocol for the Sending of Communications to Extraterrestrial Intelligence which had been drafted by SETI scientists in the late 1980's and proposed to the Outer Space Affairs Division of the United Nations, did not cover the remote contingency of someone actually *finding* alien artifacts, and most legal scholars agreed that terrestrial maritime law did not apply to the salvage of nonterrestrial objects. Thus, there was no practicable legal resource: The City seemed to be up for grabs, but by whose hands?

To make matters more complicated, American politics had taken one of its periodic swings to the right, particularly in regard to American-Russian relations. Having dragged itself from the verge of complete social and economic collapse during the early 1990's, the new Commonwealth of Independent States had entered the free-market system with a vengeance in the early 21st century. Now strongly allied to the European Common Market countries, the C.I.S. had become a strong world competitor in export machinery, agriculture, and cybernetics. As well, the newly privatized Glavkosmos had become particularly innovative in

space industry, with many of its spinoffs directly affecting the
C.I.S.'s revitalized industrial base. Although the United States
had long since ceased to be the Commonwealth's military and political enemy, America found itself rivaled in the global marketplace by the C.I.S., in everything from wheat exports and popular
films (the remake of *Battleship Potemkin* had taken the Oscar in
2028 and the action film *Six From Siberia* was breaking worldwide box-office records) to consumer cybernetics and automobiles, as demonstrated by the success of the new Zil 3000
solarcar.

Many pundits were already pronouncing the 21st century the
Russian Century, a slogan which didn't sit well with those who
had assumed that the new millennium would be a continuation of
the American Century. The discovery of the City threatened to
upset the pre-existent balance even further; if the alien necropolis yielded any important technological discoveries, the unspoken
conventional wisdom was that the nation which made those discoveries would be the primary beneficiary. The C.I.S. was desperate to solidify its new foothold in the world marketplace and saw
the City as a possible means to a greater end . . . and the United
States, its principal economic rival, was equally desperate to
make sure that the C.I.S. didn't grab that leading edge.

It now seemed to many Americans still suspicious of Russian
motives as if the C.I.S. was about to swipe a major scientific discovery from the hands of the United States. The Cooties and the
City became a sore point for the man in the street. A national boy-
cott of Russian products was begun by the Republican Party, and
the archaic-sounding "Mars Is Not Red" bumper-sticker began
appearing on cars across the country.

The nationalistic backlash reached its peak in November,
2028, when the ultraconservative George White was elected
President. During his first State of the Union address to Congress,
White alluded directly to the emerging American-Russian disagreement over the salvage rights to Cydonia artifacts (even
though, as his critics pointed out, none had yet been discovered
within the City). Referring to an "American manifest destiny in
space," President White also made the highly dubious claim that
the City belonged to the United States because it had first been
spotted by an American space probe in 1976.

The Russian leadership in Minsk was furious with White's
rhetoric. President Andrei Nasanov, a Labor Party protectionist
who took the traditional view that Russian space efforts consti-

tuted manifest destiny for his own country, struck back with an even more ludicrous claim that, because the old U.S.S.R. had accomplished the first landing of a space probe on Mars in 1971, the red planet was rightfully Russian territory. All mention of the United Nations Space Treaty, which forbade national claims to heavenly bodies, was lost in the subsequent squabble.

If the City had been found to be merely a cluster of abandoned, empty dwellings, the feud might have eventually collapsed in the usual sullen name-calling between the economic superpowers. But then, for better or for worse, the Labyrinth was discovered. . . .

2. Ultimatum

An abrupt jar woke Cassidy from his doze. For a moment, he wondered if the lander had turned around and redocked with the *Shinseiki*. When the spearhead-shaped spacecraft had departed from the cycleship and commenced its final approach, Jessup had told him that it would take fifteen or twenty minutes until aerobraking and atmospheric entry.

Cassidy had taken the opportunity to close his eyes; the less he had to deal with zero-g, the better he liked it. There was another hard bump and a slight fishtailing of the stern, like an airliner hitting turbulence at high altitude. No, he had not landed, and this was not something through which he could sleep.

He opened his eyes as he instinctively gripped the arms of his couch. In the forward cockpit, he saw Massey's head above the back of his acceleration couch. The varicolored lights of the instrument panels were overwhelmed by hot-pink light which surged through the narrow slit windows of the flight deck. "Are we there yet?" he murmured.

"Just hitting the upper atmosphere," Jessup said from the couch next to him. Cassidy glanced over at him; the NASA man looked as confident as a frequent-flyer businessman riding out a thunderstorm on a Chicago-to-New York shuttle. He glanced over at Cassidy. "How're you doing there?"

"Superb." Another swerving jar as if the lander has been drop-kicked. Cassidy felt his stomach curdle. "How much longer till we're on the ground?"

"Ten, maybe fifteen minutes," Massey said. The *Shinseiki*'s first officer didn't look away from his controls; his hands gripped the yoke, his dark skin hued red by the light through the cockpit windows. "Altitude two hundred forty-four kilometers, entry angle fourteen point one degrees, velocity about sixteen thousand klicks per hour. Things will get bumpy for a few minutes when we hit Mach Two. Just relax and enjoy the ride."

The lander skewed left-right-left-right again. "Bumpy?" Cassidy asked. "Things will *get* bumpy?" He let his head sag against the padded backrest of his couch, then decided that such indirect contact with the fuselage of the lander wasn't so comforting after all. Atmospheric friction must be causing the outer hull to blister like Texas asphalt . . . but you don't cruise down Route 82 at twice the speed of sound, nearly eight hundred thousand feet above the ground.

Just considering it, made his guts lurch. So don't think about it, he told himself. Pretend it's a roller coaster at Six Flags. Cassidy shut his eyes again and clutched the armrests, feeling a momentary respite, a little bit of calm. Breathe in, breathe out. Breathe in, breathe out, as the fuselage shuddered and the deck jumped beneath his feet. It felt as if the lander was plummeting down an abyss a million miles deep.

Presently the violence subsided; for a few serene moments it seemed as if the tiny vessel were floating on an air-cushion, suspended in time and space. "L-minus six minutes," Massey reported. "UAMS off, coming up on main chute deployment in four minutes, twenty-two seconds . . ."

Much better now. There were still small tremors running through the hull, but nothing serious. He could hear Massey murmuring radio instructions into his headset mike. No sweat, dude. You can make it. . . .

"You still have that relief bag I gave you?" Jessup asked abruptly.

He opened his eyes. Now there was a weak purple light suffusing the cockpit; everything in the spacecraft seemed to have been tinted with its lovely glow. The airline-style vomit bag was still beneath Cassidy's right thigh; he had been sitting on it since the lander had undocked from the *Shinseiki*. "Sure," he said. "But I don't think I—"

"Velocity six hundred fifty meters per second, altitude five kilometers," Massey said. "Chute deployment countdown. Five . . . four . . . three . . ."

He felt Jessup pull the folded bag out from under his ass and shove it into his right hand. "Get ready," Jessup said. "Drogue chutes first . . ."

Then the lander was then grabbed by God's own fist, wrenched into a vertical position and shaken angrily; the three drogue chutes had fired to brake the biconic spacecraft. A second later there was another hard yank as the main chutes opened, but by then Cassidy's guts had given their final revolt.

He belched agonizingly and clawed at the bag. He barely managed to rip open its adhesive seal and plunge his face against the paper maw before he vomited like never before.

"L-minus fifty seconds," Massey reported. "Velocity two hundred seven thousand klicks, altitude one point five thousand feet. Main engine ignition in ten seconds. Coming up on touchdown at Cydonia Base. Welcome to Mars, gentlemen. . . ."

Terrific. Cassidy hated the joint already.

Suspended beneath the giant main chutes, guided by short thrusts from the RCR's, the lander floated like a silver dandelion seed the last mile to Cydonia Base. At 1500 feet, the chutes were jettisoned and the descent engines ignited to slow the craft for touchdown on the base's landing pad, which was little more than a circle of sand near the habitat which had been cleared of boulders and large rocks.

Richard Jessup couldn't see the base because the cockpit windows now faced skyward, but he could imagine what lay below: eleven modules arranged in a row and buried under the red topsoil, the vehicles parked nearby and, not far away, the quadrangle of ancient pyramids which was the lost city of Mars. . . .

The lost city of Mars. He wondered how such a romantic term had crept into his mind, and then remembered. The day the City had been found by the *Burroughs* survey team, a few of the boys from NASA headquarters had gone over to the Hawk and Dove, a favorite watering hole on nearby Capitol Hill for government pen-pushers. They had spent the better part of the night celebrating the discovery of ETI so close to Earth; in fact, Jessup had surrendered his car keys to the bartender and had taken a cab back to his place in Georgetown. It had been one of those evenings.

At one point during the festivities someone who had read a lot of science fiction—it must have been old Joe Quinlan since he was the only one among them who touched the stuff—had mentioned an old pulp-era story written by Ray Bradbury. *"The Lost City of Mars,"* Joe had cackled as he reached for the third or fourth or fifth pitcher of beer which the bar girl had brought to their table. "Man oh man. If he was still around, we oughta send him tickets to Mars just because he outguessed us. Can you friggin' believe it? A lost city on Mars . . ."

Jessup smiled at the memory, then quickly shook his head. *No. Cut it out.* There was no time for science fiction dreams. He had to think of Steeple Chase first.

Mars would have to wait. He had a more important job in front of him.

Within a few minutes of the touchdown on the landing pad, Jessup walked away from the spacecraft and headed for the half-buried cluster of modules. White mists of hydrogen were steaming from the lander's vents; the ground crew was already moving in with fuel lines to drain the rest of the propellant from the tanks.

Behind him, Ben Cassidy was being helped down the ladder by Massey. Jessup told the musician to remain by the lander until someone came for him, and for once Cassidy appeared to be in no mood to argue; in fact, he seemed to be having trouble simply walking, taking tentative baby-steps in the lesser gravity. It was just as well, as far as Jessup was concerned; he was getting tired of Cassidy's lip. He left the musician in Massey's care and strode off, glad to be rid of his burden for a few minutes.

Two of the base's co-supervisors, Miho Sasaki and Arthur Johnson, had been at the landing pad as a sort of informal reception committee. They now followed Jessup, all three clad in the lightweight Mylar skinsuits which had recently replaced the more cumbersome hardsuits of the first expeditions. The white fabric overgarments of their skinsuits were soiled with red dust, and every few seconds, short steamy-cold plumes of vapor vented from their backpacks: waste carbon-monoxide, expelled from the open-loop life-support systems which extracted oxygen from the native carbon-dioxide and fed into the skinsuits' zero-prebreath environment. It rendered obsolete the frequent oxygen-tank rechargings of the older hardsuits, but it made everyone give off fumes as if they were old-style automobiles.

Sasaki and Johnson had been effusive in their greetings—quite understandable, considering it had been almost ten months since the last cycleship lander had touched down at Cydonia Base—but Jessup had brusquely demanded that they accompany him to the habitat. He shut out the expressions of astonishment glimpsed through their helmet faceplates, just as he consciously excluded all other sensory input: the strange pull of lesser gravity, the crimson boulder-strewn landscape with its short horizon, the weird pink sky and the odd feeling that, if it wasn't for the colors and the data on his heads-up display, this could all be a hot desert somewhere on Earth.

As they marched towards the habitat, Jessup paused to look at the City: four enormous, eroded stone pyramids, eerily reminiscent of the Egyptian pyramids at Giza, towering above the flat red landscape. The necropolis cast long late-afternoon shadows across the ground, their tips almost touching the habitat itself; even from here, he could see the cracks and fissures which ran across their flanks, the ravages time itself had made upon these living-rock hills which the aliens, through some undetermined means, had managed to carve into pyramids. Their sheer size was overwhelming; it caused the eye to play tricks upon itself, making it seem as if they were somehow miniaturized instead of hundreds of feet in height.

In the distance he could see the great mausoleum of the D&M Pyramid, the largest of the Cydonia artifacts. Even several miles away, its peak loomed over the tops of the two easternmost City pyramids. He couldn't see the giant crevasse in the northeastern side of the pyramid, but he knew it was there. And, farther off, out on the edge of the eastern horizon, was the Face itself, a stark profile blindly staring up into the red sky.

The lost city of Mars . . .

Then, as Jessup watched, one of the Russian autotanks clanked into view in front of Pyramid C-1. Twelve feet tall, the AT-80 Bushmaster was as ugly in its design as it was in its purpose; a robot that strode upright on two backward-jointed legs, its revolving upper turret containing a 20mm recoilless machine gun. As it walked past them, its turret swiveled towards Jessup, and the autotank halted for a moment, its cyclopean eye briefly scanning the newcomer.

Stop, Johnson's voice said in his headset. *Keep your hands in sight and don't move.*

Jessup froze. A quick burst from the machine gun could easily chop him in half, but apparently the Bushmaster's AI system determined that none of them constituted an immediate threat. The huge war-robot lumbered away, kicking up little spits of sand with its immense flat foot-pads.

Jessup let out his breath; as he did, he felt a chill surge of an-

ger. He could almost thank the robot; it had reminded him why
he was here in the first place.

Fuck romance, he thought. *This is war. . . .*

"So," Johnson began as soon as they had walked into Module
Nine, "do you mind telling me what . . . ?"

Little had been said amongst them during the long cycle-
through in the Module One airlock. Since the airlock could
accommodate only two people at a time, the two men had allowed Miho to have her privacy while they had waited in the
depressurized garage. When it was their turn, Johnson and
Jessup decontaminated and climbed out of their skinsuits,
dressing in the blue standard-issue jumpsuits which were in the
airlock lockers. Sasaki had been waiting patiently for them in
the access corridor; at Jessup's insistence, she had led them
down the tunnel-like corridor to Module Nine at the other end
of the habitat, where the science lab and infirmary were located.

"Just a second." Jessup carefully shut the hatch behind them.
Then, without preamble or apology, he unzipped a breast pocket
of his jumpsuit, pulled out a sealed envelope, and handed it to
Johnson. The astrophysicist turned the envelope over once in
his hands, grunted noncommittally, unsealed the flap, and unfolded the letter within. He quickly scanned the terse instructions and noted the signatures of the President and the NASA
Chief Administrator, then handed it to Sasaki and looked at
Jessup.

"So . . ." He paused, pursing his lips and gazing at the glass-
ware on the chemistry bench. "Is this permanent, Dick?"

"Only until the crisis is resolved." Jessup replied. "You've
got to believe me when I tell you that it's not my choice or decision. Everyone has complete confidence in your ability to lead
this mission. . . ."

"Except that they don't want someone who's so chummy
with the Russians." Johnson, a squat man with frizzled gray
hair, chuckled derisively and shook his head. "Christ. I was in
first grade when the Berlin Wall was torn down. I remember
when they called it the end of the Cold War. Now that asshole
president of ours wants to start it up again." He shook his head
once more. "Jesus and Mary, save us from the politicians."

"Art . . ." Jessup sighed and rubbed the back of his head, feeling the bump he had received during aerobraking. At least this
was all he had suffered; Ben Cassidy had been violently sick on

the way down. "I don't like it either, but this thing can't function as long as we've got a loaded gun pressed to our heads."

"Then what do you intend to do about it?" Miho Sasaki folded the letter and gave it back to Johnson, then absently shook her long, straight black hair over her shoulders. "This says that you've relieved Arthur of command because of 'military considerations.' What does that mean?"

Jessup had read Sasaki's dossier. A doctorate in astrophysics from the University of Nagoya Institute of Plasma Physics by the time she was twenty-five, a NASDA research scientist on Mars by her thirtieth birthday. Shin-ichi Kawakami's protégée. She spoke English with barely any accent. A very beautiful woman, and sharp as a tack. No demure geisha girl here. He would have to be careful of her.

"I can't tell you that right now. . . ." he began.

"Of course you can tell us that right now." Arthur Johnson feigned breeziness. "Why, Dick, the two of us go back a long way. Junior year at MIT, if I remember correctly. There's nothing you can't tell an old frat brother about, is there?"

"Okay, then, I *won't* tell you about it," Jessup replied. "First I want Sasha and Oeljanov in on this, and I want to give them a chance to remove the Bushmasters and the CAS voluntarily. That's my decision, not George White's."

"What a hero," Johnson said sourly. "What do you have up there, a nuke?"

Jessup ignored him. "I would like for the two of you to be here when I confront them. If and when—if they refuse, I want the two of you to quietly spread the word for everyone to take cover. Inside the City would probably be the best place . . ."

"That's the *worst* place . . ."

"Then at least within the habitat, just as long as they're out of range of the Bushmasters. Who's piloting the *Burroughs* these days? Is it still W. J. Boggs?" Johnson slowly nodded his head. "Okay, then, get Boggs to take the *Burroughs* up and out of here—way out of here, at least twenty kilometers—and to make sure Cassidy's on it when he leaves."

Johnson stared at Jessup for a moment, then nodded his head. "Aye, aye, sir," he muttered. "You're in charge. Right, Miho?"

"Does this mean there's going to be a military strike?" Sasaki asked.

Jessup looked at her but said nothing. The slender young woman stepped closer to him. "Who do you think you are,

Jessup? Japan and the ESA are neutral parties to this mission. What gives you the right to attack without our permission?"

"Miho, your government and the Europeans have been consulted at the highest levels." Jessup met her gaze and forced himself to remain calm. "You may think you're uninvolved, but you know as well as I do that those weapons can be used against anyone and everyone here. Paul, Shin-ichi, Art, yourself . . . you're all potential hostages. Your government recognizes this as well. That's why the *Shinseiki* is being used as the staging vessel."

"For *what*?" she demanded. "Is it a tactical nuclear strike?"

Jessup hesitated. It worked to his advantage to hold his cards close to the vest, but if Miho Sasaki erroneously believed that a nuke strike was in play, this could work against him. Sasaki's great-grandparents had been *hibakusha*, survivors of the atomic bombing of Hiroshima during World War II; distrust of American nuclear forces was traditional, but it ran deep in her family. If she spread word that the *Shinseiki* had a warhead aboard, it would not only spread unfounded hysteria, but could also prompt Oeljanov to take hostages.

"No nukes," he said. "I won't tell you what's up there, but I will promise you, a nuclear strike isn't being planned. You've got to trust me on this."

"Miho?" Johnson said. Sasaki looked at the American scientist, and Johnson solemnly nodded his head. She took a deep breath and slowly nodded her head as well.

Johnson looked at Jessup. "Okay, what's next?"

Jessup unclipped the beltphone from his jumpsuit and passed it to Johnson. "Call Sasha and Major Oeljanov and ask them to come here."

Johnson took the phone, switched to Channel Two, and tapped in a couple of numbers. "Dr. Kulejan, Major Oeljanov, please report to Module Nine at once." He gave the phone back to Jessup. "You know, Dick, Sasha hasn't been crazy about this situation either. It's been Oeljanov's doing all along. He's been caught in the middle."

Jessup nodded. "I'll try to remember that. Thanks for telling me."

A few minutes later, Sasha Kulejan and Major Maksim Oeljanov arrived together at the laboratory. The module had been crowded with only three people inside; now, with two more people present, the meeting was almost literally face to face. Kulejan had not been at the pad when the lander had arrived; the slender, bearded Russian grinned and seized Jessup's outstretched hand between both his and squeezed it warmly.

"Richard!" he exclaimed. "So good to see you once again! Welcome to Mars!"

Jessup forced an uncomfortable smile. "It's good to see you again, too, Sasha. I wish it could be under happier circumstances."

Kulejan's face changed from warmth to puzzlement, and Jessup once more felt vague, condescending amusement for his old acquaintance. Sasha was an excellent scientist, one of the very best in the Russian space community—but he could also be incredibly naive, deliberately isolating himself within an eggshell-thin sphere of theory and investigation, rarely peeking out at the harsh realities surrounding him. *Wake up, Sasha,* Jessup wanted to snap at his friend. *You've been surrounded by your own country's armor . . . don't you ask why?*

No. Sasha knew, all right. He was just unwilling to admit the facts to himself. Before the Glavkosmos astrophysicist could say anything more, Jessup turned his attention to Oeljanov. The C.I.S. Army major—tall, with a prizefighter's build and thin, receding dark hair—was standing at parade rest next to the hatch. "Dr. Jessup," he said formally.

"Major Oeljanov," Jessup replied with equal formality. "I'm here as a representative of the United States government. For the time being, I have officially replaced Dr. Johnson as the American co-supervisor of Cydonia Base."

Oeljanov gazed unwaveringly at Jessup. "Yes? Please continue."

Jessup took a deep breath. He had been rehearsing this moment even before he'd left Earth, when the duty had been thrust into his hands, but he still felt himself shivering. Making ultimatums, particularly to a Russian military officer, was not something to which he was accustomed. "We have problems . . ."

He stopped, took a deep breath, and started again. "Major Oeljanov, we cannot tolerate the presence of autotanks or combat armor at this base. They're destabilizing to the international nature of this investigation and a threat to the well-being of its members. As a designated representative of the United States of America, I'm asking to you remove all Russian weapons from Cydonia Base."

Oeljanov remained impassive. "Speaking as an official representative of the Commonwealth of Independent States"—there was a slightly ironic tone to his voice—"we believe that the deployment of our armor units leads to a greater stabilization, on the other hand. And no one has been harmed by them, have they?"

Behind him, Jessup heard Miho Sasaki move restlessly, but he did not look around. Sasha Kulejan looked uncomfortable, embarrassed. Jessup kept his eyes on Oeljanov's face. "I . . . we don't share that view, Major. Again, I ask you, please withdraw your autotanks from Cydonia Base."

The officer skeptically raised an eyebrow. "And do what with them, Dr. Jessup? Abandon them in the wasteland?" He shook his head. "No. That's unacceptable. We have gone to considerable trouble and expense to bring the AT-80's to Mars. My own CAS isn't that . . . eh, far removed from the design of your Hoplite II armor."

"It's armed. That's difference enough."

Oeljanov shrugged indifferently. "Be that as it may, I'm afraid that they must all remain operational at Cydonia Base."

"Then you refuse?"

Oeljanov's mouth twitched. "Officially, yes, that is what I just said, Dr. Jessup."

Jessup did not bother to repeat the ultimatum to Kulejan. Although Sasha was technically the Russian co-leader of the base and held equal authority with himself and Sasaki, it was tacitly understood that, in matters military, his authority was superseded by Oeljanov. Indeed, repeating the demand to Kulejan could be embarrassing for his friend, whom he had known from meetings at space science conferences on Earth. Such nuances could be reported to—and misinterpreted by—Sasha's superiors in Minsk. The old Communists might be long out of power in the C.I.S. but hierarchy of power had withstood the test of time, neo-capitalist democracy or not.

He was operating under orders. Oeljanov was operating under orders. Everyone on the goddamn planet was operating under someone else's orders . . . and, despite the political rationalizations, they had less to do with politics than with who had the most toys on Mars.

"Then . . ." Jessup paused to pick his words carefully, trying not to tip his hand. "The United States and its Mars allies will have to take appropriate measures."

Oeljanov started to say something, and then stopped. He folded his hands behind his back and stared impassively at Jessup. The challenge was clear in the expression on his face: *try it, but remember that you're outgunned.*

Okay, Jessup thought, but it's not like I didn't ask nicely first. . . .

"Excuse me," he said, and edged past the Soviet officer to step through the hatch. Behind him, he heard Johnson speaking in rapid-fire Russian to Oeljanov, apparently trying to placate the major, and Oeljanov responding in phrases punctuated by the only commonplace Russian word Jessup understood: *nyet . . . nyet . . . nyet. . . .*

Have it your way, you stubborn bastard.

Cydonia Base was a small installation; nothing in it was more than a few steps from anywhere else. Jessup walked down the access corridor until he found Module Two, the command center at the opposite end of the habitat. Shutting the hatch behind him, he immediately ordered the duty officer to radio the *Shinseiki*, using a priority frequency which the ship's command crew was monitoring. A set of code numbers established the validity of his contact and a few seconds later Captain Omori's voice came over the comlink.

Yes, Dr. Jessup? How did your meeting go?

"No go," Jessup replied tersely. "Go with Steeple Chase, code Romeo Delta two-triple-one. Repeat, Steeple Chase, code Romeo Delta two-triple-one. Please affirm, over."

A short pause. Then Colonel Aldriss' voice came over the comlink. *We copy that, Cydonia Command. Steeple Chase, code Romeo Delta two-triple-one, affirmative. We are go, repeat go, with code November Tango three-zero-nine, shall we dance?*

"Affirmative, code November Tango three-zero-niner," Jessup replied, completing the chain. "Kick it out, Steeple Chase."

Will do, Cydonia Command. Falcon Team is on the case. Over and out.

Jessup signed off and settled down in a chair to watch a bank of TV monitors above the console. Fifteen minutes, if everything went according to plan.

Now, if only Oeljanov did not wise up before then . . .

Excerpt from "Benjamin Cassidy—The *Rolling Stone* Interview." *Rolling Stone*, November 16, 2038:

You started out with The Working Blues. . . .

That's right. Jaime, Les, and Amad, plus a couple of session people we hired for studio work on the two albums we did, *Flashpoint* and *Big House*. Good bunch of guys, great musicians.

So why did you break up the band and start playing solo?

Because I didn't want to pay 'em. I'm cheap that way. *(Laughs.)* Naw, that isn't it. The Working Blues was a hot ensemble and we were making money, enough to get by at least, but I just decided after a while, y'know, just to cut loose, see if I could get the blues back to . . . back to one guy and his guitar, just that. Not to make those guys sound bad, but I began to wonder if a backup band was necessary. It's like, y'know, how John Mayall went for years without a drummer in his Bluesbreakers ensembles because he considered a percussion section to be adding just a lot of noise. After a while, I began to wonder if we were overpowering the blues with all this extra stuff, so *(draws a finger across his throat) phfft!*, I decided to get rid of the band. But I still respect and admire those guys. In fact, I'm going to be sitting in on the sessions for Jaime's next album, so this time he gets a chance to fire me from *his* band. *(Laughs.)* I bet he does, too, just to get back.

Jaime and Amad have both claimed that your cocaine addiction caused the group to split apart. Sounds like we've got two different stories. . . .

Well, no, there's not two different stories. They're just two parts of the same tale. Yeah, I was hooked on the stuff, there's

46

no denying that. It got bad enough that, when we were touring with the Cambodians, I was mainlining every time before we went onstage. First they'd hand me the syringe, then they'd give me my guitar. "Okay, Ben, go this way. Don't fall over anything now." And after the gig they'd put me on a couch in the dressing room and have someone check up on me to make sure I wouldn't O.D. I knew I was sick and they knew it too, so while I was in the clinics and the halfway houses, getting clean and deciding that maybe I should try it solo, they decided that they were fed up with my bullshit. So it was a mutual parting of ways. I don't hold any grudges and I don't think they do, either.

You once said, "Being a junkie is fun . . . all you need is patience and money."

What else would you expect a junkie to say? Man, I don't even remember when I said that. *(Pauses)* No, it wasn't because it was fun. I mean, nobody asks to be a junkie. I didn't do it for thrills, 'cause there's nothing I found thrilling about the stuff, and I can't say it was social pressure, because those guys are clean and even blues audiences are straight these days.

So why did you start shooting coke in the first place?

That's a mean, tough question. I guess . . . I think I was scared. I was looking for something, some transcendent experience that made me more of a part of the music. Just playing onstage wasn't enough. But at the same time, I was scared of what I would find. Don't ask me why, or what. *(Shakes his head)* And maybe I'm still scared. I'm over the drugs, but I'm still afraid.

3. Steeple Chase

"I hope you're not some scientist who wants to grab some rock samples 'cause I'm not putting 'em on board and we're getting the hell out of here *now!*"

W. J. Boggs, six feet of bowlegged Tennessee flyboy, did not wait for an answer as he lurched through the gondola's airlock hatch and flopped into the pilot's seat on the left side of the flight compartment. The co-pilot of the U.S.S. *Edgar Rice Burroughs*, Katsuhiko Shimoda, reached above Ben Cassidy—who was scrunched on the floor behind the seats—and flipped a switch to automatically seal the hatch while Boggs stabbed the radio button with his gauntleted thumb.

"Cydonia Command, this is the *Burroughs*, requesting permission for emergency takeoff," Boggs snapped. He did not wait for a reply. "Who gives a shit, anyway?" he muttered. "We're in a hurry here. Katsu, is that hatch secured?"

"Roger that, W.J." Shimoda calmly flipped toggles on his flight station's consoles. "Cabin pressurization cycle initiated. MPU's at one hundred percent, check. Elevators, check. Envelope integrity is copacetic. . . ."

"Yeah, yeah, yeah. Screw the checklist, let's just get out of here."

Burroughs, *this is Cydonia Command, you are cleared for emergency takeoff.*

"We copy, Command," Boggs replied. He glanced over his shoulder at Cassidy. "Hang on there, pal, this is going to be rough. Okay, Katsu, ropes off!"

Shimoda flipped two toggles which severed the airship's tethers. The 120-foot airship bobbed in the stiff breeze which had kicked up as the sun began to set on the western horizon. On either side of the gondola red dust was blown up from the ground

48

by the idling VTOL turbofans; through the crimson haze the skinsuited ground crew were running from underneath the long, ovoid shadow of the blimp.

"Elevators trimmed for vertical ascent!" Boggs called out. "Port and starboard fans grimbaled to ninety and up to full throttle! Hang on, here we go!"

Boggs jammed the two engine throttles forward with his right hand and the *Burroughs* pitched back on its stern as it bolted skyward, its 800-horsepower turbofans howling as they clawed for loft in the tenuous Martian atmosphere. A ballpoint pen which had been left loose on the dashboard skittered down the surface and plummeted to the floor to continue its noisy descent to the rear of the cabin.

"Oh, hell," Boggs murmured. "I was afraid of this." The pilot eyed his altimeter suspiciously, then glanced back again at Cassidy. "Can you fly?" he asked.

"What?" Cassidy asked weakly. It seemed as if the airship was standing on its tail. He had already been sick once today; it wasn't fair to make him go through this kind of ordeal again, less than hour after reaching firm ground. He managed to look up from the few inches of deck between his knees. "This thing?"

"No. I mean, if we have to throw you out the hatch, can you flap your arms and make it to the ground on your own? We're overloaded and this ship isn't made to take three people."

"Uhh . . ."

"Damn." Boggs turned back to his controls. "Katsu, we've got a passenger here dumb enough to think he can flap his arms and fly. Hey, keep an eye on the radar, willya?"

Shimoda looked back at Cassidy. "Don't worry about him. He's always cranky when he has to rush somewhere." He checked his gauges. "Cabin pressurization normal. We can remove our helmets."

He unsnapped the collar of his skinsuit and removed his helmet, then reached over to take off Boggs's helmet since the pilot had his hands occupied with the airship's yoke. Cassidy fumbled with his own helmet, finally getting the thing to detach from his skinsuit; Shimoda helpfully reached back to push the switch on Cassidy's chest unit which turned off the internal air supply. The Japanese co-pilot placed a headset over his own ears, then pulled a spare out of a locker to toss to the musician. Boggs managed, with one hand steadying the yoke against the buffeting of the wind, to yank a George Dickel baseball cap out from under his seat and pull it over his head, securing a headset over it. The foam-padded headsets barely muffled the engine roar, but the mikes made it a little easier for them to hear each other.

"I'm sorry we had to leave your parcel behind," Shimoda apologized. "Our cargo capacity is limited, as W.J. explained, and we're forcing matters by pulling you aboard. What was it, anyway?"

"My guitar."

"A *guitar*?" Boggs yelled again. "Are you that musician we're supposed to be sent?"

"Yeah, that's me. I'm the musician. That's my guitar you left at the base. What are you in such a hurry for?"

Boggs peered at him closely, squinching the sunburn-wrinkled corners of his eyes. "You were just up there. You tell me. All I know is, I just got high-priority orders to get us the fuck outta here *mucho pronto*. Something's about to happen back there and I was told not to have my vessel at risk." He returned his attention to his controls. "If there's anything you need to tell us, son," he said over his shoulder, "now's the time, 'cause I'm righteously p.o.'d . . . and I ain't half-kidding about those flying lessons."

"Well, ah . . ." Cassidy remembered Jessup's warning to him, back on the *Shinseiki*, to keep his mouth shut. Screw it. Something nasty was about to come down, and he was only slightly more informed than these two characters. "There's some Marines up there on the *Shinseiki*," he said, and both men darted glances toward him. "Space Infantry," he added. "They're planning something called Steeple Chase, but I don't know what—"

"Do they have landers?" Boggs snapped. "STS craft?"

"What's an STS craft?" Cassidy shrugged, feeling stupid; he was quickly getting used to the emotion. "I mean, if you know what's going on here . . ."

"Oh, I know. I know, all right." Boggs stared at Shimoda; the co-pilot nodded his head gravely. "Gotta be STS fighters. I'll be a sheep-dipped son of a—" He suddenly grinned at Shimoda, who merely smiled back and shook his head, then he glanced over his shoulder again at Cassidy. "So you're the guitar player. That's funny."

"It's better than getting another boring scientist," Shimoda remarked.

"Keep your eyes peeled on the radar, pal. Angels one-two and leveling off, course thirty-two north by four-zero-four east." Boggs pushed the yoke out of his lap and the airship's nose eased back to a more horizontal position. Cassidy decided it was safe to look up again; he raised his eyes and gazed out the port window.

A thousand feet below him was the rocky, wind-scored terrain of the Martian low plains. The blimp's tiny shadow passed over an endless red desert, falling into valleys and ancient crumbling riverbeds, passing over small hills and the eroded escarpment of an old impact crater. It was the first time he had gotten a chance to look at Mars; he hadn't seen the landscape during the lander's descent, and he had been bustled aboard the *Burroughs* before he had more than a few fleeting seconds to accustom himself to the one-third normal gravity, let alone the red-tinted landscape.

So this was Mars. It looked like . . . no, not like hell. He had been in hell, and it looked nothing like this. Like limbo, maybe. Purgatory. Kansas on a really bad day. The way your head feels after a hard summer night in a seamy bar in downtown Memphis when the crowd's been apathetic and the summer heat has sucked the cold out of your next beer before the barmaid manages to bring it to the stage, but you put down ten bottles anyway while you dumbfuck your way through Willie Dixon's greatest hits. Just like that: desolation of the mind and soul. Mars was a planet suffering from God's own hangover. . . .

"Okay, we're outta the shit and we've got some safe distance," Boggs said. "How's the envelope, Katsu?" Shimoda silently cocked a thumb upward. "Fine. Fifteen miles downrange should be enough room. Let's heave-to here and watch the show. Anything on the scope yet?"

"Negative," Shimoda said, eyeing the radar screen.

"That's *negatory*, dammit! We speak English on this ship!" He feigned a swat at the top of Shimoda's crew-cut head, which the co-pilot easily ducked. "One would think you were still hauling kangaroo meat up from Australia on *Shin-Nippon*, the way you talk."

"Beef," Shimoda corrected. "I was hauling beef, not . . . ah! Radar contact. Two objects entering the atmosphere at fifty thousand feet at Mach Two, forty-two degrees north by thirty-five degrees west . . . faint third and fourth objects dropping away from them just now, off the scope."

"That's the aeroshells breaking loose," Boggs said. "Five bucks says they've developed STS fighters since we've been gone." He glanced back at Cassidy again. "You were up there. Ain't that right?"

"I dunno." Cassidy was still transfixed by the scene outside the gondola windows. "Where's the Face?"

"Left it way back there. Shoulda been looking. What was aboard the *Shinseiki*?"

"There were a couple of Marines aboard when . . ."

"A couple? Only two?"

"Three. I meant three." Cassidy thought about it a moment. "Three from the First Space, but they didn't let me in on anything, so I don't know what . . ."

"Hell, no, but I do!" Boggs cackled and slapped his right palm against the yoke. "See, Katsu? Told you so." He looked back at Cassidy. "Musician, huh? No kidding. I'm named after a musician myself. Waylon Jennings. From Nashville, Tennessee. My hometown."

"I think that's wonderful." Cassidy burped and felt a little bit better for it. His guts were no longer in knots; there was nothing left in them to vomit anyway. "Now will somebody give me a straight answer and tell me what's going on?"

Boggs laughed. "What's happening is that Major Oeljanov and his robots are about to get smeared by the United States-fuck-almighty-Marine Corps, and if you watch out this window you can see the whole show." He motioned to the triple-paned window next to Shimoda's seat. "They've been asking for it and now . . ."

"Two o'clock high," Shimoda said, pointing out his window. "Two vapor trails."

"There we go." Boggs leaned over to stare across Shimoda's shoulders. Two thin white streaks were lancing across the dark purple stratosphere. "So," he added absently, "you're the guy who's going down into the Labyrinth?"

"Yeah," Cassidy clumsily tried to rise and balance himself on his knees, fighting the constant motion of the deck. "I guess I'm the person."

"Lucky you. I hope you make out better than the last guy who was down there."

Cassidy forgot about the vapor trails for a moment. He looked sideways at Boggs. "The last guy? What about him?"

"They brought him out of there in a bag . . . what little they could find of him, that is." Boggs stopped and looked back at Cassidy. "You mean to say that nobody told you what happened to Hal?"

"Aeroshell jettison on my mark," Spike D'Agostino said into the darkness as he curled his gloved hand around a lever next to his left thigh. "Three . . . two . . . one . . ."

He yanked the lever upward. There was a sudden lurch, a loud bang, and the aeroshell which had enclosed D'Agostino's tiny spacecraft broke apart like a clamshell. Harsh red-pink light exploded through the canopy of his cockpit, causing him to blink furiously despite the helmet monocle that was fitted over his right eye. *Woooo-ee!* Hoffman's voice shouted through his headset. *This baby bucks like a Texas bronc!*

D'Agostino ignored him. The F-210 Hornet was plummeting toward the ground some fifty thousand below; if he didn't do anything in the next five seconds, atmospheric drag on the craft's stub wings would put him into an irreversible flat spin. Grabbing the yoke between his legs with his right hand, he reached up with his left hand to the engine control panel above his head and ignited the engines. The LED lamps on the engine status panel switched to green; D'Agostino shoved the throttle forward and gently pulled back on the yoke.

The five Pratt & Whitney oxygen/hydrogen engines, mounted below and behind the Hornet's sleek fuselage, roared to life, catching the STS fighter from its deadly free fall and clutching it in the sky. The fuselage shook as the digital airspeed indicator rolled back to Mach One and the black-white ball of the artificial horizon steadied on the Y-axis. Spike breathed a short sigh of relief. He wasn't going to be splattered all over Mars after all.

"Falcon One to Falcon Two," he said. "How'ya doing there with that horse of yours?"

Copacetic, Falcon One. All stations green and we're flying. Was it good for you too?

"Just lovely, Falcon Two." The eight-ball was rising a little too far into the white; now that its airspeed had been cut, the Hornet was beginning to ascend rather than descend. D'Agostino gently pushed the yoke forward; the port and starboard engines gimbaled back to supply aft thrust, punching the STS fighter forward.

He glanced to his left. Several hundred yards away at nine

o'clock, the other Hornet was slicing through the thin atmosphere, leaving a white vapor trail behind. Falcon Two looked all right; he knew that Hoffman in turn giving Falcon One a quick visual inspection. D'Agostino had to hold tight to the yoke to counter the violent twists and lurches of the Martian stratosphere, but otherwise it was much the same as he had experienced in the simulators. All that was missing was a flight instructor chewing his ass off about slow reaction time. . . .

Fuck it. This was the real-deal now. "Okay," D'Agostino said. "Lock in weapons systems."

Roger that, Falcon One. Lock and load.

D'Agostino flipped more switches with his left hand. The dashboard fire-control panel lit up, showing him in green letters that the two air-to-ground smart missiles below each wing and the 30mm cannon mounted beneath the cockpit were armed and ready. The ECM panel showed that radar and infrared jamming were in operation; radar was tracking no incoming bogies, so the RWR screen was blank. Tiny cross hairs had appeared in his helmet's right-eye monocle; he tracked his eyes left and right, and the cross hairs followed the sweep of his vision. The heads-up display within his helmet visor copied the info shown on the dashboard multifunction display.

"Falcon Two, we're A-OK and on the beam," he said.

Roger that, Falcon One. I take it back. She's a sweet l'il pony, fresh out of the manger. . . .

"We copy." Foal or wild mustang, this was a nice little ship he was piloting, and he was all too willing to kick mongo ass with it. He grinned and pushed the yoke forward. Falcon One pitched its blunt nose forward and the red horizon rose through the canopy windows. "Okay, let it roll."

You got it, Falcon One. Let's go hunt some bear. . . .

Arthur Johnson found Richard Jessup in the command module; he didn't look away from the bank of TV monitors he had been closely watching when the astrophysicist pushed the hatch open. Johnson was about to say something—exactly what, he didn't know, except that he was still pissed off and only too willing to let Jessup know it—until he reached Jessup's side and saw what was on the screens.

Two of the screens showed scenes from cameras mounted outside the habitat. On each, a Bushmaster was quickly striding across the rocky terrain between the habitat and the City; in the background of each screen one or the other of the autotanks could be seen. They seemed to be taking up positions alongside each other.

The third screen displayed a ceiling view of the interior of Module One, the vehicle garage and airlock. Its double doors were shut; centered in the screen was Maksim Oeljanov. The C.I.S. Army major was encased in a Russian CAS; the carapace lid of the armor was open and they could see his head protruding through the suit's thick inner lining. Oeljanov was wearing a white cotton Snoopy helmet. As they watched, his lips moved silently.

"Look at that," Jessup said quietly, for the first time acknowledging Johnson's entrance. He pointed at the other two screens. The upper turrets of the two Bushmasters rotated 45 degrees, their guns both pointing east and tilting upward toward the sky.

"Bastard." Jessup's voice was an awed near-whisper. "He's figured it out and got the Bushies slaved to voice-only command. I tried to squirrel into their AI system interface, but they locked me out." He shook his head. "Maybe the Hornets can ECM the signals, but I doubt it because . . ."

Johnson didn't wait to hear the rest. He yanked his beltphone from his hip, switched to Channel One, the common band for base operations, and raised the phone to his face. "Major Oeljanov, this is Dr. Johnson," he said. "Do you hear me? Over."

Oeljanov's head cocked upwards, apparently responding to Johnson's voice. Jessup turned and made an effort to take the phone away from Johnson, but the scientist stepped back, pushing Jessup out of the way. "Maksim, this is stupid," he said. "I don't know what Jessup was planning, but if you go ahead with what you're doing, you'll be endangering the whole project. Just . . ."

"Art, don't try to—"

"Shaddup, Dick," he said. "Look, Maksim—get out of that thing and come back in here and we can talk it over. Okay? We don't have to go through with this nonsense."

Oeljanov clumsily turned around in the heavy armor and peered straight up at the camera lens. A sardonic smile appeared on his face before the lid of the CAS slowly dropped on its pneumatic hinge. Then Oeljanov raised his right arm—the one which ended in the ugly, stubby maw of a laser-sighted machine gun—toward the camera. There was a microsecond-brief flash from the barrel of the gun; the screen fuzzed out and went blank. A second later the computer replaced the TV image with a line of type: CAMERA 1.01 INOPERATIVE / 1838:32:45 / 6-18-30 / TOTAL FAILURE.

"I don't believe it," Johnson murmured. "He shot out the—"

At that instant there was a sharp *bang!* from somewhere nearby; alarms began to go off within the habitat. Johnson whirled around and checked the flatscreen readout on the environmental control station: DECOMPRESSION MODULE 1 / AIRLOCK INOPERATIVE / INNER HATCHES SEALED / INTERNAL PRESSURE STABLE MODULES 2-9 / 1838:33:01 / 6-18-30.

"Goddamn!" he shouted. "Blowout in Module One! He blew a hole right through the skin!"

"Will that keep him from opening the garage door?"

"No. He can still get out by using the manual override. . . ."

"Damn." Jessup remained calm. "And now the TV camera's gone. If you hadn't done that, we might have been able to watch what he was doing."

"Hell with that!" Johnson snapped. "Now no one can cycle through the main airlock! I've got people trapped out there!"

"Calm down. If they want to get in, they can still use the auxiliary airlock in Module Ten." Jessup reached past Johnson to switch off the decompression alarms, then turned back to the two screens which were still operational. "I'm in charge now, Art. Don't do anything like that again or we're going to have problems."

"Problems?" Johnson let the beltphone dangle from his hand; a profound sense of unreality was settling upon him. "You call this a *problem*? What the hell are you . . . ?"

Unable to articulate his rage and confusion, he floundered wordlessly. Jessup's eyes didn't waver from the screens. "If you still want to help," he said, "you can use tell everyone to take cover where they can. There's going to be a space-to-surface airstrike on the base within the next five minutes. Think you can do that?"

Arthur Johnson stared at the back of Jessup's head. There was a fire extinguisher bracketed to the wall behind them; maybe, with one good stroke, he could use it to bash in the brains of his old frat brother. . . .

But instead, he lifted the beltphone again and pecked out the digits for Channel One with a numbed forefinger.

Excerpt from the Congressional Record transcript of hearings before the United States Senate, Select Committee on Space; July 1, 2030:

MICHAEL ROSENFELD of Missouri, Committee Chairman: The committee still hasn't heard, Mr. Betano, why NASA and the White House felt it was necessary not to inform Congress that a secret military mission was sent to Mars.

ELLIOT B. BETANO, Chief Administrator, NASA: For the same reason that many people within NASA, the Pentagon, and . . . persons directly involved with the mission were not informed, Senator. We felt that Steeple Chase's covert nature, its sensitivity, precluded the public's right to know. We did not want word leaked to the Russians. I was under direct orders from the President not to reveal Steeple Chase to anyone who did not have Top Secret clearance from the FBI and the State Department.

MR. ROSENFELD: I have such clearance, Mr. Betano, and I was not informed.

MR. BETANO: I was not aware of that, Senator. I'm sorry.

MR. ROSENFELD: Yes, I'll just bet you are. The chair recognizes Ms. Crouse.

MARGARET CROUSE of California: As I understand, the strike was carried out using a new type of spacecraft, the . . . ah, F-210 Mars STS. I think they're called the, um . . .

MR. BETANO: Hornets, ma'am. The F-210 Hornet, Mars Space-to-Surface. A very efficient, effective fighting craft, as Operation Steeple Chase has proved.

MS. CROUSE: With certain reservations, I agree. But as I understand, this fighter was specially designed and built for use on Mars. The committee has heard testimony from another witness who tells us that the Hornet is too aerodynamic to be used on the Moon and too flimsy and underpowered for effective use on Earth. The only place it can be effectively used for a combat operation is on Mars. In fact, it was specifically designed for the Martian environment. My question, Mr. Betano, is whether the F-210 was conceived, designed, and built before a need for it existed.

MR. BETANO: Well, the . . . I mean, funding for the Hornet was approved by the Joint Armed Services Committee in FY '27 as a new-start program, with the possibility in mind that the plane would be needed sometime in the near term. It was approved in the DOD black budget by both Houses and was . . . could you repeat the question, please, Senator?

MS. CROUSE: Are you deaf, Mr. Betano, are do you just assume that I'm dumb?

MR. ROSENFELD: The chair recognizes Senator Leakey.

WILLIAM LEAKEY of Ohio: I believe what Senator Crouse is asking, Mr. Betano, is whether the Hornet was designed specifically for this sort of mission.

MR. BETANO: I don't understand what you're asking me, sir.

MR. LEAKEY: The F-210 seems to have been designed as a combat craft. I have the specifications here and I see where the armament includes a 30mm cannon and two solid-stage smart missiles. So the Hornet was designed not just for powered flight in the Martian atmosphere, but apparently for attacking enemy forces on the Martian surface. Even then, its limited range, because of its fuel capacity, made it capable of only short-duration missions. Once it touched down, it was effectively grounded. That's a correct assessment, isn't it?

MR. BETANO: That's correct, sir, yes, but I still don't . . .

MR. LEAKEY: What puzzles me, Mr. Betano, is why NASA and the Pentagon felt it was necessary four years ago to build a Mars STS fighter and hide it within the DOD black budget when the U.S. and the C.I.S. have been in a completely peaceful stance with each other for the past three decades, particularly in space exploration. The kind of mission for which the Hornet was intended, the circumstances for which it was built, did not exist at the time. Both countries were engaging in cooperative exploration of Mars. The Russians had not deployed any weapons on Mars in 2026, nor did they have a reason, in their minds, to do so at that time.

MR. BETANO: I don't understand what you're implying, Senator.

MR. LEAKEY: No sir, I think you do. Someone was spoiling for a fight.

4. 60 Seconds Over Cydonia

The hatch to Module Eleven, the unpressurized Ambient Environment Lab, was covered with a poster of Marvin the Martian from the old Looney Tunes cartoons; Marvin was pointing a ray-gun at the unwary visitor, his eyes narrowed menacingly beneath his Roman centurion helmet. A sign underneath Marvin read in English:

FOOLISH EARTHLING! IF YOU'RE NOT WEARING A SKINSUIT, GO PUT ONE ON RIGHT NOW!

(*and press the buzzer if you want to come in!*)

Miho Sasaki was wearing a skinsuit—the sign was redundant, since the hatch couldn't be opened unless the adjacent Module Ten auxiliary airlock was depressurized—but she had already pressed the buzzer a half-dozen times without any response. Now she was reduced to pounding on the hatch with her fists, giving Marvin worse punishment than he had ever experienced from Bugs Bunny.

"Kawakami-*san*!" she yelled in Japanese. "Kawakami-*san*, open the door!"

She stopped for a second. The absurdity of her situation had just begun to dawn on her; in the low atmospheric density of the lab, her pounding and shouting would be as audible as the sounds made by someone in a basement trying to attract the attention of a person on the third floor. But Dr. Kawakami hadn't responded to either the buzzer-light or to her appeals over the comlink.

Sasaki nonetheless pummeled the hatch again. "Kawakami-*san*, open the—!"

All at once, as if moved by her fists, the hatch popped inward on its hinges. A second later Tamara Isralilova wrenched the hatch open. *Get in here quickly!* she demanded, her voice harsh

60

through the comlink, using English as was customary when persons of different nationalities were together in the base. Without waiting for Miho to act voluntarily, Tamara grabbed her forearm and yanked her through the hatch into the module.

The lighting in the lab was dim, red-tinted on the same spectrum as the surface outside the habitat to mimic the natural Martian conditions. The AEL was designed to copy outside conditions while preserving dust-free, germless conditions necessary for exobiologic studies. On the other side of the central workbench, Shin-ichi Kawakami was using duct tape to secure a rack of flasks against a bulkhead shelf. *Have you got her in?* he asked without looking over his shoulder. *Good! Now shut the hatch!*

Isralilova immediately slammed it shut. *Sorry it took a few moments*, she apologized briskly, *but we were busy. . . .*

"Then you know about the . . ." Sasaki began.

Of course, Miho. Kawakami pulled the tape tight against the flasks, then moved to the computer terminal next to the rack. *Arthur put out the warning a few minutes ago. As the Americans like to say, there's going to be a whole lot of moving going on, so . . .*

"A whole lot of shaking going on," Miho automatically corrected him.

Jerry Lee Lewis, Kawakami said impatiently as his fingers darted across the keypad. Nobel laureate in exobiology. Senior scientist of the Cydonia expedition. Secret fan of western rock 'n' roll; he practiced *sho*, the ancient Japanese art of calligraphy, and collected 1950's rockabilly tapes with equal passion. Miho wasn't quite sure why she loved the old man. . . . *Yes, Miho, I know. . . . Now make sure the tent is secure over Hirohito, will you, please?*

Sasaki looked down at the dark form that lay on the long lab bench in the middle of the room, shrouded by a translucent plastic sheet clamped to the edges of the table. Hirohito was the scientist's nickname for the only intact corpse of a Cootie which had been found in the City. It figured that Kawakami would give it the name of one of Japan's past emperors; ironic now, considering it was Hirohito who had been forced to sign the treaty with the United States which had ended World War II.

But Hirohito the mummified alien was as important to Kawakami as his own life. All the other Cooties were desiccated fragments of chitinlike exoskeleton: a half-collapsed skull here, a foreleg there; part of a thorax from one niche which might, or might not, be matched to another partial thorax from a different part of the vast tombs of the D&M Pyramid. Of all the remains which had been thus-far located, only by freakish and as-yet-unexplained accident had Hirohito's insectlike body survived the catastrophes of time. Miho carefully checked the clamps holding down the shroud and reflected that Kawakami would gladly swap his Nobel Prize medallion for another corpse to match Hirohito. Which was not saying much, considering that the old scientist had been known to make inglorious use of that same medallion as a paperweight in the Module Nine lab . . .

For no apparent reason, she suddenly thought of another member of the science team. "Paul!" she snapped, looking up from the bench. "Has anyone seen Paul?"

Kawakami looked up from the terminal; through the visor of his helmet, his ragged white mustache twitched distractedly. *Verduin? I assumed that you knew where he was.*

Sasaki stared at him, then darted a look across the bench at Isralilova. Tamara looked back at her and shook her head. *I last saw him out on the surface,* she said. *He was checking the C-4 scanner when the lander touched down. . . .*

Sasaki hissed and bolted away from the bench; she almost made it to the outer hatch, on the other end of the AEL which led directly to the surface, before Kawakami jumped out of his chair and wrapped his arm around her waist. *No!* he commanded, stopping her more with his voice than with his frail strength. *You stay here!*

"Paul's outside!" Miho didn't fight Shin-ichi, although she could have easily knocked the sixty-year-old man to the floor. "There's going to be an airstrike! He'll be killed if he's out there!"

If he heard Arthur, then he will have taken cover, Kawakami said soothingly. *There's nothing you can do for him, Miho.*

Cocooned in his combat armor, Maksim Oeljanov looked through the built-in VR screen and studied the flat landscape separating the habitat from the edge of the City. Digital displays in Cyrillic informed him that the nearest pyramid, the C-4, lay only thirty meters away to the southeast; as he glanced in that direction, he saw someone in a skinsuit standing near one of the scanners, at the western corner of the massive stone edifice. He ignored whoever it was; if he or she was foolish enough to be out in the open like this, there was nothing he could do about it.

He returned his attention to straight-ahead, the northeastern boundry of Cydonia Base beyond the upthrust bicone of the *Shinseiki's* lander. In the far distance, near the horizon, he could see the great profile of the Face, staring bleakly upward into the darkening sky.

When they come, he thought, *it will be over the Face. . . .*

The Commonwealth's Central Intelligence Service had known about the secret American effort to build a Mars space-to-surface fighter for quite some time. In fact, the very reason why Oeljanov had been sent to this godforsaken place had been to counteract a possible American takeover of the base. If only the C.I.S. had something like the Hornets . . .

No. This was wishful thinking. He would have to depend on the autotanks which flanked him on either side. If worse came to worst and he found himself outgunned, he could always command Unit One to train its guns on the habitat's command module. Then, perhaps, he could dictate terms of surrender by the American pilots.

But that was a coward's way out. Oeljanov almost automatically ruled it out. This was to be a showdown: Russian cybernetics and armor matched against experimental American spacecraft.

Yes. A showdown . . .

He noticed his shadow stretching out before him, cast across the red dust by the setting sun at his back, and was reminded of the old American Western movies he openly adored. His fellow cadets at the Russian Military Academy used to call him "Clint" because of his predilection, and he had not minded the nickname all that much. He was a loyal officer of the Russian Army, but in his fantasy life he always wore a bandolier and two Colt six-guns; in his fantasy-self, there was a knowing squint in his eyes.

Yes, this was going to be much like a Western: he was Bob Wayne . . . *nyet,* he reminded himself once again, *that's John Wayne* . . . Gary Cooper, Steve McQueen, Yul Brynner, Clint Eastwood. . . .

"Okay, pilgrim," he said in English, imitating Bob-John Wayne's drawl, "I'm calling yew out. . . ."

As if on cue, the RWS bleeped, alerting him to something which had been picked up within radar range. Two blue crosshatches appeared on his VR screen, overlaying twin white streaks which were rising over the northeastern horizon. Very good; just as he had predicted.

"Unit One, Unit Two," he said aloud, "track and target incoming objects at azimuth fifty-five degrees nine point two minutes and lock on weapons."

There was a double beep in his headphones as the autotanks obediently followed his instructions; he didn't need to look at his heads-up to see that their guns were armed and following the track of the Hornets.

Oeljanov raised his right arm to point at the sky, feeling his index finger coil around the recessed trigger of his own built-in gun. "Continue autotargeting," he told his suit. "Fire control select on manual." He could have allowed to suit to determine the optimimum target and automatically fire for him, but that was much too unsportsmanlike. A soldier, or a gunslinger, doesn't let a computer pull the trigger for him. That's not the way Clint would have done it. . . .

As the RWS's beeps rose in cadence, signaling the rapid approach of the enemy, Oeljanov planted his feet wide apart and sucked in a deep breath.

When the sun sets, he told himself, I'll be a Hero of the Commonwealth. . . .

The first indication Paul Verduin had that something was seriously wrong was when he received a terse radio message from Arthur Johnson telling him to take cover near the City. Then the comlink went silent, leaving the Dutch scientist with little choice but to run for his life.

He'd felt certain that a showdown was inevitable, ever since the Russians had brought their weaponry to Cydonia. But he had never expected it to be so *fast*. . . .

Verduin knew something was coming out of the sky when the C-4 scanner turned its head toward the east. The scanner was a stationary robot: a tall, slender automaton fixed permanently in the ground, with a cluster of cameras, sound and motion detectors, recorders, and transmitters built into a swivel-mounted head on top of its main shaft. It had been set there to act as a sentry to the entrance to the C-4 pyramid, guarding against anyone making an unauthorized visit to the Labyrinth . . . or, just perhaps, something coming out of the pyramid.

Crouched behind the western corner of the pyramid, Verduin

jabbed a forefinger on the keypad built into the right-hand bracelet of his skinsuit, tapping into Channel Four, the scanner's frequency. WHAT IS COMING FROM THE EAST? he asked.

The reply from the AI system immediately flashed in translucent green letters across his helmet's heads-up display: 2 OBJECTS / IDENTITY UNKNOWN / NE 55.95 x 1200 M. / EST. VEL . . .

He didn't read the rest, for he suddenly heard a high thin whistle which sounded absurdly like the sound effect one hears in a cartoon when a bomb is being dropped out of the sky. Verduin looked again across the plain at the distant mounds of the habitat. Oeljanov—no one else would be wearing that combat armor suit, so it had to be Oeljanov—and the two autotanks were between him and safety inside the modules. But maybe, if he took advantage of the one-third gravity and discarded his ankle-weights which allowed him to walk normally on the surface, he could still . . .

Don't even think about it, he told himself. You have several million tons of stone block between you and whatever is coming down from the sky. If you stay here, you have a chance, but caught out in the open . . .

Verduin grimaced and crouched lower behind the corner of the pyramid. He remembered stories his grandfather, who had been a child during the Second World War, had told him about cowering in his mother's flat in Arnhem when the Nazi panzer divisions were laying siege to the Allied forces of the ill-fated Operation Market Garden. His grandfather had been among the few Dutch residents who had escaped harm when the city was eventually leveled during the combat. To the young Paul Verduin, who was then devouring all the science books he could lay his hands on, the siege of Arnhem sounded as remote as the fall of ancient Rome to the Visigoths.

He had listened to the old man's oft-repeated stories with little more than casual interest, being polite while he leafed through another astronomy text, but now he had a sense of what his grandfather had felt. A mechanized, faceless terror was descending upon him, and the only options he had were to run or hide . . . never to fight back.

The whistling grew louder. From his all-too-close vantage point, he could see the Russian autotanks tilting back on their legs as their ugly black machine guns simultaneously telescoped upward.

"Damn you," he whispered in Dutch, "get off this planet . . ."

Then, all at once, the fury of war was upon him.

The Unit One autotank opened fire first, followed milliseconds later by a continuous burst from Unit Two, the one closer to him. A dim staccato *pappa-pappa-pappa-pappa* was carried through the thin atmosphere as fire seemed to erupt from their machine guns, spent shell casings ejecting from the sides of the robots and falling, bouncing, to the desert floor. Verduin instinctively held his hands up to the sides of his helmet as he watched Oeljanov take one step forward, his own gun blazing away at something still unseen in the sky beyond the peak of the pyramid. . . .

"Get off my goddamn planet!" Verduin shouted.

Something exploded between Unit One and Unit Two, sending up a shower of dust and pummeling Oeljanov to his knees. A fraction of a second later, Verduin caught the briefest glimpse of something streaking into Unit Two. . . .

Then the Bushmaster went off like a bomb, its fuel tank detonating as an orange-red fireball, twisted metal debris spewing outward. Amid the muffled roar, Verduin saw something spiraling straight toward him; he threw himself flat on the ground, covering his head with his arms, and a moment later felt something heavy smash into the ground only a few feet away.

Verduin glanced between his elbows and saw the head of the C-4 scanner, its camera lenses pointed straight at him. A couple more feet of random velocity and it would have crushed him.

He barely had time to realize this before there was another explosion, this time from above. Paul craned his neck back as far as his helmet would permit and saw a small, stub-winged spacecraft racing across the sky, only a couple of hundred meters above the ground, its shadow passing over the ruined hulk of the autotank. Black smoke was billowing from beneath its wings; the craft canted sideways, out of control in a long downward arc, and disappeared from sight past the huge peak of the C-1 pyramid. . . .

More gunfire. Unable to help himself, Verduin rolled sideways to stare in horrified fascination as another missile lanced Unit One. The autotank's upper turret exploded and the mobile lower fuselage seemed to reluctantly collapse upon itself like the beheaded body of an animal. Maksim Oeljanov, making an ungainly struggle to his feet in his CAS, was raising his right-hand gun to take aim when a wide, dark shadow fell across him. . . .

Bullets pocked the armor like hard rain. Oxygen-nitrogen spewed outward from the CAS like fine mist—pink-tinted white mist—as the Russian officer toppled backwards, letting loose a final bit of obstinate gunfire as he sprawled into the rocky soil. His body was lost in a dusty cloud as, a second later, the second spacecraft whipped overhead, streaking against the setting sun into the dark sky.

The Greeks named this world after a god of war. . . .

Paul Verduin watched it soar upward as he waited for the next missile, the next fusillade of 30mm shells. Yet there was peace now. The western wind slowly carried the mixed haze of red dust and black smoke away from the battlefield; the fuel of the destroyed autotanks made a brief and futile attempt to burn in the sparse atmosphere. There was an unintelligible chatter of voices—unnoticed until now, but ever-present nonetheless—in his headset.

So what else should you expect . . . ?

Verduin lay prone on the ground, feeling his body shake within the tight confines of his skinsuit. There was a stinging acid sensation between his thighs where he had involuntarily pissed himself beyond the capacity of the suit's urine-collection cup. He hardly cared. He watched the little spacecraft as it banked sharply to the right, turning around and coming back toward the base. In one part of his mind he knew that it was coming in for a landing . . . but he instinctively waited for its pilot to train the cannon on him, where he lay helpless on the ground, and open fire again.

But he knew that wouldn't happen. No. It wouldn't.

It wouldn't . . .

"Get off my planet," he whispered again.

Excerpt from *Mars* (Volume 4, "The Solar System" series). Time-Life Books, New York, 2034:

The second expedition to the City found as many new mysteries as it did new discoveries.

The extraterrestrial explorers who had visited Mars in the distant past apparently never left the planet. Indeed, the red planet had become their final resting place. The giant D&M pyramid was found to be an immense tomb, its interior catacombed with niche-like compartments containing their desiccated remains. Although only one intact exoskeleton of a "Cootie"—as the alien race was dubbed by the initial explorers—was ever found, this single specimen, along with fragments of others, was enough to provide Cydonia Base exobiologist Shin-ichi Kawakami and the science team with a near-complete picture of the physiology of the insectile aliens (*see Figure 3-8*).

Why did the Cooties settle Mars instead of Earth? And why did the aliens never leave Mars, but commit themselves to mass—and perhaps living—entombment within the D&M Pyramid? While there are several theories, the leading one was first propounded by Richard Hoagland, in the 1980's before the existence of the Face and the City was verified, and later tentatively verified by Kawakami.

According to the Hoagland theory, the aliens had been colonists brought to our solar system by a sublight-speed starship from their homeworld, located in an as-yet-undetermined part of the galaxy. The starship had followed a course tracked by an earlier advance probe to Earth, but after a voyage which must have lasted hundreds, or even thousands, of years, the colonists

found Earth to be critically different from what had been anticipated.

Hoagland speculated that Earth's gravity might have been too
high to support such a colony, a factor which an advance probe
might have overlooked in its assay of Earth as a colonizable
world. From his examinations of the Cooties' remains, Kawakami
has stated that the aliens' fragile physiology may not have been
strong enough to support their life-functions for very long in
Earth's higher gravity, leading some credence to Hoagland's theory.

Other exobiologists have since questioned these conjectures—
the question of microbiological predators has been raised, for
instance, along with the obvious question of why such an advanced interstellar probe failed to report gravitational
conditions—but the Hoagland-Kawakami theory stands as the
leading explanation.

Even then, a major question persisted: why did the Cooties
leave their home system? An exploratory spirit? A need to colo-
nize other planets because of conditions in their home system?
No one knew for certain.

Nonetheless, under such conditions, the Cooties might have
reached the decision to settle Mars instead of Earth. Their starship might have been on a one-way trip, with return to the home
system impossible for reasons of fuel and resources; with the remaining planets even more inhospitable. Mars was the best and
only hope for the colony's survival.

For whatever reason, the Martian colony did not survive. The
planet's climate could not support the Cooties for long. Although
a starship has never been found, circumstantial evidence sug-
gests that it was dismantled and that the Cooties did not leave our
solar system again.

Within the City Square, Pyramids C-1, C-2, and C-3 were
found to be the vacant remains of the colony, with vast chambers
and small rooms apparently once devoted to sustaining—for a
brief time—the lives of the Cooties. Yet surprisingly few relics
were found in the pyramids, nor were there any signs of the
aliens' culture: no hieroglyphs, no examples of a written language, and most importantly, nothing which indicated from where
the Cooties had come. Indeed, it seemed as if the Cooties had
deliberately removed and hidden their artifacts before they entombed themselves inside the D&M Pyramid.

Meanwhile, there was the mystery of the Face itself. The mile-long mesa near the City had clearly been carved to resemble a human visage. From the anthropomorphic evidence, it appeared that the Cooties had knowledge of the human race's existence on Earth; why else would there be a human face on a planet where *homo sapiens* had never evolved? Extensive natural erosion to the structures—including a large chasm in the wall of the D&M pyramid caused by an ancient meteor impact—demonstrated that the Face and the City were thousands of years old, long before the human race had achieved the ability to travel to other planets. If the aliens had believed that the inhabitants of the third planet would one day venture to Mars, why did they feel it was so necessary to draw the attention of human explorers, considering that humans would arrive so long after the demise of the doomed colony?

The answers to these enigmas lay within Pyramid C-4—the last to be opened by the international team of explorers, the first to take lives. . . .

5. The First Casualty

Night had fallen by the time the *Burroughs* returned to the
base. The crew had set up portable floodlights around the perimeter of the habitat, but it was still dark enough that the airship's touchdown, guided by the flashlights of two expedition
members on the ground, was rough. Most of the floods were
centered around the wreckage of the two Bushmasters.
Oeljanov's corpse, still inside the bullet-pocked remains of his
combat armor, was sprawled near the habitat where he had
fallen during his final stand. The surviving Hornet had alighted
near the *Shinseiki*'s lander, but the other Hornet had plowed
into the desert several miles away. Miho Sasaki and Spike
D'Agostino had taken a tractor out to the crash site to retrieve
the remains of Goober Hoffman.

Ben Cassidy found Dick Jessup near Oeljanov, watching as
someone used a portable laser to slice through the CAS's ceramic shell to remove the major's body. The musician ignored
the silent, almost respectful circle of people surrounding
Oeljanov. He grabbed Jessup's left shoulder. "Jessup, I want
some words with you," he demanded.

Not now, the NASA administrator said softly. He didn't look
up from Oeljanov's body.

"Why didn't you tell me about Moberly? Or about the first
guy who went in there, the one who was killed as soon as he entered the Labyrinth?"

This is not the time, Jessup insisted.

"You son of a bitch, when *was* the time?" Cassidy's voice
rose belligerently. Overhearing the conversation through the
comlink, the people standing around looked away from
Oeljanov toward them. "Before you drafted me for this goddamn mission? Or maybe you were afraid that I wouldn't go

along with this if I knew that the last person who went into C4-20 was ripped apart like a roast chicken? *Christ, all you found was his head—!*"

Jessup, saying nothing, pulled his arm out of Cassidy's grasp and started to walk away. Cassidy grabbed his arm and hauled him back as he balled his right hand into a tight fist. For a moment, he was able to relish a look of fear through the frost-rimmed faceplate of Jessup's helmet.

Arthur Johnson, who had been standing nearby, jumped forward and pried Cassidy's fingers off Jessup's suit. *Cut it out!* he shouted. *If you even crack his helmet, he'll die before we can get him into an airlock!*

He hauled Cassidy away from Jessup, who had turned around to silently gaze at the two of them. "That's no worse than what he had planned for me!" Cassidy yelled. "What were you planning to do? Throw me in there and see if the room will kill me just like it did with Moberly?"

Johnson, still restraining Cassidy, looked at Jessup. *You didn't tell him about Hal?* he asked. Jessup said nothing; he only stared at Cassidy. Johnson shook his head within his helmet. *Is there anything else you've been keeping from us, Dick?*

Great. That's just fabulous. Waylon Boggs, who had just joined the circle after checking over the *Burroughs*, walked up behind Jessup. *The way this mission is going so far, we'll have more bodies to bury around here than the Cooties left in the pyramids.*

Leave it to NASA, Johnson murmured. *Good old Never A Straight Answer . . .*

NASA, like hell. Paul Verduin, standing on the other side of the circle, shuffled his feet in the dirt. *Any time the American military gets involved, it's never a straight answer.*

Okay! All right! Jessup lost his cool; he stepped forward into the ring of accusation which seemed to surround him. *You want to know why you weren't told about Moberly, Ben? You got it right the first time—you wouldn't have come if I had told you. Art, you want to know why you weren't informed in advance about Steeple Chase? Because the secret would have leaked to Oeljanov and he would have taken hostages, and maybe more people would have died. . . .*

I have a hard time believing that, Verduin said. *Maksim was many things, but I don't think he would have taken us hostage. If he wanted to do so, why didn't he begin the moment your gun-*

ships entered the atmosphere? He had the time. I was watching when . . .

You want to call me a liar, Jessup snapped, *go right ahead, but maybe you're all still alive because some secrets were kept.*

No one said anything for a minute; the comlink was silent except for the faint hiss of static. In the glare of the floodlight, the exhaust of their life-support systems rose like smoke from small, smoldering fires. Cassidy was reminded of all the backstage fights he had been part of, back in the days when he still had a band: then the times when he was too fucked up on drugs to go out and play, when Jaime and Amad and the session men would haul him away from the mike and into the wings, demanding to know whether he had broken his vow to stay straight for this one gig. And always, he would lie. No, I haven't touched the shit. I'm just having a bad night, that's all. I swear, there's nothing wrong with me. Just one too many beers . . .

"Truth sucks, doesn't it?" he asked aloud.

Jessup's eyes darted toward him. His gaze was murderous, but he said nothing.

I'll ask you again, this time politely, Johnson said at last. *Is there anything else you're keeping secret from us?*

No, Jessup said laconically. *Nothing.*

All right then, Johnson said. He let go of Cassidy and motioned toward the habitat. *Ben, if you'll come with me, we'll get you a cup of coffee and a bite to eat in the wardroom. Then we'll give you the whole story about the Labyrinth and what happened to Hal Moberly.* He hesitated. *Of course, after you know everything, you may not want to go in there.*

"Yeah, maybe I won't," Cassidy said. "But do I have a choice?"

Within his helmet, Johnson shook his head. *Probably not, I'm afraid.*

Module Four of the Cydonia Base habitat was a wardroom which served jointly as the galley, dining area, conference room, and recreation area. By the time Cassidy and Johnson got there, though, it had been taken over by Boggs, Katsuhiko Shimoda, Spike D'Agostino, and several other crew members. D'Agostino had just returned to the base with the remains of Goober Hoffman; he was in the mood for a wake and Boggs was only too willing to oblige. Shimoda had contributed a flask of sake and Boggs had dug a bottle of whiskey out of his locker, and they were proceeding to indulge in a melancholy bender. Neither Johnson nor Cassidy cared to join in. Johnson found some rehydrated roast beef and horseradish in the refrigerator, poured a couple of mugs of black coffee, and the two men retreated to Johnson's digs in the Module Six bunkhouse, deserted now that everyone else was getting twisted in the wardroom.

"It's been a wonderful day." Johnson settled down on his bunk and dabbed a slice of beef into the brown puddle on his plate. "First I get relieved of command, then I get to see two men killed." He shoved the roast beef in his mouth and chewed on it as he gazed at Cassidy, who was sitting on the bunk across from him. "What I'm ashamed to admit," he continued once he had swallowed, "is that I'm the guy who got you into this fix."

Cassidy stared back at him. "Come again?"

"My fault. When I listened to the tape of Moberly's encounter with the room, I thought it sounded like your improvisational work. In my report to NASA, I said as much in passing. I was suggesting that we develop an artificial intelligence . . . maybe an AI expert system of some sort . . . that would copy your guitar style, something which could communicate with C4-20. After all, the Cooties themselves must have had some sort of AI running the Labyrinth, so if there was an AI which could specifically mimic your style . . ." He took a deep breath. "But someone must have taken me literally. I didn't think . . ."

He shook his head regretfully. "Damn, Ben, I'm sorry about this. I've been listening to your work for years. The last thing I wanted was to get you into this shit."

Cassidy nodded, absently swabbing some beef in his horseradish before realizing that he wasn't hungry in the first place. He put the paper plate on the bed. "S'okay. They probably would have drafted me anyway."

"Drafted? Jeez, you're my age. You're too old for the draft. What did they get on you?"

Cassidy sipped his coffee. It was wretched and he put it down on the floor. "Taxes and drugs," he replied.

"What about 'em?"

"I didn't pay my taxes for a couple of years because I was strung out on drugs. They said I could go to jail or I could go to Mars. I think they came up with my name before they audited the books, but when they did, they found the leverage to get me here. At least, that's what I figured from what Jessup told me."

Johnson shook his head with black amusement and wiped his lips with the back of his hand. "Good old Dick. I should have let you rip his suit back there. Seldom has there been a more two-faced bastard to walk the earth . . . or Mars, for that matter." He picked up another slice of roast beef. "Guess that figures. Someone once said that the first casualty of war is the truth."

"Well, that's kind of the problem with my situation, isn't it?" Cassidy rested his elbows on his knees and cupped his hands together. "I mean, it's becoming pretty obvious that Jessup didn't tell me everything when I still had the chance to back out. So what's the real story here?"

"I don't know. What's the question?"

"What happened to this guy Moberly? I know he got killed in the room, but I don't know how or why, and that somebody else bought it in the Labyrinth. But what's so important about exploring the place?"

"Jessup left out a lot, didn't he?" Art Johnson sipped from his coffee, made a face, and placed his cup on the floor. "Hal Moberly . . . well, let me start at the beginning."

When Cydonia Base explorers opened Pyramid C-4 in early 2029, the first thing they found was a small room about the size of a large walk-in closet. The room was featureless, except for another stone door at the opposite end of the chamber. Mounted in the center of the door was a large round button.

The first man to enter the room was a Soviet exobiologist, Valery Bronstein. He had the right idea—push the button with his hand to open the door—but when he walked into the room, he stepped on a large round divot placed in the floor. The weight of his body pushed the divot down and, before he or anyone else could react, a one-ton stone block fell from the ceiling and crushed him to death.

"Oh God," Cassidy said.

Johnson nodded. "Once we hauled the block away and removed Valery's body, someone else approached the problem by extending a rod through the doorway and pushing the door-button with it. The door opened without another block dropping, and we found a corridor leading downward. We followed it to Room C4-2, and that's when we found the next little test."

Room C4-2 was larger than Room C4-1. Again, it had a door at the opposite end, but this time there was a wide slot set in the middle, with a narrow bar sticking out of the left side. Above and below the slot were inscribed two horizontal wavy lines, running parallel to each other. As well, the walls of the chamber were lined with narrow, horizontal grooves. This time, the science team cautiously entered the room and studied the slot and the diagrams at length before Johnson himself performed the task that Shin-ichi Kawakami determined was the solution to the new test: he carefully moved the narrow bar along the slot from left to right, exactly following the pattern of the wavy lines.

"I was scared to death, but the door opened," Johnson said. "Again, we found a corridor continuing downward to Room C4-3. We checked the grooves in the walls later and found spring-loaded fléchettes in them. Sharp as razors. If I had made the wrong move, they would have ripped me apart."

"And the next room was . . . ?"

"Another test." Johnson grinned. "Tic-tac-toe, if you can believe it, and another death-trap if you screwed up. This time, the whole blamed floor was rigged to collapse and drop you down a bottomless pit. And that's the way the whole Labyrinth is designed."

He traced a descending spiral in the air with his forefinger. "It goes down and down and down, room after room, and each room has its own IQ test, a degree more difficult than the last one. Mostly they involve symbology, which is the closest we've come to discovering any sort of written language of the Cooties, so the first trick has always been to determine what the symbols mean. By the time we reached Room C4-10 the tests began to involve mathematics, and C4-13 and C4-14 had tests relating to what we know as Newtonian physics. Sometimes it would take us weeks just to figure out what the Cooties were trying to ask, even if the solutions themselves were pretty simple. That seems to be the intent. The rooms want to find out if we can second-guess them."

He rolled up another slice of beef and swished it around in the sauce. "Of course, we took precautions after I went in there. We managed to get some modified Hoplite armor and shipped to us, like the ones used by U.N. peacekeeping troops. Strictly recon stuff . . . it wasn't until later that the Russians shipped up that battle armor which Oeljanov was wearing. But it gave the first person entering a new room a certain degree of safety, and we were able to monitor what he or she was seeing and doing from the control module up here. Worked fine. We didn't lose anyone else, until Hal Moberly entered C4-20."

"Okay." Cassidy held up a finger. "I know that something ripped apart his suit. You lost contact with him right before it happened, but you heard the music just before then. Is that the truth?"

Johnson nodded again. "Yep. Sounds as if the only thing they didn't tell you about C4-20 is that Moberly was killed in there . . . and that we barely found enough of his body left to fill a bucket."

"His head," Cassidy said. "Part of his armor, and his head."

Johnson grimaced as he shut his eyes. "The rest of him was missing, and damn if I know why." Then he looked up again at the musician. "But did they tell you that it looks like C4-20 is at the end of the Labyrinth?"

Surprised, Cassidy shook his head. "That figures," Johnson continued. "There's no other doors, but the walls look different. Metallic. Maybe there's something behind them. If that's the case, it would fit with Kawakami's theory that the Cooties knew somebody from Earth was coming. They built the Face to draw our attention, and then they built the Labyrinth to make sure whoever explored this place was smart enough to be able to understand . . ."

Cassidy put up his hands. "Hey, slow down. Wait a minute." He shut his eyes briefly, trying to concentrate on an unfamiliar pattern of thought. "Let me get this straight. These aliens . . ."

"Call them the Cooties. Everyone else does." Johnson peered at him quizzically. "I'm surprised you don't know about this. Everyone else on Earth seems to."

"I've only recently been living on Earth again, y'know what I mean?" Cassidy shrugged and went on before Johnson could ask what he meant by that comment. "These Cooties left behind a labyrinth in a dead city here on Mars . . ."

"That's right."

"And they built the Face to attract our attention to this place."

Johnson nodded his head. "That's correct. Go on."

"But they built it thousands of years before we even started dicking around with balloons, let alone rockets."

Johnson smiled. "You're on the right track."

Cassidy sputtered. "Then how did they know someone was coming from Earth? And even if they knew, why make it such a mystery? Why not put up . . . I dunno, hieroglyphics, a map, some sort of simple instructions? Why go through all this bull-shit if they wanted to . . . ?" He suddenly ran out of steam, un-able to verbalize his swarming thoughts.

"Why go through all this if they simply wanted to establish contact?" Johnson finished. "That's the thing of it, Ben . . . *we don't know!* Science is like that. You can't just look at it once and say, 'Ah-ha, there's the answer!' Nothing's clear-cut and obvious about this deal. There're riddles within riddles, like an old Chinese puzzle-box. It's like an onion, unpeeling in layers. We've got a city which was once occupied by an extraterrestrial race, but they leave behind nothing but a labyrinth, and at the end of it is . . ."

He paused and shrugged his shoulders. "Well, whatever it is that's down there. There might be something underneath this whole city structure, something that will explain everything we don't know about the Cooties. Like, maybe what brought them here in the first place. Why did they build the City? What's at the bottom of the Labyrinth that they needed to protect . . . ?"

"A starship?" Cassidy asked.

Johnson shrugged again. "Who knows? Both sides would love to find something like that down there. After all, we never found their vessel. It should have been left in orbit, but we don't know how the Cooties operated. We don't know what's down there, but there's more that we don't know about the Cooties than what we do know. In any case, there's something down there they felt the need to protect with the Labyrinth." He raised an eyebrow. "Whatever it is, it has to be big."

Cassidy fell back on the bunk and let out a low whistle. "No wonder everyone's so hot to lay claim to the site."

"Yup. International cooperation is fine and dandy when we're just poking through some rocks, but give them even the slim chance of finding something useful like a starship"— Johnson sighed and shook his head—"and once again politics screws around with science."

"Umm." Cassidy was pensive. "So where does that leave—?"

He was interrupted by the module hatch opening. The two men looked up to see Sasha Kulejan and Tamara Isralilova climb into the bunkhouse. They stopped when they spotted Cassidy and Johnson. Their faces were downcast.

"Whoops," Johnson said. "Sorry, guys. We'll get out of the way and let you two have some privacy." He leaned down to pick up his coffee cup, motioning to Cassidy to do the same. "Rules of the house," he murmured. "Whoever wants the house to themselves has priority. And you're sitting on his bunk."

But Kulejan quickly shook his head. "No, no, no. It's nothing like that. We were told you were in here and we came to . . ."

His voice trailed off. He and Isralilova looked disturbed, both angry and confused at the same time. "What's going on?" Cassidy asked.

Isralilova took a deep breath. "A communiqué from our country was just received at the control module," the young physician said, her voice shaking. "Orders from the President himself. The Commonwealth is formally withdrawing from this expedition. We've been ordered not to cooperate in any way with this mission. We are to prepare to return to Arsia Station, to await the return of the *Korolev*."

Johnson let out his breath. "Great. That's just great." He looked back at Cassidy. "I wonder if there's any booze left at the wake. Something else just died."

From *The New York Times* (on-line edition), June 16, 2030, page one. (Headline: "U.S. Space Forces Attack, Destroy C.I.S. Units On Mars."):

WASHINGTON, June 15—Top officials of the White Administration, the Department of Defense and the National Aeronautics and Space Administration confirmed today at a surprise press conference that a rapid deployment force of the United States Marine Corps' 1st Space Infantry attacked and "totally destroyed" mobile military units on Mars belonging to the Commonwealth of Independent States. One Russian military advisor and one Marine Corps pilot were killed in the incident, which occurred today at 1:35 P.M. EST, or 6:40 P.M. MCM (Mars Central Meridian).

According to the announcement made at the White House, the attack was carried out by two Marine Corps pilots in Space-to-Surface "Hornet" aircraft deployed from Mars orbit from the Japanese spaceship S.S. *Shinseiki*. The pilots both belonged to the 1st Space's elite Falcon Team. The two STS fighters destroyed two Russian AT-80 "Bushmaster"

autotanks before a Russian Army officer piloting a space-adapted Combat Armor Suit managed to shoot down one of the STS fighters. The remaining Hornet then killed the Russian officer before successfully landing on the Martian surface.

The raid occurred in the Cydonia region in Mars' northern hemisphere, at the site of the base camp of the international expedition which has been exploring extraterrestrial ruins recently discovered on the planet. Pentagon spokesman Lt. Col. Samuel O. Kasey identified the U.S. Marine who was killed as Lt. William A. Hoffman; the surviving pilot was not identified by name. Although the name of the Russian military advisor was not disclosed, NASA officials have identified him as Major Maksim Oeljanov.

NASA spokesman Jerome Jeffers said that no casualties or injuries were reported among civilian members of the expedition. "Everyone up there is completely safe now," Mr. Jeffers said at the press conference. "The situation has been stabilized . . . It was over and done with in sixty seconds, and the Russian armor units were totally destroyed."

White House spokesperson Mary Nile claimed that the military action, which had been covertly planned and executed, had been made in response to "pending Russian aggression on Mars which threatened the lives of the scientific team at Cydonia Base." Although she said that the United States "regrets" the deaths of both Lt. Hoffman and Maj. Oeljanov, Ms. Nile claimed that the covert operation, which was code-named "Steeple Chase" by the defense department, was "completely successful."

"We are convinced that the mission was necessary to preserve the safety and well-being of American, Japanese and European scientists working on Mars," Ms. Nile said at the press conference. "It was a dirty job, but it had to be done."

Several Russian scientists are also involved in the Cydonia expedition. At press time, no official comment has been made by officials in Minsk, although a top Russian official from the Washington embassy has privately condemned the action as "a criminal outrage" and has promised "a swift response by the people of the Commonwealth."

The same official said that it is possible that such response may include a demand for immediate action by the United Nations Security Council. . . .

From *The Washington Post* (on-line edition), June 16, 2030, page one. (Headline: "Russians Demand Reparations, Withdraw Mars Team."):

MINSK, June 16—The Russian news agency Glasnost announced today that President Andrei Nasanov has issued a formal letter of protest to President George White, demanding both an official apology and reparations for "the unjustifiable sneak attack" launched Saturday by United States space forces against armor units on Mars.

Glasnost also claimed, in a terse written statement issued to members of the foreign press here, that the director of the space agency Glavkosmos, Alexsandr Karpov, has issued instructions to Russian members of the international science team presently exploring the alien ruins that they shall "cease cooperating in the expedition" and prepare to leave Cydonia Base "at the soonest possible opportunity."

The C.I.S. is also preparing to make a formal complaint to the Security Council of the United Nations, demanding that the U.N. condemn American actions on Mars as an act of "criminal trespass," according to unnamed sources at the U.N. headquarters in New York. The C.I.S. may also ask for U.N. sanctions against American and Japanese space corporations for their support of the strike by the 1st Space Infantry of the United States Marines. (*See sidebar, page two.*)

White House spokesperson

Mary Nile gave no comment on the Russian demands and actions at the daily news conference today. Administration officials privately said that President White is studying Nasanov's demands, but that White is satisfied with the withdrawal of Russian scientists and mission support members from Cydonia Base.

"If this is what it takes to get the C.I.S. out of our hair, then we're very happy how things have turned out," said a top White House official. "We're breaking out the champagne."

Ms. Nile said that the President will address the issue during a press conference on Wednesday morning, when White is scheduled to return from vacation at Camp David. . . .

6. Music for Aliens

Okay, last stop.

W. J. Boggs halted Ben Cassidy in the low-ceilinged corridor outside Room C4-20. The underground passageway was lighted only by a few lamps; its dimness, the downward-sloping floor, the ancient stones lining the rock walls, the intangible yet oppressive sensation of the pyramid's weight above them . . . all reminded Cassidy of photos he had seen of the galleries inside Khufu's Pyramid in Egypt. The original stone door had been propped open with a hydraulic jack; in front of them, Miho Sasaki checked the LCD register on the portable airlock which had been vacuum-fitted into the doorway. She pushed down the locklever on the hatch and pulled it open, stepping to one side.

Step inside please, gentlemen, she said formally.

Boggs paused. *Miho, sweetheart, can't we try that one more time, with feeling? Like "Getcha butts in there" or something less . . .*

Please, Waylon, we're wasting time here. They all heard Shin-ichi Kawakami's voice through the comlink with the monitor center. *Mr. Cassidy, if you will please . . . ?*

"Right." Cassidy hesitated for a moment, then squeezed past Sasaki into the tiny chamber. Boggs crushed himself into the airlock behind him, pulled the hatch shut and locked it, then touched the controls which began the cycling process.

She's in love with me, Boggs murmured as they waited for the chamber to pressurize. *I'm telling you, she doesn't show it, but the lady is absolutely infatuated with me.*

Stop lying, Sasaki said coldly, invisible behind the hatch but audible over the comlink, along with Paul Verduin's distant laughter from the habitat. *Ben, we will be here. If something*

83

goes wrong, return to the airlock and we'll rescue you from this side.

Sure thing, Cassidy thought. But it didn't help Hal Moberly when he was in here, did it? Of course, this test—that was the way the science team termed it, a test—was going to be significantly different. First, C4-20 had been pressurized, if only because it would have been difficult if not impossible for Cassidy to perform while wearing a skinsuit; the suit's gloves simply weren't dexterous enough. Even if another CAS had been available, he couldn't possibly have worn it and played his guitar at the same time. And they needed the extra acoustical qualities of an Earth-normal atmosphere if this attempt at communication was going to be successful.

All good reasons, yet it meant placing Cassidy in a highly vulnerable situation. The portable airlock was a compromise, but not a very good one. If something really wanted to get into the airlock . . .

Just remember to knock first, Boggs added; Cassidy caught a sly wink from him through the faceplate of his helmet. *It may be occupied, y'know. Okay, we're at full pressure, hoss. Might as well get yourself comfortable.*

Cassidy removed his helmet and harness, then unzipped and began to peel out of his skinsuit. Going through the physical and mental procedure of desuiting helped to distract him not only from his own fear, but also from Boggs's good-ol'-boy joshing. Having observed that the pilot had struck up a rapport with the musician, Arthur Johnson had allowed Boggs to escort him into the Labyrinth, believing that Waylon could help take Cassidy's mind off the ordeal to come. It didn't help very much, though; he knew that Boggs was trying to defuse his nerves, and he only felt more tense despite W.J.'s presence.

Under the skinsuit he wore drawstring cotton trousers, high-top slippers, and an old Working Blues tour sweatshirt. Boggs, who had removed his helmet but remained suited, studied his face. As Cassidy turned to the second hatch in the airlock, the airship pilot stopped him with his arm. "Hold it there, bud," he said. "Lemme give you something for good luck. Hold out your right hand."

Puzzled, Cassidy put out his hand. Boggs reached behind him, then pulled out his own right hand, cupped as if he was holding something in his palm, and slapped it into Cassidy's hand. The musician looked down at his hand and found it empty.

Boggs winked again, although his face remained dour. "That's an authentic Tennessee cootie-catcher. Guaranteed effective against bug-eyed monsters or your money back."

Cassidy had to grin. "You finally said something funny, W.J." he replied as he slipped the "cootie-catcher" into his pocket.

"I'll try harder." Boggs turned, yanked down the handle on the airlock's second hatch, and pushed it open. "Okay, then, enough of this crap. Let's go catch us some cooties."

Room C4-20, despite pressurization, was cold; he could feel the chill cut through his clothes, see it turn his breath into fog. The room hummed. The low, monotonous sound had commenced the moment the door had been propped open and the portable airlock inserted, about three hours earlier that morning. According to Kawakami, though, nothing had happened except for a slight electromagnetic surge, detected by the sensor pod which had been placed on a tripod inside the room. The sound—like the drone of a beehive, or to Cassidy's ears like the expectant static one hears from monitor speakers in a recording studio—seemed to come from everywhere at once, from the intricately patterned metal walls of the room.

Rubbing his arms with his hands to warm himself, Cassidy let his eyes wander around Room C4-20. Rows of jury-rigged tanks fed an oxygen-nitrogen mix into the chamber. Power cables snaking across the floor led from a portable RTG generator to the lights, the sensor pod, two tripod-mounted TV cameras and, finally, to the six-channel soundboard for his electronic guitar and its two monitor speakers. The guitar itself lay on a small folding table, along with his belt unit and a communications headset. Standing next to them, like a posted sentry, was Sasha Kulejan.

"I believe all is in readiness," the Russian scientist said as he picked up the headset and fitted it on Cassidy's head, carefully adjusting the mike. Cassidy noted that his hands were trembling, and not from the cold; Kulejan had cycled through the airlock an hour earlier to set up the equipment, and he obviously hadn't wanted to be in here by himself. Yet, while the chamber door had been jacked open, nothing had disturbed him during his work. Either the door was a trigger-mechanism . . .

. . . or the room had been specifically waiting for Cassidy.

"Don't be alarmed if this fails and you don't hear anyone,"

Sasha said. "It frequently occurs during a test. Say something now."

"Test one, two, three," Cassidy said.

We are receiving you well, Tamara Isralilova replied in his ears. *You are looking good.*

"Thanks." Cassidy looked back at Kulejan. "I thought your government had ordered all the Russians not to cooperate in this. What are you and she doing here?"

Kulejan stoically *tsk*ed as he taped dime-size medical scanners to Cassidy's chest and temples. "My government is a long way from here. Besides, Russian science has a long history of . . . um, patriotic noncompliance. The military and the scientists, we often do not agree on every issue. With mutual respect, of course."

"I like your attitude. I wish some of our scientists felt the same way more often." Cassidy grinned. "Good morning, Dickie. Are you listening?"

If Dick Jessup was in the command center, he did not deign to respond to the stab, but Kulejan smiled briefly as he tested the med scanners with a hand-held instrument. Cassidy fitted the control unit in the waistband of his trousers, then picked up the Yamaha. He pulled the embroidered strap across his left shoulder and briefly ran the fingers of his right hand across the rows of recessed plastic switches before pushing the power switch on the control unit. There was the tinny *chuk* from the monitors of the guitar coming on-line. A moment later, almost imperceptibly, the hum from the walls rose a note higher in pitch.

Slight EM surge, Kawakami said. *I think your audience is waiting for you.* Everyone glanced toward the stone door. The hydraulic jack was holding firm, keeping the door open. Some other force besides simple mechanics had determined that it was time to begin the test.

"I hear 'em." Cassidy felt a cold current run down his spine. He looked at Kulejan and Boggs. "You guys better get off the stage. I think the house is getting restless."

Kulejan patted him on his shoulder, then picked up his helmet and headed for the airlock. Boggs lingered for a moment, the anxiety he felt for another expatriate Southerner now plain on his face. "Taking requests?" he asked.

"Sorry."

"That's a crummy song." His humor fell flat and he knew it.

Boggs shook his head and headed for the airlock, then paused and looked around again. "Look, Tex, if it gets hairy, get your ass out of here. You don't owe these guys nothing."

Cassidy stared down at his guitar. Boggs gave him a salute before ducking into the airlock and slamming the hatch shut behind him.

Cassidy took a deep breath, let it out slowly. Somehow, in spite of his fear, it was a relief to be alone at last. Despite the anticipatory hum of the walls, it was as if he were back in his first days as an artist. The cheap garage studio in Brownsville where he had cut his first demo tape: the walls lined with old egg cartons, the old framed photo of Sonny Terry and Brownie McGhee on one wall and the hilarious black-velvet painting of Elvis on the other. The raw days, before the fame, the concerts, and the cocaine. The good, hungry days. Everyone was gone and he was alone with his axe, his mind, and his hands. The nervous anticipation was there, but the fear was gone. He was waiting, like a master guitarist waiting for an unfamiliar road band to put down their beers and get their act together.

Now it was just him and a different room. He knew what to do.

"Come on, sucker," Cassidy breathed. "Gimme a lick I can play."

It began.

There was a inquiring trill of notes slithering up and down the scale, backed by the hum which turned into an insistent, single-minded throb. Cassidy shut his eyes and listened to the complex pattern. At first it seemed as if the notes were random, but as he concentrated, he picked up a faint rhythm. Okay, there it was. He moved his hand to the Yamaha's keyboard, inched the pitch wheel up a taste, and played the first few bars of "Crossroads Blues," an old song which seemed to match the room's rhythm.

It segued perfectly and it even fitted his own mood, but the room was apparently not satisfied. The throb rose sharply into a harsh, reverberating yowl, then lapsed into an almost rocklike three-quarter-time backbeat behind a moody chord sequence in B-flat.

Don't worry about it, Kawakami said. *Relax and try to talk to it.*

"Right," Cassidy murmured. "I'm doing Robert Johnson and it wants the Beatles." That remark gave him another idea. He thought for a moment, then switched to the fretboard, fuzzed the pitch, and burned out the simpler first refrain of "Why Don't We Do It in the Road?", playing the *rump-bum-bum-bum-bum-rump-bum* backbeat on his keyboard, then letting the memory replay the sequence indefinitely as he repeated the refrain.

It was a tasty little number and for a moment it seemed as if the room was going to mime him, repeating the bars twice. Then, in the middle of the second bar, it warbled a shrill, discordant note which arced upwards into infinity before flattening out again and resuming the near-random pattern it had begun in the first place.

Cute, he thought. But again, this particular pattern of notes inspired him. "So you like that sixties stuff, huh?" he murmured to the room. "Okay, try this one, you fucking old hippie."

Switching the bass program, he rammed out the first metronomic riffs of the Grateful Dead's "The Other One." Again, it seemed for a minute as if the room was catching it; around him, the sound followed the spooky, fast-time beat of the music, adding to the weird Halloween feel of the song. Then, just as Cassidy was beginning to relax and make his slide into the refrain, there was a loud explosion of disjointed sound, reminiscent of a bad-tempered music student whose fingers can't keep up with the tempo and thrashes at his guitar strings in frustrated anger. Sure. Except most novice musicians can't drop one-ton stone blocks on their teachers when they get pissed off. . . .

"This is getting a little difficult," Cassidy remarked.

Yes. Right. This time it was Paul Verduin who spoke to him. *We don't want to distress you, Ben, but we're seeing something rather unusual down there. Will you please look at the walls and tell us what you see?*

Cassidy looked up from his instrument at the walls and sucked in his breath. Slowly, yet noticeably, the intricate patterns on the walls were rearranging themselves. The grooves and intricately curved lines were flowing, squirming as if they were worms jammed together in a fisherman's bait bucket, or pieces of a jigsaw puzzle which were rearranging themselves. The bulges and planes moved in an organic, living fashion, as if something behind them had been revived and was struggling to get out.

"You gotta be kidding me," Cassidy breathed.

It was as if he were flashing back to one of his worst drug hallucinations: the time when he had been onstage at a club in the

Soulard neighborhood of St. Louis, his mind warped after he had just mainlined, and had glanced out into the audience to see the audience, in the twilight darkness beyond the stage lights, transformed into a hideous tangle of moray eels, gaping jaws screaming silently at him from the room.

That was the night he had torn off his guitar, rushed backstage, and had been found by his band curled up next to the toilet in the men's room. It was much like that now: claustrophobia, nausea, the abrupt suspicion that his mind was about to snap. He stared at the walls; the overwhelming urge was to do the same thing now. Get rid of the Yamaha, bolt for the airlock, pound on the hatch, and scream for Boggs and Sasaki to rescue him before the walls moved in on him.

"I have to get out of here," he whispered.

Don't look at it, Kawakami said. *Concentrate on your music.*

"Goddammit, I'm not kidding!" he shouted. "Get me out of here!"

No! Forget your songs! It wants you to communicate! Kawakami insisted.

"Communicate? What the hell am I supposed to tell it?"

Just play! Or you'll never get out of there alive!

Cassidy tore his eyes away from the undulating walls, focused on his guitar as he listened to the room and its coruscating chaotic music. Perhaps it only wanted him to improvise. He tried harmonics, holding his fingers down on the twelfth fret while turning the pitch up slowly. The speakers yowled with the feedback, and the room responded with high-pitched squeals and rumbles which culminated in a reverberating roar.

"Okay, you liked that," he said aloud. He heard his voice shake; he fought down his panic. Play or die: those were the house rules tonight. "All right, let's try this."

Cassidy thrust his right hand into his pocket and found the bottleneck slide he had grabbed from his kit bag before heading down to the chamber. He fitted the slide over the middle finger of his left hand, then pushed it against the fretboard as he adjusted the pitch wheel to its highest level. He ran the slide up the frets; the sound was like stainless-steel fingernails running down the world's longest blackboard, a painful screech which made his teeth ache. He ran the slide back down the frets, pausing to jiggle it on the eighth and third frets, then shot it back up the board again, at the same time touching the chord sequencer to repeat the backbeat he had programmed a couple of minutes earlier.

No lyrics, no tune, no preset pattern: straight improvisation, like John Coltrane wailing on his sax on a muggy night at the old Village Vanguard, or Roy Buchanan bending strings the way they had never been bent before in a London studio, or Brent Mydland making netherworldly music on his keyboards before a stadium crowd at one of the Dead's legendary late-eighties concerts. Drugs had killed Mydland, Coltrane had died at 40 of a liver ailment, and Buchanan had hanged himself when his depression became more than he could stand, but in their time they had pushed the outer reaches of the envelope, creating sounds not before heard by human ears. Music for aliens . . .

The room responded with another protracted reverberation, then began adding a not-so-random set of delicate, tinny notes of its own which sounded oddly like a xylophone being played by a hyperactive child. It became a distinct rhythm, and without thinking, Cassidy touched the rhythm control and the conga key, then used the keyboard to add his own percussion backdrop, joining but not miming the xylophone sound. The room wailed and crashed, but the xylophonic rhythm continued as Cassidy worked to keep up, matching, then surpassing the room's playing as he sought to anticipate its next moves.

He lost track of time. He was beginning to enjoy himself, savoring the experience, imagining himself as Miles Davis playing free-form jazz. For the hell of it, he ran a couple of bars from "Sketches of Spain"; the room responded, imitating him note for note. He segued cleanly into the *Twilight Zone* theme song, and the room began to improvise on that, sending the eerie ripple of notes higher and higher until Cassidy brought it back into the opening bars from "The Star-Spangled Banner," again concentrating on the twelfth fret, which the room improvised upon in a way that sounded remarkably like Jimi Hendrix's famous Woodstock jam.

The fear and nervousness were completely gone now. He was having fun. He hadn't realized that his eyes were closed until something brushed against his calves. He opened his eyes, looked down past his guitar at the floor, and saw a small Cootie standing in front of him.

It looked almost like a toy: a detailed, miniature metal model of a Cootie, a cross between a praying mantis and a termite.

While the real Cooties had been about the size of a collie, though, this one was only as large as a dachshund. At first Cassidy again thought he was hallucinating, until the pseudo-Cootie scuttled away on its six multijointed legs, its scimitarlike pincers delicately held aloft.

Cassidy panicked and jumped back a few inches, his hands almost deserting his instrument. *Don't stop,* Kawakami urged softly. *Keep playing. They've been there for a few minutes now.*

"*They've* been here a few minutes?" Cassidy repeated. Keeping with "The Star-Spangled Banner," he slowly raised his head and looked around.

The metal walls were gone, laying bare red stone inner walls like those in every other room in the Labyrinth, and moving around him were dozens of the small metallic robots. They crawled quickly and deliberately around the chamber, climbing over each other, swiftly and carefully exploring the TV cameras, the RTG generator, the air tanks, the sensor pod, his sound-board and monitors, but otherwise keeping a respectful distance from Cassidy himself.

He stared at them, mesmerized by their coordinated motions. Their pincers were briskly rubbing together, like chirruping crickets. The music was all around him now. "They were in the walls," he whispered.

They were *the walls,* Kawakami explained. *We couldn't see them because they were folded over each other. They came out while you were playing.*

"They were what killed Moberly," Cassidy said.

They won't hurt you. You're giving them what they . . . wait. What are they doing?

Now the robots were scuttling toward the sides of the chamber. Their sharp little pincers began digging into the walls, finding the hairline cracks between the blocks, gaining leverage. Suddenly, at the far end of the chamber, two of the Cooties pulled a block loose from the wall.

There was a loud, muffled *whuff!* of air escaping from the pressurized chamber; a windstorm broke loose in Room C4-20, whipping red dust from the walls and the floor. *Get out of there!* Kawakami yelled. *Get in the airlock!*

Grit in his eyes, his clothes tearing against his body, Cassidy turned and ran toward the airlock. The Cootie-robots did not try to stop him as he struggled into the tiny chamber. He pulled off his guitar and dropped it on the floor, then grabbed the hatch lever and, bracing his legs against the sill and putting his back into the effort, managed to shove the hatch shut against the escaping atmosphere.

It was quiet inside the airlock. As soon as the hatch was closed, Cassidy began to shimmy into his skinsuit, trying to remember the procedure. "I'm in, I'm in, I'm in," he babbled. "I'm safe. Just get me out of here. What's going on out there?"

Easy there, hoss, he heard Boggs say. *Just get your clothes on and depressurize nice and easy-like. We'll get you out of there in no time.*

"What's going on?" Cassidy demanded.

Nobody knows, Boggs replied, *but it's something.*

Cassidy heard him chuckle. *Hey, that cootie-catcher worked just fine, didn't it?*

"Yeah, maybe." He let out his breath and closed his eyes, feeling the sweat freezing on his face. "Why don't you go in there and try it yourself?"

From the Associated Press (on-line edition), June 17, 2030:

ANNAPOLIS, MD.—The controversial former captain of the U.S. Navy attack submarine *Boston* said today that a United States military presence on Mars is justified, not by the current Russian crisis, but because of the potential of "almost-certain extraterrestrial hostilities."

Comm. Terrance C. L'Enfant made his remarks while speaking before cadets at the United States Naval Academy, from which L'Enfant graduated in 1998. It was the first time L'Enfant had lectured at Annapolis since his much-publicized court-martial in 2019.

While speaking on the necessity of maintaining "eternal vigilance" against "enemies whose nature may even yet be unknown," L'Enfant alluded to the recent showdown in the Cydonia region of Mars between Russian and American military space forces. Although he did not remark on whether Operation Steeple Chase was a justifiable response to the deployment on Mars of Soviet munitions by the C.I.S., L'Enfant told an audience of 600 cadets and officers that the U.S. had an obligation to protect itself against "adversarial alien forces."

"Let's face it," said L'Enfant. "What used to be sheer science fiction is on the verge of becoming stark reality. We know now that there is intelligent life elsewhere in the universe, that they know where we are in the galaxy, and that they are capable of doing us grave harm. So the question is not so much what to do about the Russians. It's about what do we do to counter almost-certain extraterrestrial hostilities."

Lt. Wyatt Shippey, a spokesman for the Naval Academy, denied that L'Enfant's remarks reflected the philosophy of Annapolis or the U.S. Navy. "Commander L'Enfant was invited to speak to the cadets on the subject of general preparedness," Lt. Shippey said in a press conference following the lecture. "Anything he had to say about the Mars crisis is his own opinion."

L'Enfant was removed from active sea duty by the Secretary of the Navy following his court-martial acquittal on charges of disobedience and gross negligence,

93

which resulted from the torpedoing of the Japanese freighter
Takada Maru by the *Boston* in
2019. Although he retained his
rank as a commissioned officer,
L'Enfant has been a member of
the general staff at the U.S. Naval
Institute.

7. Beyond the Labyrinth

Cassidy leaned over Kawakami's shoulder to peer at the TV monitors. "So what are they doing now?"

He didn't really need to ask. On the TV screens in the monitor center they could see that the pseudo-Cooties were still disassembling the inner stone wall of Room C4-20. They had left all the equipment in the room intact, including the TV cameras, the lights, and the sensor pod, but the tiny robots were busily cutting away stones and piling them near the airlock.

Next to Shin-ichi Kawakami's workstation, Paul Verduin, Arthur Johnson, Tamara Isralilova, and Sasha Kulejan were crowded around Verduin's console, studying the first data to be transmitted from the sensors. The computer was already constructing an incomplete three-dimensional model of the new chamber at the bottom of the Labyrinth, as the pod's radar painted a vague picture of a seemingly endless room which the lights only barely exposed. The far wall ended in a dotted line, showing that the radar was unable to penetrate the depths of the chamber.

"It's not empty space, either." Kawakami pointed at the TV monitor in front of him, where vague shapes lay tantalizingly just out of reach of the floodlights. "See? We can barely make out something back there. Perhaps machinery. Past that may be the beginning of another tunnel or even a series of catacombs. We're not going to know until someone else goes down there. . . ."

"Not me, I hope."

"We thought we were at the end of the mystery," Kawakami said as he took a deep breath. "Seems as if we've only begun." He glanced over his shoulder at Cassidy. "And how are you, my friend? Still screaming obscenities at me?"

"If you had been down there, you would have been screaming obscenities, too." Arthur Johnson turned to Cassidy. "Good work, pal," he said softly, holding out his hand. "How're your nerves?"

"Shot, but I'll survive." Cassidy absently shook Johnson's hand, then looked around the module. "Where's Dickie? I thought he might have been here with you."

Johnson's eyebrows rose as he parodied a look of complete surprise. "Oh, you must mean Dr. Richard Jessup. I believe he got delayed in the wardroom. He went there about . . . how long ago was it, Dr. Kawakami?"

Kawakami leaned back in his chair and checked his wristwatch. "Ummm . . . about an hour and a half ago." He smiled. "I thought I heard someone pounding on the hatch, but I can't be sure."

Johnson shook his head mournfully. "It's terrible how the handle jams sometimes." His brief grin disappeared as he turned to look around at the others. "Gentlemen, lady, I think we've reached the moment of decision. All in favor, please signify by raising your hands."

Johnson put up his own hand. Kawakami and Verduin immediately followed suit. After a moment Kulejan and Isralilova reluctantly put up their hands as well. Johnson nodded his head. "I discussed this with Miho about two hours ago. She's still wrapping up things in the Labyrinth, but she added her affirmative vote in absentia, so I guess it's unanimous. Tamara, if you'll please go rescue the unfortunate Dr. Jessup? Sorry. I don't think I should be the first person to see him just now."

Isralilova squeezed past the men to leave the crowded module. As she did, Paul Verduin touched a couple of keys on his board, waited a few moments, then removed two CD-ROM disks from slots in his console. He solemnly handed them to Arthur Johnson. "Audiovisual record is on One, sensor scan and mission history is on Two," he said. "I made backups about an hour ago, but this is the complete record." He thought for a moment. "The pilot, Captain D'Agostino. Is he . . . ?"

Johnson smiled. "Disarmed. He had a pistol as a sidearm, but it made a disappearance while he was sleeping off his hangover. Since his craft is out of fuel, he won't be able to take it aloft. I think Katsu's out there now, making some more permanent changes." He chuckled and shook his head. "He and Boggs have been bitching about not having enough spare parts for the *Burroughs*, so I guess they're getting them now."

Kawakami still looked worried. "Richard might still try to get the captain to intercede."

"We'll have to take that chance," Arthur said. "But at least he's outnumbered. One combat-trained Marine against a half-dozen wimpy scientists . . . ?" He shrugged. "Well, if it gets too serious, we can always knock him over the head and threaten to toss him out the airlock. My bet is that he gets a ride back to the *Shinseiki* when the lander takes off again."

Verduin was looking at the CD-ROMs in Johnson's hands. "Don't worry, Paul. They're in good hands." Johnson slipped the two silver disks in his shirt pocket and zipped it shut, then took a deep breath. "Okay, people, let's shut it down. Paul and Shin-ichi, remember to erase everything from the memory. Leave nothing they can use."

"What are you . . . ?" Cassidy began.

Johnson held up a finger. "Wait. Just wait."

Around them, the scientists were busily working their keyboards. One by one, the TV and computer screens blinked out as the electronic hum of computer drives grunted and died. All the computers that had recorded every hard-fought inch of the journey through the Labyrinth slowly died. Within a minute, Module Eight was completely silent. All the instruments were dead, the screens completely dark.

Johnson let out his breath. "I never thought it could get so quiet in here." He put his hand on Kawakami's shoulder. "Any second thoughts, Kawakami-*san*?"

The exobiologist was staring at a blank screen. After a moment, he shook his head. "It's the only way," he said. He touched his upper lip meditatively. "Wasn't there something one of your founding fathers said about hanging together or hanging separately?"

When Jessup entered the control module a few moments later, the first thing he noticed was the inactivity. His eyes roved over dead consoles, then focused on the science team, who in turn were silently watching him. "If this is what I think it is," he said evenly, "you're all making a grave mistake."

Arthur Johnson shook his head. "No, we don't believe so. This is a strike, Dick. Maybe you could call it a revolution. Everybody here is in on it, and nothing gets done until our non-negotiable demands are met."

"Hmm." Jessup folded his arms across his chest. "Okay. I'll listen. What are your demands?"

"First, the United states and the Commonwealth of Independent States will issue formal apologies to each other for their military actions here. Second, the C.I.S. will allow its members of the science team to continue their work here. Third, the participating nations must promise not to allow any more military personnel or equipment on Mars." Johnson held up his hands. "That's all."

"That's all." Dick Jessup sighed. "Well, I'll communicate your stipulations to the President, but you know you won't get anywhere with this. All they have to do is send another science team here. They'll continue the work and your careers will be down the tube."

Paul Verduin coughed. "That will be difficult to do," he said quietly. "I've taken the liberty of erasing the memory of the hard drives. The data has been relocated to another site where they cannot find it. . . ."

"What?"

"And it will be destroyed unless all of our demands are made public and satisfied," Johnson finished. "If a new team was sent here, they would have to re-create almost two years of research from scratch. I don't think the Cooties are going to wait that long."

Jessup stared disbelievingly at Johnson. "What about the Cooties? What's going on?" Then, for the first time since entering the module, he seemed to notice Ben Cassidy. "What happened down there?"

"Room C4-20 has been solved," Kawakami said. "Mr. Cassidy here has managed to convince the Cooties that we're a sapient, creative race. That was what the Labyrinth was ultimately designed to prove. It was a mechanism to determine not only whether we were technologically advanced, but also creatively advanced. For what purpose, we don't yet know . . . but I doubt they will be patient much longer. Already their robots are working down there."

Jessup scowled at Kawakami. "Robots? As in automechanisms?"

"Activated when C4-20 was given enough proof of our intelligence. We were looking at this entirely the wrong way. The Cooties already had enough evidence of our empirical knowledge. This time, they wanted assurance that we weren't just problem-solvers." Kawakami smiled. "Now they're tearing down the last walls."

"Then why . . . ?"

"Why were we lured here? Why did they create this series of tests? What did they expect to gain from a complex game which was apparently meant to begin long after they were dead?" Kawakami closed his eyes and slowly shook his head. "I have no idea. Try to understand, Richard, that we're attempting to comprehend a completely alien perspective, and there are very few clues. There are no easy answers, and what we believe we've learned is perhaps only guesswork. Nevertheless, this is the first step to finding the answers."

Kawakami reflexively began to yawn; he covered his mouth to stifle the impulse. "The essential fact is this, Dr. Jessup . . . we were meant to be here for a deliberate reason. We don't know what it is, or what they expected to gain from our presence on Mars. At least, not yet . . . but the first layer of the mystery has been peeled away."

He stared directly at Jessup. "Beyond the Labyrinth," he said, "is yet another labyrinth. At least, that is the way it now seems. The question is, will you let us continue?"

"Will I . . . ?" Jessup began.

"They're waiting for us," Johnson said. "The door is wide open. But we're not going to do a thing about it if the boys in Washington and Minsk continue to act like children. We've decided that we're not going to allow the Cooties to become part of your little scuffle, and that's what the strike is about."

Jessup turned to glare at him. "Your work can be continued by another expedition."

Johnson shrugged. "Maybe so, but how long will that take if we destroy our research? Two, three years. I have a gut feeling that the Cooties are not going to wait much longer."

The NASA administrator was quiet for another moment. "Forget it, Art," he said at last. "It won't work. The *Shinseiki*'s still in orbit, and we've still got men aboard. Play rough if you want, but we can stage another attack whenever we want. . . ."

Cassidy had been silent throughout the conversation. Indeed, it suddenly occurred to him, he had been aloof for far too long. He cleared his throat and took a step forward, entering the circle for the first time. "He's still lying, guys."

Dick Jessup turned around and thrust a finger in his face.

"You stay out of this!" he snapped. "This is none of your god-damn business!"

Cassidy looked straight at Jessup as he continued. "There's one military guy, a Marine colonel, still on the *Shinseiki*. So far as I know, there's no more attack fighters left. They blew the whole wad when they took out the Bushmasters. Besides the command crew, all that's left up there is one rear-echelon motherfucker. He can't do a thing."

The science team was watching Jessup again. The truth was finally coming out; his aces were all used up, his lies were finally exhausted. "Maybe," he said, his voice quavering. "He could be right, maybe. But what happens when the *Lowell* gets here in nine months? You think there's not going to be another strike team on that ship?"

Johnson looked indifferent. "That's always a possibility. So what? What's to stop us from destroying the data when they show up? Doesn't help them a bit. Even in the worst-case scenario, they've got a bunch of dead renegades and nothing to show for it. Everything's lost for good . . . plus, they've got to answer to the world for a massacre." He smiled again. "Nobody wins. Somehow, I don't think even George White could be that stupid."

"Face it, Dick," Cassidy said benignly. "It's time to grow up. You can stop playing your game of beat-the-Russkies now."

Jessup's temper, held in check for so long, finally blew. "I thought I told you to shut up, you goddamn junkie!" he shouted at Cassidy.

Cassidy stared back at Jessup. Behind Jessup, Johnson smiled softly and nodded his head. Without thinking twice, Cassidy balled up his fist and slugged Jessup with a fast, hard hook to the jaw.

The NASA administrator toppled backwards, fell over a chair, and crashed to the floor. "On second thought," Cassidy said, massaging his knuckles, "sometimes it's satisfying to be immature."

He turned and walked out of the module. Johnson looked down at Jessup, who was wiping blood from the corner of his mouth and beginning to rise from the floor. No one moved to help him get up. "I'll take back command of this base now, if you don't mind," Johnson said quietly. "The lander will be launching at thirteen-hundred hours. I trust that you and Captain D'Agostino will be on it. This meeting is adjourned."

• • •

Johnson left the compartment and took a deep breath, then walked down the corridor to the wardroom. The hatch was open. Cassidy was there, gazing out the narrow window at the red terrain. Beyond the window lay the City; looming in the foreground was the C-4 Pyramid, arched high against the noon-day sky.

The astrophysicist softly padded into the wardroom, then stopped. Although Cassidy's back was turned to him, he could hear the musician whispering something to himself. Johnson stopped and listened; no, not whispering. Singing . . .

"Early this mornin' . . . when you knocked upon my door . . ."

Cassidy stopped abruptly, as if he subliminally detected another presence in the module, yet he said nothing as he continued to stare out the window. Johnson cleared his throat slightly. "Ben Cassidy, two-fisted guitarist," he said, walking up behind the musician. "Nice hook you got there. How's your hand?"

Cassidy shrugged, not turning around. "Bruised, but it should heal by the time I do my next gig. Probably in a federal prison."

The station co-supervisor joined him at the window. "Naw, Dick won't do anything like that. It'll mean admitting that he was beaten up by a liberal. I just wouldn't turn your back on him between now and the time you get to Earth."

He followed Cassidy's gaze out the window. "The lander to the *Shinseiki* takes off in about two hours. Think you're going to miss this place?"

"Hell, no. I can't wait to go home." Cassidy paused. "But I might miss the Cooties. They were good to jam with. Can you give me a tape of that performance?"

Johnson thought it over. "Sorry. Maybe in ten years, but not now. It's too sensitive."

"S'okay. Sometimes the best concerts never get heard but once." Cassidy hesitated. "Do you really think this strike of yours is going to work?"

"Maybe so, maybe not. But it'll put all the jerks back there on notice that we're not going to take it anymore. Perhaps that's all that really counts. Don't worry about us."

Cassidy snickered. "I won't . . . well, maybe I will."

"How are you doing?"

Ben Cassidy gazed out at the barren landscape, looking away from the dead city. In the far distance, on the horizon, the ruined profile of the Face stared up into space. Serenity in ancient stone. Serenity in his own mind. For the first time in years, the fear and the cravings were gone.

"How am I doing?" Cassidy closed his eyes and rested his chin on his arms.

After a while he smiled. "I feel a whole lot better," he said.

INTERLUDE

"Spying, to a greater extent than any time in the past century, will be pressed into service in support not only of government objectives but of corporate strategy as well, on the assumption that corporate power will necessarily contribute to national power. . . . The entire armamentarium of electronic surveillance may be pressed into commercial service, along with armies of trained human operatives. . . ."

—ALVIN TOFFLER,
Powershift

Anti-space demonstrators had defaced a signboard on the Red Line platform of the Dupont Circle Metro station; August Nash noticed it as he stepped off the tram and into the crowd of morning commuters. The hologram, just above a bench now occupied by a couple of Georgetown University freshmen, displayed an ad for *Newsweek*. Pictured was a photo of the Face; the ad copy proclaimed the magazine to be "not just another pretty face" or some such wordplay, but the misspelled message which had been spray-painted in a red swath across the transparent frame was much more direct:

LEAVE MARS TO THE MARTAINS!!

U.S. OUT NOW!!

Nash studied it for only a moment before he rebuttoned his trenchcoat and strode down the platform toward the escalator to the street.

The headquarters of Security Associates, Ltd., was located on Connecticut Avenue one block from Dupont Circle, in a row of commercial buildings not far from Embassy Row. There was nothing to distinguish the entrance to one of the world's foremost private intelligence agencies from anything else on the street; on the right was a bagel shop, on the left was a gay/lesbian bookstore, and in the middle was a single frosted-glass door with the firm's name etched on the glass, so innocuous and low-profile that it could have belonged to a detective agency that specialized in skip-tracing and divorce cases.

Nash pushed open the door, walked down the narrow corridor

to the foyer and stopped in front of the two elevators to remove his trenchcoat; he made sure that his face was in plain view at all times, to allow for the eyes at the other end of the hidden TV cameras to recognize him. The elevator on the right had a panel with a recessed up-button; the elevator on the left had a keycard slot. Nash pulled his keycard out of the inside pocket of his double-breasted suitcoat and slid it into the slot.

"Nash, August," he said. He thought for a second, then recited: " 'The time has come, the Walrus said, to talk of many things. . . .' "

This was enough for the computer's voice-recognition system to confirm his identity. His name was important, but the Lewis Carroll quote was unessential; he could have read the list of ingredients from the back of a cereal box and it would have satisfied the AI. The left elevator door opened, just as it would have had he not spoken aloud—but without voice-print identification he would have been gassed through concealed vents in the elevator's ceiling as soon as he entered the car.

If he had been an unsolicited client or a curious pedestrian and had boarded the elevator on the right, it would have taken him to the second floor, where a polite receptionist would have given him an application, a rather uninformative brochure, and a mild lecture to the effect that Security Associates Ltd. was a very specialized agency which catered to the very particular needs of a very exclusive sort of client. He might have heard the buzz of printers and the beep of telephones behind the partition in back of her desk—both of which were taped sound effects— but he would never have seen the TEC-9 assault pistol hidden in the half-open drawer just above her lap.

Inside the left elevator, though, there was no floor-button panel. There was no need for it, since the elevator took Nash straight to the third floor. There was a reception area here as well, but much different from the one on the floor below: no incidental furniture, potted ferns, or helpful lady at a desk. In the dim-lighted foyer a taciturn young black man sitting behind a bullet-proof window silently watched Nash as he walked to the ID station next to the elevator and subjected himself to handprint and retina analysis.

The sentry glanced at the screens below the counter, then passed a plastic badge to him through a slot in the window. "Welcome back, Mr. Nash," he said. His voice had the quasi-

British accent of a native West African; he was seated in a wheelchair. "He's waiting for you in the conference room."

"Thanks, Bart. It's nice to be home." Nash clipped the badge to his jacket lapel—its plastic coating still warm to the touch, the enclosed photo taken from the image of himself which had been captured on the first-floor TV monitor—and walked to the heavy oak door to the right of the security checkpoint. Bart buzzed open the lock as Nash put his hand on the stainless-steel knob; had he not cleared Nash through, a 50,000-volt charge through the knob would have knocked Nash across the foyer.

Beyond the door was Security Associates' inner sanctum. This was the next-most sensitive part of SA's headquarters. Beneath the building, in an underground level accessible only by a third elevator, was the Pit, the main operations center where a dozen men and women monitored every discreet move made by the agency's operatives as transmitted to them by satellite. The big Cray-10 computer was down there, too, as well as the armory and the firing range, but this was not where Nash was headed. At least not today; Control had called for a meeting with him on the third floor, and it would not be until much later that Nash would have anything to do with the Pit.

The corridor led Nash past a long row of soundproof doors, each guarded by its own keycard slot and numberpad. Anonymous young men and women—secretaries, data analysts, information specialists, and so forth—passed him the hallway, smiling politely but glancing down at the desert-tan carpet to avoid looking at him. Security Associates was not like other companies; there were no office parties at Christmas time or get-well cards for people who went to the hospital. Most employees' paychecks were drawn on the bank accounts of the adjacent bagel shop or gay/lesbian bookstore, since they themselves were fronts for the agency. Casual fraternization among employees was discouraged, if not grounds for outright dismissal. As a field operative, Nash had many allies here, but no friends; besides Bart at the front desk, he hardly knew anyone at the Washington office by name.

Aside from Control, of course, and he discouraged the use of his name except in private by his senior operatives. Nash reached the conference room at the end of the corridor, knocked once on the door out of habit, and twisted the doorknob.

Before he had opened the door even an inch, he heard Control's voice from within: "Good afternoon, Mr. Nash. Please come in. We've got quite a bit to discuss, you and I. . . ."

A dry chuckle. " 'Of shoes and ships and sealing-wax . . .' "

Of course he would have been monitoring his arrival; there was very little which Control missed. " 'Of cabbages and kings,' " Nash finished as he walked into the windowless lair. Where the sea often boiled and, at times, it seemed as if pigs *could* take wing.

Control looked like an Oxford history professor who had taken an extended sabbatical and gone slumming in the States. His baggy trousers and Irish wool fisherman's sweater were filthy with ashes from his briar pipe, and he studied Nash through his wire-rim glasses with eyes only a darker shade of gray than his longish hair and unkempt mustache. When he stood up from behind the long conference table to shake the agent's hand, he automatically reached for the silver-headed cane propped next to the table.

The cane was more of an affectation than something necessary to relieve the weight of his damaged right knee, which he claimed was broken during a polo match at Eton during his youth. The fact of the matter was that Robert Halprin had never been to Oxford; his old school tie was from a much rougher place, somewhere in Beirut where he had been held hostage by Shiite Muslim extremists for nearly two years in the 1990's before he had managed to make his escape. It was rumored that, although he had indeed been a student at Eton, he had never seen the inside of a stable, let alone mounted a saddle for a polo match. The old knee injury was the result of a mission so sensitive that, even to this day, he was forbidden to discuss it because of the Official Secrets Act.

Halprin was a veteran of MI-6, which was hardly surprising. There were at least half a dozen alumni of His Majesty's Secret Service on the payroll at Security Associates, along with various former members of the Mossad, the Russian Central Intelligence Service, the Royal Canadian Mounted Police, La Piscine and (like Nash himself) the U.S. Central Intelligence Agency. As a private intelligence agency, Security Associates Ltd. prided itself on its ability to hire former employees of various government spy apparatus; it was better than having to hire inexperienced amateurs and train them in spycraft themselves. Since the British, the Israelis, the Russians, the Canadians, the French, and the Americans were all fully aware of SA's line of work, they rarely made objections to their alumni going to work for one of the "privates" (although, in certain circles of the intelligence community, SA was alleged to stand for Sold-out Assholes). After all, it was far more desirable to have a retired agent lend his services to a firm in the private sector, where at least one could keep track of his whereabouts, than to have him go to work for one of Them or to write another embarrassing memoir.

"How was Jamaica?" Halprin asked once Nash had shaken his hand. "Better weather than up here, I might imagine."

Nash knew that Control was fully aware that a tropical storm had lashed Kingston for the better part of the last week. "Warmer, at least," he said briefly, folding his trenchcoat over the back of a chair and rubbing a hand across his wet blond hair. "A bit damp, though."

A sly smile whispered across Halprin's face. "Quite," he replied. He briskly waved Nash to a chair on the other side of the long table and resumed his own seat. "This regards your next assignment, so I hope you're well-rested from your vacation, hmm?"

Sneaky old bastard. He would have also known that Nash had spent three days bailing rainwater out of the bilge of his schooner. There was little about his field operatives that escaped the attention of Control. "Yes, sir," Nash said as he sat down and crossed his legs. "Very relaxing, Jamaica is at this time of year." He paused, and added, "You should try it sometime, sir. The fishing is excellent."

"Yes. Right." Halprin shuffled through the folders on his desk. The verbal fencing was over; it was time to get down to business. "This indirectly reflects the Cape Canaveral assignment just over two years ago. The bit of footwork you undertook for Skycorp . . ."

"Photographing the F-210 Hornets?" Nash carefully kept his voice neutral. "I hope our clients aren't still upset about my giving that technician a slap."

"Upset" was an understatement. Skycorp's chief executives had been livid when they learned that Nash had knocked out a NASA pad rat on the launch tower at Pad 2-A. Their anger was barely mitigated by the fact that the quality of intelligence they received regarding Operation Steeple Chase had been superb.

For value earned, however, there was always value received. Ever since the infamous "Big Ear" debacle of 2016, when the private space corporation had been publicly embarrassed by its affiliation with a top-secret National Security Agency operation for covert domestic SIGINT espionage—and, more recently, the labor strike at Descartes Station on the Moon in 2024 and the subsequent raid by the 1st Space Infantry—Skycorp had been attempting to distance itself from U.S. intelligence and the military. It was bad for business, overall, to have the company's interests aligned too closely with the United States government. Particularly now, when the corporation was striving to forge a multinational agreement with other space companies for the construction of the first major space colony in LaGrangian orbit.

Two years ago, Skycorp had become concerned when it learned, through the usual channels of hearsay and rumor, that a covert military payload was being sent to Mars aboard the S.S. *Shinseiki*. Skycorp had considerable capital investment in Mars, much of it still speculative. Mars had become very important to the company in terms of its long-range objectives; as a fuel resource for further deep-space exploration, it was invaluable. Skycorp had wanted to know what was going up there and why; like many other private companies before them, they had secretly retained the services of Security Associates.

SA had learned much, albeit not all, of the details of Operation Steeple Chase. Nash's mission to Cape Canaveral had been to verify the nature of the military payload which was being ferried into orbit by the *Constellation*. His pictures of the two aeroshells nestled within the orbiter's cargo bay, after study by the firm's photo analysts, had gone far to confirm everyone's worst suspicions. Skycorp had been very pleased with the information; when the inevitable crisis had occurred, the company had been forewarned and prepared to publicly disavow any connection with Operation Steeple Chase—a useful tactic, considering that the anti-space movement had gained momentum in response to the skirmish between U.S. and C.I.S. forces at Cydonia. Uchu-Hiko, who owned the *Shinseiki*, had not been so fortunate; Japanese Greens had picketed their Tokyo headquarters for months, and an unexploded bomb had been found near their Australian launch facility.

Even so, Skycorp had been perturbed by the fact that Nash had been obliged to protect his identity by punching out a launch-pad technician. It had never been charged, much less proven, by NASA that someone connected to Skycorp had been responsible for the still-unsolved assault; the FBI continued to believe that it had been radical Greens which had penetrated security at the Cape in the guise of a USAF Space Command colonel, and the small handful of people who knew otherwise weren't about to dispel that notion. Nonetheless, it had been messy. Bad for business . . . even if a partial refund had been refused.

"No, no," Halprin said hastily. "The client has come to understand that by now."

"The client wanted me fired, as I recall," Nash replied.

"Not any longer." Halprin glanced up from his paperwork. "In fact, they specifically asked for you when they contacted us. Seems they have a lingering interest in American military activities on Mars."

Nash clasped his hands together in his lap. "Another payload? Sure, I can handle that . . . at least, as long as I don't have to pose as a colonel again."

It was meant as a joke, but Control apparently didn't grasp the humor. He leaned back in his leather-backed chair and steepled his fingers together. "Oh, you'll be visiting Cape Canaveral again," he drawled. In this posture he reminded Nash of a British professor explaining the Battle of Trafalgar to a slow-but-promising undergraduate. "But you'll be going a lot further than that, I assure you. . . ."

He paused deliberately. "If you accept the assignment, of course."

Nash didn't like the sound of that last part. Control rarely gave a field operative the option of backing out of an assignment. His salary was equivalent to his former take-home pay as a CIA agent, but hazardous-duty commissions for field assignments were three times that of even a Mossad dirty-tricks operative. This was only part of the reason why the price for a Security Associates corporate contract started at one million dollars, and that was only for cheap jobs like bodyguarding corporate CEOs. It made for a comfortable living, but he was expected to earn his paycheck. Control's extending the privilege of backing out of an assignment—especially one for which Nash's personal involvement had been specifically requested by a client—was not the way Security Associates normally treated their highest-paid employees.

"I don't understand, sir," he said.

Halprin did not mince words. "For this job, you're expected to go to Mars yourself."

Nash thought about it for less than a second before he pushed back his chair and stood up. "Excuse me, Robert," he said politely; it was one of the very few times he had ever used Control's first name. "I think I have a boat that needs to be mended."

He picked up his trenchcoat and started walking toward the door. Halprin let him get halfway across the office before he cleared his throat. "If it is of any interest to you," he said, "the name of the person you'll be investigating is Terrance L'Enfant."

Another brief pause. "Commander Terrance L'Enfant, United States Navy, former captain of the U.S.S. *Boston*."

There was the sound of a match striking, then the sucking sound of Halprin's pipe. "Someone you know, yes?"

Nash stopped just before he reached the door. He took a deep breath, closed his eyes for a moment. And then, just as Control must have anticipated, he turned around and walked back to the conference room table.

"Good." Control settled back in his chair and stroked the warm bowl of his pipe. "Now that we've done with the histrionics, let's get started, shall we? Pick up your file, please, and open it to the first page. . . ."

Cydonia Base, Mars: February 14, 2032, 1359 MCM

In the vast shadow of the D&M Pyramid, a stainless-steel sphere hung suspended beneath a tripod above a crevasse, and within the sphere was a spider. The spider had been manufactured by the St. Petersburg Robotics Corporation and had cost nearly one million eurodollars. It was St. Valentine's Day, but nobody at Cydonia Base was thinking about love.

Lieutenant Charlie Akers steadied himself carefully against a leg of the tripod and reached across the open pit to yank a powerline free from the sphere's electrical port. He hauled the line away from the crevasse and the surrounding rubble, dropped it on the ground, gave the winch-cable a final yank to test its slack, then turned to give a thumbs-up to one of the three TV cameras arrayed around the pit.

Inside Cydonia Base's monitor center several miles away, Tamara Isralilova watched Akers as he stepped out of camera range. She tapped a series of commands into her console keypad. "Internal batteries charged and at maximum-rated efficiency," she said, watching the graphs on her console's flatscreens. "Power-up sequence initiated. Drop minus twenty-five seconds and counting." She quickly looked over her shoulder at Paul Verduin. "Ready, Paul?"

Behind her in the darkened monitor center, Verduin sat tensely in his chair. Multicolored lights flashed in complex patterns on his console, but he was literally blind to them; the virtual-reality helmet which covered his head except for his nose, mouth, and chin was completely opaque. "Ready to switch on," he said.

He reached out with his right hand, feeling for the master switch on the console. It was the only non-VR switch he had to use to pilot the probe, and he had carefully memorized its location at his station. But before he could find it, he felt another hand brush past him and toggle the switch. As light suddenly rushed into his dark world, he murmured, "Thanks, Shin-ichi."

You're welcome. The voice did not belong to Shin-ichi Kawakami, however. It was Terrance L'Enfant who had spoken.

Of course it would be L'Enfant, Verduin reflected; he couldn't let anything happen without muscling in somehow. *Typical pushy American,* he thought, then reconsidered. No. Not so typical. Verduin might have given voice to his annoyance otherwise, but with the commander . . .

Yet L'Enfant was only a small irritation, at least for the moment. All at once, Verduin was one with the probe, even though it was located several miles away. He could see through a small slot in the sphere, as clearly as if it were with his own flesh-and-blood eyes, the legs of the tripod, the skinsuited technician standing nearby, and, looming like the mountain before him, the broken northeastern flank of the D&M Pyramid, towering almost a mile into the pink sky. Digital readouts at the margins of his vision showed compass coordinates, attitude, battery draw, light density, and more. Unreal, and yet so real . . .

Transit capsule drop minus fifteen seconds. This time it was Shin-ichi Kawakami's gentle voice which prompted him. *How are you doing, Paul?*

"Telemetry is nominal." He gazed up at the translucent row of green lights above his forehead, focused on the second one from the left, and deliberately blinked twice; it immediately shifted to red. "Recorder on."

"Da," Isralilova reported, and immediately corrected herself: *Yes, we copy.* English was the common tongue here, even though Verduin could have understood her if she had chosen to speak in Russian. *Descent sequence on full auto. Ten seconds to drop. Nine . . . eight . . .*

Verduin folded his hands in his lap and tried to make himself relax. For the next few seconds, he had nothing to do but enjoy the ride. If, of course, one could relax while falling down a shaft five hundred meters deep, even if it was only through telepresence. He took a deep breath. . . .

Two . . . one . . . drop initiated.

He almost *felt* the tripod release the grommets on the sphere; there was a flash of motion as the probe dropped into the crevasse, its rapid descent controlled only by the cable. Verduin instinctively shut his eyes, then forced them open. In the half-light from the top of the pit, he saw the rough rock walls blur past as he plummeted into the abyss, until sunlight faded and he was thrust into darkness.

Digital numbers flickered at the edges of his vision, so fast as to be almost meaningless. Down, down, down . . .

Four hundred meters, Tamara reported.

"Basement floor, coming up," Verduin said. "Garden utensils, books, children's toys . . ."

Cut the cute stuff, he heard Marks say from the other side of the module.

Anger swept aside his anxiety. "I would like to see you try this," he replied, and almost instantly regretted it. Marks was likely to rip the VR helmet off his head and do exactly that. After five months, Verduin had come to realize that arguing with L'Enfant's bullies—*escorts*, if one still cared to use that term—was always a mistake. Shin-ichi was the only one who could . . .

Three hundred meters, Tamara said tersely. *Two twenty-five . . . two hundred . . . slowing rate of descent . . .*

The transit capsule had passed the point where the ancient meteor had collapsed part of the D&M Pyramid. Although he was still blind, the probe's cameras shielded within the protective shroud of the capsule, Verduin knew from sorties with earlier probes that the rock walls of the pit were smoother and less jagged at his lower depth, showing where the drilling machines had excavated the last few hundred feet to the underground tunnel which he himself had dubbed Mama's Back Door.

Rate of descent slowing, Tamara reported. *One hundred meters . . . seventy-five . . . fifty . . . twenty-five . . . we're doing fine . . . twenty, eighteen, fifteen . . .*

"Please don't rush on my account," he said half-jokingly.

Five meters . . . four . . . three point seven five . . . three meters . . . we're in the tunnel.

The vertical shaft had reached its end. *Point five meters to the floor,* Tamara said. *Platform attitude stable.* She paused to glance over her console, then added, *You've reached bottom.*

He let his breath out slowly as he heard her deft fingers tapping in a new series of commands. *Collapsing transit capsule,* she said. *You're on manual now. Good luck.*

"Thank you," Verduin said. "AI system engage. Spider, activate lamps and switch camera to infrared."

All of a sudden, monochromatic light rushed back into his world as the probe's voice-operated AI interface switched on its external infrared lamps and slotted the appropriate filters over its fiber-optic array. Verduin saw the curved sides of the capsule fall open, like an egg hatching from the inside. Before him stretched a long, horizontal tunnel, like an ancient wormhole, although not burrowed by any creature which had evolved on Earth; the compass told him that it led north-by-northwest. Straight toward the catacombs.

"It's dark down here," he said nervously.

We need to move quickly, Kawakami reminded him. *Any minute now they shall . . .*

"Of course." He sucked in his breath. "Spider, move forward two meters and stop."

The probe was a mechanical spider. Approximately the size of a terrier, it moved on six multi-jointed legs arranged along the sides of its low-slung body. As Verduin spoke, it clattered off the bottom of the collapsed transit capsule and onto the smooth floor of the tunnel, its way illuminated by a small, front-mounted infrared lamp. Two long whiskerlike antennae protruded from either side of the multifaceted camera array, brushing gently against the rock walls. Verduin could see, and almost feel, the slight jarring as the tiny footpads found minute cracks and faults in the tunnel floor.

Transit capsule being withdrawn, Isralilova said.

The sphere was being dragged back to the surface by the wrench-cable. Verduin was alone in Mama's Back Door now, if only in a teleoperational sense. "It feels weird," he murmured.

Don't worry about that now, Kawakami said. He paused for a second. *Picking up EMA trace near your touchdown point,* he added softly.

What's that mean? L'Enfant demanded.

His question was ignored, but Paul knew what Kawakami had meant. The probe's sensors had already registered non-background electromagnetic activity within the tunnel—EMA which was, so far, the only reliable signature of the Cooties.

The pseudo-Cooties, rather. As always, Verduin had to remind himself that the autonomous robots that lurked beneath the Martian surface were only analogues of the real extraterrestrials. Nonetheless, any activity in this seldom used part of the uncharted catacombs between the D&M Pyramid and the Labyrinth could mean only one thing at this particular time.

They knew he was here, and they were coming for him.

That was precisely the reason why he was here.

"Spider, walk forward," Verduin said. "Track and follow the *EMA* trace." He smiled to himself as the arachnid probe trundled forward, homing in on the electromagnetic signature of the pseudo-Cooties.

This time, the science team was ready for them. If everything worked according to plan, the camouflage would work and the alien robots would mistake the spider for one of their own. If the subterfuge was successful, he could enter their ranks as a Trojan horse.

He wiped his sweaty, unseen palms on the legs of his trousers. Finally, after all the failures before this attempt, they were on the verge of exploring the catacombs beneath the City.

"Here, kitty kitty kitty . . ." he murmured.

Picking up strong EMA pulses from your sensor pod, Kawakami said. *Directly ahead of you and closing . . .*

Please be careful, Tamara said softly.

Paul thought of Sasha Kulejan: how he had died down here only three months earlier, shortly after the tunnel had been discovered and opened. Sasha had attempted to explore Mama's Back Door in an armored suit, thinking that he could somehow sneak up on the Cooties. His body had never been found; like Hal Moberly before him, the Cooties had inexplicably removed all traces of his armored recon suit. His final scream, as the alien robots swarmed over his armored exoskeleton, had been the last they had ever heard of him.

No wonder Tamara had given her illogical warning; even

though Paul was in the tunnel only as an artificial presence, she had heard her lover die. How she could even stand to be in the monitor center was beyond his . . .

Something moved in the shadows of the tunnel, just beyond reach of his lamplight.

Contact! Kamakami snapped.

"Spider, stop forward motion," Paul said. The probe halted. "All right, now," he said. "Come on, come on . . ."

For a moment, there was nothing; small vague shapes scurried just outside the range of his infrared searchlight. Around him, he could hear a stillness in the module as everyone held their breath. "Come on," he whispered. "What are you waiting for . . . ?"

All at once, they came: a dozen or more pseudo-Cooties, rushing as a copper-toned wave out of the darkness. They moved so quickly, there was no way he could count their number; first there was empty tunnel, then they were upon him, a swarm of identical metallic insects, skittering on their mechanical legs as they charged the probe.

Verduin's point-of-view rocked violently as they flung themselves on the probe. He heard Kawakami yell something, then caught a glimpse of one of the spider's forelegs as it was ripped out its shoulder-socket. God, they were fast! Two scissorlike pincers swept directly in front of his eyes. . . .

Verduin jerked back in his seat . . . then the universe vanished, replaced by static gray fuzz, rapidly fading to black.

Telemetry lost, Isralilova said. *Uplink severed at source.*

"I'm dead," he sighed.

The inside of the helmet was now completely dark. He slowly pulled it off and dropped it in his lap with a deep sigh of relief, feeling cool sweat run down his forehead from his matted hair. Everyone in the module was just beginning to turn toward him, and Verduin realized that his "death" in the tunnel had lasted only a very few seconds.

L'Enfant was the first to speak. "Well?" he asked. "Did you see something?"

Verduin opened his mouth to speak, only to find that words failed him. He shrugged and held up his hands.

"Yes," he said slowly. "What a garden spider sees when a mantis is about to devour it alive." He wiped the sweat off his forehead and took a long, deep breath. "Alien. So *alien* . . ."

"Of course it was alien," L'Enfant said impatiently. "What

else do you think we're dealing with here? One of your Amsterdam window-girls?"

He bent closer to Paul, resting his right hand on the console as he grasped the back of Verduin's chair with his left hand and swiveled it toward him. "I don't want to hear subjective opinion," L'Enfant demanded, gazing straight into Verduin's eyes. "I want to know *what* you saw."

Verduin stared speechlessly at Terrance L'Enfant. During the past several months he had first learned to distrust the American; later he had come to dislike him. Only recently had he come to fear him. L'Enfant was obsessed with the Cooties. So were Kawakami and Isralilova . . . and he himself, for that matter, although he hated to admit it even to himself. Yet why else would they have remained on Mars for almost three years now?

L'Enfant's obsession had assumed a darker side, though, manifesting itself as a capacity for sudden violence. He was capable of almost anything. After all, this was the man who had sunk the *Takada Maru*. . . .

"Answer him," Marks said from across the room. He was leaning against the closed hatch, his arms crossed above his chest. "He asked you a simple question, Dr. Verduin," he added as he leisurely reached up to scratch at his thick black beard. "Can't you give him a simple answer?"

A simple answer. How absurd . . .

"We lost telemetry with the probe less than three seconds after contact," Tamara said nervously. L'Enfant's gaze turned toward her; Verduin was surprised by what she'd said. Three seconds . . . that was *all*? "If Paul managed to see anything at all," she continued, "it is nothing less than a miracle. . . ."

"It does seem to confirm, however slightly and by circumstance, the presence of a collective hive-mind." Kawakami was already downloading the data collected in the computer harddrives into a CD-ROM; his back was turned toward L'Enfant as if he didn't notice his presence, or didn't care. "Our probe, however much it physically resembled one of the pseudo-Cooties, didn't fool them for even a moment. Perhaps an advanced tropism of some sort, although that does tend to suggest organic intelligence, hmmm?"

L'Enfant had turned toward the team's senior scientist, but he said nothing. "In any event," Kawakami continued, "that may mean that they identify one another through senses which don't depend on visual recognition. Therefore, they destroyed the intruder, just as red ants seek out and annihilate black ants who attempt to invade their hills."

He slipped the little CD-ROM disc out of the slot, fitted it into a plastic jewel-box, and turned around in his chair to offer it to L'Enfant. "The record is all here, just as Paul experienced it," he said. "We may have missed something of significance, though. When you examine the record, please tell us if you have a new interpretation. We will be interested to hear your own theories."

L'Enfant glared coldly at Kawakami. The implied insult was clear: L'Enfant could no more interpret the new data than he could decipher ancient Babylonian tablets.

If he dares to strike Shin-ichi, Verduin thought, *I swear I will . . .*

He glanced again at Marks and took another deep breath, this time to make himself relax. Of all the things L'Enfant had said and done so far, he had yet to threaten Kawakami personally. Indeed, Shin-ichi was the only person at Cydonia Base who seemed to intimidate their unwanted shepherd; maybe it was Kawakami's stature as a Nobel laureate, or perhaps it was his implacable will that countered L'Enfant's unfathomable rage. Or, just perhaps, it was the fact that both men were equally obsessed, but from different directions, and therefore polarized each other.

L'Enfant did not immediately accept the disk. "And how much longer till you think you have dependable data?" he asked, his voice deceptively soft.

Kawakami gazed back at him. "As I've told you before, Commander, we don't know. We are working within entirely new territory here, and it is a very gradual and often tedious process." He slowly blinked his languid brown eyes. "Science so often is this way."

"Yes, you've said that before." There was a new edge to L'Enfant's voice. "But I'm not a gradual or tedious person."

"If you have any specific recommendations for increasing the efficiency of our research," Kawakami replied patiently, "I would be only too happy to hear your thoughts."

L'Enfant said nothing.

He reached out and took the plastic box from Kawakami's gaunt hand. Since he had been at Cydonia Station, the science team had been required to give copies of all data collected to L'Enfant—for transmission to NASA's Ames Laboratory, he had said, although it was doubtless to prevent a recurrence of the "strike" which had ended the initial investigation of the Labyrinth two years ago. L'Enfant stood up straight, tucking the box into his jumpsuit's breast pocket, and stepped away from Verduin's workstation.

"I'll let you know what I think," he said stiffly to Kawakami. He looked back at Verduin and slowly nodded his head . . . then, unexpectedly, a patronizing grin spread across his face.

"Ants," he repeated with a dry chuckle. L'Enfant shook his head disbelievingly as he turned and began walking down the narrow aisle between the consoles. "You're defeated by ants. . . ."

His grin faded as he stopped and looked back at the scientists again. "I'm losing patience," he said softly. "Come up with something new. Another way of getting down there."

L'Enfant then turned and continued walking out of the monitor center. Marks stepped aside and pulled open the hatch, giving L'Enfant a brief salute as he stepped out into the habitat's access corridor. L'Enfant didn't deign to return the gesture, but this didn't prevent Marks from favoring the science team with a smug smirk as he followed his commander out into the corridor. No one said anything until the hatch clanged shut behind them.

"Bastard," Tamara whispered.

Kawakami ignored her. He immediately swiveled his chair to face Verduin. He laced his long, bony fingers together and absently nuzzled his chin, then suddenly turned back to his computer console and touched the REPLAY key.

"For lack of anything better to do, let's look at this again. . . ."

PART TWO

"If astronomy teaches anything, it teaches that man is but a detail in the evolution of the universe, and that resemblant though diverse details are inevitably to be expected in the host of orbs around him. He learns that, though he will probably never find his double anywhere, he is destined to discover any number of cousins scattered through space."

—PERCIVAL LOWELL,
Mars
(1895)

JOURNEY TO CYDONIA

8. The <u>Percival Lowell</u>

Dim red light from somewhere overhead, seen through closed eyelids . . . cold air against his face . . . a soreness in the crook of his right arm . . . a vague sensation of constant movement . . . an antiseptic odor . . . the rhythmic digital beep of an electrocardiograph . . .

"Pulse rate eighty-eight . . . blood pressure one twenty over eighty . . ."

"Respiration normal. He's breathing all right."

"EKG activity normal . . . no sign of intraventricular defect . . . ditto for intra-arterial. . . ."

"How's the EEG?"

"Cool. We've got a winner."

His mouth tasted as if it had been stuffed with cotton. His head felt numb, like a whiskey hangover, yet strangely without pain. He opened his eyes; a young man with a sparse beard and dirty-blond hair caught under a backward-worn baseball cap was standing to his left. To his right was a woman with a chestnut ponytail, a slight overbite, and a sweatshirt which proclaimed that it, or she herself, was the Property of the Oakland Athletics.

He opened his dry mouth. "Water," he managed to rasp. "Can . . . you . . . gimme some water?"

"Say what?" the guy with the baseball cap asked. He bent over the edge of the zombie tank and grinned down at him. "You say you want some vinegar?" His breath smelled like Juicy Fruit.

"Cut it out." The woman reached behind her and brought forth a squeeze-bottle. He instinctively started to reach for it, but found that he could not raise his hands. There was mild pressure against his wrists; they were restrained by nylon

123

straps. His face itched; he had grown a beard, and he would have sold his soul in hell for a chance to scratch at it. She bent the straw and gently tucked it between his parched lips. "Sip slowly," she said. "Just a little bit . . . easy, easy . . ."

Water never tasted so good. It took all his willpower not to gulp. The lighting in the hibernation module was red-tinted, subdued. He could feel a mild turning sensation: the rotation of the cycleship's arms. The woman allowed him another sip from the bottle, then pulled it away. "How're you feeling?"

He nodded a little. Damn, did his face itch. Juicy Fruit–breath leaned over the tank again. "Mr. Donaldson, do you know where you are?"

For a moment, the question confused him. Then his memory returned; no one aboard knew him as August Nash. To them, he was . . . yes, that was it. Donaldson. Andrew Donaldson.

A glucose IV line was stuck into his right arm. Six leads from the EKG were attached to the left and right sides of his bare chest by tiny suction cups. A small tight band of pressure around the base of his penis, unseen beneath the sheet covering the tank's water bed, informed him that a catheter was in place.

"Mars ship . . ." he murmured. He thought about it for a second, then added, "The *Lowell*."

"That's right." The woman nodded agreeably. "You've been in hibernation for the last nine months. Do you understand? So we're going to have to take this a little bit at a time."

"Straps." He lifted his hands against the wrist-restraints; he was helpless as long as they were holding him down, and that bothered him even more than the hangover. He really wanted to scratch his face. "Could you please remove the straps . . . ?"

She shook her head. "Not quite yet. We've got a little more to do first."

"If you think waking up was rough," Juicy Fruit added with a smirk, "you're going to love what happens next."

"Hush." The Property of the Oakland A's reached to the tray behind her and picked up a sedative-gun. "Now, Mr. Donaldson, I'm going to inject you with a mild local sedative. You're not going to sleep again. This is just to make the next part easier. Okay?"

As she spoke, she pulled down the sheet. Juicy Fruit glanced at her, then looked at Nash and winked at him. "Jodi loves this part. I mean, when it was her turn to come down here and give you physical therapy, she . . ."

"Shut up, Lew. I'm warning you." Jodi's face reddened as she placed the blunt nozzle of the gun against the shaved pubic area just above his testicles. He barely had time to feel humiliated before she squeezed the trigger.

There was a sharp pain as the needle jabbed into his skin. As his groin began to deaden, she took an open plastic bag and pushed its sleevelike opening around his penis. Then she grasped the catheter with the thumb and forefingers of each of her soft hands. The medical officer looked up at him and smiled comfortingly.

"Okay, now," she said, "can you tell me the names of the states? Starting in alphabetical order."

"Uhhh . . . sure." Knowing what was coming, he stared up at the low, curved ceiling of the hibernation bay. "Alabama . . . Alaska . . . Arkansas . . ."

"Ngggt!" Lew honked nasally. "I'm sorry, Contestant One, but you forgot Arizona. There goes your chance at the new Pontiac Sunfire and the trip to Rome, but as your door-prize you'll receive . . ."

And then Jodi released the catheter. Despite the sedative, the agony was exquisite; it felt as if a white-hot needle had been thrust into his urinary tract. "Your first pee-break in nine months!" Lew turned to an imaginary studio audience and began to clap his hands. "Let's have a big hand for Mr. Donaldson, folks! What a guy, huh . . . ?"

As he painfully urinated into the plastic bag, Nash moved his eyes to meet those of the first officer of the U.S.S. *Percival Lowell*. "I'm . . . going to . . . kill you," he hissed between gasps.

Lew turned around and, as he saw the expression on Nash's face, his grin faded. "Right," he said as he walked toward the hatch leading to the Arm Two access shaft. "I'm going to go check out the *Sagan*. You . . . ah, should be able to handle the other zombie by yourself, Jodi?"

"No problem." The medical officer removed the urine bag and zipped it shut; she seemed relieved that the exec was leaving her domain. As she walked away to drain the bag into the recycling port and discard the plastic catheter, Nash was able to see for the first time the adjacent zombie tank in the deck. The plastic lid was open; inside lay a young Japanese woman, revived from biostasis but apparently still asleep.

Her name was written on a white strip of tape affixed to the outside of the tank. In the dim red light, Nash could barely make it out: SASAKI, MIHO.

Nash recalled something from his mission briefing about a woman by that name. He fought to pull it from his fogged mind, but his memory was blocked. Instead, his eyes closed of their own accord; within a few moments he had fallen back asleep.

Five hours later, Nash climbed down the last few rungs of the long ladder leading into the Arm One access shaft.

He still felt a little weak from biostasis; clinging to the ladder just beyond the closed hatch marked 1A-MAIN COMMAND, he paused to catch his breath and let his body readjust to the pull of one-third normal gravity. His own quarters were on Deck 3D in one of the two habitation modules on Arm Two; it wasn't far from the hibernation bay but on the opposite side of the pinwheel-shaped cycleship from the command center. To get here, he had climbed all the way up Access Two out of Module Three, crossed the zero-gravity locus at the *Percival Lowell*'s axial center where the three arms converged, then climbed down Access One to the end of Arm One where modules One and Two were joined.

A long climb, but cycleships weren't designed to accommodate cripples, let alone the recently bedridden. It was good exercise even when one hadn't been in a zombie tank for the last nine months; as it was, he was already worn out, from both the climb and from the changes in gravity-gradient.

Nash pushed his hand against the unlocked hatch and eased it open, then carefully swung his left foot off the ladder and, grabbing onto handholds within the hatchway for support, entered the command center. A tricky maneuver, even in lower gravity. A voice called out to him from the darkness: "Mr. Donaldson . . ."

"Here," he answered.

"Back from the dead already, I see. Come in and have some coffee with us."

It was the nicest thing anyone had said to him during this long trip . . . since, at least, the medic at Freedom Station had said "Sweet dreams" as he was injecting him with zombie dope, just prior to transferring aboard the *Lowell* nine months earlier. "Thanks." Nash pulled the hatch shut behind him and turned around. "Right now some coffee would be appreciated."

He stopped to let his eyes adjust. The bridge was dark, illuminated mostly by the glow of console LEDs and the few light panels in the low ceiling which were switched on; green geometric patterns wavered and shifted on the computer flatscreens, and the red crescent of Mars hung in the center of a couple of TV monitors. Like every other compartment in the *Lowell*, the ship's command center was circular and windowless, although this deck was even more cramped than the hibernation bay. But even in the dimness, he could vaguely see someone rising from a chair at the other side of the compartment. As she passed under a light, Nash realized that he wasn't the first of the ship's former zombies to be paying a visit to Main Command.

"Don't mind me," the slender young Japanese woman was saying. "I was just leaving."

James Massey, the captain of the *Percival Lowell*, was getting up from his own chair. "Sure," he said. "I'll see you again before launch. . . ." He turned and graciously extended his hand to Nash. "Mr. Donaldson, Miho Sasaki. Miho, this is Andrew Donaldson. He's the new first officer for the *Akron*. And Miho here is . . ."

"Exobiologist," Nash said as his memories from his briefing with Control abruptly returned to him. "Assistant to Shin-ichi Kawakami at Cydonia Base a couple of years ago. Yes, I've heard of you. . . ."

"You have?" Sasaki's almond eyes widened and she seemed to stiffen a little. "Dr. Kawakami may be famous, but I didn't know I had achieved such stature."

Nash stopped himself before he could blurt out more. Biostasis must have hit him harder than he had realized. First, his failure to automatically remember Sasaki—a key figure during the Cydonia Crisis two years earlier—and, just now, his loss of control, almost motormouthing info which shouldn't have been at the tip of his tongue in the first place. Unprofessional. All he could do now was try to cover.

"Sorry." Nash shrugged and looked down at the floor, feigning sheepishness. "Didn't mean to carry on like that. It's only that . . . y'know, I've been a Face buff for a while now. I've read everything about the Cydonia expedition, so . . . yeah, I remembered your name. That's all."

Sasaki smiled briefly, more out of diplomatic courtesy than real warmth. "You've got a good mind for minutiae, Mr. Donaldson. . . ."

"Andrew. Most people call me Andy."

"Andy," she finished with forced informality, her face once more turning glacial. "We'll have to get acquainted later, since you're going to be on the . . . ah, what is its name again?"

"The U.S.S. *Akron*," Massey said as came up from behind her; he took her forearm and subtly nudged her toward the hatch. "You'll be on it tomorrow, Miho, so you'll be able to ask Andy all that you want to know."

"Yes, of course," she said. "We'll have plenty of time. Good day, gentlemen."

Nash stepped aside as Sasaki squeezed past him and opened the hatch. "See you in a few hours, Mr. Donaldson," she added, her voice still cool, then she ducked through the hatchway and began to climb up the access-shaft ladder, heading for the transfer chamber in the cycleship's hub.

Massey shut the hatch behind her; this time, he twisted the lockwheel to dog it shut. "Sorry for the surprise, Mr. Donaldson, but she insisted on visiting me." He smiled as he turned back around. "We're old acquaintances, from when I was the first officer on the *Shinseiki*. Apparently she recuperated from the zombie tank faster than you did, even though you got out first."

"But she wasn't wearing a catheter, either," a familiar voice said from the other side of the compartment. Lew was half-bent over the navigation table, wearing a pair of wire-rimmed reading glasses, his right hand cupped around the earpiece of his headset. Still watching the shifting readouts on the broad LCD flatscreen, he peered owlishly over the top of his spectacles and grinned at Nash. "I gotta say, man, you had the worst case of the zombie shakes I've seen since I've been working on this tub."

Nash said nothing. Massey slid between them, as if he was deliberately trying to position himself between Nash and his first officer. "You've already met my own first officer, Lew Belotti. . . ."

"Yes, I have." Nash restrained his temper. "He's got an interesting sense of humor."

"And I'm available for weddings, company parties, and bar mitzvahs," Belotti continued, still wearing the same shit-eating grin.

Massey shut his eyes in secret pain. "And he's also available to go down to C-cube and double-check the inertial guidance platform. Right, Lew?"

Lew started to say something else, but a glimpse at Massey's expression was enough to let him know that he and his lip were not wanted on deck just then; he might have also remembered Nash's oath to him a few hours earlier in the hibernation bay. Belotti got up from his chair and avoided getting near either man by opening the interdeck hatch and climbing down the short ladder into the logistics deck beneath the bridge. Following an unspoken order from the captain, he shut the hatch behind him, giving the two men absolute privacy.

Massey sighed and shook his head. "Sorry about that, Nash," he said as he walked back to his chair on the left side of the compartment. "Lew's a little weird, maybe even for this ship . . . oh, and the coffee is in the beaker over there, behind his chair."

The bridge coffeepot rested on a jury-rigged hot plate beneath the emergency lockers; the bulkhead above it was plastered with Hawaiian surfing scenes and *Playboy* pinups. Nash found a plastic mug, stenciled with the Buck Existential cartoon characters, which looked reasonably clean. "Apparently you're aware of my real name," he said as he poured the thick, iron-black brew into it. "I trust that hasn't become public information."

The captain shook his head. "I didn't know myself until about three weeks ago, just before we went around the solar farside. We received some E-mail for you on the Huntsville uplink, and that's when I was briefed . . . don't worry, it was eyes-only for me. Jodi and Lew didn't read it."

"If you say so." Nash wasn't entirely convinced. Belotti was a little too cunning. "If you ask me, Captain, your first officer's wound a little too tight for this sort of work."

"He's a good navigator, he knows enough about biostasis to help out Jodi with the zombies, and he can bring down a lander in thirty-knot winds." Massey leaned back in his chair. "That's all that counts with me. After that, I don't care if he knows every Groucho Marx gag by heart and beats off once a day." He shrugged. "You work this job, you get used to weird people. After working the *Shinseiki* for three years, Lew's a relief. The Japs had *no* sense of humor. Hey, the beard looks good on you, by the way."

Nash had decided not to shave off the beard he had grown during biostasis. It was still uncomfortable, but it was one more bit of assurance that L'Enfant wouldn't recognize his face. "Yeah, maybe," he murmured, not interested in Massey's opinion of his grooming. He brought his coffee over to the seat which Miho Sasaki had just vacated and settled into it, then sipped his coffee and winced. It tasted like a mixture of pure caffeine and hot grease. Even crew-mess coffee from his Navy days had been better than this, but if it was intended to put a jolt into him, it did the trick. "You were on the *Shinseiki*? During the Steeple Chase operation?"

"Sort of. I piloted the *Shinseiki*'s lander down to Cydonia, when they still allowed direct flights to the base, so I was on the ground during the raid. I didn't have much to do with it though . . . up in the bleachers for most of the game, so to speak." Massey's lips tightened. "And I don't mind telling you that I'm not crazy about handling home base for another covert job, even if it is Skycorp's show."

"It's different this time."

"Sure it is. Just another variation on the same old shit. All because of these stupid dead aliens and their stupid dead city. . . ."

Nash raised an eyebrow. "Pardon me, Captain?"

"Never mind." Massey sighed again as he kneaded his eyes with his knuckles. "Jesus, I'm beginning to sound like one of those Back to Earth yahoos back home. Forget it, Nash. It's been a long trip up. Let's run this through again before I put you and Miho and the rest of the zombies on that lander, okay?"

The *Lowell*'s two landers—the unmanned cargo pod and the *Carl Sagan*, the personnel lander—were scheduled to be dropped from the *Lowell* at 1500 hours MCM. However, neither lander would descend directly to Cydonia Base; since engine-powered landings and lift-offs disturbed the sensitive seismographic instruments that monitored psuedo-Cootie activity beneath the City, spacecraft were prohibited from making planetfall directly to Cydonia, save for the occasional parachute-drop of a cargo pod from orbit.

Instead, Nash would accompany the *Lowell*'s three-person crew and the three relief scientists to Arsia Station, over four thousand miles away from Cydonia Base. The following day, at 0800 hours, Nash was scheduled to leave Arsia Station aboard the new Mars airship, the U.S.S. *Akron*. Two days later he would arrive in Cydonia.

"That gives you seven days to complete your job and get back to Arsia," Massey said. "Two days to get up there, three days at Cydonia, and two days for the return trip. That's an inflexible, drop-dead deadline."

"Sure. I understand. . . ."

"No, sir, I don't think you do." Massey hunched forward and rested his elbows on his knees. "Listen to me, because I don't want any misunderstandings. This has to do with our available launch window for the return flight. After we get our shore leave—the AIs will be minding the ship while it's parked in orbit, so we can stretch our legs a bit on the ground—we've still got to refuel at the Phobos fuel depot and check out the boat for the ride home, and seven days groundside is the longest I can stretch it. At eighteen-hundred hours on nine-three GMT, Jodi and Lew and I climb back into the lander for launch to orbit . . . and if you're not back at Arsia by then, you'll have to wait until the *Korolev* arrives in another nine months."

He smiled and shook his head. "Believe me, Nash, you don't want to be sitting around Arsia Station for almost a year. It's real boring down there."

Nash glanced at the image of Mars on one of the overhead monitors. "I can imagine."

"I guess you can." Massey drained the rest of his lukewarm coffee, made a sour face, then placed his cup on the floor. He pushed himself out of his chair. "C'mon. I've got your E-mail disk and something else to give you."

Nash stood up and followed the captain to a wall locker behind the navigation table; Massey pulled a keyring out of his vest pocket, selected an Allen wrench from a dozen others, and slipped it into the hole. "This has been in the locker since we left Earth orbit. You'll have to trust me when I tell you that nobody's messed with it. Neither Lew nor Jodi have this key. I guess it has something to do with your assignment, whatever it is."

"Maybe," Nash said. "And you're not even curious? About the assignment, I mean."

Massey opened the locker and reached inside. "Listen, sport, I just drive the bus. It's not my business to know or care what you're up to." He pulled out a small steel attaché case and handed it to Nash. As Nash took it, Massey reached into a breast pocket, pulled out an unmarked CD-ROM diskette, and handed it to his passenger. "And that's your mail from home. Don't worry about it, okay?"

Nash eyed the diskette thoughtfully. The copy-protect tab

was in place, but that didn't mean much; a good cracker wouldn't have forgotten that detail after reading the file. "If you say so, Captain."

"Yeah, I say so." Massey closed the locker and folded his arms across his chest. "Okay, now get out of here. I've got a ship to run. Be at Airlock Two at fourteen-thirty hours and your buddy Lew will fix you up."

"Right." Nash started to turn, then thought of something else. "Just one more thing . . ."

"There always is. What is it?"

"Sasaki." Massey seemed to tense up a bit at the mention of her name. "She left Mars almost two years ago on this ship after the Steeple Chase incident. People who leave Mars don't usually come back for a second tour."

Massey's face remained impassive. "Yeah. So?"

"So what's she doing back here?"

"Like I said before, Nash . . . I just drive the bus." He smiled a little. "You want to know what Miho's doing here, ask her yourself. I'm minding my own business."

Nash knew a half-dozen ways of extracting the information from Massey, most of them painful; he doubted, though, that any one of them would have worked on the captain. Instead, he turned to the hatch and undogged it. "Okay. Be seeing you," he said.

"Fourteen thirty, Airlock Two. After that . . ." Massey held up an open right palm and two fingers of his left hand. "Seven days. Believe it. Live by it."

"I won't forget."

The captain nodded his head. "Make sure you don't. And good luck . . . Mr. Donaldson."

9. Final Briefing

Nash's traveling companions in Deck 3D, two members of a relief crew which was bound for Arsia Station, were having dinner in the wardroom by the time he got back to his niche, thereby leaving him alone in the *Lowell*'s passenger quarters. Nonetheless, Nash took the precaution of closing the accordioned door to the closet-sized compartment before he placed the attaché case on his bunk.

His thumbprint unlocked the case; as he expected, it contained a notebook computer, along with accessories which had been provided by Security Associates' armory. Nash unfolded the clamshell screen, switched on the computer, and slipped the diskette Massey had given him into the disk-drive.

The first page of the screen contained a file directory with a single entry: MES/8-01-32-1500/DONALDSON. Next to it was printed: 1ST READ/8-25-32-1137. Nash let out his breath. So far, so good; no one had entered this file since it had been transmitted from the Security Associates by means of Skycorp's deep-space communications network. Nonetheless, it was a one-way message; Earth was out of radio contact until Mars emerged again from the other side of the Sun.

Nash typed in his code-number; as an afterthought, he then pulled out a pair of lightweight headphones and jacked them into the computer. He switched the playback mode to VOX so that the message would be verbally communicated through the speech synthesizer. He had a few other things in the attaché case to check out, and having the E-mail read to him would save a few minutes.

The company's logo appeared on the screen, accompanied by a sterile androgynous voice: *Good day, Mr. Donaldson. The following message was transmitted to you at 1500 Greenwich Mean Time, August 1, 2032. An extra-high baud-per-second ra-*

tio was used during transmission to prevent its being read. It is preprogrammed to play only once, then erase itself from this diskette. You are further instructed to destroy this diskette after use. When you are ready to receive, please touch any key. . . .

Further proof that the message had not been tapped. He should have known that SA would take such precautions. Nash randomly tapped the letter "J" on the keyboard; there was a brief pause, then the voice continued. *Thank you. Your message will now commence. . . .*

Again, another pause, although the screen remained static. The same AI voice continued, but the delivery, the choice of words, was unmistakably that of Robert Halprin; all that was lacking was his Oxford accent. *Good afternoon, Mr. Donaldson. This is a final briefing before commencement of your present assignment and an update of the current operating environment. You will be receiving this message shortly after you are revived aboard the U.S.S.* Percival Lowell *en route to Mars. Since extended biostasis has been known to trigger spontaneous lapses in long-term memory, this briefing will commence with a review of your assignment. . . .*

Leave it to Control to cover all the bases, even when it was redundant. Nash smiled to himself as he reached into the case; his hand found a small, bubble-celled plastic packet, which he pulled out and unzipped as he listened.

A digitalized photo of an unsmiling man—mid-fifties, craggy face, narrowed sharp eyes, thinning blond hair—appeared on the screen. Nothing about him showed any trace of warmth or humor. Nash felt something tighten in his chest as he studied the familiar face.

This man is Commander Terrance L'Enfant, Control's AI doppelganger unnecessarily explained. *He is currently the American co-supervisor of the international scientific research base at Cydonia. . . .*

Almost involuntarily, Nash touched the PAUSE key on the computer. Gazing at L'Enfant's face, he rested his arms on his knees, remembering a night long ago when he watched his former captain snuff out the lives of almost fifty men and women. . . .

In 2019, Nash had been enlisted in the U.S. Navy, serving as a seaman aboard the U.S.S. *Boston.* The *Boston* was a *Seawolf*-class attack submarine, assigned to duty in the South Pacific; at the age of twenty-five, Nash was around for the short-lived India-Japan Crisis . . . and for the *Takada Maru* incident.

When the government of Japan announced its intention of importing as much as 150 tons of plutonium, extracted from spent uranium fuel rods from east European nuclear power plants, to power its own domestic nukes, the United States, Great Britain, and Germany had led a protest in the United Nations against the proposal. The plan called for the plutonium to be transported by rail from eastern Europe and the C.I.S. to the Indian port city of Madras, where it would be loaded aboard Japanese commercial freighters and sailed along principal shipping routes in the Indian and Pacific oceans to the Japanese port city of Osaka.

Japan was in desperate need of plutonium for its nukes; the country was still heavily dependent on civilian nuclear energy, but it had lost its principal suppliers of uranium and plutonium, the United States, Australia, and South Africa, due to the Green Revolution. The C.I.S., along with Hungary and Czechoslovakia, had no such environmentalist scruples, however; they had already sold the reprocessed plutonium from their own dormant nuclear plants to India, with the Indian government anticipating a tidy profit from the subsequent resale to Japan. Although both Japan and India unofficially conceded that there was an inherent ecological danger in shipping so much plutonium across the high seas—not to mention the threat of third-world terrorist groups either hijacking a train as it made its way across the Middle East or pirating a freighter in the Indian Ocean—neither country was willing to abandon their agreement in the face of political fire. Too much money was at stake for India, and Japan's government was under public pressure to relieve the periodic blackouts in its major cities.

When both Japan and India refused to cede to binding United Nations resolutions against the shipments, push finally came to shove. Under the accords of the U.N. Environmental Protection Treaty, the General Assembly voted in favor of naval blockades of both India and Japan. The U.S.S. *Boston* was assigned to the blockade of Osaka; its primary mission was to stop any Japanese freighters bound for the seaport, search their holds, and place under arrest the crews of any ships found to be carrying plutonium.

Within a few days of the blockade's commencement, India caved in. Japan remained firm, however, calling the U.N. resolutions illegal under international maritime law. Meanwhile, an untold number of Japanese freighters were at sea between India and Japan. No one knew for certain which of them carried plutonium or not. India's pre-existing government was toppled by civil insurrection as a result of the crisis; its new Green parliament was in complete disarray, and Japan refused to provide any information which would interfere with the arrival of the plutonium it had already bought and shipped out of Madras. For the first time since the end of World War II, it was Japan versus the rest of the global community.

Then, on the night of May 29, 2019, the U.S.S. *Boston* located a Japanese freighter, the *Takada Maru*, in the Philippine Sea, apparently bound for Osaka. In command of the *Boston* was Captain Terrance L'Enfant; among the members of the boarding party was Seaman August Nash. . . .

But that was over thirteen years ago, and he couldn't afford to think about it now. A job had to be done; he could wrestle again with ghosts at another, more opportune time.

Nash restarted the message by tapping the PAUSE key again; the screen unfroze and the narrative continued. As he listened, he unsealed the packet containing a small collection of electret bugs, each with its own microtransmitter and attachable to almost any surface by suction pads, along with the tiny Sony microrecorder to be used with the bugs. Everything was neat and concealable; he could hide the whole apparatus in his underwear if necessary.

Following the cessation of hostilities between the U.S. and the C.I.S. in 2030, the voice said, *American and Russian military forces were withdrawn from the Cydonia region. As an indirect result of World Court arbitration which found that the C.I.S. had been the principal aggressors, and in accordance with the U.N. Security Council resolution which ended the conflict, the United States was allowed to place unarmed military observers at Cydonia Base as a token peacekeeping force to prevent further shipments of Russian munitions to the base. Although this was not in keeping with the initial demands made by the science team at Cydonia Base, they reluctantly agreed to the stipulation.*

A small padded box held a Seiko wristwatch; concealed in its LCD face was the tiny aperture of an autofocus lens. When pressed twice in rapid succession, the microfilm camera inside the chronometer would take a flashless picture. The film microdisc was good for seven exposures; Nash regretfully unstrapped his own Rolex Oyster and slid the Seiko onto his left wrist, making sure that the chronometer was facing out.

Because he was perceived to be a military officer capable of making independent decisions, and also because of opinions he had expressed during a speech at the Annapolis naval academy regarding the alien relics at Cydonia, Terrance L'Enfant was selected by the Pentagon for the assignment. Shortly after L'Enfant's appointment, the American co-supervisor of Cydonia Base, Dr. Arthur Johnson, resigned in protest. Several other members of the Cydonia expedition followed him off the base, reducing the science team to four persons, with no American members among them. Nonetheless, the Security Council ruling remained in effect. L'Enfant's status was subsequently upgraded and he became the new American co-supervisor, with the reluctant compliance of the European and Japanese members of the Cydonia science team. The C.I.S. issued a formal protest, but allowed two of its scientists to remain at Cydonia. . . .

The image on the screen split four ways to include the faces of three other persons next to L'Enfant's mug shot. One was a thick-bearded black man, subscripted A. MARKS by the computer. The second was a wiry, prematurely balding younger man, labeled C. AKERS. The third was a young woman with crew-cut brown hair: M. SWIGART. Altogether, Nash surmised, they looked as if they had been recruited from Camp LeJeune: tough guys.

L'Enfant has been accompanied to the base by three military officers who have been officially designated as observers: Staff Sergeant Alphonse Marks, Lieutenant Charles Akers, and Lieutenant Megan Swigart. Marks is a former U.S. Marine Corps combat instructor, Akers was trained as a Navy SEAL, and Swigart was a former Navy A-36 fighter pilot. Although all are Annapolis graduates and have some degree of college-level education in the sciences, none are scientific specialists, nor are any of them members of the Marine Corps' First Space Infantry. Their prior relation to L'Enfant is unknown, although he specifically requested them for this assignment. . . .

The screen changed again, this time to present a three-dimensional topographic layout of the City at Cydonia, including the Face and the nearby D&M Pyramid, and the smaller man-made habitat modules of Cydonia Base. The gridded map slowly rotated as the narrative continued.

Despite the successful penetration in 2030 of the labyrinth

beneath the C-4 Pyramid, during the past two years the interna-
tional science team has failed to establish further contact with
the robotic aliens—nicknamed the pseudo-Cooties—who have
tunneled beneath the alien city. The only progress made in this
time was the discovery of a tunnel that leads directly from the
D&M Pyramid to an unexplored area beneath the central clus-
ter of pyramids near Cydonia Base.

The tunnel was outlined in red light on the screen. *However,*
when a Russian scientist was sent into the new tunnel earlier
this year, all contact with him was lost. The scientist, Sasha
Kulejan, was also the Russian co-supervisor of the expedition.
He is missing and presumed dead, and has not been replaced by
the Russian space agency Glavkosmos due to continued politi-
cal protest by Minsk against the U.N. resolutions. . . .

Nash nodded his head; he was already aware of that situation.
Although the Russians were still interested in the Cydonia expedition, mainly because of possible technological benefits that
might be derived from any new discoveries, they had erred
greatly by sending military forces to Mars to back up their
claims. In the end, it had been a desperate act which had back-
fired against the C.I.S. with world opinion turned against the
Commonwealth in the backlash created by the raid; the Russian
public had voted the Nasanov government out of office and the
C.I.S. had been forced further into retreat, leaving behind only a
couple of key persons at Cydonia. Now, with Kulejan's death,
only one of the Russian scientists remained at Cydonia Base, a
final token-member of the C.I.S.'s delegation to the expedition.

Efforts to send teleoperated probes into the tunnel have also
failed, the voice continued, *destroyed upon contact with*
pseudo-Cootie drones which attack any intruders in the under-
ground network. This is one of the central enigmas of the alien
city, since the Face at Cydonia was obviously constructed to
lure humankind into a first-contact situation, just as the laby-
rinth beneath C-4 was apparently intended as a test of our intel-
ligence and ingenuity. Why the aliens are now deterring further
attempts at communication, although the Face itself initially
appeared to have been an invitation to homo sapiens, *is a mys-*
tery to the science team. . . .

A digitalized, slightly out-of-focus snapshot of a man in a
skinsuit appeared on the screen; he was half-turned toward the
camera, apparently unaware that he was being photographed. In
the background could be seen the giant, angular shape of one of

the Martian pyramids, but what was more intriguing was the fact that the man in the skinsuit was apparently cradling an assault rifle. Looking closer, Nash recognized the weapon as a 5.56mm Steyr ACR, a gun favored by several U.S. law enforcement agencies.

This photo was in a film disc which was recently smuggled out of Cydonia Base, the voice continued. *It was covertly taken by an airship pilot, Katsuhiko Shimoda, who was later killed in a flight accident near the Tharsis region. The man in the picture has been tentatively identified as Staff Sergeant Marks. He is armed with an assault weapon, a violation of the United Nations agreement since it expressly prohibited the U.S. observers at Cydonia Base to be armed. During the last several months, reports to Earth from Cydonia Base have become more sporadic and less informative, sometimes containing little more than routine statistics of consumables used by the base personnel and request forms for resupply. Direct contact with Arsia Station, the principal Mars base, has similarly diminished to monthly supply visits by the airship* Akron. *It is currently believed that Commander L'Enfant and his aides have seized paramilitary control of Cydonia Base and are prohibiting candid communication from members of the science team under threat of force. If this is so, the reasons are unknown. . . .*

The screen split again. On the right was a diagram of an enlongated, awkward-looking spacecraft which Nash recognized as an unmanned American interplanetary freighter, the type used to ferry supplies to Mars between cycleship excursions. On the left was an animated diagram of a Hohlmann trajectory between Earth and Mars. *Since you departed Earth orbit aboard the* Lowell, *there has been an unforeseen occurrence. The automated deep-space freighter* Bradbury *has been sent to Mars on an eight-month flight-path which will beat the* Lowell *to Mars rendezvous by little more than one week. We know only that a cargo pod, which was launched to orbit by a U.S. military shuttle launched from Vandenberg and loaded onto the* Bradbury *just prior to its departure from LEO, has been parachuted to Cydonia Base. The contents of the cargo pod are unknown. However, given the source of the cargo, we can only assume that the payload is military in nature. . . .*

The photo and the diagram were replaced by the Skycorp logo: a static image. *Pentagon officials have denied accusations of such military interference from the space industrial partners sponsoring the Cydonia investigation. Despite the circumstantial evidence, there is not sufficient evidence to base a claim of malfeasance by the U.S. military. None of the appropriate governments is willing to risk repeating the events of August 2030 until more hard evidence has been gathered. . . .*

The last item in the attaché case was the most important, perhaps, considering that the quarry was armed. The SIG-Sauer P230 was a deceptively small semiautomatic handgun; little more than six inches long, it could almost be dismissed as a gun for a lady's handbag. Normally, Nash went unarmed on most assignments; on the rare occasions when he did pack a gun, such as bodyguard jobs, it was usually a Glock 19. But the Glock, despite its greater firepower, was much too large to be effectively concealed in a jumpsuit, while the little P230 could easily be carried in a trouser pocket without being seen. And the very last thing he wanted L'Enfant to know was that Andy Donaldson was armed.

Your assignment is fourfold. First, to discover whether Commander Terrance L'Enfant has taken control of Cydonia Base. Second, to discover what his future plans are. Third, to determine whether he intends to use military force to accomplish those goals. Fourth, and finally, to provide an assessment of whether his operations endanger Skycorp's present operations on Mars. . . .

Nash locked the safety pin, then thumbed the magazine release beneath its blue steel barrel and reached for the box of .38 caliber ammo. As the SA armorer had promised, he had been issued fragile-nosed safety rounds similar to those used by FAA air marshals. The bullets would shatter on contact with anything more resilient than a human body and therefore not punch through a pressurized hull. One by one, he slid the seven rounds into the cartridge.

Your primary objective will be to gather tangible evidence that will either support or refute the claims, whether they be photos or taped conversation, through whatever covert means are at your disposal. Once you have returned to the Lowell, *you will immediately transmit said information to Security Associates at the earliest possible opportunity, as soon as the orbits of Earth and Mars allow resumption of direct radio contact. Again, your primary objective will be to gather information. . . .*

He slotted the loaded cartridge back into the gun's handle, then reached for the spare cartridge and began to load it as well. *However, since you will be facing armed and possibly dan-*

gerous adversaries, and because you will be operating beyond range of feasible radio contact, you are also cleared to use lethal force, with extreme prejudice, to assure your own survival. . . .

Startled, Nash glanced up at the screen; this had not been part of the initial mission briefing late last year in Washington.

Be advised that, if this option becomes necessary within the parameters of your assignment, the company's legal counsel states that you are authorized to act upon it, according to his interpretation of the seventh protocol of the United Nations Protocols for the Sending of Communications to Extraterrestrial Intelligence. . . .

"Seventh protocol?" he whispered. "What the hell are you . . . ?"

The narrative continued, unheeding of his bewilderment. *Your contact on Mars is Samuel Leahy, the Skycorp general manager of Arsia Station. Leahy will make any necessary introductions to Arsia Station staff members and give you further updates on your assignment, if you need to be provided. We anticipate your first report no earlier than twelve hundred hours and no later than twenty-four hundred hours, Greenwich time, on November 11, 2032. Good luck, Mr. Donaldson.*

With no closing other than that, the message was concluded. The screen went blank; already a self-contained virus program was destroying everything on the diskette. Nash ejected the diskette, grasped it between his fists and snapped it in half before shoving the remains down the disposal vent.

Extreme prejudice . . .

He knew what that meant. He could snuff somebody if they were trying to snuff him first. No problem with that.

The seventh protocol . . .

No goddamned idea.

L'Enfant . . .

He knew all about Terrible Terry L'Enfant.

Nash picked up the gun and studied it. Control had sent him up here on what had seemed to be a clearly defined mission; now that he was here, out of radio contact and completely on his own, the rules of the game had been changed on him. He had been given a gun, all right, but no one had bothered to ask him whether he cared to kill L'Enfant.

Or, if he did, whether he had the nerve to pull the trigger.

"Halprin," he whispered, "you old fucking bastard . . ."

10. The Mars Hotel

"Launch minus nine . . . eight . . . seven . . ."

"Final engine check nominal. We're hot. Separation at mark zero."

"Copy. Launch minus five . . . four . . . three . . ."

"Umbilical detached."

"Copy that . . . one . . ."

"Mark zero and separation." Lew Belotti's right hand, resting on the bar above his head, yanked it down. There was an abrupt jar as the *Sagan* was released from its cradle beneath the *Lowell*'s second arm. Green lights flashed across the wraparound console of the cockpit. "We've got separation," he said as he returned both hands to the control yoke. "Firing RCR's in five seconds on my mark. Five . . . four . . . three . . . two . . . one . . . mark for RCR ignition."

There was a slight sensation of motion as the flight computer automatically ignited the RCR's along the lander's biconic fuselage, pushing it away from the cycleship. From his couch in the midsection of the lander's crew compartment, Nash watched as the long trusswork of Arm Two briefly swam past the cockpit windows: the gold Mylar-wrapped habitation cylinders, the OMS engines, the oxygen/nitrogen tanks and the wide hexagon of the communications antenna and, finally, the long, black ripple of the heat radiator. Then, suddenly, the *Lowell* was gone, spinning away on its own lonesome orbit as the massive red orb of Mars drifted into view through the windows.

"Nice show, Lew." Massey was leisurely watching his first officer from the right-hand co-pilot seat. He glanced at the readout on one of his computer screens. "Four minutes to initiating primary descent sequence, on your mark."

"PDS in four minutes, Cap'n." Lew bent forward against his

straps and began tapping the next set of instructions into the computer's keyboard. Nash could hear the absent-minded snap of his chewing gum between his jaws as he worked. His check-list, loosened from its magnetic clip by the separation and unfet-tered by the loss of gravity, floated upward from the dashboard; without missing a beat, Lew snagged it out of midair and shoved it back onto the console below the window. He glanced over his shoulder at the six passengers seated behind him. "Ev-erybody okay back there?"

Nash nodded and gave him a quick thumbs-up; in the couch next to him, Miho Sasaki appeared to be completely unruffled. The medical officer, Jodi Ferrigno, seemed to be taking a nap. The same couldn't be said about the other passengers in the rear, the three scientists bound for Arsia Station for their two-year research tours. Nash heard a couple of uncomfortable burps; the sudden transition to zero-gee was unsettling, and Nash had little doubt that at least one of them would throw up during aerobraking.

Belotti's interest, though, was polite at best. He had already turned his attention back to his controls. "Arsia Control, this is *Sagan* MEM-L012," he murmured into his headset mike. "Do you copy?" A pause. "Roger that, Arsia, we are on standby for deorbit burn. All systems are copacetic. Awaiting weather nowcast and instructions for primary descent, over."

Nash looked over at Sasaki again. The young woman was perfectly relaxed, her hands folded together in her lap as she gazed at the starscape through the windows. Her long black hair was braided and caught in a tight bun behind her neck, but a few loose strands floated around the side of her face. "This must be familiar to you by now," he said.

Sasaki shrugged indifferently. "I thought it might be more ex-citing," she admitted, "but I suppose when it's the second time . . . three times if you count aerobraking in Earth's atmo-sphere . . ." She smiled a little and looked forward again. "It just feels like another trip."

"Hmm." For some reason, Nash felt much the same way, de-spite the fact that this was *his* first trip. For him, leaving the se-curity of the *Lowell* and beginning the descent to Mars was only the first phase of his assignment. It wasn't so much a climax as it was a preface. Cydonia Base was his real objective, and get-ting there was only part of the job.

"Looking forward to getting back to Cydonia?" he asked.

The question appeared to startle her—she blinked and her hands moved nervously—but only a little. "Sure," she said without looking at him. "There's much down there that I want to see. The new excavation, what has been discovered about the aliens . . ."

"And your mentor, Dr. Kawakami . . ."

"Yes." She nodded ever so slightly. "And him, too."

Nash opened his mouth to speak again, but she closed her eyes once more and tilted her head slightly away. She was clearly uninterested in keeping up her end of the conversation.

Through the windows, Mars slowly hove into view, sharply canted on its side. Nash glimpsed the long, meandering scar of the Valles Marineris and, to its left, the pockmark which was Arsia Mons. Down there, somewhere between the Noctis Labyrinthis and the beginning of the volcanic highlands, was Arsia Station. He looked over at Sasaki again, but her eyes were peacefully closed, her hands still clasped together. He watched her for a moment, waiting for her eyes to open again, but Sasaki didn't budge.

Nash cast his attention once again on the windows. He was almost certain that Sasaki was hiding something, but she wasn't going to talk about it . . . at least, not right now.

Fine. That was okay by him. Nash settled back in his couch for the long ride down. He could wait until they had landed.

Then he would make it his business to pick her brain.

"Okay, okay," Jeri Beauchamp said, steadily watching the blip on the XYZ axes of her computer screen. "Now swing it twelve degrees south, two degrees east. . . ." The blip obediently moved closer to the center of the three-dimensional axis. "There you go, Lew, you're on the dime. Looking good there . . ."

Roger that, TRAFCO, Lew Belotti's fuzzy voice said in her headset. *Main chute jettison in five seconds. Mark five . . . four . . . three . . . two . . .*

Jeri glanced up from her screen, seeking the *Sagan* through the wraparound windows of the traffic-control cupola. Past the tilted black-glass rows of the solar farm to the south, the lander was rapidly descending on its three main parachutes toward Landing Pad Three. A second later the candy-striped chutes snapped free and floated away on the cool summer wind. At the same moment, its descent engines flared and the landing gear spread outward from the oblate heat shield as the *Sagan* gradually dropped its last few hundred feet toward the pad. She could already see the scorch marks on the flat side of its hull, caused by atmospheric friction during aerobraking.

Gonna do it right on the dime and give you nine cents change, honey, Lew said. The ground crew was already unreeling the hoses to drain the last of fuel into the depot tanks.

Jeri smiled to herself: the same old brag. "Give it to me in the Mars Hotel after you land, handsome," she replied. And he undoubtedly would. Lew liked to bring down nine shiny, newly minted pennies, which he would fish out of his pocket and drop, one by one, into the palm of the traffic controller who guided him through atmospheric entry and landing. A dumb ritual, but considering the unique difficulties of landing on this world, one to which he was entitled. Now, as long as he didn't get drunk in the bar and try to get into her pants again . . .

She heard footsteps on the cupola ladder behind her, but she didn't turn to look until she felt a presence looming over her shoulder. "The lander from the *Lowell*?" a wheezy voice asked.

Jeri winced. *No, Sam,* she thought, *it's a scoutship from the Cootie invasion fleet. Better run back downstairs and protect the booze supply.* . . . "That's it," she said evenly. She glanced over her shoulder. "Any messages you want to send?"

Sam Leahy paused to massage his unshaven double chin. There was a slight reek of beer on his breath; the station's general manager, as usual, had been spending his afternoon in the Mars Hotel. "Nuuh . . ." he started to say, then quickly changed his mind. "Yeah. There's a passenger . . . uh, Andrew Donaldson. Tell him I want to see him in the bar."

That figured. Sam rarely did business in his office; he should simply make it official by having his desk lugged down from his office and setting up shop in a corner of the Mars Hotel. "Before or after he gets cleaned up?" she asked.

Another pause. The irony had missed him completely; Sam was obviously thinking over the choice. "Yeah . . . uh, after he takes a shower. But it's important that he sees me." He stepped back, relieving her from his obnoxious breath. "Remember to tell him," he added. "It's important. I gotta talk to him. Right?"

Jeri nodded. The lander's rockets were already stirring up red dust from the distant landing pad. "Sure thing, Sam. I'll get the message across to him." *And if you're still conscious by the time the guy finds you, I'll give Lew back his change. If you can even speak coherently, I might consider letting Lew into my pants. . . .*

"Good. Great." Leahy gave her a rough slap on the shoulder and turned back around. "Okay . . . uhh, carry on. I'm sure you know what you're doing." He staggered to the ladder. As the *Sagan* descended the last few feet to the pad and settled on the pads of its landing gear, she heard the general manager bang his head on the open hatch, curse, and miss a couple of rungs on the ladder.

Jeri grinned and tapped instructions into her keyboard, signaling the ground crew to begin the engine-safe operations. *No,* she thought, *I'm probably going to bed alone tonight.*

For the first several years, Arsia Station had been a row of modules huddled together beneath the Martian regolith, similar in appearance to Descartes Station on the Moon. Indeed, the first settlers had referred to themselves as the Mole Men of Mars.

Yet the base's personnel had grown more quickly than anticipated. The volcanoes in the Tharsis region had attracted geologists, and the vast canyons of the Valles Marineris where Shini-ichi Kawakami earned his Nobel prize by discovering microfossils of long-dead Martian life forms had lured more exobiologists. Most importantly, the proven capability to manufacture propellants from the atmosphere, plus the ability to extract water from the permafrost at the planet's north pole, had created an unexpected windfall for Skycorp and Uchu-Hiko. Mars was becoming the gateway to the outer solar system. Even before the permanent population of the planet reached fifty, it had become apparent that Arsia Station could not survive by simply adding more prefab modules. Like Descartes Station before it, Arsia Station was eventually forced to go native and build large permanent structures from local resources.

The first "condo-style" habitat had been constructed at Arsia Station in 2031. A fully enclosed building, shaped roughly like a bottle laid on its side, the condo was three stories tall and 180 feet in length, constructed of locally kilned brick and glass, with plastic membranes on the inside to preserve atmospheric integrity and two feet of regolith packed on the outside to provide insulation and radiation protection. At one end of the habitat were the main airlocks, salvaged from the old modules; at the opposite end was a huge, multipaned window of thick Martian glass, allowing light to filter into the spacious atrium on the ground floor. Balconies running along the upper two floors were decorated with hanging plants, overlooking the atrium where small trees were already growing in the carefully nurtured ground soil.

Although the third-floor bunkhouses were still cramped, with eight persons sharing a single barracks-style room, they were no longer the only places where a person could relax after a long day in the labs or at the fuel-farm outside. For one thing, there was the rec room on the ground floor which doubled as a watering hole. Like its predecessor in the old base before it, the place was known as the Mars Hotel, the best little bar this side of the Moon.

In fact, it was the *only* little bar this side of the Moon.

August Nash was rumpled and weary from the flight, but he had managed to grab a shower and put a full meal in his stomach by the time he pushed open the door—a discarded hatch from the original module, with MARS HOTEL painted in black handscript across it—and walked down the short flight of steps into the rec room. The first thing he noticed, besides bad lighting cast by the chintzy Japanese paper lanterns which had been hung from the low ceiling, was a row of emergency lockers behind the homemade pool table. Along with its site in a subcellar of the habitat, this confirmed his suspicion that the Mars Hotel had originally been designed as a solar-flare shelter.

Otherwise, the place looked like a frontier dive: a mismatched collection of chairs and tables, including a couple of acceleration couches which had been ripped out of old landers; a makeshift billiards table with a scratched felt cover; marsbrick walls covered with old canvas and decorated with everything from faded travel-agency posters to a pockmarked dartboard. An old Gibson guitar hung on tenterhooks on a wall next to a framed publicity photo of the now-legendary Mars Hotel, the band which had been formed by a trio of early Arsia Station personnel ten years ago and which had even managed to release two albums on Earth before the group's breakup.

Robert Johnson moaned the "Traveling Riverside Blues" from the battered CD deck behind the bar, itself little more than a couple of lengths of discarded spacecraft hullplate laid across two empty cargo crates. A number of people were hanging around the bar—the old-timers could be told apart because of the peculiar reddish sunburn on their faces but not anywhere else—and as Nash approached, Lew Belotti called out to him.

"Hey! Andy! C'mon over here and have a beer!"

The *Lowell*'s first officer was bookended by a young woman with close-cropped brown hair and a tall, lanky guy with a beard and a George Dickel baseball cap. Behind them, a heavy-set man was slumped over in his chair with his head cradled in his beefy arms, passed-out drunk. He was ignored as Belotti's friends turned to look at Nash.

Lew was already drunk himself; his voice was slurred as he made the introductions. "Andy, the beautiful lady on my right is Jeri, the traffic controller who did such a traf . . . terrfrafic . . . perfect job of guiding us to a safe landing this afternoon. . . ."

She smiled noncommittally and swatted away the hand which Lew placed on her thigh. Lew barely noticed. "And this," he added as he took the same hand and grandly clapped it on the shoulder of the man standing next to him, "Is W. J. Boggs, the legendary, estimable, too-fuckin'-perfect-for-words captain of the good ship *Akron*."

W. J. Boggs stepped around both Jeri and Lew. "You're my new first officer, huh?" Before Nash could speak, Boggs turned toward a short, bearded man who was sitting on a stool on the other side of the bar, reading a paperback. "Nuge! A bottle of Jack and two mugs!"

The bartender looked up, then silently laid down the dogeared copy of *The Snows of Kilimanjaro* and snagged a bottle of whiskey and a couple of ceramic mugs from the makeshift shelf behind him. "I'll put it on the tab," Nuge said as he placed the whiskey and the mugs on the bar. "Just don't break the mugs again, okay?" He then returned to his Hemingway.

"No sweat. Enjoy your reading." Boggs picked up the bottle and the mugs, cradled them under his left arm and grabbed Nash with his free hand. "C'mon, boy," the airship pilot said as he hauled him toward the door. "Let's blow this lemonade stand and go do some flying talk."

Nash hesitated, then reluctantly nodded his head. He still had to make contact with Sam Leahy; the message he had received upon entering the habitat was that the station's general manager would be meeting him in the rec room. Yet this Boggs character wasn't giving him much of a choice. . . .

"Sure," he said. "So long as it's a quick one."

● ● ●

They went back up the stairs, out the door, and into the atrium. Night had fallen; subdued lights along the condo's interior balconies lent a twilight feeling to the small trees in the miniature park. The atrium was quiet and completely deserted; the only sounds were the whisper of the air recycler and the soft gurgle of water moving through the nearby aquaculture pond. Through the large window at the opposite end of the condo, the irregular pale-orange glob of Phobos was rising in the black sky.

Boggs found a marsbrick bench not far from the Mars Hotel and placed the mugs on it. "Didn't want to leave, did you?" he asked as he tilted back his cap and unscrewed the top of the Jack Daniel's bottle. "Sort of looked like you were searching for someone."

"Noticed that, didn't you?" Nash smoothed out his shirt and watched as Boggs picked up one of the mugs; apparently they had been produced by the same kiln that had made the bricks for the habitat. "Actually, I'm trying to find someone named Sam Leahy. . . ."

"And, actually, your name ain't Andrew Donaldson." Boggs spoke very quietly as he poured a healthy shot into one of the mugs. "Your real name is August Nash, you work for a private-spy firm called Security Associates, and you've been hired by Skycorp to go up to Cydonia and find out what the fuck's the trouble with L'Enfant."

He held out the half-full mug to Nash. "Sam told me all about you. Did I leave out anything?"

Nash ignored the proffered mug. He took a deep breath instead, trying to stop the trembling in his hands. "Not much," he murmured. "How much did Sam tell you, or is this all over the station by now?"

"Relax and have a drink," Boggs insisted. "Go on. This stuff's too valuable to waste." Nash politely took the mug from Boggs's hand; the pilot picked up the other one from the bench. "Don't worry about your cover. Besides Sam, I'm the only one who knows about your assignment. You're going to have to settle for me."

Nash swished the liquor around in his mug; from the appearance and odor, he couldn't tell if it had come from a distillery in Tennessee or a still on Mars. He decided to take a chance and took a tentative sip. Smooth, very smooth: Tennessee whiskey, no doubt about it. "I don't know about that. I was supposed to talk only to Leahy. . . ."

Boggs chuckled as he poured his own shot and put down the bottle. "Well, you can try. . . ."

"I don't follow you," Nash said, shaking his head.

"Did you see the fat drunk at the end of the bar?" Nash nodded his head. "That was Sam. He gets shit-faced like this every night. I doubt if he remembers anything except that he was supposed to introduce you and me . . . fact is, that's the whole reason why the two of you were supposed to meet in the first place . . . but since I got the whole lowdown from him three days ago during one of his rare moments of sobriety, we can cut out the middleman."

"The station GM is a drunk?"

"Let's put it this way. When the infirmary's blood bank was running low and they asked for donations from the staff, Doc Haldeman turned down Sam because he was afraid of getting a high alcohol content in the serum." Boggs grinned as he absently played with his mug. "That's the way it is up here. Work by day, get loaded by night. Sam just overdoes it a little, that's all."

Nash was stunned by the revelation: not so much by the fact that Leahy was an alcoholic, but the incredible miscalculation SA had made in placing its trust in such a person to perform as Nash's principal contact on Mars. On the other hand, if Security Associates had enlisted Leahy through Skycorp . . .

"How does he keep his job?" he asked. "Doesn't Skycorp know?"

Boggs grinned, rolling his eyes. "The boys in Huntsville don't know shit about what really goes on up here . . . at least, not about Sam's drinking. He handles himself pretty well when he has to call the front office, and no one here wants to blow the whistle on him, 'cause this way everyone here gets away with murder on company time. That's why the company doesn't can him." He shook his head. "But he's a good old boy. He ain't going to tell anybody else about what you're doing."

Nash slowly nodded his head. Boggs's story seemed credible, and it went far to explain how SA had established contact with a drunk. His people in Washington were good at discovering pertinent background information, but they weren't precognitive. If Skycorp didn't know about Leahy's drinking problem and believed that the general manager was trustworthy, then that erroneous information would have been forwarded to Security Associates, and Halprin, acting in good faith on the information supplied by SA's client, would have asked that Leahy be recruited as Nash's liaison at Arsia Station.

It was not a good situation—Nash didn't like the fact that his security had been compromised—but the damage was done and nothing could be done about it now, short of assassinating Leahy. The mission itself had not been dealt a fatal blow. All Nash could hope was that Boggs was correct in his assertion that Leahy wouldn't spill the beans to anyone else at Arsia Station.

"Okay," he said. "Where do we go from here?"

Boggs rocked back the whiskey in one gulp, hissed between his teeth, and put the mug down on the bench. "Looky," he said softly, "here's what I know. I'm supposed to get you up to Cydonia and back again. You're supposed to be Andrew Donaldson, my new right-seater. . . ."

Boggs stopped, squinting askance at Nash. "By the way, do you know anything about LTA's, or is that just another part of the put-on?"

Nash shook his head. "Uh-uh. No put-on. I was a co-pilot on a cargo blimp in the Gulf for two years . . ."

"No shit? Anti-sub duty during the second war?"

"No. I was stationed in Bahrain, but I missed Number Two."

"Good for you. I was flying the *Macon* out of Kuwait during Two. Almost got my ass shot off by a motherfuckin' Jordanian MiG." Boggs grimaced a little. "Damn. You're probably all right, but I wish Skycorp would send me a permanent co-pilot. Since Katsu bought the farm I've hardly been able to handle the *Akron* by myself." Boggs impulsively picked up the whiskey bottle again. "Hell. Poor fuckin' Katsu . . ."

This time he didn't bother with the mug; he slugged it straight from the bottle. Nash had already been briefed about the demise of the *Edgar Rice Burroughs* a year ago, when the blimp had been demolished by a dust storm while en route back from a geological survey of Olympus Mons. Katsuhiko Shimoda had been piloting the ship; both he and his sole passenger, a British astrogeologist, had been killed in the crash. Hell of a note, as Boggs might say; Shimoda was supposed to have assumed command of the new Mars airship, the *Akron*, which was then being built at Arsia Station. Boggs had been scheduled to return to Earth, but when the *Burroughs* went down, he elected to sign another contract with Skycorp to pilot the new airship in his late friend's place.

"Anyway . . ." Boggs recapped the bottle and put it back on the bench. "We lift off early tomorrow morning. If everything goes well, we'll get there sometime early on Sunday. It's mainly a resupply sortie . . . food, medical supplies, shit like that . . . but we've got a humongous crate that was just dropped from the *Lowell* that needs to be unloaded and checked out."

That raised Nash's attention. "A big crate? What's in it?"

Boggs shook his head. "Not a clue. Something for the science team, that's all I know. Anyway, it'll help give you a little time to look around. Weather permitting, that means we'll get out of there by Tuesday morning at the latest. I usually pick up a nice headwind on the way back, so we'll do okay for the return trip . . . but we may be cutting it close, depending on the latest nowcast."

"Nowcast? What's that mean?"

Boggs looked at him askance. "Didn't they tell tell you anything about this place? Marsat II is the low-orbit weather satellite." He twirled his forefinger in a narrow circle. "Once each half-hour it completes an orbit and sends Arsia real-time pictures of the global weather conditions . . . a nowcast, as opposed to a forecast. Forecasts don't do us a hell of a lot of good down here."

Nash sipped his whiskey. "Why not?"

"Because the climate of this friggin' planet is too unstable, that's why. Things change too fast for us to do anything but fly by the seat of our pants. The best we can go by is nowcasts." Boggs jabbed a finger at him. "But I can tell you this. It may be cozy summer down here near the equator, but up in the northern latitudes it's coming into winter, and that means it's dust storm season. Cydonia is right at the western edge of the Acidalia Planitia, and some king-hell bastards tend to kick up there, just like that. . . ."

He snapped his fingers. "The *Akron's* pretty sturdy, but a hundred-knot dust storm will rip the envelope like cheesecloth, and I'll be fucked if I'm going to let happen to me what happened to Katsu. If I say we go, we *go* . . . and I don't care if you haven't done your business with L'Enfant yet."

"Hmm." Nash looked away, gazing at the window. Phobos and Deimos had already risen out of sight; it was now pitch-black outside. "What do you think my business with L'Enfant is?"

Now it was Boggs's turn to become reticent. He followed Nash's gaze to the window, speaking more softly now. "I dunno. Sam told me that you were just supposed to gather covert info for a report back to Skycorp, that's all." He hesitated. "But if it involves somehow . . . y'know, terminating his command, then I'm all for it. The motherfucker's running a bottle short of a six-pack, y'know what I mean?"

"And that bothers you?" Nash asked. Boggs looked at him sharply. "I mean, you're down here now. There's no way he an get to you even if . . ."

"Hey hey *hey*," Boggs interrupted angrily. "I used to fly the *Burroughs* out of Cydonia, pal! I've still got friends up there!"

He took a deep breath, visibly forcing himself to calm down. "Look, maybe I'm stuck here because of a moral obligation to fulfill Katsu's contract, but those guys . . . I mean, they stayed because they took on a job and they mean to finish it. It's no secret that Shin-ichi can't return to Earth because his ticker couldn't take the stress, but he could have come back to Arsia and taken over as senior scientist. And as for Paul and Tamara . . . shit, either one of them could go back home and get any fat university job they wanted, no problem. But they want to get to the bottom of this Cootie business, and they've risked their asses to do just that. I'm goddamn proud of 'em."

Once again he reached for the Jack Daniel's. "But Terry L'Enfant . . . that's one scary person, and so are the flatheads he's got with him. Two months ago I was up there on a supply run. We only had the *Akron* half-unloaded when I got a nowcast report about a big dust storm developing in Amazonis. That's a long way off, sure, but I didn't want to take chances, so I told Shin-ichi that I was going to get out of there now, get out of the area and come back to drop the rest of the supplies when I was sure that everything was copacetic."

Boggs opened the whiskey bottle, but didn't drink from it. "That was fine with Shin-ichi. He understood . . . but one of the goon squad overhears this and he tells L'Enfant, and the next thing I know L'Enfant's in the control cab, *ordering* me not to lift off without his permission. I get pissed off and tell him that nobody tells me how to run *my* ship. . . ."

He imitated a pistol with his left hand and leveled it straight at Nash's forehead. "And then L'Enfant pulls a gun on me.

Points it right at my skull and tells me that if I don't follow his instructions, he'll plaster my brains all over the seat. Those words, exactly."

Boggs dropped his left hand and raised the bottle in his right. "That's a dangerous son of bitch."

Two torpedoes streaking through moonlit water . . .

The memory came, uninvited and obscene, to Nash's mind. "I couldn't agree more," he whispered to himself.

Boggs halted in mid-sip. He gulped the whiskey in his mouth and peered at Nash. "You know something about him?"

Nash shook himself out of his reverie. "No," he lied. "Nothing that isn't part of the public record."

Before the airship pilot could ask anything more, Nash took a step away from the bench. "Thanks for the drink, but it's time for me to hit the sack . . . maybe you should, too."

"Yeah. Maybe so. I'm busting the twelve-hours-between-bottle-and-throttle rule as it is." Boggs put the top back on the Jack Daniel's and screwed it on tightly, then bent to pick up the mugs. "Just one more thing, Augie . . ."

"August. Nobody calls me Augie . . . and from here on, I would prefer it if you called me Andy Donaldson. Okay?"

"Sorry." Boggs grinned at him. "I don't like it when anyone calls me Waylon, either. Except maybe . . ." He stopped to belch into his fist. "What I wanted to ask is, what's Miho doing back here? On Mars, I mean."

That *was* a good question; Nash had almost forgotten about her. She had disappeared shortly after the lander's touchdown; although she was also staying overnight in the condo, he had not seen her since their arrival. "I don't know," he replied. "Why don't you ask her yourself?"

Boggs looked down at the bottle in his hands and shook his head. "Naaw . . . that wouldn't be a good idea." His voice thickened, either from the liquor or with emotion, or both. "We used to get along but . . . well, it's personal."

"Sure. Okay." Nash gave Boggs a slap on the arm as he walked away, heading for the stairwell to the condo's upper levels. "See you in the morning, fella. Stop drinking and get some sleep."

"At oh-seven hundred. We copy." Boggs sounded like his mind was elsewhere; Nash looked over his shoulder to see the pilot carrying the near-empty bottle and mugs back to the Mars Hotel. He hoped that Boggs wouldn't spend the night in there.

Nash was qualified to fly an airship, all right—but not on Mars, and certainly not something as unholy large as the *Akron*. If he had to take over the left seat because the pilot was too wobbly to . . .

As he looked back around, he caught the briefest glimpse of an elongated shadow, cast by an overhead source of light, flitting across his path.

Nash quickly looked up; for an instant he saw a form darting across the third-floor balcony. His first impulse was to dash to the stairs; then he heard a bunkhouse door open and shut.

He relaxed. It was much too late now, and he couldn't tell which door had been used. Someone had been eavesdropping on his conversation with W. J. Boggs; that much was certain, and he had a strong suspicion who it had been.

"Good night, Dr. Sasaki," he murmured.

11. The Flight of the Akron

The tunnel had been bored straight through the wall of a large impact crater on the northwestern periphery of Arsia Station. Long and narrow, its low ceiling lined with electric lamps, it vaguely resembled the gallery of a coal mine. As he walked through it, Nash could feel vibration through the soles of his skinsuit boots. There was a faint metallic clanking, conveyed even through the thin atmosphere, which managed to penetrate his helmet, but it was not until he reached the end of the tunnel that he discovered the source of the sound.

The airship hangar had been built inside the crater. The floor was paved with marsbricks on which had been painted a large white circle; high above, floodlights positioned around the rim illuminated the vast area. As Nash stepped through the hatch, he saw that the aluminum roof of the crater was slowly being accordioned back in two louvered sections: this was what was causing the metronomic clanking noise. As the slatted ceiling parted and bright morning sunlight washed into the hangar, the floodlights automatically switched off. This, though, was not what instantly grabbed his attention, causing him to reflexively suck in his breath.

The U.S.S. *Akron* didn't look much like its namesake dirigible, which had crashed in the Atlantic Ocean off the New Jersey coast in 1933, but it was almost as huge. Over five hundred feet long and three hundred feet wide at its stern, the new *Akron* was a sleek silver wedge, held aloft just above the hangar floor by the hydrogen gas still being pumped into its internal cells by the ground crew.

A long, spoiler-like rudder rose above and across the stern; at the tapered bow, above and to either side of the bulge of the gondola, were the long canards of its forward elevators. The top one-third of the skin was lined with photovoltaic cells which shined dull-black in the sunlight. Near the bottom of the airship, just behind the gondola, were the small windows of its internal passenger compartment. On the underside of the hull, just behind the passenger compartment, the cargo bay doors were open, while workmen moved in and out of a maintenance hatch beneath the stern. Mounted on each side of the enormous vessel were two swivel-mounted Pratt & Whitney turbofans, dormant for the time being. The ship's name and its registration number, MA-102A, were painted across the midsection.

Unlike the original *Akron*, which had been a true dirigible, the Martian airship was semi-rigid hybrid, combining features of blimps, dirigibles, and airplanes. It had a graphite-polymer internal skeleton which had been transported from Earth as collapsed rings and unfolded during construction in the crater-hangar; the outer skin was composed of layers of Mylar and Kevlar. The passenger compartment was modular, contained within the envelope and suspended by cables from the internal skeleton. Since hydrogen was readily available on Mars, but in the carbon-dioxide atmosphere didn't have its flammable properties which had doomed the *Hindenburg* a century earlier, it was used as the lifting property; the airship's delta-like "flying wing" shape lent it greater stability and payload loft than its smaller predecessor, the ovoid *Edgar Rice Burroughs*.

Nash felt something bump against his calves. *Excuse me,* Miho Sasaki said through his headset as she swung her aluminum case around him. Nash had forgotten that he was blocking the tunnel entrance; he began to mumble an apology and move aside, but Sasaki had already stepped around him and was walking across the hangar floor to the airship. She didn't seem at all impressed with the giant airship. On the other hand, she had been almost completely uncommunicative during their brief ride from the habitat to the hangar. Perhaps she had something else on her mind today—or maybe she simply didn't want to talk to him.

He hefted his own case as he heard Boggs's disembodied voice come over the comlink from the airship: *Let's move it along there, folks. Wind's beginning to pick up at ground level and I want to get out of here before it gets too hairy.*

"Coming right along, chief," Nash said, understanding what Boggs meant. Most airship accidents occur in the hangar, when wind-shear can catch the envelope and bang it against the doors during launch or landing. Although the crater made a perfect natural hangar for the *Akron*, protecting it from micrometeorites and dust storms between flights, making a vertical ascent could be tricky business if the windsock was running high. He began to follow Sasaki across the hangar floor.

Once beneath the massive shadow of the airship, though, he paused near the open cargo bay. When he had exited the condo's main airlock twenty minutes ago, he had glimpsed a large pay-load container in the bed of another rover as it was hauled out to the hangar; serial numbers on the side of the container told him it had come from the *Lowell*'s cargo lander.

The container was here, but its aluminum sides had now been collapsed and packing materials were strewn across the bricks. A couple of cargo grunts were climbing over and around a mas-sive, lumpish machine, hauling and attaching cables from the bay winch over their heads. The machine itself was almost in-visible within swatches of fiberglass padding stenciled with Japanese characters; all it needed was a bright red ribbon, a bow, and a big card reading "Do Not Open Till Xmas." One of the grunts carefully climbed off the front of the thing, looked upward into the cargo bay, and gave a quick thumbs-up; the ca-bles went taut as the winch was engaged, and the strange device was ponderously lifted from the floor.

C'mon, Andy, Boggs said impatiently. *Miho's holding the door open and we don't have time for dicking around.*

"Sorry. Coming right now." Nash walked to the ladder lead-ing up to the passenger compartment and climbed up into the airlock. Sasaki was waiting just inside; when he entered, she touched the keypad control which folded the ladder, then slammed the hatch shut and spun the lockwheel counterclock-wise to dog it.

It'll be a few minutes, she said as she tapped codes into the keypad to begin the pressurization cycles. *I expect Waylon can manage by himself.*

"I guess he can." The fact of the matter was that Nash was be-ginning to feel more like a passenger than a co-pilot. The air-ship's avionics were largely computer-controlled, so his alleged role as first officer was cosmetic.

The airlock was small and cramped; with both of them in there, it was like sharing a walk-in closet. Besides the exit hatch to the crew compartment, auxiliary hatches led into the cargo bay and, through the ceiling, into the airship's envelope. Although he was standing right in front of her, Miho avoided his gaze and steadily watched the digital indicator above the keypad.

Nash let a minute go by, then cleared his throat. "Did you sleep well last night?"

Quite well, thank you. She continued to watch the indicator. He didn't say anything; finally she turned her face toward him. *And you?*

"I'm a little hung over. W. J. and I shared a bottle of whiskey last night, so . . ." He raised his hand and wagged it back and forth. Sasaki smiled a little and looked at the panel again. "Of course," he added, "you know about that already."

Her eyes darted back to him. *Pardon me?* she said.

Nash raised three fingers, then touched the appropriate digit on his skinsuit's wristpad, switching to another comlink channel. Sasaki hesitated, then complied; they were now on a private channel. "You know that we were having a drink in the atrium," he went on, "because you were eavesdropping from the third-floor balcony."

She immediately opened her mouth. "No, don't bother to deny it," he added quickly. "I spotted you . . . but not before you heard everything that was discussed, I suppose."

The astrophysicist glared at him and didn't say anything for a moment. *So you caught me, Mr. Nash . . .* she began.

"Damn straight." It was pointless to tell her that he had been bluffing; the fact that she had used his real name was confirmation enough. "So why don't we end this charade and you tell me why you're here?"

Sasaki thought it over for a few seconds. *All right,* she replied at last. *Not now, though. Once we're underway and we're alone together, we can talk.*

"Fair enough. At least we've got that part settled." The dust was almost gone now. Nash glanced at the indicator panel and saw that the LED bar was creeping closer to the green line; he clapped his hands a couple of times and noticed that the sound wasn't quite as muffled. The pressurization cycle was nearly complete. "Switch back to One," he said as he reset the comlink to its original channel.

Boggs's voice came over the comlink at once. *Hey, where did you guys go?*

"Over to another channel," Nash said. "I wanted to tell Miho a dirty joke."

Won't work, buddy. I've told her all my best ones and she wouldn't laugh or anything. Nash noticed that Miho blushed when he said that. *As soon as you two get out of there, come straight to the flight deck and get yourselves strapped in. Don't even bother to take off your suits first. The wind's still rising and I'm getting itchy.*

"We copy," Nash said. At that instant the airlock buzzed; the panel lights flashed green. Nash and Sasaki unlatched their helmets and removed them, storing them in lockers along with their gloves. Miho pulled off her snoopy helmet and shook out her hair, then undogged the hatch to the passenger section and shoved it open.

The passenger compartment was about the size of a mobile home. A narrow passageway brought them to the gangway leading down to the gondola; Nash caught brief glimpses of the bunks, the galley, the wardroom and the miniature laboratory before Miho led him down into the flight deck. Boggs was sitting in the forward left seat, a headset clamped over his trademark George Dickel cap; he barely looked up as Nash squeezed past him and plopped into the co-pilot's seat on the right, while Sasaki took the passenger seat behind Boggs. "Took you long enough," he grumbled. "I was beginning to wonder if I was going to have to come back there with a bucket of cold water."

"Waylon . . ." Miho began.

"Sorry, kiddo. Don't mind me. I'm always an asshole before I fly." Boggs carelessly dropped the clipboard he had been holding onto the floor. "Listen, Nash . . . shit, I mean Andy . . ."

"Don't worry about it." Nash found the straps and buckled them around his waist and shoulders. "That's what we were getting straight back there." He glanced over his shoulder at Sasaki. "Right, Miho?"

"Right . . . August." Again the slight, quickly-vanishing smile.

"So we're all friends here. 'Bout time." Boggs looked as if he had eaten lemons for breakfast; Nash wondered how *his* hangover was treating him. "Okay, I didn't expect you to know how to co-pilot the thing on your first go-round, so it's all programmed auto on your side of the bench. Sit back and enjoy the ride . . . if we get out of here, that is."

As he spoke, Boggs's eyes were sweeping across the myriad digital and analog dials on his dashboard. He glanced at a board beneath his left elbow and swore under his breath. "Hey, Skip!" he snapped into his headset mike. "Skip, you hear me?" He paused, listening for a moment. "Listen, man, I got a red light telling me the rear maintenance hatch is still open . . . yeah, that one. You want to get somebody back there and close it or what?"

He cupped his hand over the mike and cast a sour glance at Nash. "Ground crew," he muttered. "They're always leaving the blamed hatch open. I swear, if I didn't have idiot-lights to tell me what's going on . . ." He stopped and listened again, looked down at the board to verify that the warning light had gone off, then unclasped the mike. "Okay, thanks. I owe you one."

Boggs grasped the twin throttle bars next to his right thigh and pulled them down one-quarter. There was a slight vibration and a rising drone as the turboprops revved up. He glanced again at the center flatscreen, which showed an overhead computer simulation of the airship on the landing grid, then touched the lobe of his headset.

"*Akron* to Arsia TRAFCO. We're vectored for launch and ready for cast-off, you copy?" He listened for a moment. "Thanks, Jeri. We're on our way. I'll bring home some M&Ms. Over."

Through the wide wraparound window, Nash saw the forward mooring cable detach from the pad-winch beneath the airship's bow; it was quickly dragged across the hangar floor and pulled upward as it retracted into the bow spindle. There were similar, lateral jerks as the port and starboard cables were released. Skinsuited ground crewmen were hastily backing out of the airship's shadow; one of them bent, released his ankle bracelets, then straightened and did a forward somersault, alighting perfectly on his feet.

"Showoff," Boggs grumbled. "Ted's going to hurt himself doing that one of these days." He grasped the yoke firmly with his left fist and gradually pushed the throttles all the way down to the floor with his right hand. "Hang on, now. Here we go . . ."

As easily as if it were an elevator, the *Akron* ascended from its landing pad. Through the window, they could see the sloped walls of the crater falling around them. Up, up . . .

The rim of the crater approached, sunlight glinting off the edges of the retracted roof. Then, all at once, the massive airship cleared the hangar and rose into the pink Martian sky.

Wind immediately buffeted the airship. The blunt prow pitched sharply forward; for a second it seemed as if the *Akron* would plow into the ground. Through the gondola windows, Nash glimpsed skinsuited people below stopping, staring up at him. The large mound of the condo seemed dangerously close. "Oh shit shit shit *shit*—!" Boggs hissed as he hauled on the yoke.

The airship almost seemed to groan as he fought for control; its shadow raced across the red dirt. Nash clutched the armrests of his chair and gritted his teeth as the *Akron* made a shallow dive toward the ground. Perhaps the six million cubic feet of hydrogen in the gas cells couldn't burn . . . but they *could* explode. He braced himself for the inevitable crash.

Boggs fought the yoke, snarling between his clenched teeth: "C'mon you fucker, climb climb *climb*—!"

Then—a precious foot at a time, then faster and faster—the bow tilted upward as the *Akron* muscled its way into stability. The creaking and shaking of the airframe lapsed; the throb of the engines became less urgent. "There we go, there we go . . ." Boggs was whispering. "Good girl, easy does it, that's my baby . . ."

The horizon appeared as Arsia Station fell away below them; clear of the treacherous ground winds, the giant airship gracefully ascended to cruising altitude. As Boggs turned the yoke to the right, they could see in the western distance the great cones of the Tharsis Montes volcano range: the vast looming mountain of Arsia Mons and, on the farthest horizon as a hazy yet insanely huge dome, the high caldera of Olympus Mons.

Then the airship was pointed to the northeast; the volcanoes drifted away to their left, and in the near distance appeared the deep, meandering canyons of the Noctis Labyrinthus. From this height, the Labyrinth of Night looked like an endless maze across the face of the planet, its steep, windswept walls falling into the thin morning fog which still lay above the floor of the chasm. Below the fog, shadows veiled furthermost depths of the great canyon. If the *Akron* had careered into that bottomless abyss . . .

Nash stared down at the canyon system until the *Akron* passed over it, then lay back in his seat and let out his breath. Behind him, he heard Miho Sasaki do the same thing. Beyond the Noctis Labyrinthus lay the equator and the vast central plains. Boggs pushed the throttle bars forward to three-quarter power, keystroked the flight computer to autopilot, then pulled off his headset. He took a deep breath himself, then tipped back his cap. There was a fine film of sweat on his forehead.

Boggs lifted the cap off his head, swabbed at the sweat with its liner, then grinned at Nash with Tennessee-style humor.

"Christ," he said. "Like having sex with a gorilla."

Nash and Sasaki took turns in the airlock to peel out of their skinsuits and stow them away; once they were dressed in jumpsuits and sneakers, Boggs sent them into the cargo bay to inspect the payload. He was concerned that the cargo might have shifted during takeoff, thereby unbalancing the airship. "It's the kind of thing you might not notice during flight," he said as he laid in their course on the navaids computer, "but it can be a pain in the ass during landing. If something's moved around, just tuck it back in the right place and lash it down again."

This was easier said than done. Several crates in the cargo bay had snapped their cords and toppled over; most were heavy enough to require handling by both of them. In addition, a large container of Russian food rations had broken open and spilled its contents across the deck. Miho righted the box and, on her hands and knees, began searching the hold for all the lost cans, wrappers, and tubes while Nash tightened the cables holding the large piece of machinery which he had seen being loaded just before takeoff.

"I had forgotten the pleasures of Russian cuisine," she commented as she pumped an armload of red-striped squeeze tubes into the container. "Sorrel soup . . . borscht . . . buckwheat kasha . . . liver with cream . . ." She found a clear plastic-wrapped bundle of dry, tasteless-looking cubes. "And, of course, rye bread."

"Sounds terrific." Nash was probing the giant Kevlar-shrouded machine; it was still suspended from the overhead winch-cables, so it had not fallen during the ascent. There seemed to be a claw-manipulator at its front end, but he couldn't be sure. At the rear, though, was the unmistakable bulge of a methane fuel tank. "I hope there's plenty of antacid tablets in the medical supplies."

"I'm serious," Sasaki insisted. "Russian food is badly underrated. Sort of an acquired taste, although this bread leaves much to be desired and I wish Glavkosmos would get away from putting the soup in tubes. They haven't improved much over what they used to send up in the old days when . . ."

She looked up from her work and watched as he tried to pull aside a few inches of the shroud. "If you must know," she added coldly, "it's a Jackalope manned reconnaissance vehicle, specially refitted for Mars work by Mitsubishi Heavy Industries. Despite its size, it's quite delicate, so I ask that you not paw at it like that."

Nash dropped the shroud and stepped back. For all he knew, it could have been the prototype of a new Mazda solarcar, but he had to accept her explanation. "Excuse me. Maybe if you came straight out and told me some of these things . . ."

She glared at him. "And maybe if you acted a little less like a spy and asked honest questions instead of snooping . . ."

"Whoa." He turned around and held up his hands. "Back off, lady. I'm not the one who was eavesdropping last night."

"This is true." Sasaki stashed the bread cubes into the crate, refastened the plastic cover, and heaved it onto the stack of containers. She dusted off her hands on the thighs of her jumpsuit and turned toward the hatch. "If you'll excuse me, I'll go prepare some coffee in the galley for Waylon."

She started toward the closed hatch, but Nash reached out and grabbed her forearm. "Not so fast, Ms. Sasaki . . ."

"Pardon me, Mr. Nash." She wrested her arm out of his hand. "And that's *Dr.* Sasaki, if you please. . . ."

"Sorry, I forgot, Dr. Sasaki. . . ." He forced himself to relax a little. "Look, I apologize, okay? But you promised you'd come clean with me once we got off the ground, and it's time we had that conversation you promised."

She hesitated, still ready to leave the payload bay. "Of course," he continued, "we've got two days in front of us before we get to Cydonia, so we can discuss all this another time. Like at dinner tonight, with W. J.?"

The sweet-and-sour treatment worked. Miho turned back around, folding her arms across the front of her jumpsuit. "All right," she said. "It's actually very simple. My government had heard many reports about the peculiar actions of your Commander L'Enfant. . . ."

Nash shook his head. "Not *my* Commander L'Enfant, believe me. Let's get that straight. He was sent to Mars by the Pentagon, and my company's client doesn't like it any more than Tokyo."

Again, that on-and-off-again smile. Nash had already noticed that Miho Sasaki was a very pretty woman; he wondered how much more beautiful she would be if she didn't keep such a tight grip on herself. "Pardon me. *Their* Commander L'Enfant. Besides the fact that Japan considers Shin-ichi Kawakami to be a national resource, there's also the large stake which we have in discovering the last secrets of the aliens, in terms of capital investment as well as possible scientific payoffs. Considering L'Enfant's past record, particularly in regard to the *Takada Maru* incident, we have much to be alarmed about."

Yes, of course: the *Takada Maru* would have to enter into this. "Sounds very much like the motivations of my clients," he said carefully.

She shook her head. "No need to be circumspect, Mr. Nash. I'm already quite aware that you're a field operative for Security Associates and that Skycorp has retained your company's services. We have our own resources."

Nash felt his blood pressure beginning to rise. Twice now in this operation his cover had been blown: first by Leahy, who had blabbed the secret to Boggs . . . and now by Sasaki, who could not have known all this simply by eavesdropping from the condo balcony the night before.

Sasaki hadn't told him everything yet, despite her promise, but he could guess that she had been enlisted by Uchu-Hiko. That, or perhaps a better possibility, JETRO. The Japanese External Trade Organization was essentially a government-operated commercial spy agency; it had been engaged in espionage against private American companies for many years now, often recruiting previously unattached Japanese nationals for the dirty work abroad. Turnabout was fair play; the CIA had done the same with American corporate officials in Asia and the Middle East.

"So your"—Nash was careful with his words—"employers asked you to return to Cydonia Base and find out what L'Enfant is doing."

Sasaki didn't fall for the bait. "Yes. Very much the same as your own assignment. Of course, I'm only supposed to be escorting the MRV to Cydonia. After I'm through, I am to return to Arsia Station to take up my new position as senior astrophysicist." She shrugged a little. "My report may be redundant to your own, but at least we'll be able to verify each other's accounts."

"We might." Nash mulled it over for a moment as he leaned

against a stack of crates. "But if your people knew about what my people were doing, why didn't they simply get in touch with Skycorp? We seem to have the same goals, and it might have saved a long trip for one or the other of us."

Her furtive smile reappeared again. "For a very good and simple reason, Mr. Nash . . ."

He grinned back at her. "C'mon, Miho. Call me August."

"Certainly, August." Absolutely immune to his charm, Miho turned again to the hatch. "The reason why we didn't contact you earlier is because we don't trust you."

As she undogged the hatch and pulled it open, she glanced over her shoulder at him. "Please, though, don't hold it against my country. I don't trust you either."

Then she left the cargo bay, shutting the hatch behind her. Nash let out his breath as he watched her go.

For the life of him, he couldn't tell whether or not she was joking.

12. The <u>Takada Maru</u> Incident

Within an hour of their departure from Arsia Station, the *Akron* entered the crater fields of the Lunae Planum. From the windows, they could see long, meandering channels leading south toward the Valles Marineris, carved by long-extinct rivers in the ancient eras when the Martian atmosphere had been more dense and the planet had free-flowing water. Boggs deliberately kept their airspeed below seventy knots to conserve fuel; when he wasn't in the gondola with his hands on the yoke, he set the autopilot so that the altitude remained constant at one thousand feet, taking best advantage of the wind.

Sunset of the first day of the journey occurred while they were still over the Lunae Planum; all three of them gathered in the control cab to watch as the sun set in the western horizon off their port side. Boggs slipped an old bluegrass CD into his jury-rigged deck, and they listened in silence as Lester Flatt and Earl Scruggs ushered out the end of the day on an alien world far from Nashville. Night on Mars was as dark and deep as the night in Antarctica: the pitch-black sky broken only by starlight, the distant ground a sullen, featureless mass without form or depth. Miho microwaved their tasteless meal in the galley, and after they ate—with little more than polite conversation among the three of them—she went to sleep in her curtained bunk while Boggs and Nash took four-hour shifts on watch in the flight deck.

Daybreak found them high above the southwest edge of the Chryse Planitia. The terrain had transformed itself overnight, abruptly changing from craters and dead river channels to a vast plain of drifting dunes and wind-scored boulders and rocks. Shortly before noon, Boggs summoned Nash to the flight deck and pointed out a metallic glint on the surface, glinting like a bit

167

of silver in a dark red sandbox: the Viking 1 lander, periodically buried under the sand and uncovered again by recurrent dust storms since its touchdown in 1976. The old NASA probe gradually receded from view, and Boggs announced that they were now halfway to Cydonia Base.

An hour later, upon Boggs's request, Nash donned a skinsuit, cycled through the main airlock, and climbed through the overhead hatch into the airship's envelope for a mid-flight inspection. It was like entering a mammoth, girdered cavern; a narrow catwalk led through the skeleton's polycarbon rings, taking him past the immense translucent bags of the hydrogen gas cells. Fiber-optic lights along the catwalk lent a dim glow to the airship's vast interior.

This was a land of giants; everything here was on a larger-than-life scale, dwarfing him like a toy play-figure left in an adult's room. Nash had to hold tight to the handrails as he toured the vast core of the airship, feeling it sway back and forth with each breeze. He went all the way to the stern of the ship, found the aft maintenance hatch and reconfirmed that it was shut tight by the Arsia ground crew; then he began to make his way forward again, the bright circle of light from his helmet lamp dancing across the inner skin as he searched for pinhole leaks.

He located one in the mid-aft section, caused by a windborne bit of gravel, and sealed it with a foam dispenser which Boggs had given him. He then scaled a long ladder to an upper gangway near the top of the airship. No more holes here; instead he found the crow's-nest: a tiny, seldom-used observation blister on the *Akron*'s upper fuselage.

Nash climbed up a short ladder into the tiny compartment and involuntarily sucked in his breath. It was as if he had been hiking a mountainside, surrounded by the forest, until he had passed the treeline and abruptly found himself at the summit. Through the Plexiglas dome, in front of and behind him, the hull of the *Akron* stretched out as a giant gridwork, rendered metallic-black by the solarvoltaic cells which covered the airship's topmost outer skin. All around the ship, he could view the Martian desert, the scarlet barrens stretching out as far as the eye could see.

Directly in front of him, past the tapering prow, he could see the great curve of the northwest horizon. Somewhere beyond that horizon, on the other side of this hellish and beautiful terrain, was Cydonia Base . . .

And L'Enfant.

He gazed into the northwest for a time, then climbed back out of the blister, secured the hatch, and began to make his way down to the cab.

Shortly after lunch, Boggs returned to his customary post in the flight deck; Nash was seated behind the little fold-down wardroom table, gazing out a window at the dunefields, and Sasaki was disposing of the last of the paper trays when she spoke up.

"Why did they send you after L'Enfant?" she asked.

The question was almost innocuous, phrased as if she'd asked him whether he was married, or what was his favorite movie. It took Nash by surprise, though; Sasaki had said little to him since yesterday's brief conversation in the cargo hold, and even less than that to Boggs. He looked at her where she was standing in the galley with her back turned toward him.

"Pardon me?" he asked.

She didn't bother to repeat the question, nor did she turn to face him. "According to your dossier, you were aboard the U.S.S. *Boston* when L'Enfant was in command. Isn't it reckless for your company to be sending an operative who might be recognized by his target?"

God, how much did this woman know about him? On the other hand, any good intelligence agency kept tabs on everyone else's known agents; unwittingly, Sasaki had proven his hypothesis that she was working for JETRO. Nash rubbed a napkin across his mouth to disguise his grin.

"I wouldn't exactly call him a target," he said. "That implies that we've picked him for assassination. I prefer the term 'opposition.' "

"Forgive my choice of words," she replied stiffly. She wiped down the counter, then opened the microwave to polish the inside. "Yet the question remains. If you were a crewman aboard the *Boston*, why would you be sent, considering the chances that you could be recognized by L'Enfant?"

Nash shrugged. "Fair question . . . but let's play on equal terms for a change." She looked quizzically over her shoulder at him, but said nothing. "That is, instead of my giving you all the answers and your avoiding my questions, why don't you be a bit more open with me for a change. A little more cooperative. Okay?"

Miho looked away; for a few moments, Nash was certain that he had lost her again. Sasaki was tough lady, he had to admit. She was capable of building fortifications around herself that no one could breach, raising and lowering the drawbridge at will. Even if she was not a professional agent, she was astute enough to have mastered one of the cardinal tricks of the trade: the ability to get others to talk while revealing only as much information about herself as she chose to give. And now, she might clam up permanently. . . .

Instead, she picked up the coffeepot and walked back to the table, stopping to refill Nash's mug before sitting down across from him. "Fair enough," she said haltingly. "We seem to be sharing the same general objectives, so there's no reason why we shouldn't be . . . cooperative with each other."

She paused, then added with frost in her voice, "At least in professional matters."

Nash looked at her closely; she met his eyes with aloof composure. "Don't take offense," he said softly, "but what you just said . . . the way you said it . . . makes it sound like you think I'm out to seduce you."

She blushed and looked away, but for a second her enigmatic smile returned. "Isn't espionage a form of seduction?" she asked.

"You're dodging again." Nash traced the rim of the hot mug with his fingertip. "Look, Miho, let's get one thing straight. I'm no James Bond and you're definitely no Mata Hari. You're a very lovely woman, but I'm here strictly on business, and that doesn't include trying to get you into bed, even if I was so inclined."

Her eyes remained locked on the window, yet she seemed to thaw slightly. "You don't mean that."

He didn't allow his own gaze to waver. "Yes, I mean that, so come off it already. It's getting in the way." He let out his breath, and added, "Besides, it's beginning to piss me off."

Sasaki looked back at him again, then ducked her head in embarrassment; her long black hair swept forward, veiling her face. He heard her murmur something; it was unintelligible and in Japanese, but it sounded like an apology. When she raised her head again, he was surprised to see a smile which didn't vanish immediately.

"Yes," she said. "I'm sorry. I understand. It's just that . . ."

She stopped, then went on, choosing her words carefully as her expression became serious again. "It's just that Japanese women have had to endure much sexism," she continued, "even more so than Western women. There's an unspoken assumption among my countrymen that, if you're thirty-two years old, have a doctorate in astrophysics, and have been assigned to Mars as a member of a scientific investigation, you must have slept with a few men to get there. It's built upon centuries of traditional values which have yet to completely die, and I've had to deal with that assumption throughout my career. After a time, you begin to assume that every man who asks you to cooperate . . ."

"And if he's a spy . . ."

Sasaki grinned sheepishly. "Yes. Especially if he's an American spy . . ."

"Then he's using double-talk for something else on his mind," Nash finished. Sasaki blushed again, but this time she didn't hide her face. "And then there's the tension between you and Boggs. An old affair, I guess."

Her eyes widened in alarm and shock. "Did he tell you?" she demanded. Her voice was an urgent whisper, despite the masking throb of the airship engines, and she glanced over his shoulder at the passageway leading to the open hatch of the gondola.

"No . . . and he didn't need to. To quote one of our great Americans, John Dillinger, 'I may be dumb, but I ain't stupid.' " He didn't add that she herself had just confirmed his suspicions. He also had to reconsider his evaluation of her; Sasaki was good at keeping secrets, but she was no pro. "There was once something between you two. A blind man could see that."

Sasaki hesitated, then slowly nodded her head. "My last tour at Cydonia Base . . . and it didn't last longer than one night spent together. I thought I had put it behind me when I left."

"But then you come back," Nash surmised, "and look who's waiting for you at Arsia Station." She winced and nodded again. "Well, it's none of my business, but you're going to have to put those feelings away. We're going into some dangerous business here and the three of us are going to have to depend on each other. If you want to slap him and me both, wait until after we've left Cydonia . . . but you're going to have to trust both of us until then."

He grinned and shook his head. "Believe me, Miho, you could throw yourself nude into my bunk tonight and I still wouldn't do a thing about it. All that testosterone just fogs the brain."

Miho gave another quick, shy smile. Composing herself, she straightened in her seat and poured coffee into her own mug. "Yes," she replied, all her former coolness having returned, "but I think you're the one who is avoiding questions now."

Nash picked up his coffee and took a sip. Unlike the brew on the *Lowell*, at least Sasaki's coffee didn't taste like caffeine-enriched motor oil. "There were ninety-eight men and women aboard the *Boston*," he said, "and most of them did little more than swab decks and polish bulkheads . . . myself included. For a year after I got off the boat I didn't want to even look at a mop. I was an enlisted man, not an officer, nor did I ever visit officer country. I was just another swabbie barely out of my teens and that's about it . . . and that was almost two decades ago. The company compared photos of me when I was in the service and recent pictures, and decided that the chances of L'Enfant recognizing me under another name were less than one in a hundred."

He rubbed at his new beard. "And that's even without the face hair, of course. Exodermic pseudoskin-grafts were briefly considered . . . I've worn 'em before . . . but those last only a little while before they begin to peel off. The company doctors determined that they wouldn't have survived biostasis, and no one thought it was necessary for me to go through permanent plastic surgery. In any case, they don't think he'll pick up on me. We're only going to be there for a few days."

"Of course," she said. "But that's only half an answer. Why did they pick you for this assignment?"

"Well, I went into the Navy airship corps after I left sub duty, so as far as establishing a workable cover, it . . ."

"I know that already. You're still not answering the question."

It was now Nash's turn to be reticent. He played with the mug as he cast his gaze out the window, watching the ancient stones of Mars as they drifted past. "Because," he said at last, "I was on the *Boston* the night the *Takada Maru* was torpedoed."

There had been a full moon on the wave crests of the Philippine Sea the night the *Boston* intercepted the *Takada Maru* one hundred and sixty miles south of Osaka Harbor; the faint lights of the Japanese mainland glowed orange-silver on the northwestern horizon. The tramp freighter had been running without lights, trying to dash through the blockade, but its hull was too big to avoid sonar contact by the attack sub.

Within a few minutes of the first pings on the sonarman's scope, the boat surfaced five hundred yards in front of the freighter. The captain ordered the radio operator to hail the vessel with instructions to heave to and prepare for boarding under U.N. General Resolution 819; an identical Morse code signal was sent by the ensign manning the spotlight in the sail. There was no reply from the *Takada Maru*'s bridge, although the freighter did slow all engines to a stop. After several minutes and more failures to establish communication with the freighter, the captain ordered an armed boarding party of twelve to launch two inflatable Zodiac boats and proceed to the ship, where they would place its captain under arrest and search the vessel for contraband plutonium.

Among the members of the boarding party was Seaman August Nash.

"The captain . . . L'Enfant . . . had strict orders about what to do if he stopped a Japanese vessel during the blockade." Nash stared down into his coffee mug as he spoke. "It wasn't made public, but he was not supposed to open fire on any ship that didn't obey the blockade. In a worst-case scenario, he was supposed to let them through and simply report the incident via FLTSATCOM."

"We never knew about that," Miho said.

"You weren't supposed to. It wouldn't have helped if Japan was aware that the blockade was a paper tiger." He sighed and shook his head. "Fact is, we had no authority to direct hostilities against blockade runners if they resisted boarding . . . just take their registry numbers and pass them to the Navy, to confirm the info being relayed by the spysats. If the ships voluntarily obeyed the blockade, we could stop them, board them, arrest the crew, and search the holds . . . but except for warning shots across the bow, under no circumstances were we allowed to engage any vessels that didn't stop when we told them to stop."

He sipped the lukewarm coffee. "Even so, it should have been a by-the-numbers operation, same as two other boardings which had been made by the *Trafalgar* and the *Bush* during Operation Sea Dragon . . . but something went wrong."

Nash raised the mug again for another sip. "So there I was, on the hull, helping to get my boat ready for launch, when I heard someone in the sail yell that the ship was moving. I looked up, and for a moment I could have sworn that the freighter *was* moving. . . ."

He shook his head again. "But it could have been anything, Miho. When you get bright moonlight on high sea like that, it can cause optical illusions. It could have been the freighter moving forward to ram us, or it could just have been the ship being rocked by the tide." He shrugged. "But in another second, it hardly mattered either way. We felt the hull tremble under our feet as the tubes were flooded and the torpedo bay doors opened. Then . . ."

Nash snapped his fingers. "The captain ordered two torpedoes to be fired."

He stopped talking as he remembered the horror of that night. Somewhere in the depths of his half-empty mug, in the black shallows of the cold coffee, he could see the twin, silver-tinted furrows of the torpedoes as they sliced through the dark water, racing toward the *Takadu Maru*. In the instant before they hit, he could hear high-pitched Japanese voices screaming in panic. . . .

Then there were the explosions, barely a second apart from one another, as the torpedoes connected with the forepeak fuel tanks in the freighter's forward section.

"There were forty-eight men and women aboard the *Takadu Maru*." Sasaki's voice was cool and nearly emotionless, devoid of either anger or accusation. "About half were killed outright by the explosion. The rest died by drowning, including the ones who jumped overboard but were dragged down by the undertow when the . . ."

Nash looked up at her. "You think I don't know that? You think I didn't hear them? I was *there*, for Chrissakes!"

For a second Sasaki was startled by the vehemence of his reply; she sank back in her seat, staring at him. Then she calmly folded her arms across her chest. "You could have tried to rescue some of them."

"It went down fast. . . ."

"Nonetheless . . ."

"Yeah. That was brought up during the inquiry. The captain—dammit, L'Enfant, I mean—gave the same reason for that as he gave when asked why he ordered the firing of the torpedoes. *Seawolf*-class boats were notoriously unstable on the surface. They couldn't maneuver very well when they weren't completely submerged. When the freighter started to move . . ."

"If it moved."

"Yeah. When it *seemed* to move, if you believe L'Enfant's testimony, he believed that he couldn't avoid a ramming other than by making a crash-drive. And since he had twelve of his men topside, he couldn't sacrifice them by giving that order." He slowly shook his head. "So he ordered the firing of the torpedoes."

The incident had caused worldwide controversy; the press, along with public opinion, was almost evenly divided between calling Captain Terrance L'Enfant—whom the British tabloids had taken to labeling "Terrible Terry"—either a courageous commander who had made a split-second decision to save his crewmen, or a war criminal and mass-murderer the like of which had not been seen since the Nicaraguan War. Subsequent investigation of the incident hadn't helped to dispel the ethical conundrum; when the Ballard Corporation, under the auspices of the World Wildlife Federation, sent deep-sea submersibles down to the wreckage of the *Takada Maru*, it was found that the freighter had indeed been carrying casks of Czech plutonium. Fortunately, none of the casks had been broken open by either the torpedo explosion or the freighter's final journey to the ocean floor, but it was charged that he had nearly caused the Pacific coastal shelf to be contaminated with the most dangerous poison known to man.

The controversy could not be ignored by the board of inquiry. There were too many ambiguities in the case for anyone to arrive at a clean verdict, especially in regard to the key question of whether the *Takada Maru* had been in motion, powered by its own engines during the critical moments when the sail watch had reported seeing the vessel move toward the *Boston*. There were no survivors of the *Takada Maru* to provide eyewitness testimony, and the *Boston*'s own sonar officer had been unable to provide a clear answer as to whether he had heard the sound of the freighter's screws in motion or—as the prosecuting lawyers charged—simply deep-sea background noise, such as whale calls, which could have been misconstrued as the cavitation of screws. In a sensationalized disclosure of the hearings, the sonarman failed a standard hearing test administered by the court; it turned out that his hearing had been impaired by wax build-up in his ear canal. Even then, it was difficult to tell whether this had helped or hurt the captain's case.

After two months of deliberation, the board acquitted

Terrance L'Enfant of charges of criminal negligence and disobedience of orders. By then, the Secretary of the Navy had already relieved L'Enfant of his command and removed him from
active sea-duty, with his naval rank redesignated from captain
to commander. He was quietly sent ashore and reassigned to a
nondescript desk job at the U.S. Naval Institute as a "senior tactical advisor"—a form of oblivion in the Navy's vast bureau-
cracy. Japan's importation of reprocessed plutonium had ceased
almost immediately after the sinking of the *Takada Maru*, and
L'Enfant's name soon vanished from public awareness, even in
Japan.

And then, many years later, he said something during a
speech at Annapolis which had captured the attention of the top
brass.

"Anyway, that's part of the reason why the company sent
me." Nash tapped his fingertips on the table, then laced his
hands together. "I served under L'Enfant and I was aboard the
Boston when the *Takada Maru* was sunk, so they figure that I
can tell whether the man has gone over the edge again."

Miho Sasaki gazed at him with remote impassivity. "So you
think he was . . . over the edge, as you say, when he fired the torpedoes?"

Nash wasn't hesitant in his reply. "Completely. That ship
wasn't on a ramming course. He was a trigger-happy paranoid
then and I think he's a trigger-happy paranoid now." He spread
his hands apart. "At least, that's my supposition."

"Then why didn't you say anything to the board of inquiry?"
Her eyes narrowed as she peered across the table at him. "You
didn't, did you?"

He sighed and looked away. "Miho, an enlisted man doesn't
go running to a high-level board of inquiry, claiming that his
captain has gone nuts, when all he did was stand on deck. It just
. . . isn't done."

Her face was as stolid as the rocky landscape passing beneath
them. "Nonetheless, doesn't your failure to bear witness make
you as culpable as . . . ?"

Nash suddenly felt his temper beginning to boil over. "Jesus,
lady!" he snapped. "You don't know what the hell you're—!"

There was a soft cough from somewhere over his shoulder;
Nash turned around and saw Boggs standing in the passageway,

looking both amused and irritated. In the heat of the argument, neither of them had heard him come up from the gondola.

" 'Cuse me," Boggs said, "but we've got a couple of standing rules on the *Akron*, and one of 'em is that if you need to have a fight, at least close the hatch so that the rest of us don't have to listen to you." He cocked his head toward the galley next to him. "The other rule is that you first remove any sharp instruments. We run a clean ship here, and I don't like having to mop up somebody's blood."

Nash's abrupt flare-up died as suddenly as it had risen. It was hard to tell whether or not Boggs was being ironic. "Sorry, W.J.," he murmured. He glanced over at Sasaki, who was avoiding looking at either of them, hiding her face with her hand, obviously embarrassed. "And it wasn't a fight," he added. "Just a disagreement . . ."

"Over ancient history," Miho said, sotto voce. She glanced at Nash. "And personal ethics."

Nash refrained from retorting to the dig. Boggs stretched his arms behind his neck and yawned. "Well, personally, I couldn't give a shit if it was over who's faster, the Coyote or the Road Runner. I came back here to let you guys know we just received a radio message from Cydonia."

Both of them instantly forgot their disagreement; Nash turned around in his seat, and Sasaki impulsively rose from the table. "What's the story?" Nash asked.

"Slight change of flight plan," Boggs said. "They've asked us to make our first landing at the D&M Pyramid instead of at the base camp. Seems they want to get that MRV off-loaded and ready to go ASAP." He shrugged slightly. "Makes good sense, since we would've had to double back to the D&M Pyramid anyway. Saves us a touchdown, so that's fine with me. Our present ETA is oh-six-thirty tomorrow, shortly after local sunrise. Shin-ichi and Paul are going to be there when we arrive, so Miho's going to have her reunion a little sooner than she expected."

Before Sasaki could say anything, Boggs raised his hand. "That's the good news. Now here comes the bad." He unzipped a breast pocket of his vest and pulled out a folded sheet of computer printout. "This just came over the mojo from Arsia," he said as he handed the flimsy to Nash. "Read it and weep."

Nash unfolded the fax and laid it out on the table. Printed across the top half of the page was a Mercator projection of the

Martian northern hemisphere; on the left side of the map, above
the Arcadia Planitia due north of Olympus Mons, was a large
dot-matrixed swirl. Arcane bar-graphs of meteorological data
were printed below the map, but Nash didn't need to interpret
them; the message on the lower half of the page spelled it out
succinctly:

ARSIA STATION TO U.S.S. <AKRON> 8-28-32 1410:37:05 MCM

*   *   *   URGENT   *   *   *

NOWCAST CENTER UPDATE FROM MARSAT-2 REPORTS SEVERE REPEAT
SEVERE DUST STORM DEVELOPING IN ARCADIA PLANITIA (MAP REF.
145 DEGREES NORTH X 43 DEGREES WEST) STOP BEARING EAST TO-
WARD ACIDALIA PLANITIA STOP ESTIMATED PRESENT WINDSPEED 55
KILOMETERS AND INCREASING STOP STORM ETA AT CYDONIA BASE BY
1800 MCM 8-31-32 AT VERY LATEST STOP NO KIDDING BOGGS THIS IS
A KILLER STOP RETURN TO ARSIA ASAP STOP END MESSAGE
8-28-32 1411:17:10 END TRANSMISSION

Nash looked up from the printout at Boggs. "It's your call,"
he said softly. "Are you turning us around, or are we still landing in Cydonia?"

"Oh, we're still making touchdown in Cydonia tomorrow, all
right." The pilot picked up the flimsy and shoved it back in his
pocket. "The storm's still on the other side of the planet, so the
leading edge won't hit Cydonia until late Tuesday afternoon.
But I'm not taking any chances with it. We're out of there by
Monday evening . . . Tuesday morning at the very latest, and by
then we'll be skinning the cat."

"Pardon me?" Miho asked. "Skinning the cat . . . ?"

Boggs's lips pursed into a grim smile. "Southern expression,
darling. Put another way, it means we'll be fucking with the
gods if we stick around here very much longer."

He looked at Nash again. "Do whatever you gotta do there in
a hurry, pal, and get back on the ship. I'm serious."

Boggs then turned and started walking back to the gondola.

13. L'Enfant

The terrain changed overnight as the *Akron* flew out of the Chryse Planitia; in the first light of dawn, the sun's amber rays fell across the craters and etched sharp shadows on crested hills of the Cydonia region. It was a rugged, inhospitable land, as unearthly as any landscape on Mars . . . yet no more alien than the D&M Pyramid which loomed before them.

At first glance, seen on the distant horizon, the pyramid looked like a natural mountain; Nash was initially unable to distinguish it from the surrounding highlands, even after Boggs pointed it out to him through the flight-deck windows. Then, as the airship gradually grew closer and the pyramid began to take on form and detail, he was stunned not only by its sheer enormity, but also by the increasingly apparent fact that the mountain was the result of intelligent labor.

Like everyone else, Nash was familiar with the thousands of photos which had been taken of this area. During the past decade, the pyramids of Mars had become engraved in the collective public psyche as a symbol of all that is mysterious and unknowable. Photos of the City had been used to the point of cliché by ad agencies to sell everything from cars to deodorant to the rock 'n' roll superstar of the month. Even so, nothing quite prepared Nash for the D&M Pyramid; it possessed a terrible magnificence which transcended familiarity with its photographic image.

The pyramid was almost one thousand feet tall. Even after millennia of wind erosion, which had pitted and scoured the once-smooth red walls, it still retained much of its original shape as when it had been carved out of a pre-existing mountain by the Cooties. Three of its four sides were sharp and even-planed, rising at 30-degree angles to its distant summit. Around

179

its base, vaguely resembling buttresses, were great piles of stone, the discards of the original construction work.

The northeastern side of the pyramid lay in ruins. As the Akron approached the pyramid, the great cavity in the northeastern slope became more apparent. Rubble from the ancient disaster rested in massive heaps around the lip of the dark gap, thrown there by the violence of the meteor strike. Sunlight gathered around the lip of the jagged crevasse, but didn't penetrate the darkness which haunted the depths below. Long after the Cooties had completed their work and entombed themselves within the giant edifice, a large meteor had struck the northeast wall, collapsing part of the pyramid and giving it a vaguely five-sided appearance. If the aliens had indeed been in some sort of long-term hibernation within the pyramid, then the meteor had been their killer; its impact had violently decompressed the vast interior chambers, ripping open their cell-like sarcophagi and exposing the aliens to the hostile Martian environment.

Why the Cooties had sealed themselves in the great pyramid was still a mystery, but the final outcome was clear: They had perished in the D&M Pyramid, perhaps without ever regaining consciousness.

The *Akron* cruised past the pyramid, making a fly-around before starting its final descent. As the airship circled the pyramid Nash forced himself to look away; he scanned the northwestern horizon. Several miles away, he could see the four smaller pyramids of the City . . . and there, due north of the D&M Pyramid, he could see the Face itself, staring up into the pink sky.

"It's beautiful," he whispered.

"Yes, it is," Miho said softly from behind him. Like Boggs, she had been quiet during the entire approach; Nash was startled to hear her voice. He looked around and saw that she had followed his gaze to the Face.

"I spent almost a year here," she continued, staring at the humanlike profile which had been carved into the mesa. "I thought I would get used to seeing it, but I never did."

"You can't get used to something like that," Nash said. She glanced at him and he shook his head. "Not when you know it wasn't made by us."

Sasaki slowly nodded her head as her eyes shifted again to the D&M Pyramid, but she said nothing. Nash gazed at the Face until it moved out of sight past his starboard window, then reluctantly returned his attention to the D&M Pyramid.

"Okay, gang, we're coming in on final approach." Boggs ignored the familiar scenery, focusing completely on the controls as he concentrated on making a safe landing. The ground was closer now as the *Akron* cruised around the western side of the pyramid; its cold shadow was thrown through the cab windows. He inched the yoke forward, gently playing the elevators and rudder to give the airship the proper pitch and yaw, while he gradually throttled back the turboprop engines. The early morning wind gently buffeted the airship as it rounded the pyramid, coming into the light again. "May be a little rough here, so make sure those seat belts are tight."

Nash gave his harness a perfunctory tug. "Heard anything from our reception committee yet?"

"Only for the past couple of minutes." Boggs had a headset clamped over his baseball cap. "They're waiting for us down on the northeast side. We passed over them a few minutes ago." He glanced over at Nash and tapped a finger against his lips; he was on a live mike and couldn't make any comments which he might regret later. "When I give you the go, drop the mooring lines and get ready to vent."

Before Nash could do anything, though, W.J. toggled the switches which opened the vent doors and prepped the lines for drop. Despite what Boggs had just said, Nash's role as first officer was camouflage; when Boggs was in the flight deck, everything having to do with the operation of his ship was strictly in his hands. The remark was strictly for the benefit of anyone listening on the comlink. "If you gotta use the head, you ought to do it now," he added with an elaborate wink.

Nash understood. He slid his left hand into his lap, slipped his right hand into the cuff of his shirt and touched the stud on his wristwatch which advanced the first frame of microfilm into the hidden camera. It was an almost useless preparation, however; once he was in a skinsuit, the camera lens would be obscured.

He looked again through the flight-deck windows; as the *Akron* completed its fly-by and slowly dropped toward the northeastern base of the pyramid, the engines tilting vertically for touchdown, he could now discern a number of skinsuited figures waiting near a clear patch of ground beyond the buttresses. The true meaning of Boggs's remark became clear.

They were now in enemy territory.

• • •

Once the mooring cables were caught by the people on the ground, they were dragged back and lashed to stakes which had been pounded into the soil. While Boggs safed the engines and went through the post-landing checklist, Sasaki and Nash donned their skinsuits. Nash let Miho go into the airlock first to put on her suit, but it wasn't entirely out of chivalry. Once he was alone in the passageway, he opened his attaché case and transferred the SIG-Sauer automatic into the right thigh pocket of his skinsuit's overgarment; as an afterthought, he put a couple of the electronic bugs into another pocket. Neither, Miho nor Boggs saw him make the transfer, and he hid the attaché case inside a galley cabinet.

Once Nash had suited up, he and Miho cycled together through the airlock, yet the first step wasn't to open the outer hatch and lower the ladder. Instead, once they had dogged shut the inner hatch and decompressed the cargo bay, they entered the compartment to unload the MRV. Nash unlocked the cargo bay doors and used the hand-crank to open them. He had barely opened the cargo hatch, though, before Miho wordlessly snatched a dangling winch cable, dropped it through the hatch, then grabbed the cable with both hands and slid down to the ground.

Nash hesitated only long enough to pat the thigh pocket in which he had hidden his gun. Not that he was expecting trouble immediately, but he wanted to make certain that it made no obvious bulge in the skinsuit's overgarment. Then he grasped the cable and skidded down after her.

Four men stood as a group beneath the wide shadow of the *Akron*; Miho had already run toward the smallest one of the group and had clumsily wrapped her arms around him, their chest units and helmets clunking as they hugged each other. Nash couldn't hear anything at first until he switched his comlink to Channel One; then he heard a fast chatter of Japanese: Miho's voice, and an older, male voice. Another man was standing nearby; after a moment, he reached out and touched her arm, addressing her in uncertain, hesitant Japanese. She turned toward him, and Nash caught her addressing him as Paul-*san* before she hugged him only slightly less enthusiastically than the first man.

They would be Shin-ichi Kawakami and Paul Verduin; that much was easy to figure out, despite the fact that they were a little too far away for Nash to see either their faces or the handwritten names on the strips of white tape affixed to their suits. The other two men, who hovered on either side of them, were neither welcomed into the reunion nor entirely ignored.

Pretending to study to the landscape, Nash quickly sized them up and found himself not regretting the fact that he was packing a gun. The one to the left, the taller man, had a Steyr assault rifle slung over his shoulder. The other man, standing to the right, was unarmed, but the man with the rifle seemed to be deferential to him, occasionally turning his way as if seeking orders.

A cold tingle surged down Nash's spine, as at that very moment the unarmed man shifted his feet slightly and turned directly toward him, as if noticing Nash for the first time. There was something familiar in his stance, the way his arms hung rigid next to his sides. A subtle presence of accustomed command. He could only be . . .

Boggs's voice suddenly came over the comlink. *Hey, Andy! You still in the cargo bay or what?*

Irritated at the distraction, and yet also relieved, Nash turned toward the *Akron* again. He couldn't see Boggs through the windows of the control cab. "Negatory, Cap. Dr. Sasaki and I are already on the ground. We . . . uh, went down the fast way from the aft hatch."

Well, don't do that again. You could skin your gloves or bust a leg or something. Was it Miho's idea?

"Roger that. She was in a hurry to see some old friends down here." He could still hear Japanese cross talk over the comlink. "The MRV looks fine," he added. "We're ready to wrench it down."

Belay that for a few minutes, bubba. The engines are safed and I'm suited up in the airlock, but I'm having a little trouble with making the ladder work. I think we got some grit in the hydraulics. If you could lower the gangway from out there, it sure would be appreciated.

"I'm on it, Cap. Hold your horses." It didn't sound likely; the idiot lights on the airlock status panel hadn't registered a foul-up of the gangway ladder. Whether Boggs was faking a minor problem—and if so why—was not his primary concern at the moment, yet Nash had no choice but to comply.

He started walking toward the outer airlock hatch, intending to manually unlock and crank down the gangway from beneath the hatch, when he felt a hand grasp his left forearm from behind. A voice which he had not heard in almost twenty years came through his headset:

Having a problem there, sailor?

"Naw," Nash replied as easily as he could. "Not at all."

He turned around and found himself looking at Commander Terrance L'Enfant, late of the U.S.S. *Boston*.

It was unmistakably the face of his former captain, the same face which had appeared on the computer screen back on the *Lowell*. Yet it was not quite the same face. Even distorted by background reflection on the helmet faceplate, he could see that L'Enfant had recently grown a thin, neatly trimmed mustache which traced his upper lip but which didn't reach the bottom of his nostrils or the corners of his taut mouth. There was a subtle puffiness around L'Enfant's normally thin cheeks, a weary darkness on the waxy skin under his eyes, as if he hadn't been sleeping well.

But these changes weren't as striking as the eyes themselves. There was a disturbing hollow depth in L'Enfant's eyes, a lack of emotional clarity, a vacant look of . . . deadness.

Not *death*; there was a fine distinction between the two. Nash had seen the eyes of men who had been suddenly killed, those who had been snapped from this life into the unknown too fast for them to make peace with themselves: the wide-eyed, disbelieving shock of the ones whose lives had been snatched from them.

No, it wasn't like that. L'Enfant's eyes held the cold, unblinking stare of a man who had accepted death as a brother of the road: a dark companion with whom he could curl up at night, telling strange tales about sailors who had lost their way at sea. Dead eyes. The fathomless gaze of an unhinged mind.

You look a little tired, L'Enfant said.

"It's been a long trip," Nash said, bringing himself back to the dangerous here-and-now. "Who are you?"

For a second, L'Enfant didn't respond. His eyes seemed to search Nash's face, and there was an instant in which Nash thought he caught a glimmer of recognition. L'Enfant opened his mouth and Nash waited for what he was almost certain would come—"Don't I recognize you? Didn't you once serve under my command? Weren't you once a seaman on my old sub?"—and he thought again of the pistol concealed in his thigh pocket.

L'Enfant, he said. *Terrance L'Enfant. I'm the commander of this base. You must be Boggs's new co-pilot. . . .*

"Andy Donaldson. Yeah, that's me." Nash held out his gauntleted hand; L'Enfant either failed to notice or declined to shake it. Nash noticed that the fourth man in the reception committee had walked closer to them. The tape on his suit read AKERS; this would be Charles Akers, one of L'Enfant's two goons. Nash did his best to ignore him. "It's my first trip up here, so . . ."

Mr. Donaldson, are you normally insubordinate to your commanding officer? L'Enfant's voice was smooth yet imperious. *The way you addressed Mr. Boggs—telling him to hold his horses and so forth—was hardly respectful.*

Before Nash could formulate an answer. L'Enfant stepped back, shaking his head slightly within his helmet. *Never mind. I should have learned by now that Skycorp's flyboys are usually rude. And if you fly with Boggs, you've got to be a loser.* He started to turn away, then stopped and looked back at him. *Nonetheless, Donaldson, while you're staying at my base, you'll be so kind as to address me as Commander L'Enfant. Understood?*

Not American co-supervisor, Nash noted, but *commander*. He wondered if anyone in the Pentagon—or on Earth, for that matter—was aware of this unofficial change of status.

Again, L'Enfant didn't wait for a reply. *I'll be returning to the base now. Dr. Kawakami and Dr. Verduin will be joining me. Charlie here will help you get that hatch open and unload your cargo. Once you're done, I expect you'll supply him with a lift back to the base camp. Correct?*

There was a six-wheeled, wire mesh-tired rover parked nearby. Apparently L'Enfant expected to drive it back to the base himself, leaving Akers to hitch a ride aboard the airship. "Yes sir, Commander." Nash found himself gritting his teeth as he replied. "We'll . . ."

Excuse me, Commander. Unexpectedly, it was Shin-ichi Kawakami who spoke up; Nash realized that he and the other two scientists had been silent throughout the entire exchange. The elderly exobiologist walked closer to the two men. *Paul and I will need some time to check out the MRV before we head back, if that's all right with you. We can ride back to the base in the airship if necessary. Perhaps if Mr. Akers could escort you back to the base . . . ?*

L'Enfant gazed silently at Kawakami for a few moments; it was as if an unspoken yet nonetheless lucid exchange were occurring between the two men. Between them, Akers looked uncertainly from one man to the other. L'Enfant finally raised his hands a little, as if in surrender to a small, token compromise. *All right then, Dr. Kawakami. You and Paul can ride back to the base with these guys. Charlie will go with me in the rover. I'll expect you back there by twelve-hundred hours. Understood?*

Quite clearly, Commander. Kawakami gave a slight, submissive bow. *By noon at latest.*

The self-appointed commander of Cydonia Base nodded dismissively, as if excusing an underling, then began to stride back to the rover. Akers fell in behind him, exposing the assault rifle on his back; they marched past Sasaki and Verduin without seeming to notice them.

Nash watched them go. "I don't know if I . . ." he began to say.

Kawakami swatted his wrist with his hand. *Having trouble with the ladder, I understand?* he asked.

Nash looked at him and Kawakami quickly raised a forefinger to his helmet, pursing his lips behind the faceplate. The meaning of his gesture was unmistakable: be quiet until they leave. *It cannot be all that difficult,* he said conversationally. *Here, let me help you.*

They walked to the *Akron*'s airlock hatch, but before Nash could reach up to push back the tiger-striped lid over the manual disengagement lever, the gangway began to unfold by itself. As it descended to the ground, the hatch opened and Boggs peered out cautiously. He raised three fingers; Nash and Kawakami obligingly switched their comlinks to Channel Three. *Is it safe to come out yet, or is Mack the Knife still in the vicinity?*

Nash looked around. The rover was trundling away from the landing site, raising a small cloud of red dust behind it as it dodged the larger rocks and boulders. He waited until it had passed out of sight beyond the edge of the D&M pyramid. At that point, he guessed, L'Enfant and Akers were out of unobstructed range of their radios, making it safe to answer. "Nice dodge, W.J., but I'd love to know why."

No reason other than the fact that I saw him sharking for you before you did. The pilot was already climbing down the ladder. *I told you the crazy fucker scares the shit out of me. If there was going to be a showdown between you two, I didn't want to get in the middle of it.*

"Glad to know I can count on you in a jam," Nash said sourly, but Boggs's description had been on target: L'Enfant had indeed come on like a shark, and Nash felt as if he had just been circled by a great white.

Another way in which L'Enfant had changed. The captain had run a tight boat when he had been in command of the *Boston*, but he had never been imperious. The old Captain L'Enfant never would have confronted a visitor to his ship, demanding that he be formally addressed by his proper rank. Nor would he have consciously insulted somebody for little or no reason. In fact, he had been known for his informal manner, even requesting that senior officers call each other—and himself—by their first names. L'Enfant had been a ramrod, it was true, but never a martinet; he was the type whose orders were couched as requests, not demands.

At least, not before the *Takada Maru* incident . . .

Nash looked back at Kawakami. "Something you said back there . . . that stuff about the rover. I don't get it."

If there's anyone to congratulate for making a good dodge, it's Shin-ichi. Paul Verduin trudged closer to them. Miho walked beside him. *He used L'Enfant's own edict against himself, and got rid of both him and his bodyguard.*

"I still don't understand," Nash said.

No. Of course you don't. Verduin halted and absently peered up at the long fuselage of the airship. *Our noble commander has made it a hard and fast rule that no one may go out unaccompanied on the surface, especially when he or she is not in the immediate periphery of the base. For our own safety, he says, although it's more for keeping us under supervision. He couldn't very well disobey his own orders, could he?* He gave a short, bitter laugh as he glanced down at his dirt-caked boots. *I'd feel safer alone in the Labyrinth than with him at my side in the wardroom.*

Kawakami smiled and reached out to give Verduin a genial pat on the arm. *You will receive your chance to do just that soon enough, Paul. Be patient.*

Verduin smiled back wanly. Kawakami turned again to Boggs and Nash, letting out his breath as a long, audible sigh. Even in his skinsuit, he looked worn-out and tired, despite the fact that it was still early morning. *Gentlemen, this may be our only chance to speak freely while you're here, and Terrible Terry has not given us much time for even this. We will talk further while we unload Paul's new toy.* He extended a hand toward the open cargo bay. *Shall we . . . ?*

14. Xenophobe

Now that, Boggs said, *has got to be the ugliest goddamn thing I've ever seen.* He thought about it for a second, then added, *Next to the Jefferson Street whore who got my cherry, I mean. Now she was . . .*

Waylon . . . Miho began.

Okay, okay, I'm sorry. Boggs walked around behind the MRV, studying the machine from its spade-shaped footpads to its high-gain antenna, and shook his head. *But if the bugs don't drop dead the moment they see this fucked-up thing, they might roll over and laugh themselves sick.*

No one disagreed with the pilot's assessment of the manned reconnaissance vehicle. It had been wrenched down from the *Akron*'s cargo bay, and as Paul Verduin removed the last of its shrouding, everyone got their first good look at the "fucked-up thing." Its aluminum/polycarbon fuselage was painted dark tan, but on the forward canopy hatch was stenciled a goofy-looking jackalope, cross-eyed and grinning stupidly as if it had just won a footrace with a bandersnatch. It was weird to see a mythical American animal pictured on a Japanese-manufactured machine, but the nickname was fitting: The Mitsubishi MRV-2 did vaguely resemble an unlikely crossbreed between a jackrabbit and an antelope.

And it *was* ugly. The semi-robotic machine stood ten feet high and moved on two backward-jointed waldo legs; to that extent, it looked somewhat like one of the Russian AT-80 autotanks which had previously been deployed at Cydonia Base. But the Jackalope's similarity to the Bushmaster was only superficial; instead of a revolving, cannon-mounted upper turret, the MRV's fuselage consisted of an elongated, ovoid-shaped one-person cab, with small portholes on either side of the enclosed canopy and various TV cameras and sensors arrayed along its fuselage. At the frontmost part of the cab, below the forward hatch and next to the swivel-mounted IR scanner, was a multijointed claw-fingered manipulator.

The Jackalope had a strange history, atypical of even the longstanding Japanese fascination with robotics. Mitsubishi Heavy Industries had designed the first prototype, the MRV-1, as a military reconnaissance vehicle, but it had not been purchased by any of the Western armies for which it had been intended; the machine was deemed to be too slow and vulnerable for use in real-life combat situations. Mitsubishi had not given up on the idea, though; the second-generation version was redesigned and adapted for noncombat use on the Moon. Uchu-Hiko had utilized a couple of the newer MRV-2's for exploration sorties to nearby Alphonsus Crater, where the company eventually established its first lunar mining colony, but with only limited success; the Jackalopes couldn't do anything that a couple of hardsuited prospectors in a long-range rover couldn't also accomplish with less expense and trouble. In either case, the MRV-2 was a classic example of the Rube Goldberg school of engineering: an overly high-tech solution to a simple problem.

The Jackalope which had been brought to Mars was the last one purchased by Uchu-Hiko; it had been mothballed in the company's warehouse near the Kagoshima Space Center, the all but forgotten relic of an enthusiastic but unwise contract. It might have remained there had not Paul Verduin remembered its existence.

And you're taking this hunka-junka down into the Labyrinth? Boggs asked.

Tomorrow morning, Verduin said, as distractedly as if he had been asked on an Amsterdam street about a bus schedule. He tugged experimentally at a power cable leading into the left leg's main servomotor. *Yes, quite so.*

Boggs whistled and shook his head. *You're crazier than you look, Paul.*

I never claimed to be sane, my friend.

As the Dutch astrophysicist began crawling around and underneath the contraption, Nash went to help Kawakami fold up the discarded shrouds. "You were telling me about L'Enfant . . . his actions after he got here."

For a moment it seemed as if the senior scientist had not heard him. His shoulders sagging within his skinsuit, he doggedly continued to gather the reams of Mylar until finally he glanced up at Nash. *Oh . . . yes, yes. I'm sorry, I was, wasn't I? I . . .*

Miho Sasaki bounded over to him, hop-skipping in the lesser gravity. She laid a hand on his shoulder and gently spoke to him in Japanese; he seemed to hesitate, then nodded his head. *Miho believes that I may be overexerting myself,* he said to Nash. *I apologize, Mr. Donaldson, but I tend to agree.*

"You don't have to apologize." They had been working hard for the last hour, bringing the Jackalope down from the cargo bay; hard enough, in fact, that they had not fully discussed the present situation at the base. Nash took a sip of water from the tube in his helmet. "Why don't you sit down over there for a while and we can . . . ?"

Sasaki laid a protective arm around Kawakami's shoulders. *We should take this into the* Akron, she said. *Dr. Kawakami shouldn't have been out on EVA for this long. Perhaps without his suit and a cup of tea . . . ?*

So long as it's fresh, Kamakami said. He glared at her militantly. *You* have *brought fresh tea, have you not?*

Yes, Shin-ichi-san. Miho laughed sweetly. *I didn't forget. It's all in my duffel bag.* She steered the frail exobiologist toward the *Akron*'s airlock hatch. Nash glanced over his shoulder, and Boggs silently gave him the thumbs-up; he would handle everything out here, including the job of lashing a protective tarp over the Jackalope.

Nash nodded, then checked the chronometer on his helmet's heads-up display; they still had more than an hour remaining until L'Enfant's deadline for return to the base. He turned and followed Kawakami and Sasaki to the airlock.

Once they had taken turns cycling through the airlock, Nash stayed in his skinsuit, only removing his helmet and gloves; he realized that he would have to go EVA again before liftoff. The two scientists, however, gratefully stripped off their suits. They did so together in the airlock, without a trace of embarrassment; as Nash had already observed, the relationship between Kawakami and Sasaki was akin to that between a father and his daughter, however surrogate those roles might be. They could not be easily discomfited by each other's disrobing.

Without the padding of his skinsuit, though, it was clear that Shin-ichi Kawakami's physical condition had deteriorated since the time the last available photos of him had been taken. His prolonged stay in the lesser gravity of Mars, coupled with lack of exercise, had shriveled his body to the point of emaciation. His gaunt hands shook noticeably as he picked up his tea mug and carefully nestled it within his palms.

Sitting across from him in the airship's wardroom, Nash wondered if Kawakami was exhibiting the first symptoms of Parkinson's disease. He said nothing, though, as he reached into his skinsuit pocket and covertly switched on the tiny Sony recorder. Within the airship, at least, it would be able to tape the conversation.

Kawakami noticed Nash's attention to his hands. "Acute muscular atrophy," he said with blunt detachment, as if explaining a curious side effect of an experiment to a grad student. "The principal reason why I cannot return to Earth now, even if I so desired." He smiled a little and took a sip from his mug, still holding it with both hands. "Whether I like it or not, I have become the first Martian . . . if you don't count our friends from Achird Cassiopeiae, of course."

Miho stopped halfway through pouring Nash's mug; the thin brown Ceylon tea spilled onto the wardroom table, but the astrophysicist appeared not to notice. "Achird Cassiopeiae? You've located the Cooties' home world?"

Kawakami put down his mug and spread his hands in an expansive shrug. "Only a supposition, perhaps in error. Achird Cassiopeiae is at least the working model for what I believe was the Cooties' home system. It's a G-zero class star, whose mass and radius are only slightly less than that of our own sun and which has equal luminosity. The Van Allen space telescope recently detected a small planetary system around it, and if the rest of my conjecture is correct, then its distance of nineteen-point-two light-years is on target."

Nash shook his head. "I don't follow you. Why would . . . ?" He struggled to pronounce the name of the star and gave up. "Why would this star be the aliens' home system? Because of its similarity?"

The exobiologist shook his head. "No. That's part of it, but not entirely." Despite his decreptitude, Kawakami was still an animated talker. "My working hypothesis is that the Cooties came to this system deliberately, but on the basis of false information."

He paused, clearly relishing the confused expressions on

Nash's and Sasaki's faces. "I think the Cooties first sent an automated space probe through this system many millennia ago, a scout in search of a colonizable planet. For some time I thought they had selected Earth as its prime candidate and simply couldn't settle there because of the differences in surface gravity, but now I believe that their probe may have selected Mars as its first choice. Indeed, when that probe found Mars, it could have still had free-standing water and an atmosphere which was far more dense. Coupled with its one-third Earth-normal gravity, which seems to be correct for the physiology of the aliens, Mars may have strongly resembled a life-supporting planet in orbit around a G-zero class star."

"Yes, but . . ." Miho hesitated, as if reluctant to question her mentor's theories. "*Sensei*, your own studies determined that it has been almost three and half *billion* years since Mars had an ocean."

Kawakami raised an eyebow. "Yes, but the distance between our system and Achird Cassiopeiae is enormous." He steepled his fingers together. "It would take more than nineteen years for even a radio signal to travel from here to that system. Even a hypothetical matter-antimatter drive can only attain twenty percent of the speed of light at its maximum velocity, and there is no reason to believe that the Cooties had developed technology of that magnitude. But if they made the journey in a generation-ship or in suspended animation . . ."

He shrugged. "Who knows? Hundreds of millions of years could have passed between the time the probe transmitted its findings to its planet of origin and the time the Cootie colony ship arrived in Mars orbit, and in that intervening period, this planet could have gone through enormous climatological changes that the Cooties simply didn't anticipate. . . ."

"Leaving the Cooties marooned on a planet which could no longer support their sort of life," Sasaki finished.

Kawakami nodded his head. "If their ship was designed for one-way travel, yes." He smiled. "I've tried to get the others into renaming the aliens the Cassiopeians, but I'm afraid that your old boyfriend's nickname has stuck." He chuckled as he picked up his tea again. "Paul thinks that they may be from 82 Eridani, but the spectral type is all wrong. Yet he remembers reading a science fiction story in his childhood about insectlike aliens from Eridani, and it's clouding his outlook."

He suddenly frowned and gazed out the window at the immense crevasse in the northeast side of the D&M pyramid. "That romanticism may yet be his undoing, I'm afraid," he said quietly. "He intends on taking that . . . ah, the machine you brought us, the MRV . . . down into Mama's Back Door first thing tomorrow morning. Tamara and I have both attempted to talk him out of it, but several months ago he . . ."

Nash gently cleared his throat. This was all very interesting, but at the moment he had matters of higher priority that he wished to discuss. Miho glanced sharply at him, then looked back at her mentor. "Shin-ichi-*san*, we need to talk about Commander L'Enfant and his men."

She hesitated, her eyes darting again toward Nash. "This is August Nash. Andrew Donaldson is only an assumed identity. He works for . . ."

"The Americans, yes." Kawakami's attention moved back from the window; he favored Nash with a long, impersonal stare. "Probably in the employ of Skycorp. No?" He didn't wait for a response from Nash, but looked again at Miho. "Just as you yourself are now working for JETRO, on behalf of our government and Uchu-Hiko. Or am I still making groundless conjectures?"

Miho was openly astonished. Nash found himself grinning. "Actually, you're only half-right," he said. "I'm from Security Associates, a private intelligence firm. I've been retained by Skycorp to investigate what's going on up here, though, so you're at least partly correct. How did you guess?"

Kawakami seemed to be insulted. He slowly shook his head and drank from his tea. "Mr. Nash, I did not receive a Nobel because I make guesses. Your arrival at this particular time is too far beyond the range of simple coincidence." He carefully placed the mug back on the table and reached out a hand to pat Sasaki's wrist. "And you, dear, should have given me coffee instead. This was a waste of an innocent teabag. Forgive me, Miho, but that was wretched."

She was completely nonplussed by now; Kawakami, on the other hand, was obviously enjoying himself. "Now that you two youngsters are through indulging a senile old man, perhaps I can explain everything which has occurred here lately. . . ."

Terrance L'Enfant's eccentric behavior did not manifest itself immediately upon his arrival at Cydonia Base. The purpose of his mission was quite clear—to prevent the science team from revolting again—and it was evident that his three "observers" were with him merely to act as enforcers should another attempt be made to derail the expedition.

Yet L'Enfant had not been a hard-liner from the outset. He had accepted his role as the new American co-supervisor with unimposing equanimity, preferring to stay out of the way and allow Kawakami to lead the further exploration of the City while he and his men took care of the more routine house-keeping chores, which had been largely neglected after most of the base personnel had left following the Steeple Chase raid. Although the science team still resented L'Enfant for being forced upon them as Arthur Johnson's replacement, and vaguely distrusted him because of his military standing, they soon discovered that he was, at least, not working *against* them . . .

By this time, however, the scientists had worse things to worry about than their new American co-supervisor. The investigation had stalled; a critical window of opportunity to establish communications with the pseudo-Cooties had been lost because of the "labor strike." Exactly twenty-four hours, thirty minutes, and 35.25 seconds after Ben Cassidy established first contact—precisely the measurement of a Martian day—the pseudo-Cooties closed Room C4-20 again.

They left alone a single sensor pod, but dismantled the portable airlock and TV cameras and rebuilt most of the chamber's walls, leaving a single man-sized opening. Yet, when Paul Verduin ventured down to the chamber in a skinsuit, he found his way barred by several of the metallic robots; they did not attack him, but neither would they permit him to go any further than the entrance to C4-20. It appeared as if an unspoken deadline had been reached, and passed, for human contact; now the pseudo-Cooties—which Kawakami now theorized were autonomous self-replicating robots, similar to the conjectural Von Neumann machines theorized in the last century—had locked themselves away in the catacombs beneath the City.

"Catacombs?" Sasaki raised an inquisitive eyebrow. "Why do you think they have catacombs down there?"

"We placed a series of seismographs around and within the City," Kawakami replied. "After monitoring them closely for some time, we observed an irregular series of vibrations emanating from beneath the pyramids. After computer modeling, we believe that this is coming from underground tunnels,

coverging in the central area between the four City pyramids."
He shrugged. "What these tunnels are for, and what the Cooties
are doing down there, is a complete mystery. We spotted what
looked like machinery when C4-20 was first opened, but what it
was, what role it performed . . ."

He opened his hands. "Completely unknown, if it was even
machinery in the first place."

However, the seismography did establish that the subsurface
vibrations extended as far as to the southeast as the D&M Pyramid, leading the science team to believe that a tunnel might lead
straight from the catacombs to the tomb of the Cooties. This
proved to be correct, and further surveys and computer modeling revealed what turned out to be a lucky break: the meteor
which had destroyed the northeast wall of the D&M Pyramid
had also formed a deep pit just above the tunnel, resting at the
bottom edge of the meteor crevasse. L'Enfant requisitioned
drilling equipment from Arsia Station, and after months of patient digging in the pit, they managed to break through into the
tunnel, creating a narrow shaft straight down from the surface
into Mama's Back Door.

Sasha Kulejan had volunteered to explore Mama's Back
Door. Wearing Hoplite II recon armor, he was lowered by cable
into the tunnel, with the intention of making his way back toward the City and, hopefully, locating the catacombs. Yet this
was not in the cards; the Russian scientist only managed to advance less than fifty yards down the tunnel when he reported
seeing movement ahead.

His suit's TV camera caught a brief glimpse of pseudo-
Cooties coming toward him. Then visual transmission was interrupted; after a final scream was recorded on the audio track,
all further contact with Sasha was lost. When a remote-
controlled spider-probe was sent down the shaft after him, no
trace of Sasha Kulejan was found—no body, no blood, no fragments of his armor—before the probe itself was attacked and
destroyed.

"It was then that L'Enfant began to be . . ." Uncommonly at a
loss for appropriate words, Kawakami's voice trailed off.

"Weird?" Nash supplied.,

Kawakami nodded, then quickly shook his head. "Paranoia is
the most accurate description, Mr. Nash. . . ."

"Call me August." He smiled tightly. "So long as you call me
Andy when L'Enfant or his men are around."

"Whenever we're in the base, even by ourselves, I will have to call you Andy." Kawakami's face was grim. "We have some reason to suspect that our quarters may now be under electronic surveillance. Our private communications have to be written on slips of paper, which we afterwards chew and swallow."

Sasaki hissed between her teeth; Kawakami glanced at her with sad eyes. "Yes, Miho, it has gone that far. We can trust no one except ourselves, and even if we could establish candid communication with Arsia, I'm not sure whom we could trust at the station." He paused, then added, "I believe L'Enfant may have informants there, but I cannot be certain."

It was a disturbing revelation, but Nash didn't want to get sidetracked now. "Go on, please," he prodded.

In the aftermath of Sasha Kulejan's death, L'Enfant took several actions, all of which he claimed were to "assure the security of the expedition." First, he assumed total command of the base; since Kulejan had been the Russian co-supervisor and Kawakami's illness prohibited him from making more than token resistance, this was an easy task. It was also enforceable by his aides; it was then that the assault rifles, which had been hidden from the science team, made their first appearance. From then on, at least one of the four Americans was awake at all times, taking shifts in the command center.

Then L'Enfant imposed a communications blackout; all messages and reports had to be cleared by him in advance. At first, L'Enfant allowed the science team to file technical memoranda with Arsia Station, until he became convinced that the briefs themselves contained encrypted communiqués. ("And he was not incorrect in that assumption," Kawakami added, "but he managed to figure out what we were doing before they were transmitted.") After that, only the most routine status reports were sent to either Arsia Station or Earth.

Then, one by one, came more restrictions. A CD-ROM copy of all new scientific data had to be given to him. No one was allowed on the surface by themselves or within the City without military escort, and an EVA curfew was imposed from sunset to sunrise. Similarly, either L'Enfant or one of his aides had to be in the monitor center during all important researches.

Finally, L'Enfant demanded that he himself be addressed by his naval rank; by now this was only a formality, since it was obvious that he had taken paramilitary control of Cydonia Base.

And there was another change, albeit one which was not imposed by regulation: at odd moments, L'Enfant had taken to referring to the Cooties as "the enemy."

Kawakami rested his elbows on the table and placed his forehead on his palms. "We have tried as much as possible to work within his guidelines," he continued wearily, rubbing at his eyes, "but it has been very difficult. Our only hope has been that someone at Arsia Station would notice the absence of regular communications and report to someone on Earth that something was amiss."

Miho reached across the table and cupped his hands within her own. "We did notice, Shin-ichi-*san*," she said soothingly. "That is why we've come."

She glanced at Nash, and he found himself nodding in agreement. Yet the word *paranoia* didn't do justice to L'Enfant's mental condition. Judging from Kawakami's story, it appeared that L'Enfant had become xenophobic, irrationally frightened by the Cooties and the vast unknown they represented.

Perhaps the condition was nothing new and had been part of L'Enfant's psyche for many years; it would account for his torpedoing the *Takada Maru*, all those many years ago aboard the *Boston*. But, like many phobias, his state of mind could have been misconstrued as something else . . . even as a positive quality if one wished to see it that way. Preparedness. Being alert to possible danger. Willingness to take charge. The good old Annapolis gung-ho spirit. The Pentagon might have known all along what he was doing up here and, taking L'Enfant's own interpretation of events as gospel truth, had quietly decided to give him a free hand. After all, in the minds of many people in Arlington and Washington, he was a responsible officer who had once already demonstrated the ability to take decisive, split-second action. This was a high-risk situation forty million miles from home, where it took fifteen minutes to transmit a simple radio message to Earth; they needed someone out there who could think for himself.

And were these not *aliens*? Their intelligence had evolved within a frame of reference far beyond the planet Earth; even the first exobiologist to receive a Nobel could not provide conclusive answers to their many mysteries. In the absence of knowledge comes fear, and fearful men are only too willing to fire blindly into the darkness. Or trust someone who will stand guard for them.

So you take this man—an undiagnosed xenophobe—and post him at the entrance of a labyrinth. You give him an open-ended mission, supply him with guns, soldiers, whatever else he needs . . .

And then you cut him loose.

"You stupid bastards," he murmured to himself.

Kawakami raised his head. "Pardon me?" he asked. Miho looked appalled.

"No. Sorry." Nash took a deep breath. "I didn't mean you."

Now, more than before, he realized exactly what needed to be done and why. If his purpose, which he had never really admitted to himself, had been simple revenge, now there was a more urgent reason for bringing down L'Enfant. The mentally ill son of a bitch was out of control, and he had to be shut down. . . .

Nash shook his head, bringing himself back to the present. He remembered his last message from Control. "I was informed that a cargo pod was recently dropped to the base from a freighter," he said. "Can you tell me anything about it?"

Kawakami shook his head and drank from his lukewarm tea. "Very little, I'm afraid. It landed due west of the base several days ago, but only Marks and Akers have been out to visit it. They attached a trailer to one of the rovers, and what they brought back was covered by a tarp. Tamara caught a glimpse of the trailer before it was brought into the garage module and believes that it contained a new combat armor suit . . ."

"Like a Hoplite?" Sasaki asked.

"Yes, but she couldn't be certain. Since then, L'Enfant has prevented anyone else except his men from entering Module One . . . that's the garage. He changed the code on the main airlock, since that leads into Module One, and has forced us to use the auxiliary airlock in Module Ten instead."

He stopped, then added, "I'm not certain if this has anything to do with it, but I've also seen them working on the Hornet."

Miho took a deep breath. Nash shook his head. "Pardon me . . . the Hornet?"

"The F-210 Hornet," Miho said. "The space-to-surface attack fighter which was used during the Steeple Chase operation. It was grounded after the mission. Waylon had been using it for a while for spare parts for the *Burroughs*, but otherwise it was useless junk." Her eyes narrowed as she considered the idea. "They might be trying to make it flight-ready again, but what good would that accomplish?"

"And why a new CAS?" Kawakami asked. "The ones which have been used in the past have been ineffectual in the tunnel and the Labyrinth. Why would they want to bring yet another one to this base? If Tamara wasn't a good observer, I would question what she reported."

"Even then," Nash said, "why would they seal off the vehicle garage? If it's just another combat suit . . . ?"

"No," Kawakami agreed, "it does not make sense." He gazed pensively out the window. "But I've also given up on making sense out of L'Enfant. It's all I can do just to reason with the man. He still accepts my role as senior scientist, but with each confrontation we have, what little control I have over him is further diminished. Soon he will stop listening to me entirely." He sighed. "This matter with Paul and the MRV is only the latest example."

"He's taking that thing down into the tunnel tomorrow morning?" Nash asked. "Isn't that risky?"

"Extremely. Yet there's nothing I can do about it now." Kawakami knitted his long fingers together on the table. "Several months ago, we sent another teleoperated spider-probe into Mama's Back Door. Paul piloted it, and his goal was to attempt to penetrate the tunnel and find his way into the catacombs."

He steepled his index fingers and tapped them against the table. "The probe was destroyed, of course, but from what very little he saw before the pseudo-Cooties tore it apart—and, judging from the tape of the encounter, I have to agree—Paul has become convinced that the pseudo-Cooties interact as a sort of hive mind, similar to that of terrestrial insects. The most appropriate analogy might be to driver ants. Given their past behavior, I have to agree with his assessment. If the original Cooties, as represented by their automechanical counterparts, are highly evolved insects, then this would seem to make sense."

He chuckled and shook his head. "The great entomologist, E.O. Wilson, would have been fascinated. I remember his guest lectures from my student days at the University of Osaka when he . . ."

"Shin-ichi-*san* . . ." Sasaki began.

"Sorry. The woolgathering of an old man." The smile disappeared as Kawakami paused to discipline his train of thought. "Paul, however, is also familiar with Wilson's theories. He has become convinced that, like ants, the pseudo-Cooties share some sort of common, central purpose, directed upon some activity deep within their lair, and that the only way to be certain of this is to personally explore the catacombs. Unfortunately, L'Enfant has also become convinced that Paul is right . . . he helped Paul get the MRV shipped from Earth. I'm against Paul visiting the catacombs in the MRV to find out whether his theory is correct, but L'Enfant has made it a top priority and has overridden my objections."

"And Paul . . . ?"

"Paul wants to go through with it," Kawakami said. "Despite my misgivings and Tamara's, he insists upon making the sortie. He thinks the MRV will be sufficient protection against the Cooties." Kawakami shook his head again. "They're both obsessed, but for different reasons. Paul sees it as a quest for scientific knowledge, however unsafe it may be, but L'Enfant . . ."

"Wants a recon mission against the enemy," Nash finished.

The exobiologist closed his eyes. "That is correct."

There was a brief silence in the wardroom as Sasaki and Nash considered all that they had been told. Kawakami slowly let out his breath. "Regardless of the outcome," he continued, "we are all in great danger. This is why I have a request to make. Mr. Nash, you plan to leave here tomorrow, is that correct?"

"If my . . ." Nash glanced at Miho. "If *our* objectives have been completed by then, yes. Tuesday morning at latest."

Miho hesitated, then nodded her head in agreement. "Very well," Kawakami said. "Then I want to have you smuggle Tamara and Paul aboard this airship and take them with you, as soon as Paul has completed his excursion."

He quickly raised a hand before either of them could make objections. "They're unsafe as long as they remain here, and I do not want either of them to become . . . ah, permanent residents of this place, as have I. It will be tricky, but we can get them both in the airship and hide them. Yes?"

Nash could not honestly disagree. Two people could easily be hidden in the interior of the *Akron*'s envelope; it was large enough to conceal a platoon. At the very least, they could hide in the observation blister he had discovered earlier. "And you yourself?"

Kawakami grinned at him. "I will remain here, of course."

Miho was aghast. "Shin-ichi-*san*, you can't—!"

"Hush, Miho." His voice was calm, almost self-sacrificial in its resolve. "After all, it is my cooperation which L'Enfant desires the most . . . and getting all three members of the team into this ship cannot be accomplished without arousing suspicions. When the proper time comes, I will create the necessary diversion . . . nonviolently, of course, but enough for you to get Paul and Tamara aboard without being noticed."

"And if their absence is noticed . . ." Nash began.

"All you will need to do is get aloft with them aboard," Kawakami said. "L'Enfant has the capability to shoot down the *Akron*, certainly, but he won't use it. Far too many questions would be raised if it was destroyed . . . especially since you two are aboard. Once you're in the sky, they cannot touch you or them. Paul and Tamara will help validate whatever you wish to tell your respective authorities back home. That alone is worth spiriting them away."

Nash opened his mouth to speak, then closed it. He could see no flaws in Kawakami's logic, and it was maddeningly clear that only logic could be used on this man; emotional arguments alone would be dismissed as simple sentiment. At the same time, he could not see Boggs raising an objection; he had been friends with Paul Verduin and Tamara Isralilova for too long for him to reject them as stowaways. Now that the MRV had been unloaded, the *Akron* certainly had the lift-capacity to ferry two more passengers back to Arsia Station.

"If Boggs doesn't have a problem with it . . ." he tentatively began, when the inner airlock hatch abruptly gave its distinctive triple-buzz, signaling recompression.

"We'll discuss this later," Nash finished.

A second later Boggs shouldered the hatch open, followed closely by Paul Verduin. "Okay, gang, we're all set to go." Boggs tossed his helmet and gloves on a bunk, but didn't bother getting out of his skinsuit. "The Jackalope's checked out, tarped up, and lashed down. Not that any one of you were of great help, of course."

"Waylon . . ." Miho began.

"Miho . . ." he replied, imitating her voice almost exactly. He suddenly bent over, ducked his head, grasped her shoulders with both hands, and planted a long, wet kiss on her lips. She was too shocked to fight it; however, Nash was surprised to note that her face held, for a fleeting instant, an expression of pleasure just before she shoved him away.

Boggs straightened and, with scarcely a look back at her, tromped through the passageway toward the gondola, ignoring Verduin's laughter and Kawakami's diplomatic cough into his hand. "After all these years, the same bitching and whining," he grumbled. "Okay, Nash . . . I mean, Andy . . . get out there and untie us. We're outta here in five minutes."

He glanced back once before he stepped down the gangway. "We've got a rendezvous to keep with the head dude, if y'know what I mean."

15. Blown

Rigging the opposition for electronic surveillance is a fairly routine part of the espionage trade. If telephones are to be miked, then all it takes is a few minutes to plant infinity bugs or induction taps, thereby transforming the phones themselves into eavesdropping devices even when they are on the hook. Concealing electret mikes, such as the ones supplied to Nash for this assignment, under or inside furniture is mainly a matter of penetrating the target area and having a few unobserved moments to do the dirty work. This can be accomplished by posing as a repairman, bribing a custodian or night watchman, or (in the worst case) breaking and entering.

In his career as a private spy, Nash had done all of the above at one time or another, to listen in on everyone from corporate research assistants to multinational CEO's to the crown prince of a certain Middle Eastern sheikdom. Yet bugging Cydonia Base was much more difficult than miking a home or office on Earth. Not counting Module Eleven—the Ambient Environment Lab, which was permanently unpressurized and thereby unbuggable by the voice-activated electret mikes—there were ten modules in the habitat, evenly arranged along a central access tunnel—including Module One, the main airlock and vehicle garage, located on the opposite side of the habitat from the Module Ten auxiliary airlock and the AEL.

Module One was a principal target; the payload which had been dropped from orbit was stored in the base garage, and Nash supposed that the garage would be repressurized when secret work was being done in there, if only for the convenience of working in a shirt-sleeve environment. In view of what Kawakami had told him about its being sealed off by L'Enfant, however, it was unlikely that Nash would be able to get into the main airlock from inside the habitat. He was forced to improvise.

After the arrival of the *Akron* at the base, where they were met by L'Enfant's three "observers," Lieutenant Akers escorted Nash, Sasaki, Verduin, and Kawakami from the landing pad to the habitat; Marks and Swigart, who had made their first appearance at the pad, stayed behind to shepherd Boggs and unload the remaining cargo from the airship. Like a guard marching prisoners into a POW compound, Akers strode behind the four of them as they walked toward the habitat. Just before they reached the auxiliary airlock, Nash contrived to pause by a rover which was parked nearby. After dropping his duffel bag on the vehicle's seat and while pretending to adjust the boot lining on his skinsuit's outergarment, he furtively slid one of the wireless mikes under the chassis.

There were fresh tire-tracks leading to and from Module One's large double doors. With any luck, the rover would be moved inside before nightfall as standard procedure; barring misfortune, the bug's adhesive backing would not be scoured by the dust and the tiny mike would not drop into the sand, where it would not only be useless but also a possible giveaway. It was risky, but it was the best he could improvise. It was important that he have a way of knowing what was going on in Module One.

Unforeseen good fortune, though, came a couple of minutes later when they reached the auxiliary airlock. Despite its label, Module Ten was not a full-sized Skycorp Type-B module, but rather a small geodesic dome not much larger than the *Akron*'s airlock. It had been intended mainly as an interconnect between the AEL and the rest of the habitat, and therefore could accommodate only two persons at a time. Once they had arrived at the auxiliary airlock, Akers unwittingly made a miscalculation: He allowed Sasaki and Nash to enter the airlock by themselves, leaving him outside with Kawakami and Verduin.

As soon as the airlock was sealed and the repressurization sequence initiated, Nash carefully examined the ceiling and walls. No TV cameras were visible, but since he was still using an open comlink frequency, he dared not say anything conspicuous. Even after recompression, when their helmets would be off, there was no guarantee that the airlock itself wasn't bugged; Kawakami had already cautioned them to that effect.

"How long does this usually take?" he casually asked Sasaki.

She glanced at him through her helmet faceplate. *About five minutes, including decontamination.* Her eyes followed him as Nash quickly opened his right thigh pocket. *It will be hard for us to talk once the electromagnetic scrub begins. We better talk now.*

Nash winced. Not good: If someone was indeed listening to them over the comlink, then that remark could arouse suspicion. He scowled at her and shook his head. "Look, Miho, I didn't mean to get . . . y'know. frisky last night, but it's been a long time since I've had anything."

Her eyes widened in shocked surprise, but his words were not so startling as the sight of the pistol he pulled from his right thigh pocket and carefully placed on the gridded floor between his feet. "Maybe you were right for slapping me," he continued, giving her a wink and a grin, "but I hope that it doesn't mean that we can't still be friends."

She nodded quickly; she comprehended the double-talk. *Sure. I understand.* Already static was breaking up her voice; red dust rose around them as electromagnetic scrubbers began to whisk their suits clean, the dirt falling into vents beneath the gridwork. *But if you need to talk about it, I can . . .*

The rest was lost in electronic fuzz-out. Nash unzipped his left thigh pocket and pulled out the rest of the electret mikes. He switched off the comlink and signaled her to do the same; then he grabbed her right hand and carefully dropped half of them into her palm. At the same time, he leaned forward and firmly touched the faceplate of his helmet to hers. "Bugs!" he said loudly. "Put these wherever you can!"

It took three attempts for him to get the message across to her; touching helmets as a means of communication was not everything that popular fiction claimed it to be. Once she got the idea, though, Sasaki nodded her head and transferred the bugs into her pocket.

A couple of minutes later the green light above the inside door flashed on, signaling that the airlock was repressurized. Without speaking to each other, they began zipping out of their skinsuits, stowing the helmets, the overgarments and the Mylar pressure-suits in the recessed lockers. Aboard the *Akron* they had given each other exclusive use of the airlock for suitup, but in this situation such privacy was out of the question. It was the first time during the long journey that Nash had the opportunity to observe Miho undressed; for the few moments in which she

was wearing only a bikini bra and panties, he had a chance to regret the vow of celibacy he had made to her. Sasaki glanced at
him, blushed deeply, then turned her back to him as she removed a standard-issue cotton jumpsuit from her locker. Nash
deliberately closed his mind to Sasaki; this wasn't the time or
the place.

He quickly tucked the SIG-Sauer into the calf-holster above
his right ankle, then climbed into his own jumpsuit, carefully
pulling the elastic cuff over the holster to conceal the gun. As he
stood up, he caught a glimpse of Miho pulling a small flat plastic case out of her skinsuit's cargo pocket and shoving it into a
thigh pocket of her jumpsuit. It seemed to be an electronic device of some sort. She looked at him, noticed his inquisitive expression, and gave a serious nod of her head as she zipped up
the front of her suit.

The woman apparently had a few secret tricks of her own;
somehow, Nash was not surprised. He was already getting used
to the notion that Sasaki was a partner in this operation. Were it
not for the possibility that the airlock could be miked, he might
have said something to that effect.

They quickly transferred the electret mikes into their breast
pockets; Nash was careful to keep his pocket unflapped, and
hand-signaled Sasaki to do the same. They picked up their duffel bags and took a moment to give each other the once-over,
making certain that everything was well-hidden.

"Ready?" he asked. She nodded nervously, then Nash
grabbed the latch and twisted it upward. There was a slight hiss
of air and their ears popped; Nash pushed the heavy airlock
hatch open.

Together, they stepped into Cydonia Base.

The access corridor was deserted; from where they stood they
could see that all the module hatches were shut. A swift glance
down the long tunnel didn't reveal any TV cameras, although
that still didn't rule out bugging devices. They had the base to
themselves for at least five minutes until the next two people
cycled through the airlock—ten minutes, if they allowed for
desuiting.

Yet L'Enfant himself was still unaccounted for; they had not
seen him since their arrival at the base. Kawakami had told
them that someone was always on duty in the command center;
Nash had to guess that he was in Module Two, at the opposite

end of the corridor. Ten minutes wasn't much time, but by planting as many bugs in the modules as they could before the next group came into the base, they might be able to steal an advantage.

"Which way?" he asked, keeping his tone casual for the benefit of any listening devices in the corridor.

"Down this way," Sasaki said. "I'll show you to our quarters." She stepped around him and began carrying her duffel bag down the corridor, passing the first two hatches: Modules Eight and Nine, respectively marked MONITOR CENTER and LAB A. He wanted to stop to conceal mikes in both of them, but she strode ahead of him before he could stop her, walking to the next two modules in the row.

The hatch to Module Six, on the right, was unlocked; she pushed it open and brazenly stepped inside. He followed her through the door, scanning the compartment. Four bunks, each with their sheets and blankets neatly tucked in to precise military-regulation, spare sneakers standing in orderly rows next to the lockers, the walls unadorned with any posters or snapshots. One bunk near the rear had a makeshift curtain around it.

"Wrong one, I think," she said softly as she jabbed a finger toward the nearest bunk.

Nash understood immediately. Sasaki had led him to the bunkhouse used by L'Enfant and his aides. He quickly knelt next to the bunk; while she watched the door, he pulled an electret mike out of his pocket and pasted it underneath the edge of the bunk, safely out of both sight and easy reach of exploring hands. A tap of his index finger against the bug's side activated it; the mike was now good for the next seventy-two hours, so long as regular voice-vibrations recharged its friction battery.

So far, so good. Nash stood up again and followed Miho out of the module.

Directly across the corridor was Module Seven; Sasaki pushed open the hatch and led him into it. As much as Module Six was spotless and pin-neat, this bunkhouse was in disarray: the two bunks at the front were carelessly made; stray items of clothing lay on the floor, posters of Earth scenes and snapshots of unfamiliar people were taped to the walls. Two bunks at the end of the module were unsheeted.

"That's yours," she said, pointing to the bare mattress on the left. "Paul and Shin-ichi use the other beds. I suppose Waylon gets the one on the right. I'll be with Tamara, at the other end of the corridor." She made a hasty motion with her hand, gesturing to the hatch; Nash dropped his duffel bag on the floor next to his bunk. "This is getting heavy," she added.

"Need some help?" he asked. He glanced at his watch. They had a minimum of two and a half minutes left before the airlock recycled. Maybe more, but he wasn't going to count on it. Maybe he could make it back to the lab or the monitor center. . . .

"Yes. Thanks." Sasaki unshouldered her bag and handed it to him; then they exited the bunkhouse and walked further down the corridor. The wardroom was in Module Four, on the right, but Miho pushed open the hatch to Module Five. Tamara Isralilova's immaculate bunk was obviously the only one occupied in the compartment; Lieutenant Swigart apparently had no compunctions about sharing Module Six with three men. Nash remembered the curtained bunk in module Six and smiled. Military field discipline.

Sasaki motioned for Nash to drop her duffel bag on the opposite bunk, then said loudly, "Let me show you the wardroom." Before Nash could reply, she bent close to him and urgently whispered in his ear: "Follow me to the main airlock! Quick, we don't have much time!"

She started to head out of the module, but Nash grabbed her forearm and yanked her back; she winced from his tight grasp and began to struggle. "No, dammit!" he hissed. "We can't do it in time . . . and how do you expect to get in there, anyway?"

Sasaki angrily yanked her arm out of his hand. "Keycard decoder," she whispered. "Hurry, while we've got the chance!"

A keycard decoder: now Nash understood the purpose of the small plastic case he had glimpsed in the airlock. It was an electronic skeleton key which could be slipped into a keycard slot to decipher the code-sequence and unlock any give door. A rather sophisticated piece of spy technology; JETRO must have anticipated a few difficulties and equipped her with one in advance. He only wished SA's armory had the same forethought.

It was tempting, yet . . . "We're flat out of time," he whispered. "Look, even if we can get the hatch open before someone cycles through Module Ten, we're not going to be able to do much before . . ."

They heard footsteps in the corridor, just beyond the open hatch.

Without thinking twice, Nash grabbed Sasaki by the waist, hauled her toward him, and planted his lips on hers. For a second she squirmed against his rough embrace, making him feel like a rapist, before her intelligence won out over her instincts. She slid her arms around his neck and reluctantly surrendered herself; for a moment he actually began to enjoy her kiss before someone outside the doorway cleared his throat.

"If you're going to do this in my base," Terrance L'Enfant said softly, "you might have the common decency to close the hatch first."

Nash quickly looked up, pretending to be startled as Sasaki uncurled her arms from his neck; she didn't have to pretend her embarrassment. L'Enfant stood in the corridor with his hands clasped behind his back, a vaguely bemused smile on his lean face. He wore a khaki jumpsuit, identical to theirs except for the pair of commander's bars which were pinned to each collar. L'Enfant studied them both with unblinking eyes, and Nash realized that he was waiting for them to speak.

"Sorry, Commander," he said. "I'm afraid we . . . uh, got a little carried away there." He could feel Sasaki trembling in his arms. "The next time we'll . . ."

The smile faded from L'Enfant's face; he closed his eyes briefly and shook his head. "Not here, no, there won't be a next time, Mr. Donaldson. We've had to make several sacrifices of personal liberty to get our work done, and this is one of them."

He paused for a moment. "You are both visitors here for the next couple of days," he continued in a condescending tone, "so I expect you to restrain your sexual impulses until you've left this base." He looked directly at Miho. "I also expect you to keep your boyfriend out of the female quarters, Dr. Sasaki," he said stiffly. "I think Ms. Isralilova would appreciate the courtesy. This isn't a college dorm. We don't have any doorknobs for you to hang a towel upon."

He glanced at Nash again and added, "But if you had to find someone for a fling with, you could have done better than choosing some blimp jockey. Sleeping with him won't advance your sterling career, hmm?"

The redness in Sasaki's face was now more from repressed anger than embarrassment. She stepped back out of Nash's arms and looked down at the floor, silently nodding her head once. L'Enfant hadn't realized how much of a verbal knife he had shoved into her with that last offhand remark; Nash admired her self-possession for not lashing back at him. Yet, more importantly, he realized that his suspicions had been correct; judging from L'Enfant's choice of words, he must have been party to their fabricated conversation in the auxiliary airlock. Kawakami was right; the entire base *was* bugged, with the primary listening post being the command module.

From the far end of the corridor, they heard the clank and hiss of the Module Ten airlock opening again. L'Enfant glanced in that direction, then looked back at Nash. He unexpectedly smiled and crooked a finger at him.

"Now, Mr. Donaldson, if you'll come this way, I have something to show you." His voice had lightened almost to the point of breeziness. "You might find it interesting. And Dr. Sasaki . . . I have a small task for you."

Kawakami and Verduin were the next two persons to cycle through the auxiliary airlock; they stood hesitantly at the opposite end of the corridor, quietly watching as L'Enfant led Nash and Sasaki out of Module Five. L'Enfant casually waved to them before turning to face Sasaki. "I'm sure you'll want more time to become reacquainted with them," he said, "so why don't you escort them into the wardroom for lunch? Mr. Donaldson and I will be joining you shortly."

At that moment, the Module One hatch opened behind them and Charlie Akers and Megan Swigart entered the habitat; Nash noticed that they both wore single-bar insignia pins on the collars of their jumpsuits. They didn't salute nor did they snap to attention when they saw the commander, yet their deference to L'Enfant was obvious nonetheless.

L'Enfant nodded to them as Akers closed the hatch. "Mr. Marks has Mr. Boggs well in hand, I assume?"

"Yes sir," Swigart replied crisply. "They're unloading the *Akron* now and they'll be in·as soon as the job's finished."

"Very good." L'Enfant stepped aside, extending a gracious hand toward Miho. "You may join Dr. Sasaki for lunch with Shin-ichi and Paul. They'll probably welcome your company." His tone was polite, yet his words left no room for refusal by anyone, least of all Miho. As Swigart walked past him, L'Enfant added, "And set an extra place for Tamara, she'll be joining you soon."

He then turned to Akers; the lieutenant was wiping sweat off

his balding pate, but snapped into parade rest as L'Enfant faced
him. "Charlie, if you'll come with me and Mr. Donaldson into
the command center, we can finish the rest of our business."

"Yes, sir." Akers said, completely deadpan. He turned and
opened the adjacent hatch to Module Two, stepping back to
hold it open for his commanding officer. L'Enfant allowed Nash
to enter first, then walked in just behind him, with Akers bringing up the rear.

The command module was cramped, dark and sullenly illuminated, filled with chittering instruments and green-backlit
LCD screens; to Nash, it had an unnerving resemblance to the
bridge of a submarine. A tall woman with curly dark hair was
seated in front of the communications station. She looked up
nervously at the three men as they entered; her eyes were shadowed, her shoulders slouched forward. One glimpse of her face,
and Nash was reminded of the look a caged rabbit gives to its
captors at petting time.

"Do you have the latest nowcast from Marsat-2, Tamara?"
L'Enfant asked.

Tamara Isralilova silently pointed at a printer next to her console. L'Enfant ripped off the top sheet of the scroll and studied
it; Nash realized that it was an update of the weather information which Boggs had received yesterday aboard the *Akron*.
L'Enfant absently nibbled at the nail of his right forefinger as
his eyes darted over the printout. "All right, Tamara, you can go
now," he murmured without looking up. "Lunch is being served
next door."

Isralilova stood up and, apparently making a deliberate effort
not to look at Nash, obediently strode out of the command center; Akers shut the hatch behind her, then stood next to it, again
assuming the parade-rest posture. L'Enfant ignored both of
them as he studied the printout for another minute, then he
dropped it on the console and took the seat which Isralilova had
just vacated. He folded his hands in his lap and crossed his legs,
gazing up at Nash with languid eyes.

"Looks as if we have a bad dust storm coming in," he said.
"Doesn't it, Mr. Nash?"

It didn't come as either an accusation or a denouncement, but
simply as a confident declaration of fact. Stated as such, it was
pointless for him to deny his identity. Strangely, Nash didn't

feel surprise or shock—merely disappointment that his cover had been blown so quickly.

"How long have you known?" he asked.

L'Enfant smiled a little. "Thank you for not wasting my time. I expected you to continue the charade until we pushed the evidence in your face."

He stretched back in his chair. "August Nash, formerly under my command on the *Boston*—no, sir, I didn't forget you—now working as a field operative for Security Associates, retained by Skycorp to investigate what's been going on here during the past few months. A spy, in essence."

"If you want to use that term."

" 'A rose by any other name . . .' " L'Enfant shrugged indifferently. "I suspected someone might come here eventually. The only real question was who and when, and that was answered by . . . well, some loose lips at Arsia Station, shall we say?"

Nash had to consider the hint for only a moment. "Leahy," he replied at once. "The general manager."

"Smart guess." L'Enfant closed his eyes and slowly nodded his head. "Yes, but not directly from him. All he had to do was get drunk and run off at the mouth in front of the right people. We have a couple of friends at Arsia who are . . . um, shall we say, sympathetic to our goals here . . . so all they had to do was relay the information to me." He opened his eyes and sighed with disgust. "A very sloppy deception on your part."

Sloppy, indeed . . . although not on Nash's part. Leahy must have been really soused to babble about a secret which had been entrusted to him. However, given the only occasion on which Nash had seen Sam while at Arsia Station—passed out at the bar of the Mars Hotel—that didn't seem unlikely. L'Enfant's confederates must have bought a lot of beer and whiskey for the witless alky that night. Bad intelligence given by Skycorp to SA had resulted in too much crucial information being given to precisely the wrong person. Larger operations had been compromised for just the same reason. . . .

Too late, though, now to blame Leahy, Skycorp, or even his own company. The fact that L'Enfant knew Nash's true identity was obvious from everything he had just said. The full extent of L'Enfant's knowledge, though, was still unknown, as was the damage it might have caused. Either way, the ball was now squarely in the opposition's court.

"I'll try to do better next time," Nash said dryly. "The question is, Commander, what do you intend to do about it?"

L'Enfant said nothing immediately; instead he unclipped a phone from his belt, unfolded it and tapped a couple of digits into the keypad. "Alphonse, your report please?" he asked.

He listened for a minute. "And you've escorted Boggs to the wardroom?" He listened again, then said, "Very good. Destroy the ones you've found, then report here."

He snapped the phone shut. "While we've been speaking, Sergeant Marks has taken Mr. Boggs to the wardroom. Don't worry, your friends are safe and under Lieutenant Swigart's supervision. Since then, Marks has been electronically sweeping the base for the bugs you planted on the way in here. Lieutenant Akers saw you put one under that rover, and my guess was that you took the opportunity once you were inside the habitat to bury a few more. Marks says he found the one you placed in my quarters, plus the few that were still on Dr. Sasaki's person."

Nash took a deep breath, trying to settle his nerves. "I'm surprised you let me get that far."

L'Enfant smiled cannily. "I only wished to see what you intended to do once you finally arrived here. This is also why you were allowed to spend some time alone with Dr. Kawakami in the *Akron* . . . I wanted you to feel more comfortable, to give you the illusion that your deception was actually succeeding. Shin-ichi couldn't have told you anything you wouldn't have found out eventually, you couldn't have caused any significant damage without blowing your cover, and it was necessary to make you believe that I was not aware of your little game."

He paused. "You can save yourself a little trouble by giving me the rest of the bugs," he added. "They won't do you much good now."

Nash winced. "No, I suppose they won't," he admitted as he dug into his breast pocket and pulled out the rest of the electret mikes. L'Enfant held out his hand and Nash dropped them into his palm; as an afterthought, he produced the microrecorder and gave that to L'Enfant as well.

"Thank you." L'Enfant cocked his head toward Nash's jumpsuit sleeve. "And your watch, if you will? Hidden cameras have been around since my mother was a teeny-bopper, but for all I know it may contain a dartgun or something similarly lethal. Please remove it for me."

Nash unbuckled the watch from his wrist and handed it to L'Enfant. "You cover all the bases, don't you?"

"Unlike yourself, we're very much the professionals here, Mr. Nash." L'Enfant glanced at the watch, then tossed it on the counter. "Seiko. How cheap. I would have thought that they might have issued you something more classy."

"Bad luck."

"Indeed." L'Enfant juggled the bugs from hand to hand, apparently waiting for Marks's arrival. When the big Marine knocked twice on the hatch and Akers let him inside, L'Enfant pointed toward Nash.

"Sergeant, please aim your weapon at Mr. Nash's back," he said softly. "Fire at will if he makes a wrong move."

Nash heard the unmistakable sound of an assault rifle being cocked into firing position; he didn't need to look behind him to know that Marks's Steyr was now poised and aimed at a spot directly between his shoulder blades. Nash kept both of his hands in plain sight next to his sides, not daring to so much as twitch a muscle.

"Mr. Nash," L'Enfant said, "you are probably armed yourself, but I sincerely doubt that you can get to your gun before Mr. Marks puts a bullet through your heart. You will now . . . very carefully . . . disarm yourself and give your weapon to me. Butt first, please."

"And don't fuck with me, man," he heard Marks murmur from behind him. "I've got a bad twitch in my trigger finger."

Moving as slowly as possible, Nash knelt, propped up his right leg and, using only his left hand, pulled up the cuff to expose the calf-holster. He gently pulled out the SIG-Sauer, making sure that he used only his thumb and index finger and that his fingers never strayed close to the trigger guard. Tilting the barrel toward himself, he extended the gun upside-down toward L'Enfant. "There's a spare clip in my duffel bag," he said.

"Shit," Marks sneered. "My grandmother carries more firepower than that when she goes to play Bingo."

"Be nice, Alphonse. Mr. Nash has been cooperative with us so far." L'Enfant reached out and took the gun from Nash's hand. He glanced over it, made a disdainful sound with his lips, and ejected the clip from the handle. "Why did you bring this?" he asked in the most conversational tone. "Were you intending to kill me?"

That was indeed, Nash reflected, a good question. . . . "No," he said, still kneeling in front of L'Enfant. "Our intelligence was that you and your men were armed, and I was given the option of protecting myself." He shrugged. "That's all. Nothing personal, Captain."

As he spoke, he prayed that L'Enfant's knowledge of his assignment didn't extend to its exact parameters. Nash didn't know how much Leahy had been told about his assignment, or how much he had drunkenly blabbed to L'Enfant's contacts at Arsia Station. This was the crucial test of how much L'Enfant really knew; so far, the commander had flaunted his knowledge of Nash's identity and mission. If L'Enfant didn't believe the bluff, there was still the assault rifle aimed at his back.

Yet there was still hope. Aside from her assistance in helping him plant the bugs, L'Enfant had yet to mention Miho Sasaki. He might be carrying on a poker bluff himself, but Nash didn't think so. L'Enfant was enjoying himself, basking in his superiority; he would have enjoyed humiliating Sasaki as well— perhaps even more so, given the fact that she was Japanese—had he tumbled to her secret affiliation with JETRO as well. If Marks's bug-sweeper had found her keycard-decoder, he would have undoubtedly brought it to L'Enfant as another trophy.

Nash felt a small bit of relief in that revelation. Sasaki wasn't much of an ace, but she was all that he had left up his sleeve. Now if he could only keep himself alive . . .

" 'Nothing personal, Captain,' " L'Enfant mimicked. He gazed at Nash for a few moments with his languid, dead eyes, idly snapping the clip in and out of the gun like a business executive playing with a desk toy. For several seconds, that was the only sound in the compartment.

"No," he said at last. "I don't believe you wanted to kill me. I think you're just a third-rate detective." He pocketed the gun. "That's everything, isn't it? I could have Charlie work you over, you know."

"That's all there is," Nash replied. "You've got the works."

L'Enfant silently appraised him again, then nodded once toward Marks. Nash heard the Steyr's safety click into position. He stood up and let out his breath, but he didn't look away from the commander.

"So what's next?" he asked. "A short walk to the airlock?"

L'Enfant blinked several times in rapid succession, then let out a peal of maniacally cheerful laughter. Marks honked his own mirthless guffaw; Akers made a sound which resembled an asthmatic sneeze. L'Enfant stood up from his chair. "Mr. Nash," he wheezed, wiping tears from his eyes, "do you think this is some low-budget spy movie? I don't intend to kill you. Skycorp sent you to discover what I'm doing here, and that information is exactly what I intend to provide to you."

His laughter gradually died off as he mopped the rest of his face. "First, though," he said, "I have to ask you . . . have you ever heard of the seventh protocol?"

Nash suddenly remembered the last important thing which Control had told him in the E-mail briefing aboard the *Lowell*. Yes, he had heard of it, but he had not understood the allusion. An obscure United Nations statute—that was all he knew.

"No," he casually replied in what was only a half-lie. "I don't know what you're talking about."

L'Enfant's face abruptly changed into a cold mask; he took a step closer, until they were almost nose to nose, and his eyes bored into Nash's like frost-covered icepicks.

"Liar," he whispered almost inaudibly.

He made a slight motion with his right hand. Nash's arms were suddenly grabbed from behind and savagely wrenched backward. A heavy first slammed into the small of his back. Nash gasped in pain; then the breath was punched from his lungs as L'Enfant himself slugged him directly in the solar plexus.

As Nash doubled over, still held half-erect by Akers and Marks, L'Enfant walked around him. "You're a disappointment to me, seaman," he said in a terse voice. "For a few minutes there, I thought I was dealing with a gentleman."

L'Enfant opened the module hatch. "When Alphonse and Charlie are through giving you remedial lessons in social etiquette, we'll continue this discussion." He held the hatch open while the two men dragged Nash toward the access tunnel. "Do your business in the storeroom. Have fun, but make certain that you don't render any permanent harm. No broken bones, please."

Nash caught a final glimpse of L'Enfant's face as he was hauled into the corridor; his smile was lunatic. "I made a promise, after all," he said, looking directly at him. "And I have better plans for Mr. Nash."

PART THREE

(August 29–31, 2032)

"I will show you fear in a handful of dust."
—T. S. ELIOT,
"The Waste Land"

IN A HANDFUL OF DUST

16. The Seventh Protocol

Alphonse Marks and Charlie Akers hauled Nash into Module Three, the storage compartment across the corridor from the command center, and there they beat the shit out of him.

They were methodical and professional about it; they knew what they were doing, and he was completely helpless. After they locked the hatch and tied his hands behind his back with a bungi cord Akers found in the skinsuit spare-parts bin, they frisked him to make certain he wasn't carrying any other weapons or surveillance items. Then, once they had taped their knuckles with a ripped-up T-shirt, Big Al held Nash up while Charlie pummeled his stomach and face.

After about fifteen minutes, they let Nash slump to the floor, barely conscious and bleeding from the mouth. He thought it was over, but the two soldiers were merely giving him time to rest; torturers know that a person can't endure extreme agony indefinitely before numbness sets in, so they waited patiently until Nash had stopped groaning before they wrestled him to his feet again. Then Marks took his turn in the boxing ring while Akers held Nash in a full-nelson.

And so on for a good hour or more. After a while, Nash lost track of time completely; he went limp, concentrated on a spot of floor between the feet of his current assailant, and tried to think of something else. His fogged mind remembered a random bit of flotsam from the past—the plastic model of an aircraft carrier he'd built when he was thirteen years old—and pretty soon he almost forgot about the pain. For their part, Marks and Akers obeyed L'Enfant's orders; they were careful not to break anything or do any permanent damage, except for the molar in his left lower jaw which Akers punched clean out of his mouth. Nor, surprisingly, did they say very much during the ordeal. For all of its brutality, it was a softening-up session, not an interrogation.

It went on like this for an eternity, until a final hammerblow to his solar plexus knocked the last of Nash's breath from his lungs and he was cast into a bottomless black pit. After they checked his pulse to make certain that he was still alive, Marks and Akers dragged him out of the storeroom and up the corridor to Module Nine, the laboratory which also functioned as the base infirmary.

Tamara Isralilova had already been summoned, in her formal capacity as Cydonia Base's physician. She carefully lifted Nash onto the examining table and scissored off his blood-soaked jumpsuit and underwear, and after she X-rayed him to make certain that no bones had been broken and that he hadn't been concussed, she did her best to heal his wounds. His midriff was a mass of purpled bruises and his face was a horror, but she administered local anesthetics, stitched the welt in his right cheek, and checked his teeth for further damage. After she dressed the bruises and injected short-life nanosurgeons into his bloodstream to repair the internal damage to his blood vessels, she dosed him with codeine to knock him out for several hours and give the nanosurgeons time to work. She then covered him with sheets and a blanket, switched off the lights and left the infirmary, allowing him to sleep off the worst of the pain.

That should have been the end of the nightmare. Instead, it was only the prelude.

When Nash finally awoke, many hours later, the darkness in the module was no longer total. At first, all he saw were the illuminated digits of a chronometer somewhere near the bed: 2337. Close to midnight, local Mars time, although he didn't immediately comprehend the fact. There was a dull ache throughout his body, and for the first few moments he thought he was still in the storeroom, waiting for Marks and Akers to begin the next round of their one-sided prizefight. Yet, as he realized that he was not in the storeroom, he also became aware that he was not alone either.

Someone shifted in a chair across the compartment. There was a small pool of light cast by a gooseneck halogen lamp, like the aura of a distant nebula. He looked toward it and, through his hazed eyes, he saw a hand reach for a plastic squeeze-bottle on the desk beneath the light. The chair softly scooted backward on the tile floor as his visitor rose to his or her feet; he heard footsteps drawing closer, then a large body opaqued the lamp. He felt a hand gently tucking the plastic straw of a squeeze-bottle between his puffed lips.

"Here, sailor," Terrance L'Enfant said. "Sip this. Just a little . . ."

Nash hesitated, then sucked on the straw. Cool water, sweeter than any wine he had ever tasted, flowed into his parched mouth and down his dry throat. He drank more greedily, but suddenly choked on the water and began to cough, spraying the sheet with saliva.

"No no no," L'Enfant cautioned. "That's too much." He pulled the bottle away from Nash's mouth, then picked up his limp right hand and placed it around the bottle, letting the cold bottom of the flask rest on Nash's chest. "When you're ready, there it is, but take it easy for a few minutes. Okay?"

Nash didn't say anything. L'Enfant was a solid black mass hovering over his bed; he stepped back a couple of feet, and now the glow from the lamp surrounded his head and shoulders like a corona, giving density to his figure but rendering no detail to his face. A dark god of madness and torture.

"They told me you were brave," L'Enfant said. His voice was a low monotone, as metronomic as the ticking of a clock. "You didn't talk, you seldom cried out. Sergeant Marks was particularly impressed with your performance. I can't honestly tell you that they're sorry for what they did, but it if makes you feel any better, the sergeant said . . ."

"Fu-fu-fuck you," Nash managed to whisper.

L'Enfant said nothing for a minute. He finally let out his breath. "I shouldn't have expected anything different." There was another pause. "For what it's worth, though, I'm proud that you were once a member of my old crew. I despise whimperers."

Nash didn't speak. He expected L'Enfant to disappear, having said his piece, but the commander remained next to the bed. "I think now," he continued, "that you were only a half-liar. That you had heard of the seventh protocol, but didn't know what it meant. When we found the gun, I was certain that you had been sent to kill me, with the protocol being used as a rather tenuous rationale. I'll ask you again, but this time I'll amend my question. Do you know what the seventh protocol *is*?"

Nash shook his head slightly. The motion made his head

ache, but L'Enfant didn't respond. He was waiting for a verbal reply. "No," Nash murmured. "I don't know."

Another long pause. "I don't think you would have the stupidity to lie to me now," L'Enfant said, "so I'll tell you."

He crossed his arms. "When the possibility of discovering alien life forms was still only theoretical," he began, "a group of SETI researchers met in England and developed procedures regarding first contact with extraterrestrial intelligence, should it ever occur. This was eventually synthesized into a declaration of principles, which was then submitted to the United Nations as a draft memorandum. Although this declaration was never formally ratified as international space law, it served as the basis for an informal treaty regarding first contact. When the Cooties were discovered, the declaration became the statute by which the Security Council and the World Court were able to judge and rule against the C.I.S. when it attempted to take military control of this base. Although it was not legally binding, it served much the same purpose. Do you understand so far?"

Nash nodded his head; this time, L'Enfant didn't require him to speak. "There were seven amendments to this declaration," he went on. "A set of protocols. The last of these, the seventh protocol, has become the most important of all in our present situation."

He raised a finger. "I quote: 'In the event that extraterrestrials appear to pose a threat to human health, well-being, or peace, no nation shall act without consulting the Security Council of the United Nations.' End quote. Do you understand now?"

Nash thought about it for a few moments, but it was hard for him to make the connection. "No," he whispered, "I don't."

L'Enfant turned and walked back to his chair. "I suspect that Dr. Kawakami told you much about the Cooties," he said as he sat down, "but since his theories tend to be rather orthodox, I doubt that he has told you of my own conjectures."

He crossed his legs and folded his hands in his lap, as leisurely as if he were enjoying a parlor conversation with an old shipmate. "Far be it from me to interpret his work for you, but based on what he and his team have uncovered since I've been in command here, I've reached my own inescapable conclusion that the Cooties pose just such a threat."

His head rocked back a little as he gazed up at the ceiling; in the dim light, Nash could see that this eyes were half-closed, almost meditatively. Nash noticed that, twice already, he had referred to the aliens as the Cooties, not pseudo-Cooties. Was this merely a slip of the tongue, or did it have a larger significance?

"And here is the irony of our situation," L'Enfant mused. "The U.N. allowed us to come here to act as a peacekeeping force against further Russian aggression. Indeed, if the C.I.S. did attempt to put military units on Mars again, we would have carte blanche to deal with them . . . the old agreement would be instantly nullified. The Pentagon even secretly provided us with guns and the necessary equipment to make the old STS fighter flight-ready again, in the case of just such an event, unlikely though it is." He shrugged his shoulders. "But the Russians are the very least of our worries. They no longer pose a threat . . . it's the Cooties which are our main concern. Several people have already died making contact with them, yet because of the seventh protocol, we supposedly cannot act to counter aggression by an advanced alien species without consultation and permission from the U.N. Security Council."

He sighed and raised his hands expansively. "This place is a beachhead, August. The safety of our race . . . the entire human race, not just the Americans or the Russians or the Japanese . . . is on the verge of utter extermination, with Cydonia Base as the starting point. Yet if this were to be brought to the attention of the Security Council, they would not act on it until the last possible moment. And by then, it would be much too late. Our window of opportunity, our chance to make a preemptive counterstrike, would be irretrievably lost. All because the politicians, the scientists, the . . ."

L'Enfant shook his head with infinite disgust. "The freethinkers," he finished, spitting out the last phrase as if it were poison on his tongue. "They want to believe that the Cooties mean us no harm. They cling to the naive supposition that an advanced species must be warm and cuddly and peace-loving, just as Kawakami waves Drake's Equation in front of me and claims that this is proof that the Cooties can mean us no harm only because they mastered interstellar flight."

He bent forward, resting his elbows on his knees and clasping his hands together, his shadowed face now looking directly at Nash. "But I'm a military man," he said, his voice growing more intense. "A soldier. I make no apologies for the way I think. This is an alien culture and therefore we cannot assume anything, least of all peaceful intent. Given the fact that the Cooties deliberately lured us to this place, then have murdered nearly everyone who has come in direct contact with them while concealing their own actions and motives, I have to assume that they mean nothing *but* harm to us."

He paused, his head turned slightly to one side, as if he was lost in his thoughts. "Are you familiar with the sundew plant?" he asked abruptly.

Nash knew of it, but he shook his head instead. "The sundew survives by luring insects onto its leaves with sweet pollenlike smells," L'Enfant explained as he spread open the palm of his right hand. "When the unwary insect alights, it gets stuck in the plant's adhesive leaves. By then, it is much too late, for the plant has already begun to close in upon its prey."

He closed his hand into a fist. "Suffocating it, then slowly ingesting it." He looked up at Nash again. "The Face is much like the sundew. Do you see?"

Nash said nothing. There was another long pause as L'Enfant gazed down at the floor. "There are those on Earth who agree with me," he said slowly, "and they have given me . . . my men and I, that is . . . the means to make certain that we do not suffer the same fate as the insect in the sundew. Do you understand now?"

L'Enfant looked up at him again, clearly waiting for an answer. Nash licked his dry lips. "The same way as you dealt with the *Takada Maru*?" he ventured.

It was a risky question, loaded to the hilt, and he was not at all certain how L'Enfant would react. The commander didn't reply at once; he looked away once more, this time as if he was embarrassed. When he spoke again, his voice was soft, almost inaudible.

"You despise me for what I did, don't you?" he asked. "Even though I acted to save your own life—yes, seaman, I know that you were on deck when I ordered the torpedoes—you still hate me for that."

Nash made no reply. L'Enfant chuckled deep in his throat. "That's all right, sailor. I've become accustomed to the recriminations, and from better men than you." He sighed. "Yes, just like the *Takada Maru*. And again, a flimsy U.N. resolution is used against me. Only this time, there will be a major difference."

L'Enfant stood up from his chair and slowly walked toward the bed. "You were sent here as a spy," he went on, "and this is precisely the role which you shall perform. You will be my witness . . . this is the sole reason why you're still alive now. I won't tell you what will be done or how, but when you return to Earth, you will carry the full record of what was done here."

He thrust his right hand into a pocket, pulled out something, and tossed it onto the bed next to Nash. "Here. It may still be useful to you, but let me know if you need better photographic equipment."

Nash prowled the bedsheet with his left hand until he found the object with his fingers; he didn't need to lift it to the light to recognize it. It was his wristwatch, with its built-in miniaturized camera.

"So what are you going to do, Commander?" he asked.

"I won't tell you now," L'Enfant replied. "I don't want you to ruin things for everyone else." He stepped back from the bed. "I trust Dr. Isralilova paid good attention to your injuries, so you should be able to walk again by tomorrow morning."

He turned and began walking toward the hatch. "Be in the monitor center, Module Eight, by oh-eight-hundred tomorrow. You'll see the beginning of the operation." He stopped and hesitated for a moment. "For future reference, its official code name is Kentucky Derby. Someone in the Pentagon has a good sense of irony, don't you think?"

L'Enfant opened the hatch; caught for a moment in the shaft of light from the access corridor, he turned and looked back at the man in the bed. "Good night, Mr. Nash," he said. "Sleep well."

Then he exited the module, shutting the hatch behind him.

Are we safe?

Miho Sasaki wrote the three words on a slip of paper and passed it to Tamara Isralilova.

They were alone in Module Five, lying in bed on opposite sides of the bunkhouse. The overhead lights were switched off, but the sullen amber glow of Deimos shined through the slot windows at the far side of the module. Each woman had a penlight hidden beneath her bedcovers, illuminating the scratchpads on which they furtively communicated.

As Isralilova reached out to accept the paper, they heard footsteps in the corridor. She snatched the note from Sasaki's fingertips and snapped off her light; Miho could hear the paper being crumpled into a wad as Tamara prepared to eat the message. Sasaki switched off her own penlight, and they lay still until they heard the footsteps pass their hatch, heading for the command module.

Marks, probably, since he was on watch right now. Or perhaps L'Enfant himself. Isralilova's penlight clicked on again; Sasaki watched as she uncurled the wadded paper, read her last question, and scrawled a reply on the opposite side. Miho's crotch itched from the small wads of paper she had already shoved down the front of her panties; when this conversation was concluded, she knew that she would have to eat a lot of paper.

Thinking of this, she pulled out one of the paper wads and thrust it into her mouth, chewing it into a pulp.

Tamara completed her note and passed it back to her. *Yes I think so,* it read in her badly spelled English, *but your new so who knows? Akers came in here ounce but I screamed loud until Swigart came to help me. Do same if he trys again.*

At first Miho didn't understand what she meant; then she hissed as she reread the note. Charlie Akers had attempted to rape Tamara; it was a blessing that one of the other Americans was a woman. But that answer wasn't to the question she had intended to ask.

Picking up her own pen, she wrote beneath Tamara's handscript: *Sorry it happened. Thanks for advice, but not what I mean. Are we safe tomorrow? All of us?* She underlined "tomorrow" to stress the point, then passed it back to Tamara.

While Isralilova read her note and formulated her reply on a fresh scrap of paper, Sasaki listened intently for the sound of the sentry in the corridor. She recalled nights like this in her teenage years, when her parents had sent her to an exclusive girls' boarding school outside Hiroshima. Lights-out in the dorms had been at nine o'clock, and although there were prefects who had prowled the halls in search of those who dared break the rules, it had never prevented her from carrying on similar written conversations with her roommate. This was not very different from those giggly nights, but she had no warm feeling of nostalgia. Back then, the subject of late-night notes in the dark had been boys and teachers and adolescent homesickness; tonight, it was the continuance of their lives.

Tamara finished writing and stretched out her hand; Miho plucked the new note from between her fingertips and unfolded the paper beneath her penlight. *No!! L. has something planned for after V.'s trip into tunnel. Dangeros. Has to do with secrets*

(?) in Mod. 1—think a new CAS in there, do not know details. A. and M. in their alot. Trouble!

Sasaki gnawed at her lower lip. Tamara knew little more than what Shin-ichi had already told her, except to confirm that Paul Verduin's sortie tomorrow morning was instrumental in L'Enfant's plans. She had the odd suspicion that Nash might have learned something new—despite the horrendous beating he had endured this afternoon, he had been separated from her for more than twelve hours now—but there was no way she could get to Module Nine, where Tamara had treated him.

She still had the keycard-decoder, though. She had continually switched its hiding place since Nash had been captured, but except for Marks's discovery of the bugs in her jumpsuit, no one had yet subjected her to a full-body search—although she now suspected that Akers would love to do so.

More importantly, she was coming to realize that L'Enfant's paranoia was his main weakness. Despite his seeming omniscience, the commander had developed a blindspot toward her, apparently dismissing Miho as a simple-minded accomplice to Nash's own schemes. Whether he had overlooked her previous role at Cydonia Base a couple of years earlier, distracted by his efforts to expose Nash, or simply believed that she didn't pose a significant threat to him, Miho didn't know know, or care—even if he'd insulted her by grossly underestimating her intelligence. L'Enfant's arrogance and ignorance were her sole advantages at this moment, and she needed to find a way to use them.

If she could only get to Module One and use her decoder to unlock the airlock hatch . . .

No. She had a higher priority, although it wasn't the one which JETRO had intended when they sent her back to Mars. She picked up her pen, hesitated, and wrote: *Most important! Destroy this at once! We leave tomorrow on the airship. B. will take you, me and others aboard after*

. . . . Again, footsteps in the corridor. Tamara immediately switched off her penlight. For an instant, Miho was tempted to ignore the risk and keep writing. Then the footsteps stopped right outside the hatch, and she quickly snapped off her own penlight and shoved it beneath her pillow.

She was barely able to wad the note into a tiny ball and shove it into her mouth before the hatch opened. Faking sleep, she squinted through her eyelids as a shaft of light came through the hatch. Her heart thudded against her eardrums as a jumpsuited figure stepped through the doorway. For a terrifying moment she thought that Charlie Akers was coming for her; she pulled her knees closer to her chest, curling into a protective fetal position. . . .

"Pardon me, ladies," Megan Swigart said as she came in. "Mind if I join you tonight?"

Feigning drowsiness, Miho sat up in her bunk, holding the dry wad of paper in her mouth. Across from her, she could see Tamara wincing in the sudden light, holding up her hand as if she, too, had been suddenly awakened from a deep sleep.

"Sorry to disturb you," Swigart said as she closed the hatch again. "The commander thought you might want a little company. That okay with you?"

In the renewed darkness, Miho heard the lieutenant walk through the module and settle down on one of the unmade bunks in the rear. If Swigart intended to sleep, she was going to do it fully dressed; Miho didn't hear the distinctive sound of clothes sliding to the floor. Indeed, Swigart didn't even take off her boots.

Miho tucked the wad of paper into her cheek with her tongue. "That is fine," she replied, pretending to be half-awake. "Good night."

Swigart didn't answer. Miho laid her head down on the pillow, masticating the note as quietly as she could. L'Enfant wasn't taking any chances; she and Tamara were to have their own personal sentry tonight, and their single line of communication had just been severed.

Tamara was right. The situation had become extraordinarily dangerous.

17. Breakout

It was much different than operating the spider. In virtual reality, death was only an abstraction, a cessation of function by the teleoperated machine at the other end of an electromagnetic channel. This time, though, the stakes were far higher; as Paul Verduin watched the canopy hatch being lowered into place by Marks, he was uncomfortably reminded of seeing a tomb being closed—from the inside.

"Cut it out," he whispered to himself. "You're not going to die."

Pardon me? Shin-ichi Kawakami's voice came through the comlink as a thin, static-filled crackle. *Did you just say something?*

Verduin let out his breath. "Negative," he replied. "Ready for power-up."

He reached up to the overhead console and toggled a series of recessed switches; there was a harsh whine from the rear engine compartment as the Jackalope's turbines engaged. Multicolored lights flashed across the consoles within the tiny cockpit, and on the secondary flatscreen between his knees, the main onboard computer scrolled a long sequence of status checks. He could hear Akers climbing off the hull; he hoped that the lieutenant didn't accidentally rip loose one of the external electrical conduits with his boot heels.

It had already been decided that he was going to ride down unpressurized; it would give an extra measure of integrity to the inner hull. Verduin switched his skinsuit's oxygen-nitrogen hoses to the cockpit's internal feed valves, then jacked the MRV's comlink into his suit's chest unit. "Can you hear me better?"

We copy. Kawakami's voice was much more clear now; the static had all but vanished. *You're coming through very well.*

Can you run through a major systems-check for us now, please, Paul? Tamara Isralilova's voice was clear enough for him to hear the strain in it. Verduin found himself regretting the fact that she was his other on-line controller for the mission. *TV and main sensors first, please.*

"All right." Verduin reached his left hand to the panel above the computer keyboard and stabbed a series of buttons. On the inside panel of the hatch, directly in front of him, the larger main flatscreen came to life; the image was blurred for a moment until the front-mounted TV camera autofocused, then he could clearly see Charlie Akers standing in front of the MRV; secondary images on the right side of the screen displayed his infrared ghost-image and the weakly fluctuating bar graph of his electromagnetic image. Verduin instinctively glanced through the small oval porthole on his left to make sure that Akers was standing there. "Do you see that?" he asked.

Yes. Fine. Isralilova sounded more businesslike now. *Switch around to your other cameras now, please.*

Verduin snapped the other buttons on the communications panel; the main flatscreen swiftly changed, sequentially moving around in a 360-degree arc as the smaller TV cameras arrayed on the MRV's fuselage kicked in: starboard, the parked rover and the distant pyramids of the City; aft, the desert, with the camera filters automatically screening the glare of the morning sun; port, the vast red slope of the D&M Pyramid, with the wrench tripod poised above the pit leading down into Mama's Back Door.

"It all looks good," he said as he returned the image to the front camera. "I'm going to test the ECM now. Hold on."

He moved his left hand down to the keyboard and, mouthing the digits under his breath, tapped the appropriate code numbers into the onboard computer. One special modification had been made to the MRV before it had left Japan: an electronic countermeasures system, similar to those used by jet fighter-bombers to foil enemy radar, had been installed in the Jackalope. Since the pseudo-Cooties were, indeed, miniature robots, then it was possible that an ECM system might scramble their AI systems. The Jackalope's ECM was designed to lock onto the electromagnetic frequencies they used and jam them, rendering the pseudo-Cooties blind and confused, or even shutting them down completely.

At least that was the general theory. If it worked, it would provide an effective shield against the aliens. There was only one drawback: it had never been tested on a pseudo-Cootie. Computer analysis said it would perform adequately—but the computers had never faced a swarm of semi-intelligent machines in an underground tunnel.

The comlink screamed with static and the main viewscreen dissolved into irregular lines until the computer dampered out the jamming signals. When the screen readjusted itself, Verduin saw Akers stagger backward slightly, apparently disoriented by what was coming through his helmet. Verduin laughed out loud; it was an unexpected pleasure to see one of L'Enfant's men so thoroughly nonplussed. "Try that for size, tough guy," he murmured.

The ECM seems to work fine, Paul. Kawakami's voice was harsh with static, but Paul could still detect some guarded humor in his tone. He reminded himself that L'Enfant himself was probably in the monitor center; if so, he was most likely not amused. *Shut it down now, please.*

Verduin reluctantly switched off the ECM. On the screen, he could see Akers recovering his composure. The assault rifle he habitually wore during EVA had slipped down its strap off his shoulder; he tugged it back into place while silently glaring at the MRV. Paul didn't like the expression on Akers's face. "Give my apologies to the lieutenant," he said formally.

All right, Tamara said. *Try to walk now.*

This was going to be the hardest part. He had done well in practice sessions on a simulation program loaded into the base computer, but that had been like playing a sophisticated computer game. Actually piloting the Jackalope would be another matter entirely. Verduin carefully slipped his booted feet into the stirrups of the foot pedals beneath the secondary viewscreen, then reached up and activated the mobility controls. There was a slight shift as the internal gyros stabilized the Jackalope's balance. Paul took a minute to grasp the joystick on his right and shift it around; he watched as the waldo manipulator on the MRV's front end appeared on the bottom of the screen, gliding back and forth like a snake.

"The waldo works well," he said. "Okay, I'm going to walk now . . . or try to, at least."

He took a deep breath, then grasped the throttle bar with his left hand, shoved it forward slightly, then lifted his right foot and set it down again. The screen tilted slightly to the right; simultaneously there was a slight jar as the massive vehicle took a step forward. Lights raced across the secondary screen, but no warning signals flashed.

Verduin let out his breath, then raised his left foot and set it down. The MRV stepped forward again, the machine trembling as the footpad found the rocky ground; the gyros kept it upright, and Verduin tried again with his right foot. The Jackalope took another big step forward; on the screen, he saw Akers cautiously backing away from the advancing machine.

"This is great." Paul grinned through his anxiety. "I feel like Baby Godzilla."

You're doing very well, Kawakami said. *Practice for a while before we . . .*

There was a muffled pause, an unintelligible background conversation, then his voice returned. *We are advised that you should take it to the winch for lowering. Are you confident enough to do this now?*

Verduin lost his grin. L'Enfant. He had to be in the monitor center, calling the shots. Paul was silent for a few moments as he considered the options. He could justifiably claim that he needed more time for practice; the Jackalope was still unwieldy, his own movements uncoordinated. He could certainly use more time in this juggernaut before he took it down into the catacombs; under normal, sane circumstances, he would have been allowed a couple of days—even another fifteen minutes—for rehearsal.

However, the present circumstances were neither normal nor sane. A dust storm was whipping out of the western plains; in another twenty-four to thirty-six hours, this area would be lashed by hurricane-force winds which could drive dust at bulletlike velocity through the MRV's hull, shredding its fine internal circuitry. Even though the machine could be covered by tarps, there was no guarantee that it would survive the onslaught.

But nature wasn't his worst enemy. The co-pilot of the *Akron*—he had to remember that his name real wasn't Donaldson, but Nash—had turned out to be a spy. Only yesterday L'Enfant had turned Akers and Marks loose on him, and according to Tamara they had nearly killed the man.

L'Enfant seemed to have something in mind; he was getting desperate, and that desperation was making him relentless and reckless. Would another person be dragged into the storeroom if Verduin refused to go forth? Paul doubted that he himself would be tortured—L'Enfant needed him to pilot the MRV—but what about the others? Shin-ichi? He could never survive the ordeal

Nash had been through. Boggs? They might spare him because they needed him to fly the *Akron* . . . but what about Tamara, or Miho?

Verduin shook his head. No, he couldn't let that happen.

And, he had to admit to himself, he *did* want to discover what was down there . . . and there was no better chance than now to find out. He had the MRV, he had the skill, and he had been in Mama's Back Door before, albeit in a remote sense. If he could make it into the catacombs, discover the secrets of the aliens . . .

"I'm ready," he said.

There was a short pause on the comlink before Isralilova returned to him. *All right, Paul. We concur.* Her voice held a nervous quaver. *Ah . . . can you please switch on your internal video? For the . . .*

She didn't finish her comment, but Verduin knew what she meant to say. "For the record"—in case he didn't come back. He stabbed another button on the communications board, then looked straight up at the little TV lens directly above his head. He grinned and waggled his fingers at the camera, hoping that it made her feel better.

As he did so, though, a dark thought involuntarily crossed his mind: they'll remember me like this. . . .

There was a long silence inside the cramped monitor center when everyone saw Verduin waving at the camera. Kawakami stoically gazed at the screen. Isralilova switched off her mike and looked away from her console and everyone else, a quiet sob escaping from her mouth before she covered it with her hand. Boggs pursed his lips together in a rare frown and pretended to study the toes of his boots. Next to him, Sasaki's face remained stolid, her back stiffly erect, but her hands were nervously curled into tight fists at her side. Boggs hesitated, then comfortingly placed his hand on her shoulder; Miho flinched at his touch, but didn't move away.

From his position behind Kawakami's chair, Nash noticed all this, but kept his attention focused primarily on Terrance L'Enfant. The commander, perched on a metal stool behind and between Isralilova and Kawakami, seemed unmoved by Verduin's gesture. Implacably silent, his narrow gaze darted from screen to screen, intent on every detail, as he absently stroked his mustache between his fingers. Nash observed that there were dark circles under his eyes; it didn't look as if the commander had slept well, if at all. At the far end of the module Marks stood like a sentry next to the closed hatch, his eyes never straying far from Nash.

On another TV monitor the POV from the Jackalope's forward camera showed the vehicle slowly lumbering closer to the pit. The big machine, as cumbersome as it looked, seemed remarkably well-suited for the Martian terrain; after a moment of hesitation, Verduin stepped over a boulder which a rover would have been forced to drive around. In the background, they could see Akers hop-skipping toward the tripod-and-wrench arrangement above the pit.

L'Enfant touched the lobe of his headset mike. "Make certain the grapples are well-secured so that they won't slip off, Lieutenant, and give him plenty of slack on the cable once he's down." His voice held an unaccustomed rasp. "We're going to need to be able to get him out of there in a hurry if we have to."

There was a firm double-knock on the hatch; Marks opened it to let Swigart inside. She quickly walked to L'Enfant, wordlessly handed him a folded sheet of computer printout, then turned and strode back out of the monitor center, returning to her post in the command module. L'Enfant unfolded the sheet and studied it for a few moments, rubbing at his eyelids, then handed it over his shoulder to Boggs, scarcely glancing in his direction.

"Current nowcast says that the dust storm is at fifty-two degrees west," he said by way of explanation. "The leading edge has just crossed into the Acidalia Planitia and it's expected to pick up speed as it moves across the hemisphere."

Boggs grunted as he skimmed the nowcast. "The new ETA is at twelve-hundred hours tomorrow. Shit." He crumpled the paper in his fist and looked at Nash. "Change of plan. If we're going to beat the sucker, we're going to have to be out of here by at least oh-dark-one-hundred tomorrow. Maybe sooner."

Nash looked back at the airship pilot, then slowly shook his head. Despite the repairs made by the clinical nanosurgeons to his bruises, he still ached from the beating he'd been given. He edged closer to L'Enfant; seeing this, Marks's hand moved toward his rifle as Nash bent over the commander.

"Call it off," he murmured to L'Enfant, ignoring Marks entirely. "Whatever you're planning, it's not going to work before that storm hits us."

L'Enfant didn't look away from the consoles. "Since you

don't know what I'm planning, seaman, how can you be so certain?"

On the screens, Akers had climbed onto the MRV's fuselage and was attaching the winch's cable-grapples to rungs on either side of the cab. The Jackalope was poised at the edge of the pit, the forward camera peering down into its shadowed, rocky maw. "The only thing I'm certain of," Nash said softly, "is that you're about to throw away this man's life. You can wait until . . ."

"Mr Nash, you are way out of line." L'Enfant still didn't look at him, but his voice gained a terse edge. "If you believe I will sacrifice months of preparation because you think . . ."

"No!" Kawakami snapped. The exobiologist swiveled around in his chair, his normally placid eyes seething with anger as he stared straight at L'Enfant. "He is correct. Paul is unprepared for this mission. He barely knows how to handle the MRV. We will stop the sortie now, or I'll . . ."

"You shall not *tell me what to do!"* L'Enfant shouted.

Everyone in the monitor center was staring at him him now, but L'Enfant's abrupt rage was focused directly upon Kawakami. "I have listened to you long enough," he continued, his voice now ragged and harsh as he thrust a finger at Kawakami, "and I've let you drag this mission into the ground! Now *I'm* in charge, and *you* will follow my instructions!"

Kawakami remained unswerved. He looked over his shoulder at Isralilova. "Prepare to shut everything down, Tamara," he said firmly. "Discontinue onboard telemetry with the MRV and . . ."

"Sergeant!" L'Enfant snapped.

There was the soft metallic *cha-chik* of a rifle being cocked. "Do what the commander says," Marks said quietly.

Everyone except L'Enfant looked toward the sergeant. Marks held his Steyr halfway to his shoulder, his right forefinger within the trigger guard. Nash raised his hands slightly, keeping them in plain slight; Kawakami followed suit, and Isralilova's hands froze above her console.

"Holy fucking Moses," Boggs said.

"Shut up, Mr. Boggs." L'Enfant touched the lobe of his headset. "Queen, report to the castle on the double. Come hot. King's knight, stand by."

He half-turned to gaze at Nash. "You're beginning to be more trouble than you're worth, seaman. I don't like troublemakers."

"Thanks for the compliment," Nash replied dryly. If it was L'Enfant's idea to suddenly assign chess-derived code names to his squad members—an absurd gesture, considering that everyone knew where everyone else was located—then his paranoia had undoubtedly reached critical mass. One look at L'Enfant's reddened face, his hyperalert eyes, and Nash could tell that the man's mental condition was deteriorating.

He cast a glance toward Sasaki. Her eyes briefly met his and she nodded ever so slightly; she had picked up the same clues. L'Enfant was on the verge of losing control. Although Nash couldn't count on her assistance, a dangerous gambit was taking form in his mind. If he could just give L'Enfant a little push in the right direction . . .

He cocked his head toward Marks. "You know, Commander, having him open fire in here would be a serious mistake. Even if he doesn't miss and cause a blowout, he might get the wrong person. You yourself, for instance."

"Like I really mind," Boggs murmured. Sasaki shushed him.

A hint of a smile appeared on L'Enfant's face. "First, the sergeant's rifle is loaded with safety bullets, same as the rounds in your own gun," he said calmly. "Second, Alphonse is an expert marksman. You should know that he was once a Marine Corps combat instructor."

"Which means you're living on borrowed time, pal," Marks said from behind the stock of his rifle. *"Comprende?"*

Nash started to say something, but Sasaki suddenly cleared her throat. "All I know, Commander L'Enfant," she said, "is that . . ."

She hesitated, her lips trembling. L'Enfant turned around in his chair, locking eyes with her. "Yes, Dr. Sasaki?" he said softly. "You were saying?"

"I know that . . . you're the sickest motherfucker I have ever met," she said with slow, carefully pronounced deliberation.

She swallowed, then added, "And it's a wonder you can walk and chew gum at the same time."

L'Enfant's face turned dark red as he gaped at her. Despite the fact that they were being held at gunpoint, everyone else stared in absolute shock at the astrophysicist. Kawakami's mouth sagged open like a father who had just heard his daughter graphically describe the loss of her virginity.

"Goddamn, Miho," Boggs breathed. "Who taught you to talk like that?"

Turning dismissively away from L'Enfant, Sasaki smiled sweetly at Boggs. "You did," she replied. Her face became mock-serious. "Did I get it right?"

"Uh . . . yeah. Sure. Especially the sick motherfucker part."

There was another double knock on the hatch, and Swigart stepped through the doorway holding her own rifle at the ready. "Is there a problem, Commander?"

L'Enfant licked his lips and slowly nodded his head without looking toward her; his gaze shifted to Nash. "Yes, Megan, there is," he said. "Mr. Nash is responsible for a loss of proper morale. Please remove him. The storeroom will be fine for the time being."

He reconsidered for a second. "On second thought, Dr. Sasaki seems equally to blame for the disturbance. Since she's nonessential personnel, please secure her in Module Five. Stand guard in the corridor to make sure that neither of them leaves without my permission."

Swigart pointed her rifle toward Nash and Sasaki and jerked her head toward the hatch. As they eased past L'Enfant, the commander took a long, deep breath, then returned his attention to Kawakami. "Now, sir, you will continue with the mission with no further protest. If you refuse me again, I will instruct Lieutenant Swigart to escort Dr. Sasaki to the airlock for rapid decompression. Is this clearly understood?"

Kawakami said nothing for a few seconds . . . then he haltingly nodded his head and, after a final glance at Miho, turned his chair back around to his console. Isralilova reluctantly went back to her own work; Boggs remained stock-still, daunted by the bore of Marks's assault rifle.

As Nash was stepping through the hatch, following Miho and with Swigart's rifle barrel almost jabbing him in the back, he heard L'Enfant address him one more time. "You've been stupid twice since you've been here, Mr. Nash," L'Enfant said. "As the old saying goes, three times is enemy action. Don't push your luck."

Nash didn't look back or make a response. He simply let Swigart goad him out into the corridor.

Module Five, the females-only bunkhouse which Sasaki was sharing with Isralilova, was located at the other end of the access corridor from the monitor center; Module Three, the storeroom, was directly adjacent to it. Once the three of them were out in the corridor, Swigart wordlessly motioned Nash and Sasaki to walk in front of her; she let a quick thrust of her rifle barrel do the talking for her.

As they marched down the corridor, Nash heard the hatch of Module Eight slam firmly shut. Good; they were alone in the corridor now. Even without Sasaki's timely interruption, this was exactly what he wanted. Everyone else was either in the monitor center or out on the surface, and the main tunnel was reasonably soundproof.

He hastily calculated his chances of getting the drop on Swigart once Sasaki was in Module Five. The odds didn't look good—Swigart was armed, alert, and undoubtedly trained in hand-to-hand combat—but since the only alternative was remaining at L'Enfant's mercy, he realized that this would probably be his only opportunity for a breakout. If he could somehow get Swigart to step just inside the storeroom with him, perhaps he could kick the hatch cover against her and . . .

"I'm not going in there," Miho said suddenly.

She came to an abrupt halt and, turning to Nash, grabbed his forearm. "No, I'm not going in there," she insisted, her eyes wide and frightened. "Paul needs me now. I can't let him . . ."

"Keep going!" Swigart snapped. She also stopped walking; standing a few feet behind them, her Steyr was leveled from her hip at Sasaki, but her eyes kept darting from Miho to Nash. "Down the hall! Move!"

"No!" Sasaki didn't even look at her; she grasped Nash's shoulders and shook him. "I'm a scientist! I'm supposed to be in the monitor center now! Paul's my friend, he needs me!"

Nash glanced at Swigart, then looked back into Sasaki's wild eyes. "Miho, you're not doing him or us any good," he whispered urgently. "If you fight them, they'll take you in there and give you the same treatment they gave me. C'mon, just go into your . . ."

"No!" All at once, Sasaki turned around and began striding purposefully back the way they had come. "I have to help Paul! He needs me to get out of there alive! I'm the only one who can—!"

Startled, Swigart raised her rifle slightly, but not to shoulder height, as she took a single step forward, "Ma'am," she ordered, "you will turn around and—"

"Get out of my way!" Sasaki unexpectedly grabbed the barrel of Swigart's rifle and angrily shoved it aside as if it were a toy.

Thrown off-balance, mentally and physically, by Sasaki's reckless move, Swigart turned her back on Nash as she moved to block the Japanese scientist from stalking past her.

Now!

Nash whipped around and kicked his right leg upward, slamming his foot straight into the woman's stomach just above her groin. Swigart didn't see it coming; she gasped and doubled over as the blow knocked her against the corridor wall. The rifle barrel dipped slightly. . . .

Ignoring the sharp pain in his battered gut, Nash leaped on Swigart while she was still helpless. He grabbed the rifle with both hands, wrenched it upwards, and pinioned Swigart against the wall with its stock. Swigart's face twisted in rage; with eyes squinted and teeth clenched, she clutched at her weapon, pushing it back against Nash.

Her left knee lashed upward toward Nash's groin, but he turned sideways and caught the blow on the side of his thigh. A good countermove, but it hurt like hell where her knee had connected, and the dodge left him off balance. Swigart captured the moment; with an animalistic snarl, she shoved him backwards with the rifle, causing Nash to fall against the opposite wall of the corridor.

His bruised muscles screamed in pain and his hands jerked free of the rifle. The lieutenant tore it from his grasp. He glimpsed the rifle barrel sweeping around to aim straight at his face, Swigart's finger darting within the trigger guard. . . .

Sasaki's right hand, her knuckles curled into the palm, hammered a ruthless karate chop to the side of Swigart's neck. The lieutenant staggered, her knees crumpling as the Steyr sagged in her hands. Nash surged forward and slammed a right hook into her jaw, then followed it with a vicious punch to her solar plexus. Sasaki added another blow to her neck for good measure; Swigart fell face-forward to the floor, her rifle clattering from her hands.

Nash glanced down the corridor. The hatch to Module Eight remained shut; no one had overheard the fight. Luck was finally on their side. He immediately knelt beside Swigart and gently laid his fingertips against the carotid artery under her right ear. He felt a slow pulse, telling him that she was unconscious but still alive. Good enough; he had no personal score to settle with Swigart, as he did with Marks and Akers.

He looked up at Sasaki. "Nice moves there, kid."

Miho was already scooping up the rifle. "Get her out of here," she whispered, wasting no time on comebacks. She checked the corridor again, then pointed toward Module Three. "In there. Hurry."

Nash grasped Swigart under the arms and hurriedly dragged her down the passageway to the storeroom. He felt sick at the sight of the dry bloodstains on the floor, but there was a certain poetic justice to be found: also on the floor were the same bungi cords that Marks and Akers had used to tie him up. Nash pulled Swigart's hands behind her back and knotted them together with the cord; he felt no remorse when Sasaki gagged the lieutenant with the ripped-up T-shirt Akers and Marks had used to bind their fists. Turnabout was fair play.

"Okay," Miho said as she stood up from her work. "We're out. What do we do now?" She looked in the general direction of the command module across the corridor from the storeroom. "If we go in there, we could try taking control of the base. Shut down the airlocks, take out the AI mains . . ."

"We could." Nash picked up the Steyr and checked the clip. Fully loaded. "But we could also get cornered that way. Besides, I first want to see what L'Enfant's got stashed in Module One. Then we figure out what's next. You still have the keycard decoder?"

Miho nodded; she unzipped her left thigh pocket and pulled out the small plastic case. Nash smiled. "Good deal," he said. "It'll take us a couple of minutes, but we need to see what their ace is. Still with me?"

"No argument," she replied. Nash stepped over Swigart's inert body and started toward the hatch, but she placed a hand on his chest to stop him. "But I wasn't kidding about Paul," she added. "After we're finished in the garage, we stop them from harming Paul Verduin. Do you understand me?"

Nash remembered the enormous armored hulk of the Jackalope; the MRV looked as if it could take every round from the assault rifle he now held and keep coming. "If you ask me, I think Paul's the least of our worries right now."

Sasaki shook her head. "No, he's not," she said gravely. "Not even Commander L'Enfant is the most of our problems." Before he could ask what she meant, she turned toward the hatch. "Quickly now. We have no time."

18. Mama's Back Door

There was no need to switch on the infrared lamps to avoid detection; the pseudo-Cooties were aware of his presence almost the moment the MRV's legs touched the floor of the tunnel.

Bar graphs on the cockpit's secondary flatscreen arched upwards. "Strong EMA pattern approaching from the northeast," Verduin said. He switched on the floodlights; on his main screen the tunnel ahead of him was suddenly awash in their white glare, lending a pinkish hue to the smooth-bored walls. "I anticipate their arrival in only a few moments."

We copy, Kawakami's voice said in his earphones. *Is the ECM still operational?*

"Yes, Shin-ichi," he sighed, "it is quite functional, thank you." It was only the third time that Kawakami had inquired about the Jackalope's electronic countermeasures. Verduin had switched on the system before the Jackalope had been lowered into the pit, but Kawakami was still worried that it might have been damaged in one of the many slight collisions the Jackalope had suffered with the shaft walls during the descent. "Have Lieutenant Akers give me a little more slack on the cable, please."

There was a long pause; then Verduin saw the loop of winchcable slide a little further down the side of the starboard porthole. The cable was still attached to the top of the MRV; when his exploration was finished, Verduin would return to the bottom of the shaft and Akers would haul the Jackalope back up to the surface. Until then, the MRV would drag the cable behind it as an umbilical cord. He hoped that the cable wouldn't get tangled with one of the machine's legs.

"All right," he said, "I'm beginning my reconnaissance."

Gently pushing down the throttle bar, Verduin pressed his foot down on the right pedal, then followed it with pressure on the left pedal.

One ungainly step at a time, the semirobotic vehicle stamped forward into Mama's Back Door. He heard a harsh scrape across the top of the canopy and glanced through the portholes; the tunnel ceiling was precariously close, but he wasn't in any immediate danger. Besides, there was nothing he could do about it now except pray that the tunnel didn't narrow very much more before he entered the catacombs.

Your telemetry remains nominal, Tamara said, *but we have just lost the image from one of your cameras. Are you having problems?*

"Oh, it's a tight squeeze," Verduin replied, "but I think I'll make it." The scraping must have been one of the TV cameras being sheared away. "Don't worry. I have more where that came from."

He was fifty yards down the tunnel now, and it was still empty. He was struck again by how much it resembled a wormhole . . . or perhaps it had once been an underground river channel? He was about to comment to that effect when he glanced again at the secondary screen and sucked in his breath. The EMA surge had almost filled the graphic display; he switched to radar and immediately saw a blur of white dots inching down from the top of the screen.

"Here they come," he murmured.

One moment, the tunnel in front of him was vacant. An instant later, it was filled with a solid, scuttling wave of pseudo-Cooties. Rank upon rank of huge metallic insects, sweeping toward him like a column of driver ants, clambering over each other, their antennae and sharp pincers flashing in the harsh floodlights . . .

Heading straight for him.

Until now, Paul had been surprised at his own calm; he had been anticipating this moment for so long, he had almost forgotten the deadly peril he faced. Now his feet froze on the pedals as his pulse hammered in his ears and his mouth gaped open. Once again, his mind flashed to those who had died down here, their armored suits ripped apart by these same creatures. He heard Shin-ichi and Tamara both shouting through his headset, but his tongue was a numb muscle in his dry mouth. His hands instinctively jerked up . . .

And then, quite suddenly, the pseudo-Cooties stopped.

It was as if they had run straight into an invisible barrier only five feet in front of the MRV. The ones at the head of the column halted dead in their tracks, as if paralyzed; the ones in the rear comically piled into the leaders, then backtracked a little. As far as the floodlight beams could reach, there was a solid carpet of the metallic-red creatures, twitching and moiling as if they were a single organism. . . .

But they didn't come any closer then the five-foot line.

Paul! Kawakami was shouting. *Paul, are you all right? Do you copy?*

Verduin slowly lowered his hands. He took a deep breath and let it out, feeling his heart thudding against his chest. "I hear you, Shin-ichi, ah . . ."

He licked his dry lips and smiled despite himself. "The ECM works: The Cooties have stopped their charge."

He heard cheers and shouting through his headphone, loud enough to make him tone down the volume. "I'm going to see if this takes complete effect," he said. "Two steps forward . . ."

Verduin pushed down on the foot pedal, and the Jackalope took a tentative step forward. The pseudo-Cooties in the front of the column retreated a few feet, inching backward until they collided with their brethren just behind them. All the way to the rear echelons he could see the little robots scuttling backward. He took another step forward; the pseudo-Cooties seemed to be in gradual retreat, pulling back to keep away from the Jackalope.

"They seem confused," he observed. "They're still functional, and I think they're still communicating with one another, but they obviously don't like the jamming." Paul shook his head. "I'm not sure I understand why. Since they're not organic creatures, I can't imagine how they could feel pain, so it must botch their internal homing systems to some degree so that they can't . . ."

Don't look a gift in the horse's mouth, Kawakami scolded, and Verduin almost laughed. An avid fan of American slang, Shin-ichi must be thoroughly rattled to curdle a cliché like that. *We can analyze it later. For the time being, continue going forward. Make it slow enough to give them time to retreat, but keep going forward.* There was a pause, then he added, *Be careful, please.*

"Never charge blindly into a gift horse's mouth," Verduin replied, snickering slightly. If Kawakami had a retort in mind, he kept it to himself. "All right, I'm going again."

He carefully took two more steps forward; it felt as if he was pushing the invisible curtain in front of him, steadily forcing the pseudo-Cooties back down the tunnel as he advanced. Verduin heard more scraping from above as the top of the MRV's canopy scraped against the rock ceiling, but he chose to ignore it. The cab was unpressurized, so he didn't have to risk a blowout if the hull was punctured.

Three more steps forward. The pseudo-Cooties continued to fall back, practically fighting each other to stay out of his path. Verduin remembered a vintage, pre–Green Revolution TV commercial he had once seen, of cartoon bugs fleeing in screaming panic from the spray of an American household insecticide; if he had known it would be like this, he would have painted over the jackalope on the MRV's fuselage and replaced it with a can of Raid. *It's too easy,* he thought as he continued to march forward.

He was a hundred yards down the tunnel now. By his own reckoning, Verduin estimated that he was directly beneath the D&M Pyramid. Akers was continuing to feed him slack from the cable; no indication of tangling with the MRV's legs. So far, so good. Watching the main screen, it now seemed to him as if the rear echelons were in full rout; they had turned and were scurrying back the way they had come.

Just within range of the floodlights, though, he could see that the tunnel made a sharp 45-degree turn to the left; nothing could be seen beyond that point. This was a feature that had not been detected by any other robotic sorties into Mama's Back Door— but then again, no man or man-made mechanism had ventured so far into the alien lair.

"Approaching a bend in the tunnel," Verduin said. "Might be the start of the catacombs." He glanced down at the secondary screen. Damn, the radar didn't penetrate the bend; it was too sharp to get a return signal. "Radar doesn't give us anything, but . . ."

Verduin looked up at the main screen again and was stunned to see that the pseudo-Cooties were now in full retreat. Even the front ranks had done an about-face and were streaming up the tunnel, racing away from the Jackalope as fast as they had come. He felt a chill race down his back and shuddered within his suit.

"Looks like our little friends have given up," he said.

We see that, Kawakami said. *Do you have an EMA signature beyond that point?*

Verduin switched back to the original display on the secondary screen; it showed the same bar graph he had seen when the pseudo-Cooties had first arrived, although he noted that it seemed to be fluctuating more strongly now. "Strong trace," he said, "but it's probably my reception committee on their way home."

The tunnel was almost deserted now. The ceiling remained high enough for the MRV to walk under; Verduin's way ahead was now unhindered. He heard a soft rasp through his headphones—a hand covering the mike?—then Kawakami's voice returned. *Recommend that you proceed with caution,* he said almost formally. *Repeat, with extreme caution.*

Verduin frowned as he heard the emphasis in Kawakami's warning; again he wondered what was occurring in Module Eight. There had been some sort of argument in the monitor center just before he was lowered into the pit, but he had been unable to tell what was happening. Was L'Enfant forcing a decision of some sort? For the first time, he also realized that he hadn't heard a word from Miho Sasaki; she had been in the module when he'd first signed on, and it wasn't like her to remain mute. . . .

No. He couldn't worry about that now. After almost three years of studying the pseudo-Cooties, they were close to getting a definitive answer to so many unsolved mysteries. His suit felt close and binding; sweat trickled down from his armpits. Verduin took a sip of cool water from the straw inside his helmet. "All right, Shin-ichi," he replied. "With extreme caution."

He pushed down on the throttle again and walked the Jackalope down the tunnel. The searchlight danced across the grooves and shallow hollows of the walls; he could feel the tremble of the MRV's motors behind his seat. Abruptly, he imagined a crowd of black-tie dignitaries in Stockholm rising to their feet in a standing ovation as he walked to the podium to accept his Nobel medallion. . . .

He forced the notion from his mind. Do the dirty work first, he told himself. There will be plenty of time later to write your acceptance speech.

The Jackalope arrived at the bend. Grasping the joystick in his right hand, he vectored it to the left, gradually shifting the

yaw of the footpads to make the turn. The searchlights flowed
across the rock, turning with the MRV as they reached into the
abyss. Closer, closer . . .

Then the searchlight beams landed on a huge dark form in the
tunnel.

For a moment, Verduin irrationally thought that the tunnel
had caved in; the shape filled the passageway, blocking it completely as a near-solid mass.

Then it surged forward, and in the brief instant in which he
realized that the shape was humanoid, an almost absurdly long
arm lashed upward. He caught a glimpse of an enormous four-
fingered claw.

He shouted in fear as he grabbed for the waldo joystick, but
he barely managed to raise the manipulator before the claw
slammed into the canopy of the Jackalope, ripping through the
fuselage as if it were paper. . . .

One instant, they saw Verduin on the TV monitor, frantically
grabbing for support inside the Jackalope's cockpit as an immense claw—vaguely glimpsed for a half-second on another
screen as belonging to some dark and amorphous form—
gouged through the canopy of the MRV. They heard a
scream. . . .

Then, in the next instant, the screens flickered and went
blank.

"Paul, come in!" Kawakami shouted, hunching forward in
his chair to stare at the dead TV screens. "Do you copy? Paul,
do you hear me? *Paul!*"

In the adjacent seat, Isralilova's hands flew across her console as she sought to establish contact with the MRV. "Complete loss of telemetry!" she snapped, her face ashen as she ran
across all the possible frequencies. "Comlink severed at the
source! Zero modulation, no source-EM! I'm not receiving a
carrier signal!"

Kawakami spun around to face L'Enfant. "Have Akers winch
him out of there *now*! There may still be a chance for him!"

For a moment, it seemed as if L'Enfant might refuse. Then he
tapped the lobe of his headset. "King to king's knight," he said
with almost absurd calm. "We've encountered hostile activity
in Mama's Back Door. Pull him out of there, Charlie, right
now."

He listened for a moment, then nodded and looked back at

Kawakami. "The lieutenant has re-engaged the winch. He reports getting some tug on the cable, so your boy is probably still attached to the other end." He looked away from the Japanese exobiologist and added, "I can't guarantee what condition he'll be in, however."

Kawakami's hands clenched into trembling fists. "I told you not to let him go through with this," he hissed, barely able to suppress his rage. "The danger was only too apparent, but instead you—"

"Shin-ichi!" Tamara suddenly shouted. "Look there!"

Kawakami's eyes darted back to her. The Russian scientist was pointing at a computer flatscreen above her console; a red line had spiked sharply upward, tracing a rising curve on the screen. A telltale electromagnetic signature, indicative of pseudo-Cootie activity.

He stared at the screen. "I thought you said we had a complete loss of telemetry," he murmured.

Tamara looked back at him. "That's not from the MRV," she said softly. "That's from the sensor pod in C4-20 . . . *in the City!*"

Kawakami's mouth dropped open. It had been almost countless months since any alien activity had been registered in the Labyrinth. But there could be no mistake. It was a pseudo-Cootie trace—an incredibly strong one, more intense than any they had seen before.

"Something's coming out of the Labyrinth," Tamara said, "and it is very large."

One by one, a series of six digits appeared on the LCD of the small black case in Sasaki's hand. As the last number appeared, she hastily tapped the sequence into the keycard decoder's numeric pad. There was a soft buzz and a metallic *clunk* as tumblers within the hatch slid back; Miho slipped the decoder's plastic tongue out of the keycard slot, folded it back into the unit, and tucked it in her breast pocket.

"Okay, we're in," she whispered.

Nash took a final glance over his shoulder before he gripped the lockwheel and turned it counter-clockwise, tugging the hatch open. Recessed ceiling lights automatically flickered on as they hurried into the airlock chamber. He glanced up at the indicator panel and saw that Module One was unpressurized. "Suit up," he said as he laid the assault rifle on the floor and

shut the hatch behind them. "Make it quick. We can't count on
our luck holding out much longer."

Miho was already pulling open skinsuit lockers. "What
next?" she asked as she unzipped her jumpsuit and let it drop to
the floor around her ankles. "Take over the command module?"

Nash discarded his own jumpsuit; he heard her gasp as his
bruises were revealed, but paid no attention. "Truthfully? We
can't go back in there. That's for certain."

She stopped and stared at him. "But Paul—"

"I'm sorry, Miho, but Paul's on his own." He cocked his head
toward the closed hatch. "Even if we got control of the command module and fucked up things from that end, we'd be
trapped in there. Not only that, but L'Enfant can take the others
hostage. It's a no-win situation either way. And I don't think
Terry's going to be too happy about us punching around one of
his people." Nash shook his head. "It all leads back to the
same thing. We inevitably surrender, L'Enfant is still in charge, and
the next time we see this airlock, it's without the benefit of
this." He held up the rubbery mass of a skinsuit. "You understand?"

Sasaki hesitated, then reluctantly nodded. "All right. Then
what are we going to . . . ?"

"I'll let you know as soon as I come up with something." He
began to shimmy into the skinsuit. "Now hustle. We don't got
all day."

In fact, he did have a vague plan. If they could make their
way unobserved to the *Akron* and climb aboard without anyone
spotting them, he could lead Sasaki into the airship's envelope
and up to the unused observation blister in the upper fuselage.
He doubted that L'Enfant or his troops were aware of its
existence—at least, he hoped that was the case—so it was feasible that they could hide up there until Boggs lifted off again.

It was chancy, but the only possible alternative would be to
steal a rover and attempt to take it all the way back to Arsia Station. That, however, meant driving the vehicle over four thousand miles through a Martian dust storm, without maps or even
water. He had no illusions about their chances for survival
under those conditions. . . .

That, he considered as he sealed the front of his skinsuit and
reached for the helmet, or try to directly take on L'Enfant and
his men in a firefight. Nash glanced at the Steyr on the airlock
floor. Sure, he was armed now—but he was also outgunned

four-to-one, and in unfamiliar territory besides. This was L'Enfant's home turf; he and his team had been here for many months now, while Nash himself had only once walked through part of the area. Injured, running for his life in strange surroundings, trying to protect an unarmed non-com . . .

No, he thought. We'll make for the *Akron* . . . and if that fails, we'll have to take our chances with a rover.

Just before Nash tucked his right arm into the suit's sleeve, he glimpsed the Seiko on his wrist. As an afterthought he unbuckled it, held it in his left hand until he had pulled on the skinsuit, then cinched it around the outer right sleeve of the suit's overgarment. He still might need to take some pictures, although he was beginning to wonder if the film would ever make its way back to Washington.

Sasaki opened a service panel and disabled the airlock's electromagnetic scrubber—exit-decontamination would only waste precious time now—then started the decompression cycle as soon as they had sealed their skinsuits and switched to internal pressure. As the airlock voided its atmosphere, Nash picked up the rifle. The Steyr was fully loaded with thirty 5.56mm safety rounds. Under the circumstances, he could have wished for the rocket-propelled gyrojet bullets normally used by 1st Space special-ops infantry, but he recalled L'Enfant telling him how safety shells were used by his men inside the base. All right; so long as he didn't have to open fire on anyone in the first place, it hardly mattered. All he wanted to do was get him and Miho out of there in one piece. . . .

And what about L'Enfant? Didn't he have a score to settle with him?

No. His score with L'Enfant could wait until later. Screw the assignment. Right now, basic survival was his only consideration.

A green light flashed above the hatch, signaling that decompression was complete. Deliberately staying off the comlink—the frequencies could be scanned and eavesdropped—he raised a gloved forefinger to his faceplate, signaling Sasaki to remain silent. She nodded her head; then he undogged the exit hatch and kicked it open, raising the gun in case someone was waiting for them on the other side of the airlock.

Module One was vacant; no one had come in through the garage doors to surprise them. He carefully looked both ways, sweeping the unpressurized compartment with the barrel of the gun, before leading Sasaki into the module. A rover was parked in front of the open double doors, but that wasn't what immediately caught his eye.

Propped against the far right wall was a CAS. However, the aircraft-gray exoskeleton was of an entirely different design from either the Hoplite-style combat armor commonly used by the U.S. or Russians; this suit had triple-paned tinted windows in the front and sides, allowing the wearer to see directly out of the suit without having to use either VR systems or a periscope. It was also heavier than a Hoplite; the rear section bulged outward in a way that seemed more than necessary to house the usual internal fuel cells and open-loop life-support systems. Nash also noticed that the suit's left arm contained a built-in machine gun.

It was a radically different design than previous combat armor. Except for the gun, it looked as if it had been custom-built, intended more for reconnaissance than for combat. But why the difference?

Remembering his spy-watch, Nash raised his right arm to his chest, pointed the face toward the CAS, and clumsily pressed a forefinger against the tiny shutter-button, snapping a picture for posterity. His curiosity aroused, he then started forward for a closer look, but Sasaki suddenly grabbed his free arm. He looked back at her and saw that she was pointing to a workbench on the left side of the garage.

Abandoning the CAS for the moment, Nash stepped past Sasaki and walked around the parked rover toward the bench. A couple of small, foam-padded aluminum equipment cases lay open beneath the bench. It appeared as if unassembled parts of something had been packed inside the cases; the padding was cut to precise measurements. He guessed that the cases had been in the cargo pod which had been parachuted from orbit just previous to their arrival at Cydonia Base.

The object on the bench itself was both indistinct and yet annoyingly familiar: a long, slender metal tube, painted neutral gray, approximately the length and diameter of a baseball bat, but with a large handgrip on its midsection. At one end of the tube was a large, irregularly shaped sphere, about the size of a basketball. The sphere was sealed, but he noticed an open service panel on the tube just in front of the handle; the panel exposed a miniature bay, enclosing a recessed keypad and an

LCD. The whole assembly was clamped into a cradle on the bench; the number of tools spread around the object showed that it was still being worked upon.

Nash walked closer, then stopped. Printed on the sphere was an all-too-familiar red hexagon: the international symbol for hazardous radiation.

Seeing that, everything suddenly meshed together. Nash realized exactly what he was looking upon. He numbly raised the Seiko and snapped another picture.

"Goddamn," he breathed. "They've got a nuke."

The winch was dragging something up from the pit; whatever it was, it was threatening to rip the machine apart.

Even through the sparse atmosphere, Charlie Akers could hear the high, coarse whine of the winch motor as it struggled to raise the MRV from the pit. He kept the operating lever in reverse, gritting his teeth as he mashed it down with both hands. The spool turned slowly as the cable was reeled in, a few precious meters at a time. His back turned to the pit itself, Akers kept his eyes fixed on the cable, alert for signs of fray and praying that it didn't snap; if it did break, it could possibly whiplash and hit him, perhaps fracturing his helmet. That would be a stupid finale to a promising military career.

The fate of Paul Verduin was the least of his concerns. Akers had overheard the exchange from the distant monitor center through the comlink, and he had already surmised that the Dutchman was toast. But the commander had ordered the MRV retrieved, and since it was undeniably still attached to the umbilical cable—whatever was left of it, that is—Akers had no choice but to reel it home.

Fine, he thought as he fought to keep the lever pinned down. Bring the sucker back up. Then we'll go ahead with Kentucky Derby and get rid of the little shits once and for all. Like, y'know, the only good Cootie is a dead Cootie. . . .

The spool started to turn faster now; the winch's whining took on a slightly higher pitch. It looked as if he was reaching to the end of the line. As the last few yards of cable appeared, Akers noticed that it looked shredded and torn, almost as if something had been chewing on it.

"Jesus H. Christ," he whispered under his breath. "What happened down there?"

He barely had time to reflect upon this disconcerting observation, though, before the cable halted. Okay, it was up. Akers yanked the winch back into neutral, banged the lock-lever into place, then turned toward the pit. Okay, time for the messy part of this. . . .

He stopped dead, staring at the abomination which hung beneath the tripod.

He recognized the battered upper fuselage of the MRV only because of the little cartoon Jackalope painted on the side; everything else, from the legs on down, was completely ripped away. There was no sign of the man who had been in the cockpit except for a wide streak of blood beneath one of the shattered canopy portholes, but hanging beneath the fuselage was . . .

"Oh my God," Akers muttered.

The huge shape—reddish-black, humanlike yet seemingly mechanical—let go of the wreckage and, with terrifying agility, threw itself forward. It landed, hunched forward, on the edge of the crevasse, its dagger-shaped claws sinking into the rocky red soil for anchorage. For a second it looked as if it might lose its balance and fall backward into the pit.

Then its splayed feet found purchase on the ground and it hauled itself away from the shaft. The giant stood erect on its massive, double-jointed legs; as its monstrous claws tore out of the ground and its long, almost simian arms stretched upward, a cyclopean red eye beneath the cowl of its neckless head swung toward Akers . . .

And locked on.

It was nine feet tall, and it looked like a demon straight from hell.

For the single instant that the creature stopped, Akers managed to shake off his paralysis. As he dove for the Steyr he'd left propped against a boulder, he yelled into his headset: "King's knight to king! Mayday, Mayday! Bogey at the D&M—!"

With horrifying swiftness, the monster lurched toward him, its arms extended outward.

"I'm under attack—!" Akers howled as he grabbed the assault rifle. He crouched and brought the Steyr into an awkward firing position. "Jesus, get somebody down here, it's—!"

Then it was on top of him. Screaming with incoherent fear, Akers managed to squeeze off a few futile rounds before the behemoth, with one swift and violent swipe of a claw, decapitated him.

19. The Running of the Minotaurs

"When I get my hands on that son of a bitch, I'm going to rip out his . . ."

"Knock it off." Marks glanced up at the indicator above the airlock hatch. He had to repressurize Module One before they could go in there; otherwise, he wouldn't be able to climb into the CAS, since it was not designed to be used with a skinsuit. "You'll get your chance, okay? Just ease off and do your . . ."

"Ease off, my ass." Swigart was struggling into her skinsuit; once Marks was in the armor, she would have to depressurize the garage again. It was a time-consuming procedure; they were both in a rush and her anger was making her clumsy. Marks had to watch her carefully to make sure she didn't miss any steps in the suitup procedure. "And if I see that slant-eyed cunt, I'm going to . . ."

"I said, *knock it off!*" Marks grabbed her arms and threw her against the bulkhead wall. For a moment it looked as if Swigart was going to flail at him: her gloved hands were balled into fists at her sides and her teeth were clenched in naked rage. "Get it straight!" he shouted in her face. "I'm gonna need you out there, and I'm gonna need you chilly! You copy that?"

"They beat me up!" she yelled back at him; her voice was almost a childish wail. The bruise on her jaw was livid. "They punched my clock and tied me up in a goddamn closet!"

"Then we'll punch them back!" Marks kept her arms pinioned against the wall. "*After* we get rid of the bugs! I promise you, we'll do it . . . but we gotta take care of business first! You got me?"

An annunciator buzzed and the green light above the hatch flashed on, indicating that the garage module had been repressurized. Marks barely glanced at the indicator. At least

Boggs had done his job; he had cycled through the auxiliary airlock and had re-secured the outer doors so that Module One could be used by Marks for CAS suitup. He was out on the surface now, waiting to help Swigart get the Hornet airborne.

"We don't got time for this shit, Megan," Marks said, more calmly now. "Something out there scragged Charlie and now it's coming our way. We're next for lunch unless we wax 'em first. So TCOB, okay?"

Swigart took a deep breath and let it out; she seemed to relax a little. "Okay, okay. TCOB." She pushed Marks's hands off her, then zipped up the overgarment and pulled a helmet out of a storage bin. "But when this is over, they're history, man," she added as she pulled the helmet over her head and latched down the neck-ring.

Marks nodded grimly as he quickly adjusted the oxygen-nitrogen flow on her chest pack. When she had failed to report back to the monitor center, Commander L'Enfant had sent him to look for her. By the time he had found her in Module Three—bound and gagged, consciousness regained and madder than hell—the commander had called a full alert. Marks sympathized with his teammate; getting mugged by a couple of unarmed civilians was, in itself, a serious wound to one's self-esteem. And considering that one of them had been this dude Nash . . .

"I'll be more than happy to help," he murmured. He pulled his Steyr off his shoulder and handed it by the strap to her. "And this time, ain't gonna be no mercy. I'll break his fucking neck."

Swigart grinned and he grinned back at her, and for a few moments they were so tough that they managed to forget that they were both scared out of their wits. Because they *knew*, if only instinctively, that Charlie Akers must have gotten off a few rounds at whatever had killed him . . .

And it hadn't slowed the bastard down. Not one inch.

Kawakami felt the slight pressure of the gun barrel at the back of his neck. "You don't need that," he said softly.

"I'm afraid I do, Dr. Kawakami," L'Enfant replied from behind him. However, the smooth metal bore lifted away from the scientist's neck. "More comfortable? Good. Now get those cameras switched on so we can see what's happening out there."

The gun was Nash's .38; L'Enfant had hidden it in a thigh

pocket of his jumpsuit, and no one had known it was there until he had pulled it out, the moment that Marks had discovered Swigart bound and gagged in the storeroom. He had then ordered Boggs out onto the surface to seal the Module One outer hatch and assist Swigart as the Hornet's ground crew. As soon as Marks and Swigart had stepped into the main airlock and he had received assurance from Boggs that he was outside the habitat, L'Enfant escorted Kawakami from Module Eight, leaving Isralilova behind in the monitor center to watch the screens.

Even then, the commander had left nothing to chance; once they were out in the corridor, L'Enfant had slammed shut the hatch to Module Eight and used his keycard to lock it from the outside, effectively imprisoning the Russian scientist inside the monitor center. Then he had ushered Kawakami down the corridor to Module Two.

As Shin-ichi Kawakami switched on the array of external TV monitors and selected from the array of cameras positioned around the habitat and the nearby pyramids, he could hear L'Enfant speaking into his headset. "Okay, Alphonse, how're you doing there?" he asked.

Kawakami noticed that L'Enfant, apparently without realizing it, had discarded the ridiculous code words he had used earlier. It seemed as if the commander had been shaken by Akers's death more than he cared to admit. "Okay, depressurize Module One ASAP and let Swigart get to her craft."

Kawakami reached for the headset that dangled around his neck, and immediately felt the sharp pressure of the gun return to the base of his skull. He hesitated for a moment, then slowly pulled the headset on. "If you're going to kill me," he said, "go ahead, but I think you need all the help you can get right now."

He gave him a sidelong glance; L'Enfant's face was lost in the deep shadows of the darkened command module. After a second the gun was lifted away from Kawakami's head once again. "No tricks, Dr. Kawakami. I'm not playing games anymore."

"I never was, Commander L'Enfant." Kawakami touched the lobe of his headset and suddenly he could hear cross talk on Channel One:

. . . Okay, I'm in tight and powered-up. Internal electrical is copacetic. Now depressurize the garage and get out there. . . .

. . . External CAS power off. Emergency air flush on Module One initiated . . .

. . . CAS fast-start checklist commencing . . .

. . . I've got the shroud off your craft, lady, so hurry your ass up in there before I fly this fucking thing myself. . . .

. . . Primary servos check, hydraulics check, gun locked and loaded, auto TADS on/off circuit check . . .

. . . Don't you get near that thing, Boggs, or I'll rip off your balls. . . .

. . . Onboard ECM is hot and checks out. Watch your gauges, Megs, I'm popping it now. . . .

. . . Don't get bothered, lady, I'm just trying to . . .

A sudden, sharp squeal of electronic feedback. Kawakami hissed painfully as he clapped his hands over his headphones until the main computer system automatically dampered the interference.

. . . Watch it, Al, you almost fried the comlink. Rapid flush nearly zeroed-out. I'm opening the main doors. . . .

Kawakami lowered his hands. He glanced over his shoulder again at L'Enfant. "Your CAS has its own ECM system? Why would you . . . ?"

"Nothing you need to worry about." L'Enfant leaned forward; he was now visible in the half-light on the TV and computer screens. His face was rigid and dispassionate in the soft purplish glow. "Just a little surprise we had worked up for our friends down there. Now get me a picture from the City."

Kawamaki returned his attention to the console, switching from camera to camera. A montage of live-image TV pictures fell across the screens—a close-up of the habitat, a distant shot of the Face, a quarter-distance view of the D&M pyramid, a stern-angle picture of the *Akron*—until he found a shot of the C-4 pyramid, taken from a camera positioned close to the primary entrance to the Labyrinth. . . .

There. Shadow-cast, indistinct movement.

He caught his breath and froze the camera. Yes. Something was moving in the stone doorway. He zoomed in as much as he could; the image blurred and became indistinct, but the motion wasn't lost. Kawakami breathlessly tapped a code into the computer keyboard and the image was enhanced.

A giant was coming out of the Labyrinth. It lurched forward on pillar-like legs into the cold red morning light of the Martian sky, dragging its enormous claws through the soil.

Just behind it, another was coming through the doorway.

And, on another screen, yet another juggernaut had just ap-

peared as a grainy image, approaching from the direction of the
D&M pyramid.

Kawakami suddenly remembered the ancient Greek legend,
of the monster that haunted the island of Crete. As in that legend, these creatures came from a labyrinth . . . only this time,
there was more than one, and there was no Theseus around to
slay them. But the similarity was too striking to be ignored.

"We've found the minotaurs," he whispered.

Get away from that thing!

W. J. Boggs was standing next to the F-210 Hornet; he had
just pulled away the protective aluminized shroud and was bent
over to remove the landing skid chocks when he heard
Swigart's voice through the comlink. He looked up to see the
Navy pilot bounding toward him from the habitat, her assault rifle held at the ready as she made broad-jumping bunny-hops
across the sand.

"Easy, Lieutenant." He stood up from the forward skid, holding up his empty hands. "I was just getting your plane ready
for . . ."

*Nobody touches this craft but me. 'Specially not some blimp
jockey.* Swigart ran to the stubby port wing, kicked the remaining chock out of the way, then glanced around the one-seater
aircraft; Boggs noticed that she was particularly careful to
check the nozzles of the rocket engines, as though she expected
to find that he had deliberately clogged them with something.
Apparently satisfied, she stepped around to the starboard side,
passing the slogan EAT SHIT AND DIE! which had been hand-
painted beneath the cockpit, and began climbing up the fuselage
rungs to the cockpit.

Swigart pushed open the tinted canopy, then hesitated for a
moment, looking down into the tiny cockpit. *Damn hell,* she
muttered. She then half-turned on the top rung and held out her
assault rifle to him. *No room in here for this,* she said. *Take it . . .
and don't get any ideas.*

Boggs didn't reach for it. "Gee, are you sure? I might decide
to shoot you in the back or . . ."

Just take it, asshole! she snapped. *I don't got time for this!*

"Since you ask that way, sure . . ." Boggs extended his hand
and Swigart tossed the rifle to him. She gave him one last mean
look, then scrambled the rest of the way into the cockpit. "Hope
you have a real good flight."

Fuck you. She reached up to grab the interior handle and slam the canopy down into place. *Now get out of here. Go play with your toy balloon or something.*

Boggs stepped back a few feet, carefully keeping away from the exposed muzzle of the Hornet's 30mm cannon, then cocked his left fist upward to give her the bird. If Swigart noticed, she didn't make any response; through his helmet, he could hear the thin whine of the F-210's engines being powered-up for launch.

Okay, now what? He glanced toward the *Akron*, remembering the last time his ship had been caught in a fire zone. Toy balloon or not, the *Akron* was an even larger target than the old *Burroughs*; it was probably a good idea to get the dirigible out of here before the shooting started.

"Goddamn," Boggs muttered. "I don't get it, Waylon. How can the same shit happen to you twice in the same fucking place?" Slinging the rifle over his shoulder, he began to bound toward the *Akron*. . . .

He suddenly heard, from the general vicinity of the City, the sound of popcorn popping: distant, muted by the thin atmosphere, yet unmistakably the echo of gunfire.

Startled, Boggs ground his boot heels into the sand; he fell over backwards, but barely noticed as he stared in the direction of the pyramids. Nash and Sasaki were missing from the habitat, and since Swigart had told L'Enfant that her weapon had been taken from her when they had made their escape . . .

"Oh, no," he whispered. "Miho."

Boggs lurched to his feet, yanked the Steyr off his shoulder, and began to race across the red sands toward the City.

They had stayed off the comlink channels to avoid giving themselves away to L'Enfant and his men, so they had to touch helmets and use hand signals to communicate with each other. As soon as they had exited the base through the Module One garage doors, Sasaki had suggested that they hide in the C-4 pyramid.

It seemed like a good idea. Nash knew that it would only be a matter of minutes before their absence was discovered. He also realized that L'Enfant would probably have the *Akron* searched, possibly before any place else. Like it or not, the plan for smuggling the science team aboard the dirigible was now dead, as was his scheme to hide himself and Sasaki in the observation blister. All they could do, at least for the time being, was make a run for the City.

Escaping into the City was almost equally risky, though, since monitor cameras ringed the site. Yet if no one was watching the screens in the command module, they just might be able to get into the C-4 pyramid and hide inside the Labyrinth until it was time for the *Akron* to depart. Boggs had to get the dirigible out of Cydonia within the next twelve hours; if they could hold out inside the City for just that long . . .

Grabbing Sasaki's hand, Nash ran for the distant pyramid. It hurt like hell to make the ten-league hop-skips in the lesser Martian gravity; every time his boots touched ground, his swollen stomach muscles shrieked in agony, yet it was the quickest way to cover the long distance between the base and the ancient necropolis. Sasaki didn't have any trouble keeping up with him, although she hesitated when they approached the first of the stalk-mounted surveillance cameras. Nash was tempted to shoot out the lens, but then he realized that the next time someone attempted to use that particular camera, it would provide a clue to their whereabouts. He let it go and kept running.

They had almost made it to the pyramid when something came through the doorway.

It was nine feet tall, metallic and jet-black, although odd streaks of dark red ran chaotically across its seamless form like imperfections in a sheet of mica. Humanlike in its general form, it had trunklike legs which shifted on double-jointed knees, and wide footpads which oddly resembled the MRV. In fact, the behemoth vaguely resembled a CAS: wide, massive body, rotary joints, a low sloped head, a vaguely hunched back. But its accordion-jointed arms were gorilla-like in their length, almost touching the ground as it lumbered forward, and the hands were massive, sharp claws.

Nash stopped dead in his tracks, his mouth gaping open; Sasaki halted with him, grabbing onto his suit for support. A single, cyclopean eye moved toward them within a narrow eye-slit and stopped as it locked onto them. The leviathan paused for a moment, then ponderously began to advance toward them. Behind it, a second creature—identical to the first, except for a different pattern of red markings—was emerging from the stone doorway.

"Back off," he said softly. Freeing himself from Miho's

grasp, he took two steps backward, warily raising the Steyr into firing position. "Take it slow, but back away . . ."

Sasaki didn't respond; she stayed in place, staring at the black monster. Nash remembered that his comlink was switched off and she couldn't hear him. He hesitated for a moment, then stabbed the appropriate button on his right gauntlet's wristpad. "Miho!" he snapped. "Back off!"

She jerked a little at the sound of his voice, then switched on her own radio; however, she still didn't move away. *August, I don't think it's . . .*

At that instant, the first creature raised its vast arms and lurched toward them.

Nash heard Sasaki's scream through his headset. He lunged forward, shoved her out of the way, then raised the Steyr to his shoulder and clenched the trigger with his right forefinger. There was the muted noise of firecrackers next to his ear; he felt the rifle stock recoil against his shoulder, almost knocking him off-balance, as spent casings danced across the back of his forearm.

His aim was good; a jagged line of thumbhole-size pockmarks appeared in the creature's wide chest. The thing jerked back slightly, its movements less fluid, more mechanical—now, for the first time, Nash realized that it was some sort of robot—but it didn't fall.

The second robot, unharmed, continued to advance steadily as the first behemoth recovered itself. Claws outstretched, it stalked toward the two of them.

"Get out of here!" Nash yelled. He opened fire again, still focusing his aim on the closer of the two creatures. Sasaki finally reacted; as she flung herself out of the way, the robot's right arm swung at her, its immense claw viciously slashing through the space where she had just been standing. If she had still been there, she would have been disemboweled.

Nash took a couple of steps backward, still firing at the first robot. More bullet holes marred its thick skin; it seemed to have been slowed down, but it still kept coming at him. Now the second leviathan had turned and was heading straight for Nash. He let loose another few rounds, then whirled around to make a leap. . . .

The toe of his right boot snagged a rock; he tripped and pitched forward to the ground. Nash instinctively threw his arms up in front of his helmet to protect his faceplate from being cracked; his bruises shouted with agony as he smashed into the rocky soil. Ignoring the pain, he grabbed for his gun—

Nash! Sasaki screamed.

—And found it missing. It had been flung aside in the fall. In near-panic, he glanced about and saw it lying on the ground about six feet away to his right. He could hear his own breath rasping in his helmet as he scrambled for it. . . .

Roll left! Sasaki shouted. *Left!*

Nash didn't think twice; he tucked in his arms and twisted to the left. He caught a glimpse of a clawed fist ramming into the ground where he had been lying.

He looked up and saw one of the robots towering above him, its dark form eclipsing the sun. It tore its claws out of the ground and raised them above its head. . . .

There was the rapid *poppa-poppa-poppa-poppa* of full-auto gun fire. The creature staggered back and suddenly Boggs was shouting in his ears: *Move it, move it, move it—!*

Nash gasped and heaved himself off the ground, hastily crawling on hands and knees out from under the unexpected fusillade. He felt hands grasp his wrists and haul him forward; his feet found the ground and he barreled forward, catching Sasaki in the midriff. She grunted as the breath was almost knocked out of her, but let herself be carried backward past Boggs, where he stood spraying bullets at the advancing creatures.

Haul ass! Boggs yelled. *Get out of here! Move, move, move!*

Nash had a fleeting wish to go back and retrieve the lost Steyr, but Sasaki was already pulling him away. He glanced back and saw that the robots were still on their feet; they were less than a dozen feet away from Boggs, who still had his gun wide-open on them.

"Get out of there!" Nash yelled. "You can't kill 'em!"

No fucking shit! Boggs threw down his Steyr, turned and leaped away from the monster in the lead, barely in time to escape another slashing swipe by its claws. *Out of ammo! Run for it! They're gonna . . .*

They ain't gonna do jack shit, a new voice said in their headphones.

Nash looked around. A hulking figure in a combat armor suit stood behind them; the maw of the integrated machine-gun in its left arm was raised and pointed toward the three of them. He could see Marks's scowling face through the tinted glass of the canopy.

They barely had a chance to dodge aside before he opened fire.

Kawakami had an eerie sense of detachment as he watched the TV monitors. One screen displayed one of the minotaurs and Sergeant Marks, the image caught by the camera positioned near Pyramid C-4. On another screen, replacing an earlier view of the habitat's exterior, was a close-up shot of the same robot as seen throgh the fish-eye lens of another camera mounted on the carapace of Marks's CAS; in the background lurked the massive form of a second minotaur. It was as if he were watching an action movie on TBS back home in Osaka; all that was missing was a melodramatic music score.

He could, however, hear the brash rattle of gunfire over the comlink, which threatened to drown out Marks's voice. *They're taking the rounds,* Marks said in an almost calm voice, as if he were narrating a documentary. *I've stopped 'em, but they ain't falling. What's this damn thing made out of anyway?*

"Lay down suppressive fire and hold them in place." L'Enfant was bent over Kawakami, balancing himself on the back of his chair. Kawakami glanced up at him; the commander's face was completely stoical. "Let the civilians get out of there, then . . ."

On the screens, they could see the first minotaur take a lumbering step forward; its armor almost seemed to absorb the bullets, like an ebony sponge soaking up water. *They're not staying put!* Marks's voice rose in panic, his matter-of-fact tone suddenly gone. *I'm giving them the works, but they're not—!*

"Sergeant!" L'Enfant snapped. "Your suit's ECM will keep them at bay. Now hold your position and lay down more fire. Lieutenant Swigart has lifted off in the Hornet and she can take them out with her cannon. Just . . ."

Goddammit, Commander, the ECM isn't doing shit to them! The robot took another step forward; its long arms were rising menacingly, almost as if to embrace the CAS in a bear-hug. *I can't—!*

Hang in there, Al. The new voice belonged to Swigart. *I'm coming in for a strafing run right this minute, so just . . .*

Commander L'Enfant! Now it was Tamara Isralilova on the comlink. *Motion detectors have picked up movement near the periphery of the base! It's coming our—!*

"Not now, Dr. Isralilova," L'Enfant said. "Keep monitoring its movements."

Holy shit, Megan! The minotaur almost filled the lens of the CAS camera. *Get in here and save my ass! This fucker's about to—!*

"Hold your position, Sergeant," L'Enfant insisted. "That's an order." He paused, then added with absurd calm, "And both of you . . . watch your language."

Watch my . . . ? Sweet Jesus, sir, it's only six feet away!

"That's far enough. Just keep your . . ."

"Madman!" Kawakami's temper, held under tight rein until this moment, snapped in that second. He slapped his headset lobe and shouted, "Get out of there, Sergeant! The ECM will not deter them! They're too big for the—!"

"Shut up!" L'Enfant screamed. *"Shut up!"*

He grabbed the back of Kawakami's chair and wrenched it upward, and Kawakami was suddenly spilled to the floor. As the Japanese scientist hit the carpet, his headset was torn off his head, breaking his radio contact. Stunned, his breath knocked out of him, Kawakami looked up to see that L'Enfant had already taken his place in front of the console. "Sergeant, this is Commander . . . !"

Kawakami mercifully could not hear the rest; lying on the floor and staring up at the screens, though, he could still see everything.

In a single, violent thrust, the minotaur hurled its right claw straight through the transparent canopy of Marks's CAS.

Marks . . . ! L'Enfant howled.

As one screen went blank, the other monitor continued to function, displaying the horror of the moment: frosty oxygen-nitrogen, tinted scarlet by the sergeant's blood, exploding from the shattered canopy as the massive exoskeleton fell backward, its arms and legs twitching either from shorted-out servomotors or Marks's death-throes.

As the CAS collapsed, the minotaur withdrew its arm from the wreckage; its claw was bathed in blood. . . .

"Swigart!" L'Enfant shouted. "Get in there and waste 'em!"

In that second, Kawakami caught a glimpse of something on the remaining active TV screen. The robot which had destroyed the CAS was already lurching onward, passing out of range of the camera. But then, the second minotaur—which, up until now, had done little more than advance behind the first one—strode to the ruined CAS and stopped.

Then, incredibly, it bent over slightly, grasped the thick armored ankles of the CAS, and began to drag it backwards towards the doorway of the pyramid.

All at once, as a white-hot flash of insight burned through his mind, everything became clear to Shin-ichi Kawakami.

His eyes locked on the screen, he fumbled for the lost headset, found it, slapped the mike against his face. "Lieutenant Swigart!" he shouted. "This is Kawakami! Do not fire on the second robot! I repeat, *do not open fire on the . . . !*"

"What are you doing?" L'Enfant whirled on him; his face was a mask of anguish and rage as he reached down to grab a handful of the scientist's jumpsuit. Before Kawakami could speak, he ripped the headset from his head and threw it aside.

"I thought I told you to shut up!" L'Enfant snarled, hauling the elderly man upward as his right arm pulled back into a fist. "Do you see what you did? *You killed my men, you fucking—!*"

"Look at the screen!" Kawakami shouted, pointing at the console behind the commander. "Don't you see? Look at the screen! The other one, it's . . . !"

He stopped. On the screen, he could see the first minotaur being kicked backward, its carapace splitting open as high-caliber bullets pounded into its armor. Arms flailing spasmodically, it staggered for a couple of seconds before it fell, like Marks, into the red sand as an inert mass of metal.

In another instant, the second minotaur was similarly riven by a long burst of 30mm shells; its claws released the CAS as it was violently thrown backward by the bullets. If it could ever have been described as being alive in the first place, it was now dead.

"It's over," L'Enfant breathed, his tantrum suddenly leaving him as he watched the display. "It's over. . . ."

He carelessly released Kawakami from his grasp, letting the scientist crumple back to the floor. His rampage halted, he let out his breath and blindly stumbled backward, finally collapsing into a chair as he capped his right hand over his headset. His face seemed to have lost all its blood; the man looked older now, no longer invincible.

"Swigart, how did it go?" L'Enfant rasped. He listened, then nodded his head. "Confirm two kills. Good job. Okay, you may stand down. We can . . ."

Then he stopped, listening intently to something through his headphones. He leaned forward in his seat. "Dr. Isralilova," he said impatiently. "I don't think you're . . ."

Then his mouth gaped open, and Kawakami caught a rare expression of astonishment and utter speechlessness on the commander's face. "Oh my God . . ." he whispered.

Kawakami crawled across the floor, reaching for his headset. As he groped for it, he suddenly heard a high-pitched scream.

Not from the headset . . .

From the other end of the habitat.

He jerked his head up. "Tamara!" he shouted.

"It's attacking the base!" L'Enfant bellowed as he lunged out of the chair toward the windows at the end of the module. "Swigart, take out the other robot! No, the *third* one! *It's attacking the* . . . *!*"

The rest was lost in a sudden, loud *bang!* from within the habitat and the module shook as if the base had been rocked by an earthquake. L'Enfant was thrown backward, less by the force of the explosion than by his own surprise, as decompression alarms squalled and all the flatscreens flashed red-alert signals. He hit the floor, still conscious, clamping his headset against his ears as his eyes went wild in terror. Kawakami instinctively threw his arms over his head; from somewhere not far away, he briefly heard another insane cry, now blotted out by a louder cyclonic roar.

"Tamara—!" he screamed.

Triggered by the main computer, candy-striped ceiling panels automatically opened as oxygen masks fell downward on their plastic hoses; the aluminum emergency hatch irised shut in front of the module doorway, sealing them off from the access corridor. "Fire! Fire! *Fire!*" L'Enfant was shouting. . . .

Something had just broken through the habitat's hull.

20. Boot Hill

It was the saddest and most lonely place on Mars: a row of grave-markers, made of scrap sheet-metal and parts of old cargo containers, held erect by small cairns of rock. Each was marked by dust-scoured paint with a name: MOBERLY, BRONSTEIN, HOFFMAN, OELJANOV, and KULEJAN.

And now there were four new markers.

The graveyard had been established on a small hillock behind the habitat. It was not practical to bring the dead back to Earth for burial; the space taken up by a corpse aboard a cycleship, plus the penalty paid for transporting what was essentially inert mass, could be used for more valuable payload. And since cremation was also ruled out in the carbon-dioxide atmosphere, the only recourse was to bury the deceased where they had fallen. The Cydonia Base cemetery had been nicknamed Boot Hill, but it was not the first graveyard on Mars; that dubious distinction belonged to Arsia Station, where more than a dozen men and women were buried.

Yet the population of the boneyard at Cydonia had been almost doubled today; alongside the markers of Hal Moberly, Valery Bronstein, William Hoffman, Maksim Oeljanov, and Sasha Kulejan had been added three fresh graves: the remains of Charlie Akers, Alphonse Marks, and Tamara Isralilova.

The way I figure it, Boggs commented as he pounded a fourth marker into the ground with the flat of his entrenching tool, *the Russians are way ahead of us.*

Nash looked up from his own work of shoveling sand over Isralilova's grave. The fourth marker bore Paul Verduin's name, although there was no body beneath it; like Sasha Kulejan before him, he was missing and presumed dead. At least there had been something left of Hal Moberly to be buried. *Right now,*

Boggs continued, *the Russians are running four-to-three over the Americans up here, with one each for the Brits and the Dutch. The Japs are running way behind. Enough for a half-decent baseball team, but the Americans are going to have to do some catching up before . . .*

"If you're trying to be funny," Nash said, "you're not succeeding."

Boggs gave Verduin's marker a final whack, folded his entrenching tool, and tossed it on the ground. *I'm trying to be funny because if I allowed myself to take it too seriously, I just might lose my mind.* He dusted his gloved hands against each other as he gazed at the row of markers. *I've helped dig more than half of these holes, and most of these people were my friends. That, plus the one at Arsia where I planted Katsu. Makes me feel like more like a part-time gravedigger than a pilot.*

He turned and looked back at Nash. *Four in one day. Jesus Christ. So you'll excuse me if I make a joke or two. Sorta takes the edge off things, y'know what I mean?*

Nash threw a last handful of gravel on Tamara Isralilova's final resting place and folded his own shovel. "Sorry. My apologies. I guess you're right."

He turned and let his eyes travel to the nearby pyramids and, further away, near the eastern horizon, the Face. Regardless of the violence of the just-passed morning, it was actually turning out to be a pretty day. The clear sky, the still-calm winds, the long shadows of the pyramids across the placid red desert . . . indescribable beauty. One could almost imagine a caravan of camels slowly emerging from the City, devout Muslims embarking on a long pilgrimage to Mecca.

"Not a bad place to be buried, though," he murmured. "Great view."

It sucks. Boggs followed his gaze to the City. *You ever hear of King Tut's curse?*

"Funny you should mention that. I was just thinking it looked . . ."

Like Egypt. Yeah, everyone says that. But I'm beginning to wonder if the Cooties copied more from the Egyptians than their architectural style. Boggs sighed and shook his head. *In case you missed the news, buddy, you and me almost bought a lot on this friggin' hill ourselves today.*

Nash didn't have to be reminded of how close they had come to being killed—or, for that matter, how close it had been for everyone else who had been inside the habitat. The third and last of the minotaurs—as Kawakami had dubbed them—had ripped apart Module Eight before Swigart had used the last of the Hornet's ammo to destroy it in a final strafing run. He she not succeeded, the robot might have demolished the rest of the habitat.

Even then, she had been too late to save Isralilova's life. Locked inside the monitor center, the Russian scientist had been killed when the module had suffered explosive decompression; her final scream, as near as anyone could determine, had been when she had glimpsed the black leviathan outside the module's window in the instant before it had punched through the glass.

Swigart was now standing at the bottom of the hill, an assault rifle cradled in her arms. As Nash watched, she looked over her shoulder again at Kawakami and Sasaki, who were kneeling beside the remains of the minotaur where it had fallen next to the ruins of Module Eight. If the lieutenant had anything on her mind, she'd kept it to herself. Indeed, after she'd landed the Hornet back at the base, she had done nothing more than to take L'Enfant's next order: escort Nash and Boggs while they retrieved the corpses of Akers, Marks, and Isralilova and took them up to Boot Hill for burial. There had not been a word from her since, not even when they had found Akers's headless body near the D&M Pyramid.

As for L'Enfant himself, he had not been seen or heard from by anyone except Swigart in the last two hours. As far as anyone knew, he was still inside the command module. No one knew what was going on inside his head except that he'd ordered Swigart to keep the surviving civilians together and at gunpoint.

Hey! Boggs called out. *Lieutenant!* Swigart slowly looked around at them again. *We're done up here. You wanna ask the commander if he wants to say any last words?*

Behind her, Kawakami and Sasaki paused in their examination of the minotaur and gazed expectantly at Swigart. *He's the boss around here,* he went on, *and there's a couple of his guys up here, so maybe he'd care to . . . y'know . . .*

Swigart simply stared up at the two men, her right hand never straying far from the trigger of her rifle. Nash wondered if she was playing the role of a good soldier; it was possible that she was shell-shocked, having just seen two of her fellow officers wiped out in combat. Either way, she said nothing. . . .

And if L'Enfant was listening in on the exchange, his voice remained unheard over the comlink.

Guess not, Boggs murmured. *Damn flathead.* He put his hand on top of Paul Verduin's marker and gave it a fond pat. *Rest easy, dude, wherever you are.* He picked up his entrenching tool and walked slowly past Tamara Isralilova's grave. *See you 'round, sexy. Hope you and Sasha are having a good ol' time.*

Ignoring the graves of Marks and Akers, he then gave Nash's arm a slap and began to trudge down the hill toward the habitat. *C'mon. Let's get out of this place.*

Nash paused to take a last look at the graves he had just dug, then followed Boggs down off Boot Hill. He felt sick over the four lives that had been snuffed out today . . . even for Marks and Akers, strangely, although they had beaten the hell out of him the day before. No one deserved to die in such a miserable place, so far away from home.

But if he had his way, there would be a tenth grave up here today. It wasn't difficult for him to imagine Terrance L'Enfant's name on the marker.

"They've got a bomb in the garage," Nash said. He paused to sip his squeezebulb of orange juice and added, "A nuclear bomb. Anyone want to make bets on what they intend to use it for?"

He was in the Module Nine lab/infirmary, sitting on the same examination table where, only twenty-four hours earlier, Isralilova had sought to heal his wounds from the beating he had taken. Sitting or standing around him in the cramped module were Boggs, Sasaki and Kawakami. The hatch was shut, but Swigart was standing guard just outside; after he and Boggs had completed the burial detail, she had escorted the four of them back into the habitat, where they had been confined together in the lab module. Nash had little doubt that L'Enfant was eavesdropping on their conversation, through the bugs which were still hidden in the module. Everyone's cards were on the table now, though; there were virtually no secrets left for anyone to hide.

"If it's a nuke," Boggs replied, sitting on a stool next to a computer terminal, "then all bets are off . . . but *is* it a nuke?" He looked around at the others. "I mean, I've never seen a nuke up close, have you? Maybe it's a . . . I dunno, a laser-powered pogo stick or . . ."

"I saw it too, Waylon." Miho Sasaki was leaning against a bulkhead, next to where Kawakami sat next to a lab bench. On the bench was a large piece of the minotaur which they had collected from the wreckage and wrapped in a thermal blanket before carrying it inside. "I've never seen a thermonuclear weapon either, but if August says it was a nuke . . ."

"Believe me," Nash interrupted, "I know what I'm talking about. Simply put, it's a small, two-piece plutonium core surrounded by a cadmium sphere, with conventional explosives mounted on either side of the shell . . . probably *plastique* shaped-charges, if it follows conventional form." He held up his hands, a few inches apart from each other. "The whole thing's rigged to a timed electronic detonator. When the timer goes off, the *plastique* explodes and drives together the plutonium inner core, causing instant critical-mass and . . ."

He clapped his hands. "Believe me, W.J.—I know one when I see it. I was briefed on the things when I worked for the CIA. It's a standard-issue nuclear mine, similar to the type developed for use during Gulf War II. From the size of it, my guess is that it's a low-yield tactical nuke. Ten kilotons, maybe."

Boggs shrugged. "Ten kilotons isn't much," he murmured. "Shit, I could blow my nose with it."

No one laughed. Sasaki glared at him. "My great-grandparents were *hibakusha* of the Hiroshima bombing," she said softly. "That was caused by a ten-kiloton warhead. It did more than blow their noses."

Boggs looked down at the floor in embarrassment. Shin-ichi Kawakami diplomatically cleared his throat. "It certainly makes this operation . . . what did you call it, Mr. Nash? Kentucky Race?"

"Kentucky Derby," Nash corrected him. "That was the code name L'Enfant told me last night. Sort of makes sense, considering that the first covert U.S. military operation here was called Steeple Chase. It's upping the stakes a little."

"Yes, whatever." Kawakami gave a dismissive wave of his hand. "It begins to make more sense now. The commander wished to have Paul reconnoiter the catacombs in advance of planting this bomb. Once this was accomplished, he intended to have Sergeant Marks penetrate the area in the new CAS and place the bomb. They were counting on the suit's internal ECM to allow Marks entry into the underground tunnel system without being harmed."

He smiled slightly, shaking his head. "But what he didn't anticipate was the ability of the pseudo-Cooties to grow a defensive system which was too powerful for our ECM to defeat. The . . . ah, minotaurs, if you wish to use my term . . . seemed to have been grown in advance of whatever threat we might have . . ."

"Whoa. Wait a sec, Shin-ichi." Boggs held up a hand. "I'm not the swiftest kid on the block, but I know a buzz-word when I hear it. You just said *grow* twice now. Don't you mean *manufacture*?"

Kawakami slowly shook his head. "No, Waylon, I chose the word quite deliberately. I meant *grow*." He stood up from his stool and turned to the workbench behind him. "Miho, perhaps it's time to show our friends our most recent discovery, hmm?"

Miho nodded and began to carefully unwrap the fragment they'd retrieved from the destroyed minotaur. "Normally we would keep this under quarantine in the AEL," she explained, "but we considered the threat to be minimal. Besides, it seems that Commander L'Enfant does not wish to have us separated any longer, so we . . ."

"Hush, Miho." Kawakami gestured for Nash and Boggs to come to the bench as he telescoped a large magnifier-lens close to the fragment and switched on its light. "Take a look, gentlemen. I'll attempt to explain."

Nash put down his squeezebulb and walked over to the bench. Under the lens was what appeared to be a large, four-foot-long fragment of one of the minotaur's arms; each end was raggedly severed, violently torn apart by a salvo of 30mm shells from the F-210 Hornet's cannon. He noted, now that he could see it more closely, that the arm was multijointed and accordionlike, similar to the segments of a worm, with each section only a few inches apart from the next. He was immediately struck by the precision of its manufacture . . . or growth, if one wanted to use Kawakami's mysterious phraseology.

Kawakami beamed at him. "You're already intrigued, Mr. Nash. Here, see . . . ?" He picked up the fragment and, with little apparent effort, flexed it between his hands. The arm bent smoothly, like a fine-tooled machine. "And observe its sides, around the joints," he continued. "No seams, no welds. Not one. Totally solid-state, as if it had been built as one complete piece. The best-made microcircuitry we have doesn't have this sort of refinement. And see here . . ."

He pulled one severed end into the light, exposing the inside of the arm. Under the lens, Nash could see that its interior was astonishingly detailed and compact: no dangling wires, no servomotors, no solenoids or cog-and-wheel linkages. It reminded him uncomfortably of a severed human limb. "It's . . . almost like . . ."

"Like organic tissue," Miho finished. "Yes, it's integrated that way, isn't it? But it's not organic." She gently prodded the inner workings of the arm with her fingertip; it pushed inward slightly, but not in the way animal flesh might react. "Without a complete chemical breakdown, we can only speculate what this is made from, but our best guess is that it comes from various ferrous oxides, silicates and carbonaceous polymers, just as the outer shell is chiefly composed of iron and carbon. All native Martian elements."

"I don't get it." Boggs was staring through the lens at the fragment, at once fascinated and bewildered. "I mean, it ain't like anything I've ever seen, but if it wasn't built . . ."

"The point is," Kawakami said impatiently, "is that this machine was neither manufactured nor built. It was grown, as a single corporate entity, much as you and I grew in our mothers' wombs. Yet this was part of an unliving being. It *is* a mechanism."

"Biomechanical," Sasaki said, "although even that's a clumsy term for what we're seeing here." She let out her breath and stepped away from the counter, sweeping her long ebony hair back from her shoulders. "There's only one sort of technology that can accomplish something like this, and it's . . ."

"The *form!*" Kawakami interrupted. He dropped the arm back on the bench and pointed at it; his voice rose with excitement as he spoke rapidly. "We have been here for three years and, except for the Face, this is the first time we have seen something which resembles a human being! It is completely anthropomorphic! It's bipedal, it has two manipulative limbs, it's oriented toward forward movement, it has binocular vision . . . nothing about it resembles a Cootie! Not only that, but its exoskeleton resembles a CAS! *Look at it!* It's—!"

"Please, Shin-ichi-*san.*" Sasaki closed her eyes. She said something admonishing to him in Japanese, and Kawakami stopped himself, although his mouth trembled with anticipation. When he was silent, she opened her eyes and looked straight at Nash.

"This is a . . . a paradigm of a human being," she said, carefully selecting her words. "Just as much as the pseudo-Cooties are imitations of the real Cooties, this was a construct of a true human . . . or, at very least, the closest they've yet seen to a living human being—a combat armored suit."

Nash glanced at Boggs. Although the airship pilot was still confused, Nash was beginning to catch on. "You started to say . . . ?"

"Yes," Sasaki finished, "it was made to perform like a human being. And before you ask, it was made by nanotechnology. *Alien* nanotech, far beyond the rudimentary nanites we've developed thus far. Nothing else is capable of this sort of precision."

She looked up at Boggs and favored him with a wry, humorless smile. "And if that's the case, Waylon, then our nuclear bombs really are something which we can use to blow our noses."

Kawakami crossed the compartment to the computer terminal where Boggs had been sitting. "The fact that this thing was grown—or biomechanically manufactured, if you prefer—is only part of the solution," he explained as he quickly typed instructions into the keyboard. "First, we have to look at the pseudo-Cooties themselves and why they . . . ah, yes, here we go."

Nash walked over to the terminal and peered over Kawakami's shoulder at the screen. The exobiologist had interfaced the terminal with the base's mainframe; the flatscreen was divided in half, the left-hand side showing a diagram of a Cootie, the right a scale model of a pseudo-Cootie. As Sasaki and Nash gathered around, Kawakami rotated the two images on an imaginary three-dimensional axis.

"When we first encountered the pseudo-Cooties," he said, "I assumed that they were mere robotic copies of the original aliens, mainly because they so closely resembled the remains I had unearthed in the D&M Pyramid of one of aliens . . . Hirohito, remember?"

Boggs nodded vaguely, but the reference was completely lost upon Nash. "I also assumed that the robots were self-replicating," Kawakami explained, "but I did not go any further than that. After all, the only persons who had come in contact with the pseudo-Cooties and survived to tell about it were Ben Cassidy and Arthur Johnson, and neither had been in Room C4-20 long enough to make any detailed observations. Nor had we ever been able to capture a pseudo-Cootie and subject it to detailed examination. So my assumption was that they were simple-minded, mechanical analogs, no more complex than our own factory-line robots which are programmed to interact with each other but nonetheless are no more intelligent than grasshoppers."

He coughed into a fist and pointed at the screen. "I now believe that I was partially in error. Yes, the pseudo-Cooties are self-replicating, but they are neither simple-minded nor mechanical."

He cocked a thumb over his shoulder at the fragment of the minotaur. "Like that monster over there, they were grown by nanites . . . microscopic robots, much like the nanosurgeons we use in hospitals, yet far more intricate. In theory, at least, they can construct complex objects from whatever raw materials are at hand. The nanosurgeons are the first step we've made in that direction, but . . ."

"Wait a sec," Boggs interrupted. "You're telling me that nanites built *that* thing?"

"Not ones like we have, no," Sasaki said, shaking her head. "This is apparently the end-product of nanites which are presently in use . . ."

"But not by humans," Nash said.

"Yes." Sasaki looked at him and slowly nodded. "If this is true, then the nanotechnology of the aliens is far advanced from anything we've developed so far. Our nanosurgeons can repair internal tissue damage, like broken blood vessels and so forth . . . the way your own wounds were healed last night, in fact . . . but what Shin-ichi-*san* has postulated goes far beyond that."

Listening to his protégée with obvious pride, Kawakami nodded his head in agreement. "Indeed. The Cooties seem to have mastered nanotechnology to a degree we've only imagined so far. The robots that attacked us earlier are an example. Yet there's an important difference . . . what we encountered today resembled a *human being*, not a Cootie."

"So?" Boggs shrugged. "They're copying us instead of one of them."

"Exactly!" Kawakami jabbed a finger at the pilot. "The minotaurs were inexact copies of ourselves! Like the Face, they are approximate imitations of the human physiology, constructed through nanites!"

"The Face?" Boggs remained skeptical. "But if they used these . . . whatchamacallit, nanites . . . to make the Face, then they must have also used them to make the pyramids. . . ."

"Not beyond their capability," Kawakami said. "They could have used them to transform pre-existing mesas and mountains into the forms they desired. It explains much about their construction techniques." He turned around in his chair and spread open his hands. "Yes? So it becomes apparent, does it not?"

"No." Nash folded his arms above his chest. "No, it doesn't. I don't get it either."

"Think!" Kawakami demanded. "We were lured to this location by an edifice which was a copy of a human face, which in turn led us to structures which were copies of the ancient Egyptian pyramids. When we passed a rudimentary intelligence test . . . a test designed to prove that we were not only a sapient species, but capable of innovation and creativity as well . . . the pseudo-Cooties were awakened from their sleep."

He held up a hand before Nash could interrupt. "Yes, that's what I believe it was . . . a long sleep, perhaps lasting for millennia. Our final, correct response to the Labyrinth activated a long-dormant program within their slaves, the pseudo-Cooties."

"Like a . . ." Boggs shrugged. "I dunno. A wake-up call?"

Sasaki covered her mouth with her hand to disguise a laugh, but Kawakami vigorously nodded his head. "Yes, if you want to call it that. A wake-up call." He stood up impatiently from his chair and paced past them, his hands clasped together behind his back. "Yet when we failed to make an immediate response, they locked us out of the catacombs."

"Why?" Nash asked.

"This I do not know." Kawakami rocked his head back and forth. "Perhaps we failed to make the next appropriate response. Nevertheless, when we finally did investigate further, they captured all manned and unmanned probes we sent down there. This is the reason why we've never found any remains of the combat armor or spiders we've sent down there." He held up a finger. "However, when we were attacked today, it was by human-like robots, not insect-like pseudo-Cooties . . . and even then, they attempted to salvage the CAS which Marks had been wearing. I saw that on the monitors in the command module."

Boggs sputtered and looked at the ceiling. "Jesus, Shin-ichi, I still don't get what you're . . ."

Kawakami whirled around and glared at him. "Don't be stupid!" he snapped. "Don't you see? *They're imitating us!*"

Nash found his mouth dropping. "God," he whispered as he suddenly realized the point Kawakami was attempting to make. "They're mimes."

Kawakami let out his breath and briefly shut his eyes. "Yes.

Mimes. Like some species of insects on Earth . . . and, after all, the Cooties are highly-evolved insects . . . they mimic the abilities of other creatures, such as those species that camouflage themselves to resemble their prey, or emit identical pheromones to capture their attention. In this instance, the Cooties used advanced nanotechnology to accomplish their goals, imitating things on Earth which they once observed very long ago—a sculpture of a human face like the Sphinx, a form of architecture like the Egyptian pyramids—to attract our attention."

He hunched his narrow shoulders. "Who knows for certain? It may even be that they didn't develop nanotechnology on their own, but simply copied it from another alien race which they previously encountered. This may be their basic tropism, the inherent behavioral pattern of their race . . . attracting another race to their worlds, then pirating their technology through entrapment."

Nash remembered the conversation he'd had the night before with L'Enfant, here in this same room. "L'Enfant said something to me about sundew plants. He told me that you thought . . ."

"That the Face was a lure." Kawakami sighed as he rested against the examination table. "Yes, I did think so then, as I do now . . . but for entirely different reasons than he believes. He sees everything in terms of hostile invasion from space, like a plot from an old science fiction movie. But I believe we're onto something much more complicated, if not more benign, than his paranoid conjecture."

"Yeah," Nash agreed, "but you haven't answered the question. Is this a trap?"

Kawakami slowly nodded. "Yes, it's a trap of sorts, like the sundew. We were deliberately lured to this place." He shook his head again. "But for what reason . . . I still don't know."

Everyone was silent for a few moments as this sank in.

Boggs winced and sat down. "Shit, this is giving me a migraine." He rubbed his eyes with his hands. "Okay, I'm getting it so far, but . . . I dunno, maybe I'm stupid, but why did they start so long ago? I mean . . . if they started off by copying the Egyptians, why did they think a bunch of Arabs would come to Mars? I mean, it ain't like the Pharaohs were into building spaceships."

Sasaki picked up the thread. "Look, Waylon, this is all strictly theoretical, but . . ."

She sat down on the table next to Kawakami. "It could have been that, when the Cooties first explored this solar system and discovered the existence of the human race on Earth, they may have assumed too much of us."

"Sounds like one too many assumptions on everyone's account," Boggs interrupted. "You know what 'assume' means? It stands for making . . ."

"An ass out of you and me," she finished. "Yes, I know. You've told me countless times." Kawakami lowered his face and snickered, and Nash had to hide his grin before Boggs spotted it. "But let's suppose that the Cooties found our species more than five thousand years ago," she said. "If they were shipwrecked on this planet, they might have . . . ah, assumed, for lack of a better word . . . that our technological progress would be in an unbroken upward curve."

With her fingertip, she traced a line in the air, rising along a 90-degree angle from the floor toward the ceiling. "Perhaps this was the way it was with their ancestors, if they were indeed natural mimes. Given the technological prowess of our own ancestors, they may have determined that we would also be capable of interplanetary travel within a few centuries . . . a single millennium at most . . . and that our culture would continue to use the same basic forms of architecture throughout our cultural ascent."

"And they planned accordingly," Kawakami continued. He extended a hand toward the unseen City and the Face. "They copied the Face and the pyramids to resemble the largest man-made structures on ancient Earth, believing that modern man would immediately recognize these edifices as being similar to their own." He glanced at Sasaki. "Correct?"

She nodded. "And they were correct, to a certain extent," she said. "But they didn't anticipate that our progress would take so long. Perhaps the Cooties made the technological jump to spaceflight as a straight, even line, but we . . ."

Again, Miho traced an upward line in the air, but this time as a ragged series of dips and halts. "We were not so fortunate. Our history has been retarded by many factors. Wars, plagues, famines, politics. The long Dark Ages in which the western world lost most of the science of the Greeks and Romans . . ."

"The destruction of the Great Library at Alexandria," Nash supplied, "the Crusades . . ."

"The rise of a stifling feudal culture in the eastern world, the isolationism of China and Japan," Sasaki supplied. "Yes, and so on. After the Renaissance and the rediscovery of the solar system, it still took several centuries for the first liquid-fuel rocket to be launched . . . and even after the Viking probe initially sighted the Face and the City, it was yet another half-century until the first manned expedition arrived at this site."

She looked at Boggs and smiled. "Don't feel so stupid, Waylon. If we're right, the Cooties had been waiting for you to come for more than five thousand years."

He grinned and stared her straight in the eye. "Hey, Miho, I usually come a lot quicker than that." Her face reddened as she quickly glanced away. Kawakami appeared to be embarrassed, although he pretended not to catch the cheap joke.

Nash had no time for innuendo. "That's all very interesting," he said, "but that still doesn't answer the basic question. Why did the Cooties . . . ?"

He was cut off, not wholly unexpectedly, by the sound of the hatch opening. Nash turned around and watched as Swigart pushed the hatch open and stood out of the way to let Terrance L'Enfant step into the compartment.

"Why did the Cooties cross the galaxy?" he asked, not completely without a trace of humor. "Why, to get to the other side . . ."

L'Enfant looked hollow, as if something vital had been sucked out of him in the last few hours. His eyes were shadowed as if he hadn't slept in days; his shoulders were slightly stooped, his hands thrust deep into the pockets of his jumpsuit. Swigart silently followed him into the lab, not bothering to close the hatch behind her; she stood with her back to the hatch, her Steyr cradled in her arms.

For a few long moments, L'Enfant studied the four persons in the module, scowling as he appeared to size them up one at a time. When he finally spoke, his voice was a taut, harsh rasp.

"No more games," he said. "No more subterfuge. You all know about Kentucky Derby now, what we were intending to do with the nuke. That plan is still in effect."

"Pardon me?" Boggs looked simultaneously amused and perplexed, as if someone had just suggested that he perform an unnatural act with a farm animal. "You and who else, pal? Your CAS is scrap metal now. You can't . . ."

"Shut up, Mr. Boggs."

Boggs winced. "Aw, man. I wish people would stop saying

that to me," he muttered, his eyes rolling upward. "I'm beginning to think my first name is 'Shut Up.' "

L'Enfant made a small gesture toward Swigart. "Lieutenant,
if he speaks again, shoot him." As she raised her rifle and
trained it on Boggs, he added, "In the leg, though, please. We
will still need him to pilot the *Akron* once we're done here."

Boggs opened his mouth to say something, but he carefully
reconsidered whatever retort he had been about to make. For
once, he shut up. Everyone else froze in position, not daring to
move or utter a word. L'Enfant was not fooling around; it was
clear that Swigart would unquestioningly obey an order from
him to open fire on Boggs or anyone else in the lab.

"There. That's better." L'Enfant straightened his back a little.
He pulled his right hand out of his pocket, and now they could
all see that he was holding Nash's gun. "Mr. Boggs has raised a
salient point. Sergeant Marks had been intending to use the
CAS to carry a thermonuclear mine into the catacombs. That
option, of course, is no longer open to us. However, the basic
plan is still in effect."

L'Enfant raised the gun to his hip and pointed it at Nash.
"Seaman Nash, I'm afraid your role in this affair has been
changed. You will carry the weapon through the Labyrinth."

His eyes shifted to Miho. "Since the device is quite heavy,
though, you may need some help. Dr. Sasaki, you will assist
him."

Miho stared at him, her mouth agape in disbelief. "We would
never survive," she protested. "The pseudo-Cooties will . . ."

"The enemy will tear you apart as soon as you enter C4-20.
Yes, I know." L'Enfant smiled condescendingly at her. "But
that's close enough for the purpose of planting the device. What
little usefulness you've had for me in the past is at an end, but
for this single function you'll serve rather well. I need Boggs,
and Dr. Kawakami is a little too frail for this task."

Nash carefully cleared his throat, if only to telegraph his intent to speak. "It's a nice try, Commander," he said calmly, "but
it's not going to work. If either of us refuses, what are you going
to do? Shoot us?" He shrugged. "Then there's nobody left to
carry the bomb down there. As you just said, Shin-ichi's in ill
health and you need W.J. to fly the *Akron*."

L'Enfant barely blinked at his argument. "I said that Dr.
Kawakami is too ill to help you carry the device," he replied. "I
didn't say he was entirely useless."

He slowly lifted the SIG-Sauer, steadied it with his right hand, and deliberately aimed it straight at Shin-ichi Kawakami's face. The physicist blanched and his hands trembled, but he said nothing. "If you refuse," L'Enfant said, "I will kill him. Plain and simple."

"No!" Miho shouted. She jumped off the table and rushed protectively toward Kawakami. Nash grabbed her by the arms and pulled her back. "You can't kill him!" she yelled, fighting against Nash. "I won't allow you to—"

"Miho!" Kawakami snapped. "Hush now!"

He looked over his shoulder at her, calming her with a single glance, then returned his steady gaze to L'Enfant. Kawakami seemed shaken; his hands were trembling, and when he took a breath it came as a soft rattle from somewhere deep in his emaciated chest. He stared back at L'Enfant, seemingly ignoring the gun which was aimed directly at his forehead; then he closed his eyes and shook his head in disgust.

"Commander L'Enfant," he said in a measured tone, "you are an ignorant man after all. You can't blackmail someone if he refuses the role."

He then began to walk toward the commander, heading for the hatch. "And I refuse to play along with your stupidity."

For a moment, L'Enfant appeared completely startled; as if caught in indecision, he allowed the gun in his hands to dip downward a little. He gazed down at the floor, apparently humbled by Kawakami's inescapable logic. Swigart raised her gun and spread her legs slightly, blocking the exit from the compartment. Kawakami paid no attention to her. He strode past the workbench, stepping around L'Enfant as he headed for the door. . . .

Then L'Enfant looked up again, and in that instant Nash caught a glimpse of absolute madness in his eyes.

"Shin-ichi!" Nash yelled. *"Stop—!"*

Then L'Enfant whipped around, jammed the gun against the silky white fringe of hair covering Kawakami's right ear, and squeezed the trigger.

The roar of the gunshot was still reverberating off the metal walls as Sasaki, screaming in horrified anguish, tore away from Nash and hurled herself across the compartment.

Unmindful of L'Enfant, she threw herself over Kawakami's limp body, kneeling in the pool of dark cranial blood and sobbing hysterically. Swigart had already rushed forward to guard

L'Enfant, covering Nash and Boggs with her assault rifle. Boggs was completely petrified; his mouth worked silently as his eyes moved back and forth from the blood-drenched ichor splattered across the bulkhead wall to L'Enfant and back again.

L'Enfant's hands, his sleeves, the front of his jumpsuit—all were soaked with blood. He stood stiffly erect next to Kawakami's corpse, the gun still clasped in his hands. Somewhere in the compartment there was the tinny metallic sound of a spent cartridge rolling across the floor. His eyes—wild, totally lunatic—were locked unblinkingly on Nash.

"Last chance, Nash!" he shouted. "The Jap didn't believe me! You want to make it two?"

Without taking his eyes from Nash, he placed the gun barrel against the back of Sasaki's skull. She didn't notice the slight pressure on her head; she was still crying uncontrollably, hugging Kawakami to her chest and rocking back and forth as she murmured something in Japanese.

"I'm not shitting, Nash!" he shouted. All his earlier pretense and posturing—the role-playing of the erudite gentleman-soldier, the perfect Annapolis graduate—had completely vanished. A raving maniac had taken his place. "I'll blow her brains all over the place and you'll *still* have to carry the fucker down there . . . by *yourself* if you have to!"

Boggs seemed to awaken from his trance. "Christ, August," he whispered, his eyes now fixed upon Miho. "You can't let him . . ."

"Shut up, Boggs," Nash said.

"He means it, man. He'll do it. He's—"

"Just shut up!" Nash took a deep breath and gazed unwaveringly back at L'Enfant. It took all his willpower to keep from flinging himself at his former captain; at that moment, he would have sold his soul to get his hands around the maniac's neck.

"You didn't need to do that, Commander," he said softly. "He was just trying to make a point. You could have . . ."

"Gimme a *yes* or a *no*!" L'Enfant snarled. "I'm not interested in anything else!" He thrust the gun more firmly against Miho's head. "Do it *now*!"

Nash took a deep breath. He had no choice.

"Yes," he answered. "I'll do it."

21. Kentucky Derby

The stone door leading to Room C4-20 was propped open with a pneumatic jack, as were all the chamber doors in the Labyrinth. Under the beams of their helmet lanterns, they could see the scratches and abrasions on the rock walls of the corridor where a portable airlock had once been inserted, before it had been dismantled by the pseudo-Cooties. Beyond the doorway lay a deep, fathomless darkness: the anteroom of the catacombs.

Lieutenant Swigart knelt on the floor of the corridor next to the nuke. Several pages of scrolled computer printout were resting on her upraised right knee; she meticulously consulted the single-spaced rows of instructions as she entered the arming codes into the bomb's keypad. She was taking her time, double-checking each step of the procedure, and for obvious reasons. Any slip-ups, and the nuclear device would fail to detonate. Or worse, explode prematurely.

Such as in the next second.

You know you're not going to get away with this, Miho Sasaki said. *Don't you, Commander?*

She was standing between Nash and Boggs in the corridor on the other side of Swigart and the nuke, directly in front of the entrance to Room C4-20. They were so close to one another that the exhaust from their skinsuits' backpacks clouded the face-plates of one another's helmets. Her hysteria of less than an hour ago had been replaced by cold implacability; were it not for the fact that L'Enfant had continually kept his gun pointed at her during the entire trip from Module Eight to this place deep beneath the C-4 pyramid, Sasaki might have hurled herself upon the commander.

Don't be melodramatic, Dr. Sasaki, L'Enfant replied. *Of course I'm going to get away with it.* He was standing behind

Swigart, blocking escape from the Labyrinth with the Steyr he kept trained upon them. L'Enfant had recovered his air of arrogant condescension, but he had not lowered his guard for a single instant since they had left the lab. Even their suitup had been done with extreme caution; he had forced the three civilians to climb into their skinsuits, together in the open Module One airlock, before he and Swigart had taken their own turns, one at a time, while the other maintained a gun on the prisoners. Nothing had been left to chance; once they had all cycled through the airlock and left the habitat, L'Enfant had ordered Swigart to search their overgarments, making certain that no useful items had been surreptitiously concealed in their suits.

She's correct, Nash said. *When the nuke goes off, Marsat-2 will detect the explosion from orbit. Even if you get out of here in time, there's nothing you can do to stop people from asking all the right questions.*

He paused, hoping to let the facts soak in. *Especially about what happened to us and the rest of the science team,* he added, *not to mention your own men.*

Swigart seemed to hesitate in her programming; her fingers hovered above the keypad as she glanced up at him. *Keep going, Lieutenant,* L'Enfant said easily. *He doesn't know what he's talking about.* As Swigart returned to her painstaking work, L'Enfant went on. *Mr. Nash, we had already taken this into consideration when Kentucky Derby was planned, long before your interference. We were counting on a seasonal dust storm to occur at about this time of the Martian sidereal year and had made our plans accordingly. In about an hour, Marsat-2 will develop an onboard glitch which will render its cameras totally inoperative. A small computer virus, effective only for the next forty-eight hours, but long enough for the explosion to occur. By the time the dust storm dissipates, the base will have ceased to exist, buried beneath tons of wind-borne sand. Any fallout from our underground explosion will have been dispersed throughout the northern hemisphere.*

And the City? Miho asked. *How will its destruction be . . . ?*

Oh, no no no . . . L'Enfant shook his head within his helmet. *You overestimate the power of this bomb, Dr. Sasaki. Think of the sheer mass of the edifice above us. This explosion will be deep underground, within the catacombs. According to computer projections, Marsat-2 will detect a new pit within the center of the City, yes . . . but the pyramids themselves will remain intact. Shaken a bit, but not destroyed. This is why a tactical nuke is being used for this mission. Only the Cooties will suffer.*

"Besides Miho and me, of course," Nash said.

If it helps to ease your mind, L'Enfant continued, *my guess is that your demise will be quick and relatively painless. The enemy will kill you as soon as they've detected your presence, then seize this strange thing you've brought to them and take it deeper into their catacombs. So you'll be long-dead by the time the device detonates.*

"Imagine my relief," Nash replied dryly.

Swigart looked up from the nuke again. *Timer setting, Commander?* she asked.

L'Enfant considered the question. *Two hours . . . no, make it three. Just to be on the safe side.* He hesitated again. *Mr. Boggs, can you have us out of here in two hours and at a safe distance within three?*

Boggs didn't say anything for a few moments. *Yeah,* he muttered reluctantly, *I can get you . . .*

L'Enfant cleared his throat meaningfully. *Pardon me, Captain Boggs?* he asked.

Yes sir, *Commander L'Enfant,* Boggs amended. His stiff tone of voice suggested that he was on the verge of grinding his teeth. *The* Akron *can be ready to leave in two hours.* He paused, then added, *Call it seventeen-thirty hours, sir.*

Nash glanced at the illuminated heads-up display inside his helmet. It was now 1515, local time: mid-afternoon in the central Mars meridian. Perhaps Boggs was only conveniently rounding it off a bit, but it was possible that the pilot was trying to buy them a little more time. As if it mattered; as soon as they entered C4-20, he and Sasaki would be at the mercy of the pseudo-Cooties. Mercy was one trait that was in demonstrably short supply among the alien mechanisms.

Even so, those extra fifteen minutes might make all the difference. . . .

L'Enfant appeared to be mulling it over, and Nash didn't want him to notice the slight discrepancy. *You still haven't answered the question, Captain. What about Kawakami and Verduin and Isralilova and the others . . . ?*

And us? Miho added. *What will be your alibi for our absence when you get back to Arsia?*

For a moment, L'Enfant seemed to be distracted; through his helmet faceplate, Nash could see his eyes unblinkingly locked onto some point midway between the floor of the tunnel and the ceiling. Swigart's right hand remained poised above the keypad as she gazed up at him expectantly, awaiting a final order. Nash was wondering if he should risk a last-ditch attack on the commander when L'Enfant appeared to shake himself out of his reverie.

Yes, that's fine, he said absent-mindedly, as if a consensus agreement had been reached while he was woolgathering and he was making the final call. *Arm the detonator for eighteen-thirty hours, Lieutenant.* As Swigart bent over the nuke once more, carefully tapping the parameters into the digital timer, he went on. *I hardly need an alibi, Dr. Sasaki. During the dust storm there was an accident . . . say, a piece of rock was hurled through the window of the wardroom. Because everyone was in there having an early dinner, they were all killed in the blowout. Only Lieutenant Swigart, Mr. Boggs, and myself were spared, since we happened to be aloft in the airship, surveying the Chryse Planitia. . . .*

Aw, c'mon—! Boggs blurted out, before he remembered the precariousness of his own position and shut up.

"He's right," Nash said. "It's total bullshit. No one will believe you for a second."

True, it's not a likely story . . . but, then, it hardly matters how implausible the fabrication may be. There was gloating in L'Enfant's voice now. *Much like the* Takada Maru, *isn't it? Since it is the cover-story for this operation, the Pentagon will support my allegations, and the contrary evidence will have been buried by natural forces. Everything else is circumstantial. Nothing will happen to us, at least in the long run.*

He chuckled. *Besides, this sort of tragedy has happened before on Mars, has it not? If anything, the anti-space movement will make it into one more reason for us to get off this planet. A disastrous waste of lives and so forth. That's fine with—*

The timer has been set, sir, Swigart interrupted, glancing up from the nuke. Looking down at the bomb, Nash noticed that the top LCD read 1830; below it, a second chronograph displayed a row of zeros. *Awaiting your command.*

You may arm the device, Lieutenant. L'Enfant gave the order without hesitation, yet for a moment Swigart's hand lingered over the keypad. She stared at the two people she was condemning to death; for the briefest of instants, Nash thought he glimpsed an expression of remorse through her helmet faceplate. Then her face hardened again, and as she entered the final code sequence into the nuke's detonator, the bottom LCD blinked and a new string of digits appeared: 03:14:59:00.

The countdown had begun.

Swigart closed the access panel and resealed it with a portable electric screwdriver; they could hear a faint whine as the screws were driven back into place. *If you're thinking of prising open the shell and deactivating the bomb,* L'Enfant added, *I should warn you in advance that it has—*

An auto-destruct override that will detonate the bomb if the proper codes are not entered, Nash finished. *Yes, I know. I've been briefed on this sort of mine.* He felt sweat drooling down the inside of his skinsuit as he watched Swigart finish her work and stand up. *And that's it? You've got nothing more to say to us?*

Brave to the very end. I respect that. L'Enfant mulled over the question for a few seconds. *You should consider what you're doing is not a sacrifice, but a service,* he said solemnly. *Not just for your respective countries, but for the entire human species. For this, I salute you.*

"Yes," Nash replied. "And fuck you, too . . . Captain."

L'Enfant made no verbal response, but his right forefinger twitched near the trigger of his assault rifle. Swigart silently stepped away from the nuke, unshouldering her own rifle and aiming it at Boggs. *Mr. Boggs, you'll come this way, please,* she said.

Boggs started to step forward, then halted and turned back to Nash and Sasaki. Their suit lamps cast a harsh glare over his helmet faceplate, so they couldn't see his face, but his voice over the comlink was choked. *Hey, man, I'm sorry it worked out this way,* he said to Nash. *I didn't think . . .*

"Don't sweat it," Nash replied. "You didn't know. Just straighten up and fly right, okay?"

Yeah. Can do. Boggs was at a loss for words as he turned toward Sasaki. *Babe . . .* He let out his breath as a mournful sigh. *Maybe it's too late now, but I just want to say that I'm sorry for all the dirty jokes.*

He hesitated, then added, *And that I love you . . . always did.*

Miho didn't respond at once. She reached out and briefly took Boggs's gloved hands in her own. *We'll meet again, Waylon,* she said very quietly. *Then I'll listen to your apology.*

She stopped, then said something in Japanese which might have meant *I love you, too.*

Sasaki released his hands; Boggs gazed at her one last time, then reluctantly turned and stepped carefully around the nuclear mine. Swigart immediately grabbed his arm and pulled him out of firing range, pushing him behind L'Enfant. Even if Boggs had considered overcoming the commander in that brief moment when L'Enfant's back was turned toward him, the notion was quickly quashed when the lieutenant swung around to cover him with her rifle.

All right. So much for the long goodbyes. L'Enfant tipped the muzzle of his Steyr toward the nuke. *Pick up the device, Seaman Nash. You too, Dr. Sasaki.*

Nash bent down and took one end of the handle in his right hand. Sasaki grasped the other end with her left hand. As they hefted the mine, Nash was vaguely surprised at its lightness; it weighed not much more than a heavy suitcase. The bomb was cumbersome, but he could have hauled it by himself; L'Enfant had ordered Sasaki to assist him only because it was a convenient way of eliminating two of the last three persons who could cause him problems.

Now turn around and carry it into the chamber, L'Enfant said.

It was the very last thing he wanted to do, but Nash wasn't about to demean himself by making empty gestures of rebellion or contempt. Boggs was being held at gunpoint, and Nash had little doubt that L'Enfant wouldn't hesitate to kill another hostage, although he also intuitively knew that the pilot's life was forfeit once the *Akron* returned to Arsia Station.

Yet, as they lugged the mine through the doorway and into the darkened crypt, he was surprised that L'Enfant had no final words for him. As they entered C4-20, he heard a metallic clang from behind him, then a faint grinding noise. He looked over his shoulder and saw the pneumatic jack had been kicked away, and the massive portal was sliding shut.

They were alone in the Labyrinth.

As soon as the door had closed completely, Sasaki swiftly gestured with her free hand for Nash to put the mine down. He glanced toward a narrow opening in the far wall of the room; in minutes, if not seconds, the pseudo-Cooties would be swarming into the chamber. Miho kept jabbing her finger urgently toward the floor.

"What are you . . . ?" he started to say.

She shook her head; her hand now made a shushing gesture, urging him to be quiet. Nash fell silent. Following her lead, he bent over to gently lower the nuke to the floor. As soon as their hands were off the device, Miho grabbed his right wrist, pulled his wristpad toward her and, unexpectedly, switched off his comlink.

She did the same with her own unit, then grasped his shoulders and pulled him close until her helmet faceplate touched his own. "Stay off the radio!" she shouted, her voice a muffled murmur inside his helmet. "They home in on electromagnetic frequencies!"

Nash was confused, but he nodded his head. "Stand against the wall over there!" she shouted again. "Lie flat against it and stay absolutely still . . . and turn off everything in your suit! Your lamp, the heaters, the oxygen recirculator . . ."

"The life-support system?" He gaped at her. "How are we going to breathe?"

"The reserve tank will cut in!" she snapped. "You can draw air from it for a few minutes and your suit will retain your body heat! Don't argue with me! Go!"

Miho released him, then hurried to the wall farthest away from both the nuke and the entrance to the catacombs. Nash glanced again at the opening in the wall; several of the stones were moving inward, as if being pried loose from within.

The pseudo-Cooties were already on their way.

Nash rushed to the wall and put his back flat against the hard surface. His heartbeat pounded in his ears as he fumbled with his chest unit, tapping his fingers against the recessed buttons. Red emergency lights flickered on his heads-up display as he hastily switched off the skinsuit's primary life-support system; he heard a thin hiss of air as the oxygen reserve tank automatically kicked in, taking up the slack from the deactivated oxygen extraction system. He would have to breathe shallowly; the reserves were intended to be used only in case the OLLSS experienced a power failure, and it was expected that the wearer would already be dashing to the nearest airlock.

The suit began to go cold as he turned off the internal heating system. Last to go was the helmet lamp; Miho had already turned off her own light, and the chamber was plunged into darkness, broken only by the dim red illumination of his battery-powered heads-up display.

Nash flattened the palms of his hands against the wall, forcing himself to remain still. It was more difficult to remain calm; he could hear a thin, scraping noise from the general direction of the opening, presumably more blocks being hauled away. He didn't want to think about what was invading the chamber, so he concentrated on getting his respiration under control.

Breathe shallow, he told himself. Breathe shallow . . . little bit in, little bit out . . . little bit in, little bit out. . . .

The scraping noise rose; either imagined or real, he thought he felt a slight vibration on the floor beneath his boots, as if something was moving into the room. He peered into the frigid blackness, trying to see something, but everything was rendered invisible. For all he knew, one of the minotaurs could be standing directly in front of him, one of its massive claws rearing back to make a fatal strike. . . .

Stop it, he thought. *Don't assume anything. Just work on your breathing. Little bit in, little bit . . .*

Something scurried across the toe of his right boot.

He stiffened, involuntarily sucking in his breath, but he caught himself before he could move. More vibrations from the floor, but this time from all around him. Now he could hear vague, tinny metallic movements, as if the chamber had come alive with nocturnal insects.

Take it easy, he commanded himself. Don't freak. Just remain still. Breathe in . . . breathe out . . . breathe in . . .

Something else moved across his feet, but this time it didn't leave. Nash didn't have to see it to know what it was. His bladder was suddenly full and he desperately needed to urinate, but he knew that if he whizzed now, the pissoir would flood because he had turned off the fluid waste-removal system. *Don't wet your pants, August. Just hold it until . . .*

Another pseudo-Cootie crawled across his feet. He felt a tug at the calf of his left leg, then another at his right. More pseudo-Cooties danced across his feet, but he hardly noticed because tiny little legs were clinging to the fabric of his suit's outergarment, grasping each fold and wrinkled as they scuttled up his knees, up his thighs, scaling towards his groin and hips.

They were climbing up his body.

He struggled against the sharp impulse to scream, to throw the creatures off his suit and dash . . .

Where? He was locked in this chamber. L'Enfant had caused the door to close. There was no way out.

Easy, man . . . easy . . . easy . . .

Now they were all over him. Six? Ten? A dozen? Nash had no idea. He could feel them scurrying up his chest, like minia-ture rock-climbers making an assault on a cliff-face. Their com-bined weight threatened to drag him to the floor; he locked his knees and hips and forced himself to remain rigid. Pretend you're a statue, he told himself. He tried to bring forth the im-mense bronze sculpture of Abraham Lincoln, forever seated within the Lincoln Memorial in Washington, and instead his mind flashed to Control, sitting in the third-floor boardroom of SA's headquarters, sucking on his filthy stinking briar pipe.

Keep control, he thought crazily, almost on the edge of hysteria. Just keep . . .

Caught in the amber glow of his heads-up display, a shad-owed alien countenance rose in front of his helmet: a pseudo-Cootie, staring straight in through his faceplate.

Nash held his breath, not daring to even move his eyes. No more than a few inches separated him from the pseudo-Cootie. He wanted to blink, so badly that the corners of his eyes itched, but he struggled against the impulse. Eerily, he could see his own face reflected in the multifaceted eyes of the little robot, miniaturized and multiplied as tiny mirror-images. Its antennae flicked back and forth, lightly brushing against those of the other pseudo-Cooties crawling around it on his shoulders. Nash was acutely aware of its sharp, mantis-like forelegs digging into the nylon fabric of the overgarment on either side of his helmet.

He waited for the pseudo-Cootie to move onward, perhaps to climb to the top of his helmet. Maybe it would plant a little flag up there, open a tiny bottle of champagne, take some pictures for the folks back home.

But it didn't move.

He couldn't breathe. His lungs needed to exhale. He couldn't breathe. His lungs were aching. If he didn't breathe . . .

The hell with it.

"Boo," he whispered, and cautiously sucked a breath of air.

The mechanical insect jerked backward slightly, as if startled, but continued to cling to his chest, peering into his helmet like a climber who had found a snake lurking within a cave. All at once, the other pseudo-Cooties went motionless. Nash was all too aware that their pincers could rip through his skinsuit within seconds.

On the other hand, the heads-up display told him that the oxygen reserve was almost exhausted. Asphyxiation or having his skinsuit shredded; either way, it added up to the same thing. He was about to die.

Might as well get this over with . . .

"What are you waiting for?" he murmured under his breath, addressing himself as much as the pseudo-Cootie. "If you're going to do it, get it over with."

The pseudo-Cootie remained still, yet its antennae lashed back and forth madly, rubbing against those of the others around him. Nash remembered what Kawakami had told him about the possibility of a collective intelligence—a hive-mind—existing amongst these creatures. Maybe these were the equivalent of soldier-ants, searching their environment for enemies or food. He hoped that he was neither. . . .

Then, abruptly, the pseudo-Cootie vanished from his faceplate, and at the same moment he again felt the crawling sensation around his body . . . but this time, it was heading downward, as if in full retreat.

As swiftly as they had come, the creatures were abandoning him.

He remained stock-still until he felt the last of the pseudo-Cooties leave him; then, very cautiously, he moved his fear-stiffened left hand to the chest unit, groped for the proper buttons, and reactivated his life-support system. There was a rush of cool air through his helmet, clammy against the perspiration on his skin; he hadn't realized that he had been sweating. He sucked greedily at the air, taking it in as deep draughts, wondering if Sasaki felt the same . . .

"Miho," he rasped. Did she also . . . ?

Helmet lamplight lanced out from a spot next to him, dazzling him with its unanticipated brightness. He squinted against the glare and almost switched on the comlink before a hand laid itself over his wrist unit. As he blinked and covered his faceplate with his glove, he felt a human form move against him and a now-familiar shape thump against his helmet.

"It's me!" he heard her yell through the inductive connection. "We made it! Go ahead and turn on your light!"

● ● ●

There was no telling how many pseudo-Cooties had been in C4-20, but the chamber was now completely vacant. One thing was immediately apparent, however.

The nuke was missing.

Sasaki pointed toward the dismantled wall. "They must have taken it that way," she said, stating the obvious. She glanced at the still-closed door leading into the Labyrinth. "Unless we want to stay here . . ."

"We're going to have to follow them," Nash finished. Although they had reactivated their skinsuits' life-support systems, they cautiously remained off the comlink. The helmet-touch system was cumbersome, but in the stillness of the chamber they could hear each other plainly. "I don't get it. Did they crawl all over you too?"

Sasaki nodded her head; he felt her shudder at the recollection. "Then why didn't they kill us?" he asked. "I had one of them looking straight through my helmet, and it couldn't have mistaken me for anything but a human."

She shrugged her shoulders. "We weren't wearing combat armor."

Of course . . . Nash closed his eyes. "Miho," he said, "I wish you wouldn't speak in riddles whenever I ask you a question. *Why* didn't they kill us because we weren't wearing armor?"

"The only people who have survived encounters with them in this room were Ben Cassidy and Arthur Johnson," she replied. "They both came down here in skinsuits. Everyone else who came in here was wearing armor . . . and didn't Shin-ichi observe that the minotaurs vaguely resembled CAS's?"

"So you thought that they might home in on combat armor?"

"Yes. Something like that." She looked straight at him, smiling slightly. "I had a hunch that might be the situation. That's why I had you turn off everything and stand still. They must perceive combat armor—in fact, anything mechanical and emitting electromagnetic frequencies, like the probes or the Jackalope—as a threat, and immediately act to neutralize it. Probably another one of their autotropisms."

"Uh-huh." Nash was still regaining his breath. It sounded like a plausible explanation. "When did you arrive at this conclusion?"

Her face became solemn. "About ten minutes ago," she said almost inaudibly.

Nash slowly exhaled as he sagged against the wall behind

him. "Better late than never," he muttered. He wasn't about to split hairs with her. He looked dubiously at the gap in the wall. "The point is, if we go in there, will they attack us?"

Sasaki hesitated. "I don't think so," she said uncertainly. "They could have killed us a few minutes ago and they didn't. Maybe without the armor we're not interesting . . . or perhaps there's nothing they can salvage from our suits."

"That sounds too much like guessing."

"It is," she admitted. "Either way, we don't have a choice. If we can find our way to Mama's Back Door, we could make our way to the D&M Pyramid. There's bound to be a way up to the surface from there."

Nash glanced at the digital chronometer on his helmet's heads-up display; he was surprised to see that only ten minutes had elapsed since L'Enfant and Swigart had forced them into the chamber. "We've only got two hours until the *Akron* takes off. If we're going to make it out of here before the bomb goes off, we're going to have to hurry." He looked back at her. "You ready?"

Sasaki slowly nodded her head; despite her outward composure, it was apparent that she was shaken by her near-death experience. Nash gave her hand a reassuring squeeze. "Okay," he said, "let's go."

He stepped back, breaking contact with her helmet, but Sasaki continued to clasp his hand. Nash smiled and nodded, then led her across the empty chamber to the broken wall.

Beyond lay darkness, the beginning of the catacombs. Hand in hand, they stepped gingerly across the border into the undisturbed domain of the Cooties.

22. Underworld

Beyond Room C4-20, the tunnel became both wider and higher than the one in the Labyrinth. Instead of narrow corridors of smooth rock, it resembled the passageway of an underground river, with smooth, sloping walls of eroded stone leading further into the depths of the catacombs. Nash was struck by its similarity to cave-systems on Earth; he wondered if the Cooties had indeed built the City on top of an ancient underground waterway, one which had once fed water into the shallow sea where the Acidalia Planitia now lay.

Yet that wasn't what immediately attracted his attention. On either side of the tunnel rested large, almost shapeless metallic hulks, some the size of trucks although they could hardly be mistaken for vehicles. Discarded machinery of some sort, yet they all looked oddly stripped-down, as if they were great engine-blocks which had been cannibalized for functional parts. Nash approached one of the hulks and carefully wiped away a patina of red dust from a flat surface; caught beneath the ray of his helmet lamp was a series of tiny holes and grooves, resembling attachment-points for something which had long since been removed.

"What do you think these . . . ?" he started to ask before he remembered that he wasn't sharing a comlink with Sasaki. He turned around and saw her kneeling on the tunnel floor, apparently studying something. As he walked closer, she stood up and clamped her helmet against his.

"Tracks," she said, pointing down at the floor. The red dust was sifted and dragged, showing where hundreds of tiny legs had recently moved through the tunnel. They led straight ahead, past the reach of her light into the darkness.

"They went thataway," he drawled. She looked at him

strangely, and he grinned back at her. "Let's head 'em off at the pass, pilgrim."

"Ah, yes." Miho smiled tightly. "John Wayne. The old American cowboy star. Maksim Oeljanov was a big fan of his movies." Her face went serious again. "Never mind that now. We need to catch up with them."

Sasaki broke contact and began walking down the tunnel, carefully keeping the oval spot of her lamp centered on the tracks. She displayed no curiosity about the alien artifacts around her, and Nash couldn't blame her. She was onto much bigger game now; why waste time in what amounted to an auto graveyard when there was the potential of discovering the source of these relics?

In any case, he had no choice but to follow her. Nash fell into step beside her, making certain that he didn't lose sight of the tracks himself. Despite the fact that they were running against the clock, he found his own curiosity aroused by what little he had seen thus far. They were the first human beings to have ventured so far into the Cooties' lair. Not only that, but following the trail of the pseudo-Cooties was their best bet of finding a way out of the catacombs.

The tunnel was sloping gradually downward; as they walked, he was increasingly aware that it was taking them further away from the surface. After several hundred yards, they came to a junction where another, seemingly smaller tunnel to their right converged with the first one. More tracks led from that junction. Miho stopped, consulted the compass on her wrist and matched it against the larger line of tracks; she decided to stick with the main tunnel since it led directly southeast, where the D&M Pyramid lay. After another hundred feet, they came upon a second convergence where another branch intersected the tunnel. Again, after studying the tracks and her compass, Miho decided to remain on the present course.

"I think those are secondary tunnels," she said. "They may have once been tributaries in a subsurface river system that the Cooties—"

"I figured as much," Nash interrupted, and she gave him a sharp look. "I'm not totally stupid, Miho. I just want to make sure that we don't get lost in this maze. We don't have time to backtrack if we do."

She shook her head. "I understand . . . but those seem to be secondary arteries, and even if they might lead to one of the other pyramids, there's a chance they could branch into even smaller veins before we reach an opening." She pointed toward the larger set of tracks leading into the main tunnel. "There has been much recent motion this way. They probably carried the nuke in this direction, and it corresponds with the seismic activity we've already detected. It is our best hope."

Nash checked the REM counter on his heads-up display. No clues there; it showed only the nominal background radiation typical of any place on Mars. It figured; the Kentucky Derby nuke was well-shielded, so there was no telltale gamma trace of its passage through the catacombs.

"If you think you're right," he said.

Sasaki said nothing. She stepped away from him, pointed straight ahead, and continued the long march. They were in completely unknown territory, unmapped by humankind. Nash could only hope that she remembered this, and pray that they didn't get confused. He glanced up at the rock ceiling above them and felt a brief chill; he didn't want to be beneath all that mass when the nuke detonated. They had to find their way out of the catacombs, or remain sealed in here forever . . .

Buried alive, beneath a city of the dead.

The convergences became more frequent as the main tunnel became more serpentine, winding downward into the rocky mantle. Each time they came to a junction, Sasaki had to stop and check the compass. After the fourth intersection, though, the width of each tunnel and the tracks in the dusty floor began to look almost identical, until it was impossible to differentiate between the main artery and its tributaries except for the southeastern compass heading. The disassembled machinery was left behind by the time they passed the fourth convergence; the tunnels were now vacant of everything except the furrowed places where extraterrestrial footprints now lay. A claustrophobe would have been shrieking in terror.

As they rounded a bend and came upon the seventh junction, they saw something completely unexpected. The new tributary converged from above, and from it flowed a steady stream of pseudo-Cooties. Two streams, rather: one coming down from the new tunnel, heading for the main artery, and the other marching in the opposite direction, into the tributary.

Nash stopped and grabbed Sasaki's arm as soon as they saw

the alien robots. "What's . . . they're . . . ?" he stammered, tapping his helmet against her own.

"I think I know." Her voice was almost inaudible, yet strangely calm. "Look at the ones coming down from the secondary tunnel. See what they're carrying?"

Nash's helmet lamp flashed across the pseudo-Cooties. The ones emerging from the tributary each held a large rock between their pincers. Rock. Nothing apparently more significant than that . . . yet the ones headed back into the tributary were empty-handed. As Nash watched, it seemed to him that for each pseudo-Cootie that emerged from the secondary tunnel another came to replace it from the main branch. He was reminded of something Kawakami had said, comparing the pseudo-Cooties to driver ants. They had that sort of intrinsically mechanical, inhuman precision.

"They're miners," Sasaki said. "Raw materials being dredged out of the planet's crust. All they do is select and bring back what they need." She paused. "But why from above . . . ?"

Her voice trailed off into an unconscious flow of Japanese. Nash glanced at her; through his faceplate, he could hear that she was transfixed by the pseudo-Cooties. He grabbed her arm and gave her a hard yank. "Can we get through them?" he said.

Sasaki's eyelids fluttered as if she were coming out of a trance. "I don't know . . . yes, maybe we can, but I don't . . ."

"Only one way to find out." Nash broke away from her. He took a deep breath, then strode forward and, one careful step at a time, walked into the midst of the pseudo-Cooties.

For an instant, the metallic creatures were bewildered; they swarmed around his legs, bumping into him and against each other, some prodding and touching his calves with their antennae and pincers. Watching them carefully, Nash prepared to leap free in case one of them attempted to slice through his skinsuit. Yet nothing happened; in a few moments, the pseudo-Cooties docilely accepted him as an unforeseen obstacle in their path. They began to move around him, avoiding contact with his legs.

Nash sighed with relief, then gestured for Sasaki to join him; she hesitated for a second, then timidly stepped into the swarm. Again, there was confusion as they jostled against her legs for a few moments; then both the incoming and outgoing ranks parted on either side of them.

She touched her helmet against his. "They're like worker-ants in an anthill," she said. She pointed at the pseudo-Cooties who were just now entering the junction. "Notice how the ones who weren't here at first are also avoiding us. The message must have already passed through the ranks. Paul was right. They've developed a collective consciousness which allows them to instantly communicate with each other and . . ."

Her voice trailed off as her face suddenly paled. "The minotaurs!" she snapped. "They could already be on their way! August, we've got to get out of here!"

Sasaki started to bolt, but Nash grabbed her shoulders and held her close. "Don't run!" he yelled. "They're not coming! Nothing's coming this way!"

He could see her panic-stricken face inside her helmet; she fought to wrench herself from his grip, but he held on tight. "Miho, *think*!" he demanded. "Just stop and think for a minute! If there were any minotaurs left, they would have been sent to the base with the rest of them. Right? If there were any more, why weren't they in the Labyrinth when we came down? Right? *Right?*"

She stared back at him as mute comprehension crept into her eyes. "Trust me!" he shouted, giving her a ruthless shake "There's no more of them! They're all gone!"

Then her muscles relaxed as her anxiety attack faded away. Almost limp, she swayed against him; Nash wrapped his arms around her, feeling her tremble. He thought he heard her say something in Japanese, but he didn't ask for a translation. "It's okay," he said, clumsily patting the life-support unit on her back. "It's all right, it's okay. . . ."

He waited a minute until she had calmed herself, then he gently pushed her away. "We've got to get out of here." He glanced at his chronometer. "We've got only about an hour left until the *Akron* takes off. We need to hustle now."

"Yes. You're right." Sasaki quickly nodded her head, then unexpectedly smiled at him. "Thank you, August. If we weren't wearing helmets, I'd give you a kiss."

"Save it for your redneck boyfriend," Nash replied. He dropped his hands from her shoulders and pointed toward the upward-leading tributary tunnel. "If they're coming from above, then it might lead straight to the surface."

"Possibly." Miho checked her compass again. "As a rough guess, I say we're beneath the City's center, the open area between the pyramids. It might take us up there . . . or we could get lost."

"So do we try it or not?"

She gazed at the new tunnel for a moment, then slowly nodded her head. "Yes, perhaps we should . . . but I still want to see what's down there. We're getting close."

Nash hesitated, then nodded his own head. "Okay, I'm with you. We'll check it out . . . so long as we make it quick." He turned towards the main tunnel, heedless of the pseudo-Cooties which mindlessly moved on either side of them. "C'mon, let's go. I want to see what's so important to these little guys."

Even before they reached the end of the tunnel, they could feel vibrations running through the stone floor. The tunnel had now widened to the point where it could have accommodated two freight trains. Nash was reminded of the rail yards outside his hometown in Fitchburg, Massachusetts, where his father had sometimes taken him when he was a kid to see the trains come and go. He could now hear vague noises through his helmet, as if great forces were working just ahead of them; indeed, the pseudo-Cooties around them seemed to be moving with greater speed, impelled to operate with more alacrity toward their mysterious objective.

They passed another bend and suddenly saw weak, diffuse light seeping from a large opening just ahead. The pseudo-Cooties were marching in and out of the tunnel mouth, yet they could make out no details beyond that point. Walking between the metallic insects, they strode quickly toward the tunnel's end . . . and abruptly halted in their tracks, dumbfounded as they saw what lay before them.

"Oh my God . . ." Nash heard himself whisper.

They were in the bottom of a vast bowl-shaped cavern, easily the size of an enclosed baseball stadium on Earth.

The sloped rock walls were hundreds of feet high, extending outward as far as their lamplight could reach. Above them stretched a smooth, yet irregularly dappled, concave ceiling, as if they were looking up at the bottom of a great opaque lens. The cavern vaguely resembled the enclosed crater at Arsia Station where the *Akron* was hangared between flights, but it was much larger; the *Percival Lowell* could have been dropped in there, with plenty of room to spare.

Yet the circular edge of the ceiling didn't quite touch the

walls of the cavern, as if the ceiling was hanging free above the floor. It was from that fissure that sunlight indirectly penetrated the cavern, from an unseen opening far above the floating ceiling, as if from an obstructed skylight.

Multitudes of pseudo-Cooties scurried across the stone floor in the shadowy half-light, moving between what at first appeared to be great triple-trunked trees—or maybe stalagmites—which grew randomly from various places on the bottom of the cavern. The miniature robots were dwarfed by the huge structures; many of them were drawing large metallic-looking objects from big round pits near the walls of the cavern and passing them to each other, pincer to pincer, as if they were in an old-style fire-bucket brigade.

Not just pseudo-Cooties either. Larger, spiderlike creatures, vaguely resembling immense daddy-longlegs except that they were the size of cattle, carried bigger objects away from the pits. Many of them scaled the cavern walls toward the curved ceiling, their fragile-looking legs clinging precariously to minute cracks and crevices in the rock, hauling their cargo toward the mysterious ceiling.

Then, all at once, something lowered itself from the nearest stalagmite-tree, which towered above them like a mutant redwood: a three-clawed arm, like that of one of the minotaurs except much larger. Startled, Nash took a step backward, but Sasaki remained still; they watched the arm as it moved to a flat plate-like object held aloft by a dozen pseudo-Cooties. The claw clasped the edges of the plate and, as it raised it upwards, Nash was astounded to see one of the three trunks *take a step forward*.

His breath caught in his chest, Nash peered upward, following the progress of the great arm as it hauled the object toward the ceiling. At the apex of the three trunks—which, he now realized, were mobile legs—was a saucerlike centerpiece, from which two giant arms extended. As the left arm brought up the plate, the right arm steadied it and, with careful ease, pushed it into place against an opening in the ceiling which matched its dimensions precisely.

It was a machine. All of them: machines. Nash didn't realize that he was mesmerized until he felt Sasaki's hand close around his left wrist and pull him closer to place the side of her helmet against his own.

"H. G. Wells was right," she said. "There *are* tripods on Mars."

He could now see, through the diffuse light filtered from above, that each of the tripods was taking flat plates from the pseudo-Cooties and raising them to the high ceiling of the cavern. His mind reeled from the notion that something so immense could be mobile; he swallowed hard, feeling his mind teeter on the edge of imbalance.

"It looks like they're building something," he said, and was instantly aware of the stupidity of his remark. "They're ... I don't know. Assemblers. They can barely move, but that's what they are. Like big mobile cranes, specially built ... grown, I mean ... for one purpose." He pointed toward the nearest spider, which was halfway up the wall of the cavern. "Like that one there, taking something up to the ceiling. It's as if it was designed for this job."

"I agree," Sasaki said. "Like the pseudo-Cooties and the minotaurs, each has a specific function." She paused, then added. "Look up. Tell me what you see."

He stared at the ceiling again; the beam of his helmet lamp danced across its irregular surface. He now noticed, in its exact epicenter, the round opening of a narrow shaft. He also realized that the ceiling was not made of rock, but of metal; it was composed of platework, almost as if it was ...

"A hull," he said aloud.

"Yes. An outer hull." Sasaki's awestruck voice was barely intelligible. "We've been looking for their starship ... and here it is."

They began to cautiously make their way across the cavern, skirting the sides of the vast chamber to avoid contact with the pseudo-Cooties or the tripods in the center of the floor. Their subterfuge barely mattered, though; the pseudo-Cooties and spiders they encountered paid absolutely no attention to them as they single-mindedly scurried back and forth, carrying parts from the pits, and they were beneath the notice of the tripods.

Although Nash was in a hurry to return to the tunnel from which they had come, Sasaki insisted on checking out the pits. The first one they came upon was completely empty; shining his helmet lamp down into it, Nash saw that it was a smooth round bore, made of polished red stone, about twelve feet wide and twenty feet deep. He noticed that its walls were lined with tiny, pinprick-size holes, but if the pit itself had ever served a purpose, it was apparently obsolete now.

Yet, fifty feet away was another pit; dodging the pseudo-Cooties gathered around it, they went closer. The second pit had the same dimensions as the first, but this one was filled with a viscous scarlet fluid. Unsettlingly enough, it resembled an enormous vat filled with blood; Nash supposed that if it could be smelled by human nostrils, it might also smell like blood.

Yet the fluid was not still; it swirled of its own accord, subtle eddies and currents flowing through the dense mixture as if something deep within the pit was alive. Miho knelt next to the lip of the pit, staring intently down into the morass; she suddenly reached up, and grabbing Nash's wrist, hauled him down next to her so that their helmets connected again.

"Microassemblers!" she exclaimed, jabbing an excited finger at the mixture. "It only looks like liquid, but it's not! Those are millions of nanites!"

Nash gazed into the vat; upon closer examination, he now saw the fluid had an almost granular texture, somewhat similar to quicksand. He remembered what Kawakami had postulated about the construction of the minotaurs. "Are you trying to tell me . . . ?"

He stopped and studied the pit. "You're trying to tell me that something's being *grown* in there?"

"Yes!" Miho eagerly replied. "Exactly! If it was a true water-based liquid, it would have been instantly evaporated by the lack of atmospheric pressure. No, those are microscopic, self-replicating robots . . . the largest may be no bigger than a rice-kernel."

She stood up and strode quickly toward the next pit. Several pseudo-Cooties were dropping chunks of rock—probably dredged from the near-surface quarries from where they had earlier seen the robots carrying the stone—into a three-quarters-full pit of the same fluid. Here, the pit was churning more rapidly, as if tiny piranhas were devouring the rocks. Heedless of the pseudo-Cooties, Sasaki approached the edge of the pit and watched for a minute before she turned back to Nash.

"Raw materials are being fed into the vats," she said quickly, her words coming out as a breathless rush, "which in turn are being broken down into their basic elements by the nanites and reassembled into solid-state components for the starship."

Sasaki pointed toward the immense hull above them, where

the tripods were sealing more plates into position. "Everything in this cave . . . the pseudo-Cooties, the tripods, the vessel itself . . . is a product of nanotechnology, yet one so far beyond the grasp of our species that we've only theorized these possibilities."

Nash followed her gaze. "Then . . . this is not the original ship?" She shook her head. "Then the junk we saw in the tunnels . . ."

"Unsalvageable scraps of their first starship," she finished. "Things they either couldn't break down or didn't need to copy. It hardly matters. If Shin-ichi was right, then the Cooties came here in a sub-light-speed vessel which was only intended for a one-way voyage across the galaxy. In order to get home, they've been forced to build another like it."

"But the Cooties are all dead!" he snapped.

"Yes," Miho said, "but that doesn't matter to them." She stared straight at Nash's face. "Don't you see? They're obeying a biomechanical tropism . . . programming, if you want to call it that, but it's far more complex. When the Cooties went into hibernation, they told their slaves what to do and how to do it. Everything they've done . . . everything *we've* done . . . must have been thought out beforehand and anticipated thousands of years ago. They don't *care* if their programmers are now dead. This single purpose is all that matters to them."

She closed her eyes, shaking her head inside her helmet. "L'Enfant was right. This *is* a trap . . . but not for the reasons he believed."

As she spoke, Nash's gaze wandered back to the pit next to them. Already the nanites were busily constructing something in its depths. Nearby, he could see another crowd of pseudo-Cooties hauling a completed hull plate out of the adjacent pit; sanguine liquid seeped off it as it was tugged into view, a few hundred nanites who had remained fixed to their end-product. If all this had been made from raw native materials . . .

Abruptly, he realized where all the men and human-made items that had been lost in the Labyrinth and Mama's Back Door had gone. The combat armor, the Jackalope, the various probes, the bodies themselves: all dumped into the pits and reduced to their most elementary substances. Oxygen, hydrogen, carbon, nickel, zinc, copper—there were many useful trace-elements to be found in a corpse, if one only knew how to extract and refine them.

His stomach lurched as the full horror hit him. Somewhere up there, within the innards of that vast machine, were the decomposed remains of Hal Moberly, Sasha Kulejan and Paul Verdiun—now scattered parts of an alien vessel.

"When the first ship landed here, they dismantled it completely," Sasaki went on. "They had to, in order to survive for as short a time as they did. That's why we never found their ship. But this is a duplicate of that vessel, constructed from natural resources by the pseudo-Cooties. They might have—"

She suddenly stopped talking as she stared up at the vast ceiling. Nash looked back in the direction of her gaze. For a moment, he couldn't see what had caught her attention. Then the beam of his helmet-lamp landed on the outstretched claws of one of the tripods, and what he saw grasped between them caused his heart to freeze.

The tripod held the unmistakable, elongated shape of the Kentucky Derby nuke. It was being carefully raised toward the shaft in the center of the outer hull.

"Of course." Sasaki's voice was a monotone inside his helmet. "Plutonium . . . an element which doesn't occur in nature. Uranium ore they can find on Mars, even refine in the pits, but if they needed plutonium to get off the ground . . ."

"What are you trying to . . . ?"

"They've built an Orion ship," she murmured.

"I don't understand," Nash said, although he was beginning to get a hunch. "If they have uranium, then why would they want . . . ?"

"Uranium they could use for reaction-mass once they've gotten off the ground, but they needed a more potent fuel-source for liftoff. All this time, they've been waiting for plutonium." Miho seemed not to be talking to him as much as she was thinking aloud. "The Face was intended to attract us here, the City to contain the remains of the original passengers . . . they instinctively knew that we would have to possess advanced nuclear technology if we were capable of achieving interplanetary flight. So they built their new vessel for the voyage home, and waited for us to deliver what they needed the most, yet couldn't find on Mars. Plutonium."

Within the hull, Nash could see the tiny figures of spiders as they reached down to grasp the nuke with their long legs and pull it up into the vessel. Transfixed by the sight, Sasaki shook her head in wonderment. "Thousands of years, waiting for just one thing to take them back from where they came. Maybe if our landers had used nuclear engines, they would have stolen them and stripped out the fuel cores, but instead they had to wait a little longer. Biding their time, building their new ship, watching us from a safe, protected distance. Finally, L'Enfant brought a nuke here to Mars and we delivered it to the catacombs. They don't even need to construct the engine to . . ."

"Cut it out," he said as he gave her a hard shake. "What do you mean by an Orion ship?"

Miho blinked, her trance broken. "Something a group of American scientists dreamed up in the last century," she said. She looked back at him, her eyes wide with mixed elation and fear. "An absurd idea . . . or at least it seemed so then. If you could build a spaceship with an immense pusher-plate at the end, then detonate a hydrogen bomb of sufficient kilotonnage beneath it . . ."

"It'll lift the ship off the ground," Nash finished. "Give it escape velocity, by brute force."

He suddenly perceived the source of the indirect sunlight which illuminated the cavern. The pseudo-Cooties were disassembling its roof, making way for the launch of their ship and using the nanite-processed rock as material for the final pieces of the ship. And if they were this far along to be clearing the way for liftoff. . . .

He felt a surge of panic. "We're getting out of here," he said coldly as he glanced again at his chronometer. A little less than thirty minutes remained until the *Akron* was scheduled to fly, but that was now the lesser of his concerns. In approximately an hour and a half from now . . .

He grabbed her wrist. "C'mon, let's go. I'm not sticking around to see if you're right about all this."

Miho didn't protest as he tugged her away from the nanite-vat and, taking her by the hand, began to haul her back the way they had come. It was too late to seek out the entrance to Mama's Back Door; even if they located it and successfully found their way to the D&M Pyramid, they would emerge several miles from the base. The side-tunnel to the surface was their only real chance of escape.

Nash hustled Miho toward the mouth of the main tunnel, running past the pit where the pseudo-Cooties had just brought forth a new hull plate. All he wanted to do now was get the hell out of there before . . .

He felt something slide beneath his boots, as if he'd suddenly stepped into a shallow rain-puddle; he slipped backwards, instinctively jerked himself forward, lost his balance, and came down on one knee. He hissed in pain—another bruise!—and almost fell over completely before Sasaki grabbed his arm and hauled him erect.

Nash glanced down at his leg, alert for a rip in his suit, and saw that he had stepped into a puddle of the nanite-liquid. The soles of his boots and the lower left calf of his skinsuit were stained with the blood-colored liquid.

If Sasaki said anything, he couldn't hear her. He studied the blotches for a moment, but nothing seemed to be eating through his boots or the fabric of his overgarment. There had to be something about the taste of skinsuits that aliens didn't like.

It didn't matter. He dismissed the accident from his mind as he took Miho's hand again and resumed their run toward the tunnel mouth.

23. Pikadan

W. J. Boggs watched the digital chronometer mounted above the pilot's seat: the green-lit display told him it was now 1725 hours. His gaze shifted down to a status board next to his left elbow, to a single LED which stubbornly remained dark. He stared hard at the tiny light, willing it to blink, but it defied his silent admonition to come alive.

C'mon guys, he thought, *you can still make it. . . .*

The indicator next to the one in question suddenly flashed red, fooling him for a moment until he realized that it was the main airlock light. He let out his breath and looked over at L'Enfant; the commander was sitting in the left-hand co-pilot's seat, apparently watching the last scarlet glow of sunlight fading over the western horizon. Although L'Enfant's mind seemed to be focused elsewhere, the palm of his right hand still rested on top of the gun in his lap.

"Has Lieutenant Swigart come aboard?" he asked without looking away from the sunset.

Damn, but the bastard hardly missed a trick. Boggs prayed that L'Enfant hadn't noticed his attention to one particular idiotlight. "She's cycling through the airlock now," Boggs replied. L'Enfant didn't say anything, but a corner of his mouth twitched downward and his hard eyes darted toward him. "Sir," Boggs added.

"Hmm. Very well. You may initiate lift-off as soon as she's with us." L'Enfant's gaze moved back to the gondola windows. "You know," he said conversationally, "it has always amazed me how the autumn sunsets here are so much like those on Earth. Just as there, the sun goes down a minute earlier each day as the winter solstice grows closer, until we begin to see dark-

307

ness in late afternoon. All we miss are the leaves changing color. . . ."

He looked toward Boggs again. "Quite a bit of synchronicity between the two worlds, isn't there, Mr. Boggs?"

"If you say so, sir." Boggs glanced up at the chronometer again; 1727 now. "We ought to wait until the sun's completely down, y'know, before we take off. The wind picks up quite a bit right at sundown, so taking off before it gets calm could be tricky. I had sort of the same trouble a few days ago when we were leaving Arsia. The ship bucked like a . . ."

"No." L'Enfant's response was cold and flat, leaving no room for argument. "We lift off at seventeen-thirty precisely, as we agreed earlier. No later. I'm certain you'll be able to manage the wind-shear, Mr. Boggs."

Boggs silently nodded his head, pretending to study the checklist in his lap. L'Enfant's eyes moved away once more; Boggs surreptitiously checked the status board again. The indicator had yet to flash red.

Goddammit, Nash, get in there! Don't tell me you've forgotten already . . . !

He heard footfalls on the gangway leading down into the gondola, then a heavy weight was dropped into the passenger seat behind him. Boggs looked around to see Megan Swigart—still wearing her skinsuit sans helmet and gloves—pushing an airtight aluminum attaché case the rest of the way into the seat. "I've gathered the remaining records, Commander," she said, "All the CD-ROM's from the command module are in the case and the mainframes have been scrubbed."

"Good work, Lieutenant," L'Enfant said distractedly, still watching the sunset.

"Nothing to it." Swigart smiled casually as she tugged the strap of her Steyr off her shoulder and carefully propped the assault rifle against an armrest. "Piece of cake."

Boggs clamped his jaw together as he forced his eyes away from the attaché case. The bitch had just destroyed all the hard data gathered by the science team over the past three years, and she called it a piece of cake. All records of their labor were collected in the attaché case. Although only L'Enfant knew what he intended to do with the CD-ROM's, Boggs could well imagine their final fate: a small creche of information, classified Top Secret and hidden within some Pentagon AI system, where the names of Kawakami and Isralilova and Verduin and all the others would appear only as minor footnotes and indices.

Perhaps that was the whole point of Kentucky Derby, the hidden agenda of those who had sent L'Enfant to Mars in the first place: to steal information, carrying it off in the night like a half-ass thief snatching gold-plated candlesticks from a church altar. All this, just to gain a temporary advantage over imaginary enemies . . .

"Very well." L'Enfant sat up straight in his seat, shifting the gun around in his lap as he began to buckle up for takeoff. He paused halfway through pulling down the harness straps and glanced over his shoulder at Swigart. "And, ah . . . just to be on the safe side, did you . . . ?"

"Yes sir, I checked the base perimeter." Swigart was seating herself behind L'Enfant, obviously to keep Boggs within gun-range in case he had any homicidal notions. "Nothing moving in the vicinity. All clear."

"Very well," he said. "Just checking." Was it his own imagination at play, or did Boggs detect the slightest hint of relief in L'Enfant's voice? The commander buckled his waist and shoulder straps, then looked over at the pilot. "Mr. Boggs, it's now seventeen-thirty hours. Please take us out of here."

Oh, Christ. Miho . . .

For an instant, Boggs was tempted to reach across the aisle, grab the smug asshole by the throat with both hands, and ram his balding skull straight through the cockpit windows. Even if he or Swigart managed to plug him during the act, at least he'd have the satisfaction of seeing the sick fuck die before instant decompression snuffed out all of their lives. If Boggs was going to hell, he might as well take this raving maniac down with him. . . .

"Yes, sir," he murmured instead. He let out his breath and swiftly buckled his own seat harness. The blind obedience of a coward who wanted to stay alive just a little while longer.

The *Akron* was already refueled and powered-up; all he had to do was sever the mooring cables, vector the engines, and throttle up. Boggs deliberately forced all thoughts of Miho Sasaki from his mind as his eyes swept across the myriad gauges, screens, and LCDs, automatically checking to see that all systems were flight-ready. Everything was copacetic, except for the stone in his chest.

As he grasped the yoke in his left fist and curled his right hand over the throttles, he stole one final glance at the aft maintenance-hatch indicator near his left elbow. . . .

The LED was pulsing a vivid, bright red.

He stared at it, blinked . . . and, just as suddenly as it had appeared, the indicator went dark again.

Someone had opened the aft maintenance hatch in the lower stern of the *Akron* and closed it again. Just like all those times at Arsia Station when he had to bug the ground crew about making sure the damn thing was latched. Except, this time, there was no flight crew on hand to resecure the hatch.

Nash was alive . . . and he had remembered.

And if Nash had made it out the Labyrinth, there was a good chance Miho had escaped as well. No way to make sure that they were both aboard, though, without tipping off L'Enfant and Swigart. All he could do was hope.

Nonetheless, it was difficult to refrain from grinning. Boggs quickly coughed into his fist to hide an involuntary chuckle, then forced his attention back to his controls. "All right," he said. "Everyone strapped in? Okay, let's hit it. . . ."

He reached up, grasped the cable-detach bar, and yanked it down.

There was a sudden lurch as the airship freed itself from its mooring lines. Nash had already anticipated it, but Sasaki was unprepared for the abrupt motion. Caught off-balance, she was thrown across the catwalk railing; it caught her in the stomach and she nearly toppled over before Nash grabbed her by the hips and hauled her back. Through her helmet, he caught a glimpse of her blanched face.

No wonder. If she'd gone over the rail, she would have fallen twenty feet until she ripped through the skin of one of the internal gas cells . . . and then it would have been another fifty-foot drop through the cell itself until she smashed against the *Akron*'s internal skeleton, or even hurtled through the Mylar outer fuselage.

She grasped the opposite railing with both hands and placed her feet firmly on the gridded catwalk. Already they could hear the drone of the engines as they were throttled up; there was the familiar rising sensation as the *Akron* began its ascent. Miho started to place her helmet against Nash's, but he signaled for her to reactivate her comlink, raising three fingers to indicate the third channel.

They had deliberately continued radio silence even after they had reached the top of the secondary tunnel and climbed through the partly disassembled roof of the great cavern. As Miho had predicted, they had emerged from the catacombs in the City square, amidst the four major pyramids. It hadn't been difficult to climb through, since most of the groundcover had already been removed by the pseudo-Cooties. Even then, however, they had barely been able to reach the *Akron* in time; they had been forced to hide behind a corner of the C-4 pyramid until almost the last minute, when Swigart finally boarded the airship and enabled them to make a frantic dash for the maintenance hatch beneath the dirigible's stern.

Sasaki hesitated, then tapped her fingers against her skinsuit's right gauntlet. *Are you certain we should be doing this?* she asked.

It was a relief to be able to hear her voice distinctly again, without the muffling effects of helmet-to-helmet communications. "Positive," Nash said. "They won't be using the comlink themselves while they're down there, and I doubt they'll wander up here."

She still looked worried. *What about Waylon?*

"If he's been paying attention, he must know we're back here. He won't get them to make an inspection." Nash could only hope this assumption was true; they were running on thin luck already. "C'mon, we have to get to the blister. Just make sure you always keep one hand on something firm."

She shook her head, grim-faced. *Don't worry. One lesson was enough.*

It was dark inside the envelope, but not completely opaque; the luminescent fiber-optics that lined the central catwalks and ladders radiated an orange glow across the mammoth gas cells. Nash led her down the center of the *Akron*, retracing the path he had taken during his previous in-flight inspection of the envelope, pulling against the railings to compensate for the upward tilt of the deck. The airship shuddered as it gradually ascended to cruising altitude, its engines moaning on either side of them. It was the second time in the last hour that they had been forced to make such a steep climb; first the upper galleries of the Cootie underworld, now this. Again, Nash felt his battered stomach muscles stretch painfully. He clenched his teeth and forced himself onward.

He located the central ladder and began to make the long

climb to the upper gangway, pausing now and then to look down and make certain that Sasaki wasn't running into any more trouble. If she was having any problems, though, she didn't show it. She carefully clung to the ladder rungs, never once looking down. She paused on the ladder, resting for a moment, and glanced up at him.

Much further? she asked, her exhaustion plain in her voice. Her breath was coming in ragged gasps; the woman had been through a lot today.

"Not much." Nash was whipped as well. He waited another few seconds until they had both caught their breath, then continued to scale the ladder. "We've only got a little further to go. Then we can relax."

They reached the upper gangway several minutes later; once they were there, Nash gave Sasaki a few minutes to get her wind again before he retraced his steps to the topside observation blister. There was room enough for both of them to squeeze inside comfortably; unfortunately, though, it wasn't pressurized. Nash regretted that omission. The inside of his skinsuit was already beginning to smell, and he had no doubt that Miho's suit also had the odor of stale sweat.

"No food, but I guess that can't be helped." He bent down and pulled the hatch shut behind them. "You'll have to ration your water intake, too." He grunted as he dogged the hatch shut. Now that it was closed, the rumble of the engines was effectively muffled. "It's going to be a long ride home, that's for sure."

She didn't answer. When he looked up, he saw that she was standing beneath the Plexiglas bubble, silently gazing toward the rear of the airship. He stood up and huddled against her to look out of the dome.

Darkness had fallen over the Martian landscape. During their long climb, the *Akron* had reached cruising altitude and had leveled out. The ground below them was completely invisible; the airship's navigational beacons flashed blue and red on either side of the delta-shaped fuselage, reflecting dully off the solar cells. Above them, the stars were beginning to appear in the night sky, cold and unwinking in the black depths of space.

When it comes, she said, *shut your eyes and turn away. Don't look at the flash, whatever you do.*

For a moment, he didn't know what she was talking about.

Then the chill realization hit him and he glanced at his heads-up display. The chronometer read 1829:45:38 . . . fifteen seconds and counting.

Had it taken that long to make it up here? Worse yet, he had almost completely forgotten about what they had left behind.

"God . . ." he murmured.

God has nothing to do with it, she said, her voice low and tense. *Get ready.*

Nash instinctively fastened his arm around her shoulders; after a moment, he felt her arm slide around his waist, yet he felt no comfort in her embrace. Had Boggs been able to gain sufficient distance in time? It was impossible to tell. He fastened his gaze on the changing digits of the chronometer.

Five . . . four . . . three . . . Sasaki repeated the countdown in a steel-voiced monotone. *Two . . . one . . . don't look! Get down!*

He caught the briefest glimpse of a silent white-hot flash in the far distance, illuminating the line of the western horizon, before Sasaki savagely yanked him beneath the lip of the dome. Nash hugged her against him as they crouched within the dome, squinting against the sudden glare that surged through the blister.

Even though his eyes were tightly shut, for an instant it seemed as if he could see through his eyelids: a silent blast of nuclear light, bright as a supernova.

The glare intensified, then seemed to recede. He started to stand up, but Miho held him tight against her. *No!* she shouted. *Wait for the noise! Wait for the—!*

An immense sledgehammer of sound, impossibly loud and dense, swung solidly against the airship. He felt the *Akron* careen forward as the shockwave slammed into its broad stern, its nose tilting toward the ground.

Still clinging to each other, he and Sasaki were hurled against the far end of the blister. He barely heard Miho scream through the comlink as the impact knocked the air from his lungs; there was a sharp, ragged pain in his ribs as his skinsuit backpack drove itself against his bruised rib cage. He gasped, fighting for breath, feeling his bladder involuntarily void itself. . . .

They were going down. The blast had nailed them. The *Akron* was going down. . . .

Then the violence and the roar faded away, and as it did, he felt the airship slowly begin to rise again. The floor of the observation blister gradually became horizontal once more.

Nash hesitantly opened his eyes. There was a suffused reddish-white light coming through the blister, spreading outward from the direction of the detonation. Sasaki disentangled herself from his arms; he let her go and struggled to his feet, staring out of the bubble at the unearthly light.

The false dawn of the nuclear explosion was already diminishing, but that wasn't what attracted his attention. Against the black sky, a new star was quickly rising into the heavens: a small, indistinct orb, strangely flattened at the bottom, was climbing into space atop a streak of fire. Hurtling towards an escape velocity it had awaited since the dawn of human civilization.

Pikadan, Miho said softly.

He looked at her, but said nothing. *They called it the* pikadan, she said in response to his unasked question. *The survivors of the Hiroshima bombing gave it a name . . . the "flash-sound" of the bomb going off.*

Her eyes remained fastened upon the ascending alien vessel. *My grandfather used to tell me about it when I was a child. He was blinded by the explosion, but he could still remember the last thing he saw before he . . .*

She stopped talking as her legs suddenly buckled beneath her. Nash grabbed her in his arms as she collapsed; he carefully lowered her to the deck and laid her on her back, then checked her oxygen feed and examined her face through the light of his helmet lamp. For a minute, he was frightened that her life-support system had somehow failed. He checked the digital readings on her chest unit and let out his breath. No, that wasn't the problem. She had simply fainted.

"It's okay," he muttered. "Sleep now . . . you deserve it."

Nash stretched her legs out and folded her hands together over her stomach, then squatted next to her within the blister. The glare of the explosion had disappeared; looking up through the bubble, he could see the shooting-star ascending into the galactic heavens.

"You're going home," he whispered, watching the new star. His eyes felt heavy-lidded. "I hope it was worth it."

He let his eyes close and his head fall backward as a warm, comforting darkness reached in to take him for its own.

24. Contamination

Nash and Sasaki slept through most of the night, curled up against each other on the floor of the observation blister, as the *Akron* raced southwest out of Cydonia and into the Acidalia Planitia. From time to time, Nash was stirred by an abrupt motion of the airship; he would awaken to take a drink of water, move himself around a little, look up at the bright starlight through the transparent dome . . . then he would allow himself to slide back into sleep once again. He was more exhausted than he had realized; crammed in as they were, he slept soundly.

Bright sunlight was shining through the blister when he next awakened. Miho was still asleep; sometime in the night she had managed to embrace him, although less as a lover than as someone who was trying to make herself comfortable in a cramped situation. Nash smiled as he carefully unwrapped her arms from around him and stood up, stretching as much as he could in the little cupola.

It was already late morning. Judging from the appearance of the cratered terrain that stretched out below the *Akron*, he was surprised that they were already above the Chryse Planitia, just northeast of the Lunae Planitia. That would mean that they were more than halfway home; he noticed the speed at which the airship's triangular shadow was rushing over the ground and guessed that the *Akron* was moving at more than eighty nautical miles per hour.

Boggs was keeping the engines throttled up. Nash got a bearing from his suit compass, then looked toward the northwest. At the farthest edge of the horizon he spotted a dark reddish-brown haze, as if a ghostlike mountain range had been dropped from the sky and was gradually moving across the plains. The leading edge of the dust storm; from the looks of it, the storm had already entered the Acidalia Planitia, and was probably already in Cydonia. Boggs was undoubtedly taking the *Akron* below the storm belt in an attempt to outrun the hurricane-force winds which could slash apart his ship.

Good morning, he heard Miho say. Nash looked around and saw that she was awake and was beginning to stand up. *What are you looking at?*

"Dust storm. Over there." Nash pointed at the faraway haze. "Looks like your boyfriend is doing his best to get us out from under it. They'll probably have to completely overhaul the engines, the way he's cooking them, but at least we'll make it out of here in one piece." He checked his chronometer and made a rough computation in his head. "In fact, at the rate he's cruising, we may even reach Arsia Station shortly after nightfall. We've probably picked up a good tail wind. That'll help."

She nodded her head, but said nothing. Her face was solemn as she stared at the distant storm, her mind apparently elsewhere. "I can't promise you breakfast," he added, attempting to force some levity from their situation, "but we might be able to catch last call at the Mars Hotel."

Yes. Her voice sounded distracted as she gazed out of the dome. *But when we land, there's still L'Enfant and Swigart to contend with.* She looked at him. *They'll kill us, you know. All three of us. We're the only witnesses.*

Nash let out his breath and shook his head. "No, they won't . . . not now, at least. If they knew we were up here, they would have come for us already. The fact that we're standing here means that L'Enfant is sure that we're dead. W.J.'s living on borrowed time, but L'Enfant has to keep him alive until they reach Arsia. He's the only one who can bring the *Akron* home."

Lieutenant Swigart's a pilot. . . .

"Not the same kind of pilot. It's one thing to be able to fly a one-seater Hornet, quite another to handle a five-hundred-foot dirigible." Nash shook his head again. "Boggs is safe for the time being, or at least until we reach the ground. Maybe even after that. Who knows? L'Enfant's crazy, but he's not completely ruthless. He's the type of person who respects talent. He might not kill W.J. just because he managed to get him out alive."

Then our lives are still in jeopardy, she insisted.

He shrugged his shoulders, feeling his skin chafe inside his skinsuit. Nash would have given anything to get out of it; he had been dressed for EVA for almost a full day now. It was probably because of this that he still felt fatigued. "Maybe, maybe not. If we stay up here until we've landed, then there's not much opportunity for him to do anything to harm us. Even in the hangar, there will be too many witnesses around for him to attempt to knock us off."

But if he gets us alone inside the base, he could . . .

"Look, Miho, there's all sorts of variables in this thing." Nash felt himself becoming irate. He took a deep breath, forcing himself to calm down. No point in snapping at Sasaki because she was worried about Boggs. "All we can do is play it by ear and . . ."

Play it by ear? she repeated, sounding a little confused. *I don't know what you're . . .*

He grinned and sat down again on the deck. "Play it by ear. Make it up as we go along. Improvise."

Oh. Right. Miho turned around and slumped down next to him. *Shin-ichi would know what you . . .*

Her voice trailed off as her eyes closed in grief. She bent forward and hugged her knees between her arms, suddenly remembering the grotesque death of her mentor. Nash heard her sobbing over the comlink; he reached out and took her gloved hands between his, but said nothing. She needed a good cry; it was long overdue.

After a short while, she gave his hands a brief squeeze, then rested her back against the curved wall. *August . . .* she began, then hesitated. *What do you intend to do about L'Enfant?*

Nash didn't say anything. He gazed up at the pale-pink sky passing overhead. He had Control's permission to act with extreme prejudice. L'Enfant had violated the seventh protocol; the proof was there, not only in the lives which had been wasted and the destruction which had been wrought, but also on the microfilm which was sealed in his camera.

Not that Nash needed anyone's permission to kill his former captain.

"I'll deal with Terry," he murmured. "You don't have to worry about that."

He felt his eyes beginning to close again. God, was he tired. Every muscle in his body seemed to ache; he still felt the bruises he had received from his beating. Nash laid his helmeted head back against the side of the cupola and stretched his legs out as far as he could. Sasaki didn't continue the discussion, for which he was grateful. They still had a long journey ahead of them; if he could doze through the next eight or nine hours . . .

Just before he fell asleep again, though, his half-shut eyes fell across his boots and his lower left leg, and he noticed something curious. The last time he had consciously looked at his legs, the soles of his boots and the left calf of the skinsuit overgarment had been stained crimson. That had been down in the Cootie underworld, when he had slipped in a puddle near one of the nanite-vats; he had been lightly splashed with some of the liquid from the pits, but he had been in too much of a hurry to escape the catacombs to even mention it to Miho.

Like the rest of his skinsuit, his boots and calf were filthy with dust . . . but now there was no sign of the stains. They had completely vanished, as if they had never been there in the first place.

An indistinct thought tickled his mind. *So . . .*

He shook his head. So what? It had been a long hike to retrace their steps through the catacombs, followed by a steep climb through the secondary tunnel to the surface. After that, he and Sasaki had been forced to jog through the wide City square in order to make the covert rendezvous with the *Akron.* The stuff must have rubbed off during all that; the Martian dust was abrasive enough to scour anything clean. . . .

So it was nothing important.

He couldn't think anymore. Nash let his eyes close.

He was awakened by the *Akron* lurching violently to one side as if it had been kicked by a massive foot; before he could even open his eyes, he was slammed against Sasaki as both of them were pitched against the side of the cupola.

Miho's left shoulder was wrenched backward by the impact; as she screamed in agony, the airship lurched again, this time downward. Nash had barely an instant to throw his arms and legs out and pin Sasaki beneath him to keep her from being hurled against the dome. Her face was twisted in pain, but she held on to him as the *Akron* abruptly bucked sideways again.

The dust storm—! she shouted.

Nash heard a loud ripping sound below them, as if something deep within the airship's hull was fighting to get loose. However, the airship seemed to steady itself; Boggs was apparently still in control of the rudder and was fighting to stabilize the massive craft. Grasping the inside ledge of the dome with his fingers, Nash hauled himself to his knees and stared out of the blister.

The sunlight was much dimmer than when he had gone to sleep; it was late afternoon now, and he realized that he had been asleep much longer than he had intended. Yet the evening sky was completely clear, unmarred by the sirocco of red sand he had expected to see. He looked to the west, toward the setting sun, and was astonished to see a great cone towering above the western horizon: Pavonis Mons, one of the three shield volcanoes of the Tharsis region.

Another sudden jolt, less violent than the first three, passed through the fuselage of the *Akron.* It almost knocked him off his knees, but Nash held tight to the edge of the dome. *What's going on?* Sasaki demanded, her voice high-pitched with fear. *Isn't it the dust storm?*

"No," he said, trying to remain calm in spite of his own confusion. "I don't know what it is." The deck was tilting forward now, but Nash hung on and forced himself the rest of the way to his feet.

In the farthest distance beyond Pavonis Mons, he could see the great bulge of Olympus Mons. He glanced toward the tapering bow of the airship and saw, many miles away and yet rapidly approaching, the chaotic canyons of the Noctis Labyrinthus. They were less than a hundred miles from Arsia Station, yet he could also see that the *Akron* had lost altitude; the airship was no more than six hundred feet above the ground.

Miho shouted something else but he ignored her. Nash swung his gaze toward the stern and felt his heart freeze. The fuselage was still largely intact, but it had lost much of its rigidity; there were great dimples in its aft sides, as if massive hands had squeezed its flanks, and the long spoiler-like elevator was partially collapsed on its support pylons. One glance at the main elevator, and Nash knew that the *Akron* had lost much of its control. And even though there were no apparent rents along its silvery skin, he had little doubt that the airship was slowly leaking hydrogen from somewhere along its hull.

They were almost home . . . but for whatever reason, the big ship was floundering and in serious trouble. Minute by inexorable minute, the *Akron* was going down.

"Get the hatch open!" he shouted. "We gotta get below!" When he looked around, he saw that Miho had already undogged the hatch cover and was halfway down the ladder. She had switched on her helmet lamp; its beam danced back and forth as she hurried down the rungs.

Yet another tremor swept through the ship; he fell to his knees and braced himself against the lip of the hatch. He waited until he caught a glimpse of Sasaki stepping off the ladder, then he gripped the hatch tightly and swung himself headfirst through the opening, making a clumsy half gainer to the gangway below. It was a risky move, but he didn't want to linger in the observation blister for a second longer.

His boots hit the gridded gangway deck at the same moment there was another hard lurch; off balance, Nash began to topple forward, but Miho grabbed him from behind and hauled him back. They fell together onto the gangway, tangled in each other's arms and legs.

What's happening? she yelled, on the verge of panic. *Are we crashing? Why are we . . . ?*

She suddenly stopped shouting; instead, Nash heard a startled gasp over the comlink. His eyes darted in her direction; she looked unharmed, but the stark bright oval of her lamp had caught something: the side of one of the slender frame-rings which ran laterally through the skeleton of the airship. Disentangling himself from her, Nash fumbled with his wrist controls until his own helmet lamp flashed on; he swung his shoulders until the beam landed on the same ring. . . .

"Oh my God," he whispered.

The surface of the ring was bleeding.

Red liquid streaks were oozing down its curved gray sides, as if the metal itself had developed ulcerous stigma. No, not oozing . . . *crawling*, as a solid mass of near-microscopic lice ran up and down the polycarbon girder. Feeding upon it . . .

The nanites, Miho said. *They're aboard the ship.* She swung her face toward Nash. *When you slipped in that puddle in the cavern . . .*

"I know," he murmured. "Some of that stuff got on my suit. I thought it rubbed off me, but I . . ."

Never mind that now. She was already clambering to her feet, grabbing the gangway railing for support. Another shudder ran through the fuselage, but they were prepared for them now. *They've probably replicated billions of times by now, making endless copies of one another. If they're following their original purpose . . .*

"You don't have to spell it out." There was a sickening drop in his stomach as the full magnitude of the situation came home to him. The micro-Cooties—if they could be called that—had hitched a ride on his skinsuit; they couldn't consume his suit's outergarment, but once they had been carried into the *Akron*, they had found a rich source of basic materials to disassemble for their own innate purposes. It didn't matter to them if the Cootie starship had already been completed and launched; their programming was simple. Tear it apart and rebuild it.

If the Akron *returns to Arsia Station,* Sasaki continued, *they'll be beyond our control. We'll never be able to contain them.* Her voice was beginning to rise. *They could even contaminate the* Sagan *and be transported back to Earth aboard the* Lowell, *where they could . . .*

"No. You don't have to worry about it going that far." Nash hauled himself to his feet and stumbled toward the ladder leading down to the central gangway. "Believe me, the *Akron*'s never going to make it back to base. They'll . . ."

The airship quivered like a wet dog shaking off water. He grabbed a rail for support and felt it give a little; he looked down and saw that it had bent inward slightly, as if it was made of half-hardened putty. The palm of his glove was covered with redness. He lifted it for Sasaki to see.

"They're destroying the ship from the inside out!" he yelled. "If we don't get out of here, they're going to take us with her! Now *c'mon—!*"

The climb down the ladder was frightening; individual rungs had turned soft and threatened to collapse, plunging them into the dark chasm beneath their feet. The airship occasionally gave another violent surge which almost loosened their tenuous grip on the ladder. But it didn't take long to get to the bottom; they were too scared to take their time making a careful descent.

Once Sasaki had reached the central gangway and was out of the way, Nash took a deep breath and jumped the rest of the distance. He landed on all fours, his breath huffing out of him. He picked himself up off the desk and looked around. In the translucent half-light cast by the fiber-optic safety lines, he could see the airship's skeleton collapsing inward, its support rings and trusswork melting as if made of wax. All around them, the giant gas cells were sagging like old pillows as hydrogen leaked through their dissolving skins. Nanite liquid dripped all around them, as if the *Akron* were a hemorrhaging leviathan. He could hear a vast groaning, grinding sound throughout the massive envelope; every few seconds there was a distant crash as a support gave way and another piece of the internal frame toppled downward.

The *Akron* was dying. It was a big ship; although infected with billions of micro-Cooties, its destruction was taking some time to complete. But it was dying nonetheless.

Sasaki was hugging the gangway rail, staring speechlessly at the chaos erupting around her. Nash turned toward her, pointing toward the bow of the ship. "Get to the cargo bay!" he shouted. She looked toward him. "If we can blow the hatch and drop the cables, maybe we can . . .!"

Look out! she screamed.

He instinctively ducked and whipped around, expecting a girder to come crashing down upon him. Instead, a human form lunged out of the semidarkness behind him, arms outstretched to shove him over the railing. . . .

His reflexes took over. Nash grabbed his assailant by the forearms as he simultaneously kicked his right foot into the figure's midriff; at the same time, he allowed himself to fall backward, still grasping the other person's arms. His backpack slammed into his spine and he almost lost his breath, but he managed to hurl the other person up over himself.

The judo throw took Megan Swigart completely by surprise. In the half-instant before Nash released his grip, he caught a glimpse of her shocked face through her helmet. Then she was over the railing, her arms and legs flailing helplessly as she was pitched off the catwalk.

If she screamed, he couldn't hear her; she was on a different comlink channel. Yet, as he glanced down from the catwalk, he saw her helmet faceplate shatter as it slammed directly into a crossbeam twenty feet below; there was a brief spout of instantly frosted air amid the shattered glass, then Swigart's body fell into the impenetrable darkness of the lower hull.

A second later there was another slight jar through the fuselage; without looking, Nash knew that her body had just punched through the outer skin of the *Akron*. The airship might be falling, but it was still a long way down. . . .

He pulled himself to his feet, gasping at the renewed pain in his ribs. It was the first time he had ever killed anyone. Strangely, he felt no remorse. He couldn't help remembering how taciturn she had been when he had buried three people on Boot Hill yesterday; maybe she'd thought she was immortal and had only contempt for the dead.

"Any last words now?" he asked.

You killed her, Miho whispered.

"Yeah. Uh-huh." Nash didn't dare look at Miho, but he wasn't about to argue the point. He reached out and grabbed her hand. "Let's go. Maybe we can still get out of here."

Pulling her along, Nash stalked toward the prow of the dying airship. They now had only a few minutes left until the slow demolition of the *Akron* reached critical mass, when the mass of the airship simply wouldn't be able to support its own weight in the frail Martian atmosphere. If they moved fast enough, they still might be able to make an escape through the unpressurized cargo-bay hatch.

And if they weren't quick, they would certainly be dead. Even so, Nash knew there was one last matter to be resolved. . . .

L'Enfant.

It was time for the man to die.

25. The Labyrinth of Night

Once they reached the end of the gangway, Nash found the access hatch to the main airlock open; Swigart had apparently left it that way when she'd gone into the envelope. As soon as they climbed down the ladder into the small compartment, though, he saw red emergency LEDs blinking on the airlock control panel. He only had to study the panel for a moment to realize exactly what had been done.

"Damn it," he hissed. "The bastard froze the airlock shut."

The hatch leading into the crew compartment was sealed from the inside; either L'Enfant had forced Boggs to override the automatic controls or the commander himself had monkeyed with the main fuses. The result was the same either way; Nash could not open the hatch from his side of the airlock. Not only that, but another LED told him that the crew compartment and the gondola had been depressurized. At first he thought that the nanites had managed to blow out the pressurized parts of the *Akron*—in which case both Boggs and L'Enfant were already dead—but then he noticed that three of the skinsuit lockers were open and empty.

His mind was still racing as Sasaki opened the hatch leading into the cargo bay. Yet another tremor ran through the vessel as he stared numbly at the disabled control panel. *I can still manually open the bay doors and drop the cable,* Miho said tersely, *but how are going to get Waylon out of there before . . . ?*

"Do it!" Nash snapped without looking back at her. There was one small chance. . . . "Just get it ready to go . . . and be prepared to bail out if this doesn't work!"

Before Sasaki could ask what he meant, Nash switched the comlink to Channel One, the common-use frequency. "Captain L'Enfant," he said. "This is Seaman Nash. Open the hatch, sir."

He could hear the static hiss of an open channel, but nothing more. "Captain, this is Nash," he said. "I'm still alive. Both of us are still alive. You blew it, sir. Now open the hatch."

For a few moments there was no reply; Nash was about to switch to another band and try again when L'Enfant's soft voice come over the comlink.

On the contrary, Mr. Nash, I didn't blow anything.

Nash's hand froze above his gauntlet's comlink control. L'Enfant sounded ridiculously calm, even taunting. *Except for a nuclear warhead, and of course that was my main priority. I'm only sorry that you and Dr. Sasaki are still alive, but I suppose I can't always prevent stowaways from . . .*

Nash broke in. "You didn't finish off the pseudo-Cooties, if that's what you mean," he said. "They were building a starship down there and they used your nuke for its launch. The big flash you saw last night was their ship lifting off. We watched the whole thing from the topside blister." He paused, then deliberately added a touch of irony to his voice. "Nice try, but Miho and I helped them get away. Hope you don't mind."

Again, there was silence over the comlink. Nash wondered why he hadn't yet heard anything from Boggs. The pilot had to be alive—someone must be keeping what little control still remained over the *Akron*—so it was most likely that L'Enfant was keeping him quiet at gunpoint. "If you haven't noticed already," he went on, "this ship's going down."

Your powers of observation remain acute as ever, Mr. Nash. It was hard to tell, but L'Enfant's voice seemed to have lost its smoothness. *Lieutenant Swigart reported that something was causing the ship to deteriorate before she met her untimely demise. I assume it has something to do with the aliens.* Another pause. *Did you bring something aboard, Mr. Nash? If so, then you're responsible for whatever . . .*

"Christ, you're long-winded!" Nash retorted. "You're like some plebe who keeps trying to talk his way out of not having his bed made in time for inspection!"

Oh, please. Spare me your inconsequential . . .

L'Enfant's voice was condescending, yet Nash instinctively knew that he was hitting a raw nerve. "Yak yak yak, that's all we ever hear from you," he said, sticking the needle in hard. "Always trying to pin the blame on someone else. The senior cadets must have had fun hazing you, you incompetent loser. I bet they had you down on the bathroom floor doing push-ups until you were begging for—"

That's enough! L'Enfant snapped. *I won't have a swabbie questioning my . . .*

The gambit was working; despite the immediate danger, Nash found himself grinning. "Enough?" he asked. "I haven't even begun! It's just like when you fucked up during the *Takada Maru* . . . you can't get anything right, can you?" He allowed a sneer to enter his voice. "I screwed up your whole operation, Captain L'Enfant fucking *sir.* I enabled the Cooties to make their getaway, then I brought some of their little friends aboard the *Akron*, and I just scragged one of your officers. How's that for a swabbie?"

He stopped for a second, letting it sink in. "And I gotta tell you," he went on, "I took considerable pleasure in chucking the bitch off the gangway. You should have seen the look on her face when she took that last big dive. Did you hear her scream? She just . . ."

You goddamn cocksucking—! L'Enfant's scream was pure infantile rage; the megalomaniac had been challenged. *I'm going to kill you! I swear to God, I'm a commissioned officer, I'm going to . . . !*

"Kill me?" Nash forced a laugh out of his throat. "You *coward*! You don't even have the balls to face me!"

He took a deep breath. "All you can do is hold hostages and throw them in front of the guns when the flak gets heavy," he added with calm, heartfelt contempt. "So fuck you and your commission. I piss on 'em both from a considerable height."

A height which was decreasing with each second. He waited. Nothing. He couldn't play this game for much longer. "Try this, you pompous dick," he continued. "Open the hatch and let Boggs out of there. He can put the ship on auto-pilot. It won't matter, we're all doomed anyway. So let's you and me settle our bill, once and for all. Man to man, if you think you can take it."

Again, Nash waited. He heard only static over the comlink. He glanced over his shoulder into the open hatchway of the cargo bay. Sasaki had cranked open the cargo doors and had lowered the cables; she was hanging on to a couple of bulkhead grommets and staring at him. Through the open cargo hatch, he could see the rocky ground scudding past, less than a hundred feet from the underside of the *Akron*.

In another few minutes, the airship would crash; at this velocity, nobody would survive.

He yanked his eyes back to the airlock hatch. "C'mon, L'Enfant!" he barked. "Let's see if you have the nerve to . . . !"

One of the red lights on the panel was suddenly extinguished; at the same moment, the hatch popped open slightly as its internal gaskets were relaxed. The airlock had been unsealed.

Nash immediately grabbed the handle, then hesitated. L'Enfant was still armed; he had to keep that in mind. The bastard could have his gun—Nash's gun—aimed straight at the airlock. He stepped aside, pressing his back against the bulkhead, then licked his dry lips and reached out to gently push the hatch open. On the count of three, he thought. One . . . two . . .

The hatch was yanked open from within; Nash yanked his right fist back, ready to slam it into L'Enfant when he came through the doorway, but instead it was Boggs who charged into the airlock.

He skidded to a halt as soon as he saw Nash; he stared wide-eyed at him as he steadied himself on the sloping deck. *God-damn, man!* he brayed. *You scared the shit outta . . . !*

"Get out of here!" Nash grabbed Boggs by the shoulders and shoved him through the airlock toward the cargo bay. "Miho's got the cable dropped to the ground! Follow her down, she'll—!"

The *Akron* pitched violently again; they could hear the tortured screech of metal rending itself apart from somewhere high above them as the two men toppled against each other. "Get going!" Nash yelled. He thrust Boggs toward the cargo bay. "You can make it down! I'll take care of him! Now get—!"

No! Miho screamed. *Waylon, make him . . . !*

Nash angrily pushed away from Boggs and hauled himself through the open airlock hatch into the passenger compartment; he caught a final glimpse of the pilot's face just before he slammed the hatch shut behind him. As an abrupt afterthought, he stabbed the recompression button on the inside control panel; although the command was useless, now that the airlock was open to the cargo bay, it would keep the hatch shut.

"Sorry, gang," he whispered, "but Captain L'Enfant and I have a few private things to discuss."

• • •

He had started to turn around, when the *Akron* made another sickening yaw to the left. Nash was flung forward through the companionway; he collided with the edge of the mess table in the galley and his tender stomach muscles howled in anguish as he doubled over, clutching his gut as he fell to the floor.

You're quite correct, seaman. L'Enfant's voice was once again smooth and confident. *We do have many things to discuss, you and I . . .*

It felt as if a rib or two had been fractured. The agony was murderous. Nash tasted blood on his lips; he impulsively raised a hand to his face, but his gloved fingers met only the faceplate of his helmet. Alphanumeric codes flashed irrelevantly across his heads-up display.

I seem to remember a little bit of Alice, L'Enfant continued. His voice was madness itself: monotoned, infinitely banal. *Do you know Alice? Or perhaps her old tutor, Lewis Carroll . . . ?*

Nash gasped as he struggled to his knees. A spike seemed to have been hammered into his chest. The aisle was littered with trash which had been torn loose by the sudden decompression: foam coffee cups, pens, shredded pillows from the bunks, log-book pages, part of a nudie calender with a voluptuous model teasingly draped across the hood of a sports car. The deck jumped again, but he was braced on his hands.

No? A little worn out, perhaps? Let me refresh your memory . . . .

Nash grasped the table with both hands and dragged himself to his feet. He made himself trudge forward, step by weary step. Just beyond the short aisle was the gangway leading down into the gondola. Hugging his chest with his left arm, he hauled himself toward the open hatch. Already he could see down into the flight deck. It seemed to be empty.

"The time has come," the Walrus said, *"to talk of many things . . ."*

No. There. L'Enfant was sitting complacently in the right-hand co-pilot seat, his hands relaxed upon the armrests. Nash couldn't see his face; he was looking directly ahead.

"Of shoes—and ships—and sealing wax . . ."

Through the wide gondola windows, Nash could see the jagged edge of a vast wound hurtling toward them: the Noctis Labyrinthus, the western end of the Valles Marineris. The Labyrinth of Night.

The last traces of sunlight gleamed across the sharp, rugged wall of its far rim: mammoth bluffs higher than those of any canyon on Earth, falling down into a dark nothingness where the sun only reached in the earliest hours of the morning. The *Akron* was only a few hundred feet from reaching the precipice.

"And cabbages and kings . . ."

His gun lay on the bottom step of the gangway.

Nash half-fell down the gangway, almost tripping over the SIG-Sauer. He bent over painfully and picked it up. The gun was already cocked. An invitation to end the battle once and for all . . .

If he had the nerve.

"And why the sea is boiling hot . . ."

The memory of torpedoes slicing through chill, moonlit waters, in a place and time only a few scant years ago, yet many millions of miles away. A sea which had not yet been turned into a barren, windswept wilderness. A young man whose innocent belief that authority equaled righteousness was irreversibly shattered by the screams of dying sailors . . .

" 'And whether pigs have wings,' " Nash finished. "*Alice In Wonderland.* My boss loves it."

L'Enfant said nothing. Nash could now see his profile through the faceplate of his helmet, yet he wore an expectant smile as he gazed upon the abyss hurtling toward them. It was far too late for either of them to escape their shared fate.

He hugged his chest with his left arm and slowly raised the gun.

Your boss has good taste, L'Enfant murmured.

"No," Nash replied. "He's just a jerk like you. Talks too much."

L'Enfant sat still in his chair, saying nothing. Patiently waiting for the bullet.

Nash closed his eyes; he placed the barrel of the gun against the side of L'Enfant's helmet and squeezed the trigger.

He felt the recoil, heard the shot and the sharp crack of L'Enfant's helmet shattering. Yet he didn't look at what he had just done; he had seen enough blood. The satisfaction of getting the job done was good enough to last the rest of his life.

Nash dropped the gun to the deck and sat down on the gangway. He was exhausted beyond belief. Behind him, he could hear the muted crashing of the airship falling apart, collapsing in on itself. Had it been this way inside the *Takada Maru* when she went under the waves?

He would know soon enough.

The edge of the canyon was just before him, clearly visible through the gondola windows. Beyond was the vast dark chasm, a bottomless pit as old as time itself. Nash grabbed the gangway railing for support and forced his eyes shut. There was a violent, grinding lurch as the bottom of the gondola scraped against rocky soil. He wondered for a half-instant if he might survive after all—perhaps the airship would be stopped at the penultimate moment—then the windows shattered and broken glass lacerated his arms and chest. There was an endless scream of metal, then silence except for the harsh Martian wind and the sensation of falling, falling, falling. . . .

He had a chance to murmur a final prayer as the *Akron* crossed the edge of the precipice and plummeted into the Labyrinth of Night.

EPILOGUE

"If all this has been happening, they should have arrived here by now. So where are they?"

—ENRICO FERMI,
on extraterrestrial intelligence,
Los Alamos, 1950

Arsia Station, Mars; September 1, 1050 MCM, 2032

Pewter-colored minnows chased each other in and out of her reflection in the aquaculture pool, turned silver by the midmorning sunlight which gleamed through the high windows of the central atrium.

Miho Sasaki had chosen a stone bench by the pool to sit while she composed her report, but the cool waters had distracted her. The datapad she'd carried with her into the garden lay open on her lap, its keys untouched since she had created a file . . . how long ago had it been?

She glanced at her watch and sighed with frustration. A half-hour ago. She was wasting time.

Miho moved her feet restlessly through the grass planted near the artificial pond, favoring her bandaged left ankle, as she gazed again at the blank flatscreen of the pad. She absently tapped the cap of her stylus against her lips as she once again sought for the opening words to her report. How could she possibly describe, with the rational detachment and scientific objectivity requisite for such a report, all that she had seen in the past several days?

Eight people dead . . . an alien race whose technology stretched the limits of man's understanding . . . the needless loss of so many friends . . .

It was impossible to write about these things. The memories were too fresh. Miho put the pad down on the bench as her eyes wandered again to the dancing minnows. Lucky little creatures. They had been born in this small, quiet pond; they didn't know that their ancestors had evolved on a planet many millions of miles away, that they belonged to a species that could never have been produced on Mars without the aid of a higher intelligence. For them, their miniature ecosystem circumscribed the known universe; Miho was a vague shadow hovering over their world, frightening perhaps but otherwise part of something of which they could remain cheerfully ignorant.

"You're so fortunate," she murmured aloud as she watched them play. "You have the liberty to be stupid. . . ."

"Now, that's not a very nice thing to say to a fish," said a voice from behind her.

Sasaki was not surprised to hear W. J. Boggs; she had been expecting him to turn up sometime today. The only surprise was that she had spoken in English; on the rare occasions when she talked to herself, she usually spoke in Japanese. She looked over her shoulder as he approached from the living area. "Good morning. What did the doctor say about your leg?"

Boggs hobbled toward her, clumsily riding the two aluminum crutches he'd been given late last night in the station infirmary, the last place she had seen him. He wore a pair of denim overalls over a worn-out Grand Ole Opry sweatshirt; the clothes had come from his locker in the station-crew bunkhouse, but the right leg of his Levi's had been cut up to the top of his thigh, making room for the white plaster cast which encased his entire leg from his hip down to his calf.

"Same as before, I reckon. Multiple fractures in the tibia and femur, busted kneecap . . . I forget what else, but I sure as hell ain't walking without these damn things for a while." He grinned at her. "If you plan to get romantic with me any time soon, please be careful. I'm a hurtin' old hound dog."

Hurting old hound dog. She smiled slightly at the thought; he was lucky to be alive at all. She herself had come away with a sprained ankle after their desperate evacuation from the *Akron*, only because she had clung to the cable until her feet had touched ground. Boggs had been on the cable behind her, but he had been forced to jump the last thirty feet before the airship fell into the Noctis Labyrinthus. His good fortune was that his skinsuit hadn't been split open by his fall. But, of course, he always found a reason to complain. . . .

Miho picked up the datapad, making a place for him to sit down. "Much obliged," he said as he made his ungainly way to the bench and carefully settled down on it, pulling up his crutches as he thrust out his rigid leg. He gently massaged the plaster. "Damn thing itches like a bitch . . . hey, you wanna sign it?"

"Sign it?" Miho shook her head. "I don't understand. . . ."

"Fine old American tradition. Like getting a baseball autographed, but you don't have to pay anyone for the privilege. Collected one already, from my best bartender." He tapped a fresh ink-scrawl located just above his knee. Miho looked closer. CRIPPLES DRINK FOR FREE!—NUGE.

"All I have is the stylus," she said, holding up her light-pen. "I'll autograph it later." Boggs looked mildly disappointed, but he nodded his head. "What I meant was . . ."

She hesitated. "Are you going back on the *Lowell*?" she asked quietly.

Boggs took a deep breath. "Well, I guess that all depends," he said slowly. "It's gonna be at least another six months before this leg is fixed-up again. Even if they had another airship for me to fly, I couldn't handle the thing anyway . . . and my guess is that it's going to be at least two years before they replace the *Akron*. There's not much for a blimp jockey to do up here until then, so . . ."

He looked at her sharply as another thought appeared to cross his mind. "Did you talk to anyone about the *Akron*? I mean, about the crash site?"

Miho felt rebuffed; her question to him was unanswered, whether he meant to be evasive or not. "Yes. I spoke to the station general manager and the resident scientists this morning."

Boggs chuckled. "Was Leahy sober?"

"So far as I could tell, yes." She smiled a little. "I think he was hung over. He didn't say much. . . ."

"Typical. I smelled booze on his breath when they were working on me last night." Boggs shook his head in disgust. "All he could say was, 'You crashed *my* airship? You crashed *my* airship?' Wetbrain sonnuva . . ."

"They wanted to send a team into the canyon," she went on, "but I told them to quarantine the crash site and gave them the reasons why."

She paused, kneading her hands together. "I don't know whether they will obey my wishes. Some of them were eager to collect samples of the nanites, regardless of the danger. But, at least for the time being, they have agreed to place remote monitors near the canyon ledge and not to venture down to the wreckage."

Miho placed her hand on the datapad. "That is why I'm try-ing to write a report and send it to my people as soon as the communications window reopens. Perhaps when they see the inherent risk in trying to develop the Cootie nanotechnology without proper safeguards, they will proceed carefully."

"Uh-huh." Boggs had become more somber. He rested his el-bows on his knees and clasped his hands together, staring into the aquaculture pool. "And what did they say about L'Enfant . . . ?"

He stopped. "And Nash?" he asked more softly.

Sasaki licked her lips. "Commander L'Enfant, they agreed, was completely insane. Paranoid-schizophrenic. His actions were completely without authorization. No one had heard of Operation Kentucky Derby. He was a . . ."

She rolled her hands around each other. "Loose cannon? Loose gun?"

"Loose cannon." Boggs closed his eyes and grimaced in dis-gust. "Figures. Complete deniability, right on down the line. The fucking assholes . . ."

He spat into the pool; the minnows feverishly swam toward his cob until they realized it was not a snack; then they mean-dered away, almost as if embarrassed. "And as for Nash . . . ?"

"They never even heard of August Nash," she said. "Even Leahy denied having heard his name before. They expressed surprise that he was anyone except . . ."

"My co-pilot." Boggs put his face between his hands. "I can't even remember his fake name, and the poor bastard . . . the guy will probably have it carved on a marker in the graveyard. So far as they're concerned . . ."

"He never existed," she replied. "He never lived."

"He saved our lives," he said, "and the assholes will never even admit that he was here. The bastards will never . . ."

"Hush. Be quiet now." Miho laid her head against his shoul-der, feeling the tears she had suppressed flow freely now as she remembered all the two of them had been through. For once, Waylon J. Boggs shut up when he was told to shut up. He put his arm around her shoulder; this time, she didn't pull away from the touch of his hand.

For a few minutes, they clung silently to each other. A man and a woman, sitting together on a garden bench, a long way from home. Remembering all the lies, the wasted resources, the banalities of politics, the distortions of truth, the sacrifices . . .

"The lives," she whispered. "All the lives . . ."

Harvard, Massachusetts; November 11, 2230 EST, 2032

A cool evening wind blew across the hilltop, scattering dead autumn leaves which covered the paved asphalt lot surrounding the giant radiotelescope. Down the road from the big dish, past the signs asking drivers to switch off their headlights, astronomers were opening the white-painted dome that covered the sixty-inch optical telescope which had already been maneuvered to point toward a certain direction in the western sky. Meanwhile, the eighty-four-foot radiotelescope was being rotated to face the same celestial coordinates.

The sound of a blues guitar floated from within the concrete shed at the base of the radio dish. In the clear night sky, a bright red star hove into view above the naked treetops.

Although the Harvard-Smithsonian Astrophysical Observatory had been in operation on this rural Massachusetts hilltop for close to seventy-five years, it was a rare moment when both the radiotelescope and the optical telescope were used simultaneously for a joint project. Yet now that Mars was emerging from the far side of the Sun, the opportunity was too good to miss. The Project META radiotelescope had been scanning the northern hemisphere sky for over fifty years, searching for signs of extraterrestrial intelligence.

Finally, the astronomers had a definite direction in which to search. Not only that, but tonight they also had a means of talking back to the stars.

Inside the radiotelescope's blockhouse, Arthur Johnson listened for a few moments to a telephone, then cupped his hand over the receiver. "They've acquired the starship," he said aloud. Behind him in the bare concrete room, the sound of the blues guitar abruptly stopped in mid-chord. "Looks like it's point-five AU's past Mars orbit, out in the belt somewhere. Do we have anything on the spectrum analyzer yet?"

Inside the adjacent glassed-in computer center, two other Planetary Society scientists were crouched over a computer terminal. Next to them was the heart and soul of the Megachannel Extra-Terrestrial Array, the 8.4-million-channel radio receiver and spectrum analyzer which was capable of eavesdropping on radio frequencies from deep space. Diodes flashed like tiny Christmas lights across the mammoth steel-cabineted computer; displayed on the terminal's flatscreen was a regular pattern resembling a series of slender rectangles.

One of the scientists look up from the screen. "We have a definite ET signal," he announced, his young face flushed with pride. "Same azimuth and everything. We're right on the money."

"Good deal. Frequency?"

"Fourteen-twenty megahertz," the other scientists murmured. "I'll be damned if it ain't right in the ol' waterhole itself." He looked up from the screen and grinned. "Think it's time for our concert, Dr. Johnson."

"Right, then." The astrophysicist tapped another number into his phone. "Cape, this is Harvard META . . . code word is Bravo Whiskey Echo two-three-two."

He waited a moment, then smiled broadly. "Yes, Nathan, this is Art. Glad we've dispensed with all that password stuff. Listen, we've got a positive fix on the Cooties. The frequency is fourteen-twenty megahertz. Are you ready down there?" Again he listened, then nodded his head. "Fine, fine. We've got him all hooked up and he's been practicing for the last half-hour or so. All right, if you've got a clear feed from us, we'll get started. . . ."

Johnson put down the phone and turned to face the man standing in the back of the room. "We're ready whenever you are, Ben." He sat down on a table beneath a poster-map of the Milky Way. "Let's hear some tunes."

Ben Cassidy sat on a stool at the other end of the room, his Yamaha perched on his lap, a harmonica held within a brace strapped around his neck. Except for a small monitor speaker, the only other pieces of equipment were a microphone and a hardwired soundboard for his guitar; both, though, were hooked into a shielded telephone hookup.

Several thousand miles south of the hilltop observatory lay the other end of his communications relay: the giant dish-array of the NASA Deep Space Communications Network at Cape Canaveral. The DSCN was usually dedicated to maintaining communications with spacecraft in Earth orbit, but tonight— like the Harvard-Smithsonian telescopes—it was oriented toward a certain point in the night sky.

Out there, far beyond Mars, the Cootie starship was making

its way out of the solar system, heading straight out from the red planet on a course which, until this time, had rendered it invisible to human observers on Earth. The starship was transmitting a steady signal of unknown content as it left the humankind solar system; that much had already been ascertained by Arsia Station.

The time had come to say farewell, in the only way to which the Cooties had ever paid any attention.

Cassidy swallowed and touched the strings of his instrument. He played a couple of random notes, but found no inspiration. He glanced up at Arthur Johnson; his old friend waited expectantly but said nothing. The musician looked toward the computer room.

"Excuse me," he said. Through the window, the other two scientists were still staring intently at the screen. "Excuse me," he said more loudly, and they looked over their shoulders at him. "Would y'all mind standing out of the way for a minute? I want to see what's on that thing."

The two men glanced at each other, then at Johnson. Arthur made a shooing gesture with his hand; the radio-astronomers stood erect and stepped back from the terminal, allowing Cassidy to have a clear view of the oscillating signal-pattern from the Cootie starship.

Cassidy watched it for a moment: a rhythmic series of ups-and-downs, almost like patterns on a music scale. Like B-flat jumping up to F, then to G, and back to B-flat . . .

He tapped the appropriate commands into the guitar's memory, then hesitantly placed his fingers on the strings and began to play a deep-throated, melancholy song, one so old that no one knew its exact origins, yet so familiar that every seasoned musician had performed it at some time or another. He started with a thumping, repetitive bass-line, then essayed a quick run from the low end of the scale to the high, then back again. . . .

Cassidy closed his eyes as he concentrated on the opening bars; then he placed his lips against the harmonica and tramped through the refrain once again, this time accompanying his guitar licks with the brassy railroad-blues sound. When he was through with the harmonica, he raised his head and sang to the aliens. . . .

> *"I know you rider,*
> *Gonna miss me when I'm gone.*

> *Well, I know you rider,*
> *Gonna miss me when I'm gone.*
> *Gonna miss you, babe,*
> *From rolling in your arms. . . ."*

Across the room, Arthur Johnson nodded his head in time with the music; inside the META room, the two scientists turned their attention from the pulses on the screen to watch Cassidy as he dished out the timeless song.

> *"I'm goin' down the road*
> *Where I can get more decent care.*
> *I'm goin' down the road*
> *Where I can get more decent care.*
> *Goin' back to my used-to-be rider*
> *'Cause I don't feel welcome here. . . ."*

Cassidy accented the second stanza with another refrain on his harmonica, a sassy comment to an extraterrestrial vessel leaving the confused realm of humanity forever. A nanosecond later it was transmitted to the asteroid belt, hurled at the speed of light toward an invisible lifeboat making its way back home across a trackless void. A last goodbye from Earth.

When Cassidy was through with the song, they waited for a reply, watching the terminal screen for a change in pattern, an alteration in the interplanetary static. A sign that they cared. None came. As before, the human race was left only with themselves for conversation.

No farewells, no promises to return. No comfort from a hard, remorseless universe. Only the memory of an old, sad tune, lost somewhere in deep space, falling through the labyrinth of night.